Make

Mission

by

J N Cleeve

For Brenda
with best wishes

Juniper Cleeve

I am the master of my fate,
I am the captain of my soul.

24 July 2014

William Ernest Henley (1849–1903).

The front cover is a computer generated composite of a period cottage typical of the style found as gatehouses to large country estates in England. The characters are presented in American wartime aircrew headdress and the English female hairroll clear of the neck. The aircraft is a representative Lockheed P-38 in example camouflage paint scheme.

www.fast-print.net/store.php

The moral right of the author has been asserted
A CIP catalogue record of this book is available from the
British Library

ISBN 978-178035-489-7

First Edition

First published 2012 by
FASTPRINT PUBLISHING
Peterborough, England.

Acknowledgments

I am indebted to my rigorous editor, Deanna Freeman, for her advice in converting my early attempts to construct a manuscript fable into a readable tale. She helped me strike a balance between history, high level politico-social pressures of the period — real or imagined, a measure of contemporary technology, revision of certain geographical settings in the interest of literary pace, documentary and correspondence styles used at that date and a degree of gender interaction. The syntactical presentation is hers, any textual imbalance is mine. Equally important, the continuity within the fictional family across eleven generations and, now, three continents, has been rigorously addressed with the aid of Deanna's unfailing memory thereby allowing the saga's literary hooks to relate to episodes in the four previous *Warranted Land* novels. That we remain friends is a testament to her encouragement and support. And she is watchful for the similar opportunities which have been laid for the forthcoming next novel *Piers' Cadetship*.

Gladys Page, Jill Iredale and Jackie Renfrey each encouraged my continuance at the keyboard when the author's energy appeared to flag. As the nine year cycle to construct the *Warranted Land* saga clocked away, these ladies showed interest and support when it was most needed — and asked me why stop now?

The images of All Saints Church, Snodland are used with herein under licence   http://www.creativecommons.org/licenenses/by-sa/2.0/   by the photographer.

The meteorological charts and other 'UK weather actual' information used in this novel was obtained from, and is used herein under licence from, the National Meteorological Library and Archive (see http://www.metoffice.gov.uk/).

And to my ever-patient wife, Jean, who gave me the space and freedom — and not a little encouragement — to convert the first glimmer of '…there's got to be a story there…' to setting the whole thing down on paper.

Throughout the novel, various commercial brand names or trade names have been used in appropriate context. I have labelled each with the symbol ^{tm} thereby attempting to give recognition and credit where due, irrespective of the nationality specific trademark where the service or material is used. If I have missed any, please let me know and I will make the appropriate change in subsequent editions of the novel.

J N Cleeve

31 August 2012

INTRODUCTION

The Warranted Land Saga, of which this is a part, tells a story of a fictional English-origin family determined to make a new life in the American colonies set against the intriguing characters, episodes and lifestyles of the period spanning the four centuries from the arrival of King James I in England, through the extended chapters of the Anglo-American Wars of Independence between 1771 to 1815, up to the war in Europe between 1943 to 1945 and on towards the 21st century.

The title Warranted Land derives from the inducement of promised wealth by the 17th century English Crown to persuade emigration from an over-populated England to the New World. In exchange for immigration, at the rate of 1 head per 50 acres, the Governor of Maryland was empowered to warrant undeveloped colonial land to any who could raise the funds for the hazardous Atlantic crossing. Later, when Australia replaced America for the exodus from overcrowding in England, the principle of land settlement for population displacement continued and touched on the trading area of the East India Co.

By the date when this novel opens, the powerful United States of America has its own reasons for going to the aid of war torn Great Britain. This novel, the fifth within the saga, continues the tale of one example family, who were not always harmonious, who faced many happy and a few tragic episodes under the umbrella of World War II, as the decades of the mid 20th century rolled by.

The Ploughman family is entirely a fictional creation of the author's imagination. Any resemblance between the fictional characters and any person, living or dead, is unintentional. The historical characters are portrayed for the purposes of this novel within fictitious settings and are not intended to be biographical. Many are mentioned in the historical notes at the conclusion of this work. Historical events shown with a full anglicised date: dd mm... yyyy are historically accurate according to public archives; any other date format implies fiction. There was an RAF Snodland, actually at nearby Halling between 1939 and May 1942, storing ammunition for the Fighter Command aircraft in south-east

England; it closed on the transfer of its responsibilities to an adjacent facility. Certain liberties have been taken with geography for the sake of fictional pace. Family names have retained the old English contemporary spelling; some of the fictitious documents and letters retain the style of the time. In some cases an element of dialect has been used to differentiate between speakers in dialogue sequences.

In this saga, the pivotal decision to emigrate is made in 1659, by a former naval surgeon with a successful London practice. When members of the Ploughman family decided to emigrate to the new American colonies, their lives intertwined with unstoppable forces driving their new communities towards conflict, independence and yet further travel. They could not have foreseen that, within three centuries, fate would place an American Ploughman back on the same land quit by his ancestor and once more handling the family heritage documents written in the 1600s.

The saga tells of the proud heritage sustaining the family and its continuity, through 3 previous and 10 subsequent generations, in England, America, the East Indies and on the high seas. The full saga is planned to be presented in six novels, each designed to be free-standing. Any novel in the saga could be read individually, or the whole sequence could be taken in any order, although there is a chronological structure to the six titles:

Warranted Land	broadly 1605 to 1662
Bernard's Law	broadly 1662 to 1730
Rosetta's Rocks	broadly 1752 to 1799
Ada's Troth	broadly 1770 to 1840
Makepiece's Mission	broadly 1943 to 1965
Piers' Cadetship	broadly 1938 to 2001.

The Makepiece of this — the fifth — title is a son of the eighth generation immigrant family of a plantation, in Maryland, built on original warranted land granted to the Ploughman family. In 1943, he is a colonel in the US Army Air Corps, working an intelligence desk assigned to understand and counter Hitler's advanced weapons programme. Under Presidential decree, he is given command of a reconnaissance aircraft group to operate from an airfield in Kent, England, which is subject to unremitting enemy threat. Where once stood the family residential hall, there now stands an Anglo-American facility which contains Colonel Ploughman's top secret buried headquarters.

On one of his infrequent days of relaxation, Makepiece seeks out family history records in the county archives only to discover that he is not the only researcher with an interest in a folio of 350 years old papers written by his nine greats grandmother. Makepiece will have to wait until he returns to Maryland to access a copy of the 1659 original Land Warrant, but the folder in the Maidstone archive does contain a transcription of its text. And war has taken the colonel a long way from the comforts of home…

The Land Grant Warrant

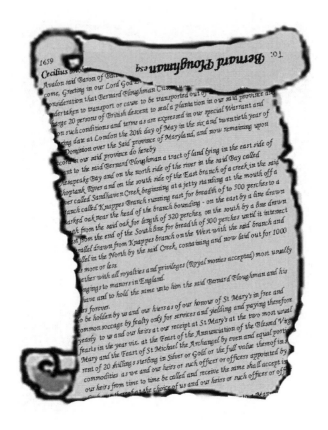

An illustration of the Warrant for land issued under the authority of Cecil Calvert, Lord Baltimore, Governor of Maryland in 1659. The original survived the owners' generations to be a framed, treasured exhibit at the Homestead. The complete, original spelling, text is opposite.

To Bernard Ploughman esq

1659

Cecilius absolute Lord and Proprietary of the provinces of Maryland, and Avalon said Baron of Baltimore to all persons to whom these presents shall come, Greeting in our Lord God Everlasting. Know ye that we for and in consideration that Bernard Ploughman Citizen and a Chirurgeon of London has undertaken to transport or cause to be transported out of England at his own charge 20 persons of British descent to seal a plantation in our said province and upon such conditions and terms as are expressed in our special Warrant and bearing date at London the 20th day of May in the six and twentieth year of our Dominion over the Said province of Maryland, and now remaining upon record in our said province do hereby

Grant to the said Bernard Ploughman a tract of land lying in the east side of Chesapeake Bay and on the north side of the river in the said Bay called Choptank River and on the south side of the East branch of a creek in the said river called Sandhaven Creek beginning at a jetty standing at the mouth of a branch called Knappes Branch running east for breadth of to 500 perches to a marked oak near the head of the branch bounding - on the east by a line drawn south from the said oak for length of 320 perches, on the south by a line drawn west from the end of the South line for breadth of 500 perches until it intersect a parallel drawn from Knappes branch on the West with the said branch and Parallel in the North by the said Creek, containing and now laid out for 1000 acres more or less.

Together with all royalties and privileges (Royal monies accepted) most usually belongings to manors in England. To have and to hold the same unto him the said Bernard Ploughman and his heirs forever.

To be holden by us and our heirs as of our honour of St Mary's in free and common soccage by fealty only for services and yielding and paying therefore yearly to us and our heirs at our receipt at St Mary's at the two most usual feasts in the year viz. at the Feast of the Annunciation of the Blessed Virgin Mary and the Feast of St Michael the Archangel by even and equal portions the rent of 20 shillings sterling in Silver or Gold or the full value thereof in such commodities as we and our heirs or such officer or officers appointed by us or our heirs from time to time be called and receive the same shall accept in discharge thereof at the choice of us and our heirs or such officer or officers as aforesaid.

And we do hereby Deed the said one thousand acres into a Mannor by the name of the Mannor of Ploughman.

Together with a Court Baron and all things thereunto belonging by the law and custom of England. Given at Saint Mary's under our great Seal of our said province of Maryland the seventeenth Day of January in the eight and twentieth Year of our Dominium over the said province of Maryland Anno Domini 1659.

Witness our trusty and well beloved **Josias Hendall** esq our Lieutenant of our said province.

Prologue

"Good of you to make time to see me, Colonel. You gotta be busy preparing your outfit for England. Don't forget to pack your tin hat!"

It was 1:00 pm on May 23rd, 1943 that Colonel Makepiece Ploughman passed through the door into the Oval Room in the White House. President Franklin D. Roosevelt and Secretary of War Henry L Stimson were alone in the room with the small wizened figure standing behind the seated President at his familiar desk. FDR was taking time out of the war planning conference convened in Washington since 12 May. The portrait of George Washington looked down on the scene. The colonel made certain the door was firmly closed and moved to the indicated chair.

"Mister President. I'm able to tell you the aircraft are ready, tried and tested, the world's best. The hangar to park them, over there, is now camouflaged with grass growing on its roof. The technical processing apparatus is being fitted into the bunker..."

"You've been spending our valuable dollars wisely, I hope? I wanna steal a march on Winston with information about Hitler's wonder weapons. Have you brought a map of where this snoddy place is?"

"Snodland, Mister President. By the River Medway, in Kent County England." The colonel, dressed in his best pressed uniform, was pointing at a map he had laid out on the President's desk. "The Brits fly pursuit fighters, day and night, from near there to guard London and there's a barrage balloon outfit sharing our compound to give us some depth away from prying eyes."

"You got enough good American boys to do the job, Colonel?"

"The best, Mister President. Boys and a dozen girls too. Lockheed and Allison have come up trumps; your personal letter helped stir hearts and minds."

"Thought it might!" There was a sense of fun in FDR's spectacled eyes.

"The Brits think you're over there taking photos with special brownies." Henry Stimpson knew what the 1574th Special Projects Security Group's real mission capability was and how it extended beyond photography into signals intelligence and beyond.

"Kodak's finest, Mister Secretary," replied Colonel Ploughman with a smile. "We're going to give them copies to keep in their albums!"

1

"Good. I like a good photograph myself. Now, colonel, I want you to know that I shall personally read every goddam report that comes out of the snoddy..."

"Snodland..." prompted Stimpson.

"Yeh... Snodland outfit, Colonel, so that I can tell General Spaatz where to go drop his bombs. You know about MANHATTAN, Colonel?"

"Enough, sir, to know that we've gotta have it before the Germans, or the Japs, get it."

"Well Colonel..." Henry Stimpson was beginning to fidget with unease about what the President was about to say about the atomic bomb project. The President noticed the secretary's disquiet.

"It's alright, Henry. The colonel's gonna keep his mouth shut. What I was gonna say was... this MANHATTAN bomb might make a hole bigger than the state of Texas... and I don't want Adolf dropping that thing here. If you are right, Colonel Ploughman, and the Kraut corporal's gotten something worse on the slate, he's gotta be stopped. If there's anything you need, or if anyone... and I mean anyone... gets in the way of finding out, you've got an open channel right to my desk, here." FDR thumped his desk. "Right, Henry?"

"Right, Mister President." The Secretary of War grimaced at the thought of a middle ranking officer being given right of access to the President of the United States of America. He was positioned behind FDR's line of sight so his concern did not register with the President. However, Makepiece noticed it.

"I know the value of staying in channels, Mister President." It was the right thing to say to avoid putting Stimson's back up. "I won't misuse my privileged access. As I was coming out of Arlington Street, I just got sight of a MAGIC cypher transcript, hot off the press. The Japs in Rome are telling Tokyo that the Italians have got wind of Hitler's war winning weapon, but they don't know what it is. I would be surprised if the top German brass would share too much with Mussolini, but maybe Berlin wants to stiffen the Axis spaghetti for the battle ahead. There's nothing better than the ultimate weapon to do that."

"I'm interested in hard facts, Colonel. You go get me some evidence and the nation will be grateful. I might even screw something out of Churchill if can I stop him smoking those infernal Havanas. He hasn't let on that that he knows Gerry is planning something new on the bomb front. He's a wily bird and I had to concede a liaison officer from their air force as part of getting use of West Malling airfield, so I guess he thinks we're up to more than I've let on."

Stimpson added, "Winston gave us the data on the German flying disc machines — they call them *Hauenbau* — as a sweetener. These discs use a novel power plant with no obvious propellers and are reputed to be pretty fast."

"I know a little about the *Hauenbau*, Mr Secretary. In the absence of decent photographs, the folks in the Pentagon think the concept is too far fetched and will offer no threat to 1574th Special Projects Security Group's mission."

"I'm meeting with Churchill tomorrow; I'll let him know that your boys will be landing on his field within a week. Now good luck, Colonel — and don't drink too much of their warm beer, it rots your socks. When do you move out?"

"Final roll call is in 72 hours, Mister President, and the advance party will be at Snodland 24 hours after that."

"Make it happen, Colonel. Just make it all work."

A smart salute and Colonel Ploughman left the Oval Office. Now the room was occupied only by the President and his Secretary for War.

"Want to add anything, Henry?"

"Mr President. The Japs and the Gerries are doing a fine job of disassembling the British Empire. But the commies have had a hell of a pasting and if you are going to butter their bread, you've got to protect Joe Stalin from being A-bombed or worse. I'm not suggesting you give Uncle Joe an ABLATIVE clearance but equally it is important that he doesn't get out of step on our parade."

"I get your drift, Henry." The President's face was wreathed in smiles. "I'll get Cordell Hunt at State to have Ike make some concession to keep the reds on-side when we come to divide up the goodies at the endgame. The reds have got to draw some of the heat off Macarthur's boys if they want influence in the Pacific. But we don't want commie red taking over British pink on the maps of Asia."

"I like the line, Mr President. We can let history take their empire apart and finish the job..." pointing at the life size portrait on the wall,

"…that George Washington started 180 years ago. Winnie ain't gonna like it!"

"Winnie ain't gonna know! I want America to come out of this war as top dog. Heh, the Brits were the first to show this nuclear fission thing works with a mighty bang; we had no choice but to bring them over here to work with our boys. So, bomb-wise, we're one up on the Brits and, Hell, we've gotten Einstein sending me letters saying a bomb's feasible too. If all this means understanding what makes Stalin tick, that's OK. And if it means we have to stop Hitler blowing the soviets away, that's OK too. Right, Henry?"

"Right, Mister President!" Secretary Simpson swallowed while he thought. "Your executive order on 28 June 1941, only six days after German troops invaded the Soviet Union, creating the Office of Scientific Research and Development, makes it quite clear we in the federal government take this whole thing seriously. The timing won't escape the Kremlin; they're bound to be trying to work out this nuclear thing for themselves. But, if this Colonel Ploughman's study has any basis… that the Krauts are going for something that makes nuclear bombs old hat… well… we just gotta try to find out."

Chapter 1
1943 ~ Mission Briefing

The view from the aide's window over Bushy Park, 12 miles west of London, was obscured by rain. It had been raining in England since Makepiece had flown in from Iceland. He had some idea why he was waiting outside the General's office. Senior officers, particularly those at staff headquarters level, liked to believe they were in charge of the forces nominally under their command. Colonel Makepiece Ploughman knew different. He was one of only 12 men in the United States of America who knew the real reason why a bird colonel from the Office of National Intelligence (Special Projects) was in England and why four modified Lockheed P-38M twin-seat reconnaissance fighters, together with one unmodified P-38L, had been assigned to the task. The aircraft were en-route while he was transiting through Reykjavik. When he entered the general's office, at what the Americans called Camp Griffis, he would learn if the general had been told the facts by Washington.

The aide had offered coffee. Makepiece was suffering from a surplus of caffeine and had politely refused. Washington to England, via Iceland, was not a comfortable journey and there were security, political and military issues which weighed heavily on his shoulders. This was an occasion where he wished he smoked — something to relax the tension. But the constraints of flying at extreme altitude took precedence. This was no time to pick up a habit that could ignite his lungs from the inside. Extended breathing of pressurised pure oxygen could do strange things to the body.

While waiting, Makepiece reflected that it was just seven days since he had met the President in the Oval Room. Not many colonels had one to one interviews with the President of the United States. FDR had invited Makepiece to sit in an armchair opposite and had spoken very quietly.

"Colonel Ploughman, your paper on Hitler's vengeance weapons makes worrying reading. I can tell you that Churchill shares my concern that the Allies must take control of this issue before Hitler and his gang can unleash these dastardly devices on our democracies. Churchill won't tell how he knows, but the wily fox has somehow got wind of scientific

5

developments deep inside Germany and behind so many layers of secrecy that even ULTRA cannot break."

Makepiece knew the President was referring to the breaking of German coded messages at the British Bletchley Park facility. "I have to tell you that our MAGIC attack against Japanese ciphers has no success either."

Colonel Ploughman knew this lack of success. He did not know that FDR and Churchill had discussed the matter although he suspected that a British source in the Vatican was making sure that 'the Yanks were kept up to speed' with the British understanding the latest German technology.

"The Krauts have got these projects sewn up tighter than a duck's arse. Our boys and girls on the ground can't get a look in." The President paused. He knew that Colonel Ploughman was his best shot at getting the information he needed — short of interviewing Hitler that is! That is why he had used Executive Discretion to authorise the $15 million dollar budget that the Joint Chiefs had said they needed.

FDR spoke again, "Colonel Ploughman, this German plane they call the V-5, the *Amerikabomber*, or that rocket ship the A-4, if they ever use either against America there will be so much panic that we may have to drop out of the war. I cannot, I will not, allow that to happen." FDR was thumping his desktop with a clenched fist.

"You have been selected by the Joint Chiefs to lead our reconnaissance mission to find out what is really going on. I want you to know that your President, your Commander-in-Chief and your Nation expect you to do duty and bring back the evidence which will allow our bomber groups to remove this threat terminally. I shall be reading every word you send back from England; there will be no middle men on this mission. Churchill knows you are coming and there will be someone you know when you get to England to introduce you to cleared folks at Dawes Hill over there to ensure the Brits give you all the support you need."

"Mr President. I will do my best to justify the trust you have placed in me."

"The Joint Chiefs are having your travel orders cut as we speak, Colonel. The classified mission orders will be couriered to Dawes Hill in time for your arrival. I want you to read them very carefully and abide by their requirements. Do I make myself clear?"

"Very clear, Mr President. Thank you for time. Good day to you, sir."

Makepiece's interview in the White House was over.

'Why had the President insisted so strongly that I had to stick to rules? Why would he expect me to do anything different? He has sent me over here to find something a bit stronger than Hitler's V-5 or the A-4. I am not about to tell anyone anything they don't have a need to know, no matter who. Marybeth has not even the vaguest inkling of what my mission is about; why she doesn't even know its codename. In fact, she doesn't know where in England I am going to be. Does the general here know about Operation ABLATIVE? If he mentions it then he does, if not, it's not for me to tell him!'

Makepiece was brought back to army reality with a jolt. Here in England, the general's aide said, "Colonel Ploughman, the general will see you now."

Makepiece stood, smoothed down his uniform, adjusted his headdress and approached the closed door. He knocked under the name plate General Airlift Planning Group, did not wait for summons, and walked in.

Chapter 2
1943 ~ Departure

Marybeth Ploughman stood at the top of the three steps down to the kerb. The tree lined suburb of Alexandria was a pleasure to behold, even at six in the morning. Husband Makepiece was off to meet the President, in his smartly pressed uniform and under a close haircut. She knew that tonight would be their last night together before he did his 'colonel's thing' and went off to war. A neighbour was coming in to look after the children while they went for a special meal down by the river. A military car would be coming to take Makepiece away very early tomorrow.

Makepiece came from within the house. He had gone back to collect his briefcase. Marybeth did not understand why her colonel carried a briefcase. He said it was empty, as indeed it was, except for five blank sheets of paper and three pens just in case. Makepiece did not bring work home, he just came home late, every night it seemed, every week since he told her he had been given a command and it involved a flying unit in England. The men would be going over to England without their wives and they did not know how long their mission would keep them there.

One evening he had told her that he had been summoned by FDR. "...to make sure I don't upset the Brits," he had said. But Marybeth guessed that colonels in the Office of National Intelligence did not normally get summoned to the White House. Makepiece would not talk about where he was going or why. She just had to accept that America was at war and demands were being on everyone. Even the wives in Officers' Club had no gossip about her husband's secret mission. Rumour control was not working, at least in the Ploughman's case.

A military car drove up and stopped alongside the Ploughman address.

"I'll be home prompt tonight, Marybeth. We are ready to go and it's all over bar the shouting."

"I'll be waiting for you, Makepiece." Marybeth stood on tip toe to kiss her husband. He reached around her narrow waist, lifted her clear of the ground to prolong the kiss. "Good luck with the President and don't be taking any nonsense from him, ya' hear!"

Makepiece moved to a step lower than Marybeth's, the better to sustain the sweet kiss. She treasured the moment.

"Um, not bad for a mother of four. I'll tell Mr President that Marybeth Ploughman will be a-calling on Eleanor Roosevelt if I leave the Oval Office without a good word for my little excursion to England. Now you go inside and hustle the kids off to school and I'll be about my business. I'll see you sooner than you think."

Makepiece leant forward to plant another kiss on his wife's mouth and turned away down the steps to the car. His height emphasised a broad back within his uniform jacket under a peak cap. The driver opened the rear, kerbside door saluting the officer and Makepiece climbed in. Marybeth, touching her lips to remind her husband to check for lipstick, waved goodbye as her husband was carried away. As she turned indoors she remembered that her closest friend, Anna, would be calling for coffee about 10 am. A good gossip would kill the time until Makepiece came home. Would he tell her what had happened in the Oval Office this morning? She half expected that he would say nothing. But surely, what it felt like to be in that famous room could not be all that secret. Could it?

Chapter 3
1943 ~ Interview at Bushy Park

"You got some orders, Colonel?" The general's greeting was curt. Makepiece had saluted his superior and received a cursory response. Makepiece delved into his briefcase and removed the only piece of paper from it.

"Park your butt, Colonel, while I see what the great chiefs say about you."

Makepiece sat while General Packer cursorily scanned the familiar paperwork. It was a formality. He already knew that this Colonel Ploughman was his in name only, for budget management purposes. Packer did not want to add to his pile of trouble with oddball experimental planes buzzing around combat zones.

"You seem to have gotten yourself some pretty powerful friends in the Pentagon, Colonel. Word here is the Secretary for War is keeping his eye on you. You bringing in four P-38 for the Brits to evaluate as night fighters ain't going to cut much ice hereabouts. They, the Brits, have already been stateside and turned down Lockheed's finest. So what's so special about your planes?"

"These are two seaters, General," replied Makepiece being economical with the truth. "Our technical guys reckon a second pair of eyes gives the night pursuit fighter an edge. It's the way the British Royal Air Force is going. And we are both going for two engines."

"I've been given the word that I am to give you every assistance, Colonel. Pretty important folks in America think you can sell these P-38 to Churchill. You go about your duties, Colonel and don't rattle my cage none. I'm a four screws man, myself. If it don't need four propellers to lift it, it ain't worth the juice fetchin' it. It's a busy life here and I've got an invasion to plan. There are sealed orders for you on the desk outside, with my aide. Sign for them on your way out."

Makepiece took the cue that the interview with the General of the Military Air Transport Service had ended. He stood, saluted and began to advance for the return of his duty assignment papers.

"Aren't you a bit long in the tooth to be flying fighter combat missions? It says here," he dabbed the travel orders Makepiece had given him, "that you are 43. I would say that's pushing it." His chin had risen so that he appeared to be looking down his nose jealously looking at an officer of certain years who had gotten a flying command.

"Oh they are giving me a couple of young navy pilots and some RAF jockeys to steer these things around the sky." Makepiece's face creased into a smirk and his shoulders shrugged. "I don't expect I'll be doing anything too strenuous, General."

"Make sure you know the way we indent for spares over here. My aide will give you the low down. I have appointed Colonel Carrel to be your interface with my staff. A good man, Carrel, knows how to get blood out the proverbial stone. Knows his way around airlift, so he's a kosher mover and dumper in my book. Cultivate him, Colonel Ploughman. Yes, I like that. Cultivate him! Now, Colonel, I've a war to win." The general reached out to return Makepiece's travel orders.

This time Makepiece did not delay in moving through the door. Even as he was closing it, the aide was holding out a sealed package and a document receipt book. "Colonel Carrel will see you in his office, Colonel Ploughman. The orderly will show you the way — after you've signed for that package — Colonel."

The buzzer on the desk was indicating the aide's presence was required behind the closed door.

While he was signing for the sealed pack, Makepiece reflected, 'So they haven't told this general what I'm supposed to do. Life around here is going to get interesting...' His thoughts were interrupted by the aide speaking.

"Oh, Colonel Makepiece, I ought to warn you. The Brits spell the name of this 'ere country-park-cum-Kraut-bomb-target as 'Bushey' with an 'e'. Us'un Yanks spell it without the 'e' as in B U S H Y — like 'bushy tailed'. If you're confused just think how bad it must be for Hitler!" The buzzer sounded too insistent to continue the discussion. The aide was already rising from his chair and the orderly was indicating the visitor should follow him.

As he moved through the corridors, Makepiece wondered if the aide was trying to be funny or if he was already 'bomb happy'. It was of no consequence, he'd another staff colonel to get around to his way of thinking.

Chapter 4
1943 ~ Camp Griffis, Teddington, Middlesex, England

It was through the corridors, up some stairs and down to the end of another corridor that the orderly escorted Makepiece Ploughman to the office door marked Colonel Logistics (Special Projects). A bold notice warned: 'Knock but do not enter until invited'. The orderly knocked, waited, knocked again more insistently and was about to repeat with greater vigour when the door opened.

"Yeah! What?"

"Colonel, sir, there's a colonel sent up to see you by the general, sir."

"What general, boy? You got ID, Colonel?"

"General Packer, Colonel, sir. Down the corridor aways."

"Uh!" The colonel was inspecting Makepiece ID card. "You got any orders, Colonel?"

Makepiece handed the colonel the same sheet that General Packer had looked over. His inspection of the document was more detailed.

"Ok, Orderly, that will be all. I'll look after Colonel Ploughman from here. You don't want a receipt for his body, do you?"

"No, Colonel, that will be all right, Colonel. I'll tell the general that the colonel's got the colonel as required. With the colonel's permission..." The orderly saluted, did not wait for acknowledgement, and hurried away.

The office door opened wide. "Come in Colonel Ploughman. Park your butt on anything that doesn't move and I'll pull you a coffee. Cream and Sugar?" The office door closed.

"Sorry about that — got an image to uphold. My name's Able Benjamin Carrel. Folks call me 'Easy' after my initials... ABC... easy as... geddit?" Beneath a balding head and wire framed glasses, his face broke into an ice-breaking smile.

"Good day to you Easy, folks call me Makepiece on account of that's my name." Makepiece offered a handshake. "General Packer's aide gave me a pack from Washington which I would appreciate a little space to read and then, perhaps, we could have a talk about what is going on? I'll take that coffee, both please. Does it ever stop raining in this God-forsaken country?"

Easy's right hand seemed to hesitate. "Only on Tuesdays and when there's a 'y' in the month. Then it snows or fogs. You'll love it. Makepiece it is then. Welcome to Camp Griffis aka Bushy Park not to be confused with the other Bushey Hall, way up north of here, where the 8th Fighter Command pursuit jockies sit next to the RAF's HQ Fighter Command at Bentley Priory, that of Battle of Britain fame."

The two men grinned, two professionals going to war, feeling each other out before the real business began. They shook hands. Makepiece, at 6 feet 2 inches tall, towered over the other. Both grips were firm, reassuring and confident; both noticed the other's palm was slightly hardened through fair wear and tear. These men could work together with mutual respect. Makepiece noticed that Easy's uniform did not carry aircrew wings; this man was a professional ground officer.

"By the look of the seals on that pack, you ought to come with a government health warning. Tell you what — my major has gone to Dawes Hill and won't be back until late afternoon. Dawes Hill aka Pinetree to the Yanks and High Wycombe to the Brits — it helps confuse the enemy; it's where the big cheeses of our 8th Bomber Command hang out. Here's the key to his office, make yourself comfortable through that door while you read those 'burn before reading' secrets from the Stateside's big white chiefs. Come back when you're ready and I will clear a hole in this paper. We can talk about how I can help you with whatever it is you're up to. I've a feeling that my life just could be about to get more interesting. Oh, if the air raid warning goes, come out and leave everything and lock the door. I'll show you where we go. Krauts haven't dropped their calling card for a week now so it might happen. We go for lunch chow in the O-club about noon."

* * *

The most important document was succinct and to the point: on headed notepaper from the Chairman of the Joint Chiefs of Staff it read:

From: Office of Chairman of Joint Chief of Staffs, Washington DC
To: Colonel Makepiece F. Ploughman
May 25th 1943.

With effect June 1st, 1943 you are to take command of Number 1574 Special Project Fighter Group, to be based along with the British Royal Air Force at West Malling, Kent, England. You will be assigned four P-38M and one P-38L fighters to undertake operational duties associated with OPERATION ABLATIVE. You will be assigned such aircrew and ground maintenance staff as necessary to complete your mission; these may be American or British nationals for whom security clearance will be notified through the Office of National Intelligence (Great Britain Detachment), Dawes Hill, England.

Your operational and technical mission tasking will be directly from the Office of National Intelligence (Special Projects) to which office all results, on whatever medium is appropriate, are to be couriered with all due speed commensurate with the ABLATIVE security directive. You will use the services of the ONI located at Dawes Hill, England for this purpose and to interface with any British Royal Air Force formation for any purpose.

You are to adhere to the ABLATIVE Security Directive and will be supported by a dedicated group of US Army field security soldiers who will remain under your command while ABLATIVE operations continue in Great Britain.

Your administrative command for any American national as may be assigned to your command will be through the General Airlift Planning Group, Bushy Park, England. Your requirements for fuel, aircraft spares, consumables, vehicles and other transport, and for accommodation will be through Camp Griffis, England.

Your administrative command of any British nationals as may be assigned to your command will be through the RAF Liaison Officer nominated to you through ONI(GB det), Dawes Hill, England.

You are to occupy your assigned command by June 14th, 1943 so as to work up your capability towards declaration of operational readiness by 23:59 EST on June 30th, 1943.

Signed

Chairman, Joint Chief of Staff

In the pack was an abbreviated version of the ABLATIVE briefing paper that had been delivered to the President. There were nominal rolls of six American aircrew, he knew them well from training at Patuxent, of intelligence analysts and of ground crew experienced on the Lockheed P-38 fighter. There was a separate roster of a 30 strong US Army security and guard forces headed by a named officer Captain Jodell Lee Grant. Makepiece chuckled at the name; he hoped there would be no conflict of loyalties between the 'Lee' and the 'Grant' components of this young officer. A third list was a register of the enlisted men and the attached specialist contractors who would be at West Malling.

There was a letter of introduction to Colonel Julius Knapp US Army at the ONI(GB det), Dawes Hill. Julius Knapp happened to be his brother-in-law, brother to Marybeth. Makepiece knew Julius was in the European theatre but he did not know where or doing what. Now it became clear; if he was on ABLATIVE duties then he would have kept silent about everything. What on earth did Julian tell his wife back home in Alexandria? Makepiece would ask him when they met. Now there, in that letter, was another solution to the hanging questions following that strange interview with FDR. The President had said, "Churchill knows you are coming and there will be someone you know, when you get to England, to introduce you to cleared folks at Dawes Hill over there to ensure the Brits give you all the support you need." There had been some background planning going on before he was tasked with briefing the President! Was he going to have to visit Churchill too?

There was a map of central Kent County, England attached to typed notes. He had looked up West Malling before leaving Washington. Located about 4 miles west of Maidstone, the RAF base was under the Luftwaffe's approach tracks for their bombing raids on southern London. He had not shared this news with Marybeth but he knew she would have been interested by another detail if he could have told her. Makepiece would be billeted in Snodland, three miles north of the airfield. It was from Snodland that the Maryland Ploughmans heralded in the 1660s. Or, to be more specific as befits an intelligence officer he thought, 10 times great grandfather Bernard's father had been born there before becoming a grocer in London and producing the Bernard who was buried in the Homestead's plot back home. He foresaw that much of any spare time would be trying to resolve the family history questions Marybeth would dream up.

'I can't not tell her where I'm living, can I?' Makepiece knew he could be between a rock and hard place. 'My life will be a misery if I try to hide it from her.' He had not yet become acquainted with the censor's rules, but that was for the future.

The typed notes pinned to the map informed Makepiece that a reconnaissance processing complex was being constructed near the accommodation huts for his group. The aircraft would be given a dedicated hangar located sufficiently far away from RAF activities to deter casual visitors. The nominated RAF liaison officer promised to be fully familiar with the West Malling area.

Makepiece repacked the papers, except for the introduction to Julius Knapp, and knocked on the Colonel Carrel's door. Arrangements were made to secure Makepiece's papers.

"Before we break for lunch, I've been informed that the British have appointed a liaison officer to help you through the red tape at their RAF West Malling airfield." Easy Carrel was feeling more settled now. "They are using a codename ABLATIVE. Does that mean anything to you?"

"It's the codename Washington and London are using as shorthand for why I'm here. I'm flying four P-38s to investigate using a sort of telescopic viewfinder, like a star gazing telescope looking horizontally, to see if we can improve success in night fighting."

"Well they're putting you in the firing line in Kent, old lad."

Makepiece replied, "It's what it's all about. Churchill wants to do something to sort out Göring's bombers and FDR wants to be seen as helping. And not so much of the old lad if you don't mind! What with you and the general going on about my collection of anno dominii, I'll be drawing my pension before we knock off Hitler."

"Don't count on it. The RAF are telegraphing me with a name of their man and contact details. Tell you what, I fancy a day out. Why don't I take you off to West Malling airbase tomorrow and show you the ropes? It will give me an excuse to meet their blanket stacker or whatever they call their stores chappie."

The two men set out for the O-club and lunch. "Tell me, Makepiece, have you flown one of these P-38 things? It's not another widowmaker, is it? I have enough problems getting caskets for our younger birdmen."

Makepiece left the question hanging. Time enough for flying stories in due course.

"Do you know my brother-in-law Julius Knapp, Colonel in the Air Corps? My orders say I have to go to a place called Dawes Hill to meet him. Perhaps you'd have your clerk find out how to get there from West Malling. I presume I'll get my own car...?"

Chapter 5
1943 ~ Alexandria, Virginia

It was serviceman's wife's lot. Off he goes to war and leaves running the family to his woman. Four children was a handful, but they were good kids and helped around the home. There had been some tears, except from their eldest son who wanted to join the US Navy and become a submariner. 'Well, at least there is brother Julius's wife along the way; Antonia is missing her husband and more so now their boy is flying off carriers in the Pacific. Antonia guesses that Julius is in England but at least he doesn't fly. I do hope that Makepiece doesn't take any unnecessary risks.'

The memory of their final embrace, his kissing away her tears and his soft tender withdrawal from their final contact, and the wave as he went away to war with his mouthed mute, "I love you, Marybeth," all persisted in yet another cup of coffee. She knew he would not look back as the car drove away. He loathed goodbyes as much as she. But there, in the rear window, was his left hand opening and closing twice and clearly visible before the staff car turned a corner to go out of sight.

Marybeth decided that the best way to involve the children was to have a family conference. Now that would not be easy because daughter Antonia, named after her aunt and godmother, was courting and the boys were forever in the gym with their basketball. However, a special cherry pie should hold the four long enough for them to think they thought of going back to Annapolis to be close to the Homestead.

The mother's subterfuge worked for 20 seconds. It was youngest daughter, Sue Ellen, who cracked it. The special pie with luxury ice cream did not fool her and her siblings were quick off the mark.

"OK, kids, you cracked it. We all gotta have a serious conference." There was just time to remove her kitchen pinafore and be seated before the started.

"Awh, Mom. Do we have to?"

"I gotta go to the rest room."

"I just knew there was a reason for cherry pie." The eldest could be trusted to blow her story wide open; he wanted to get out and throw some baseball.

"Right. Girls, you stack the dishes in the sink, and all, while you boys clear the table. It's alright; I won't keep you from your friends long."

"Mom's cracking the slave whip, boys, so you get on with your chores."

The place was tidy in no time and the five sat around the table for Mother to tell them what was so urgent as to spoil their entire evening with their friends.

"Did you like my cherry pie?" as she smoothed her short blond hair away from her face.

"Mom!" moaned the family in unison.

"Well, alright then. Now we don't know how long your father is going to be away, do we? And we don't want to stay in stuffy old Washington when there's fresh air out on the bay. Right?"

"Right," replied the boys. Was she talking about the prospect of getting some sailing in?

"But I like it here," intoned Antonia.

"That's 'cos you've got a boyfriend!" interjected Sue Ellen.

"Look who's talking," replied her elder sister. The boys just grimaced at the exchange.

"You've all got friends up in Annapolis. And there lots to do out at Rosetta's Rocks. So, I thought… while your father is away winning this horrible war… we'd go and open up the Annapolis house and maybe spend some time with Grandmother Ploughman out at the Homestead. What do you say?"

"Sound great." The boys concluded that their mother knew exactly how to get her way and, so long as that meant getting out on the tidewater with rods, then it was OK by them. The girls were less keen.

"But Mom." Antonia could see that separation from boyfriend Mark was looming and tears were already beginning to show. There was no such reaction from the younger Sue Ellen.

Marybeth reacted to her daughter's adolescent tears. "Antonia, my dear. Annapolis is only a bus ride away and Mark could visit. And you can write to each other. And there is the phone. There's no need for tears. Imagine how I feel about being separated from your father and not expecting him to be allowed to phone."

"But Mom," started Sue Ellen. "You're older than us and don't have so many friends to leave behind."

"Tcch! Child, sometimes there are things you just have to do. All of you, would you like me to arrange to move home back to Annapolis in time for the summer holidays? We could arrange for you to finish your schooling up there. And you could invite your friends over to Rosetta's Rocks, for the day, when the new the bridge is open and go riding and fishing and perhaps shooting on the plantation. What do you say?"

"They're not going to open the bridge. Someone complained there is a war on and the project has been cancelled." Youngest son Bernard was airing his knowledge. Marybeth just shrugged. There were reliable ferry routes to cross the bay.

Within two minutes the children had came around to Mother's way of thinking. With tears wiped away, Antonia went up to her mother and whispered, "Thanks for a good pie, Mother. I won't be out late, promise. I've just gotta tell the girls our news."

The eldest came round the table and kissed his mother's cheek. "Don't you worry, Mom. I'll take good care of you till Father comes home."

"Thank you, Frisby. I just knew I could rely on you." She reached for her son's hand and held it to her cheek. She was so lucky to have such lovely children.

Privately, she thought a little prayer, 'Makepiece, my darling man, take care of yourself and come home safely to your family. We miss you so much already.'

*   *   *

At that moment, across the Atlantic divide, Colonel Makepiece Ploughman was settling into yet another unfamiliar bed in the Officers' Quarters at Bushy Park. His thoughts were about the family he'd left behind. Would he ever see them again? England didn't look so safe to him! He faced an extraordinary challenge ahead, using remarkable machines and excellent men. But, somehow, he could not escape the loneliness of separation from Marybeth and the unmitigated love and support she gave him — through thick and thin. 'I'll say a little prayer for her before I go to sleep. Perhaps it'll help…'

Chapter 6
1943 ~ RAF West Malling, Kent, England

Waiting for the two USAAC colonels at the guardroom of RAF West Malling was Wing Commander Cliff Battel. Makepiece Ploughman was the first to dismount the passenger seat of the jeep, put down his collar, and thrust his right hand forward in greeting. Standing before Makepiece was a uniformed pilot with bad burn disfiguration to the right hand side of his face. The RAF officer saluted with a gloved right hand, showing the flat open palm forward as was customary, to his peaked cap which enclosed most of his hair. The gesture seemed to emphasise his pilot's wings on his chest above a row of medal ribbons. Observant Makepiece noticed a brief wince of pain before responding with the American salute touching his forehead just above the eyebrow with open palm face down. The RAF officer offered his ungloved left hand for the handshake.

"Welcome to RAF West Malling, gentlemen, colonels. My name is Cliff Battel, one time Hun slayer now mahogany desk jockey and host nation minder. I hope you had a good drive down." Makepiece had overcome the surprise of the awkward left-to-right handshake. He was about to speak when Colonel Easy Carrel spoke.

"Hi," he started, "I'm Able B Carrel from COSSAC. We spoke yesterday. This here is Colonel Makepiece Ploughman of the United States Army Air Corps and selected by FDR himself to help us win the war." Easy was not sure whether to offer his right hand or his left. He chose right, which was vigorously gripped and shaken by the other's left.

"Good. Let's go and meet the Station Commander, get the formalities over, then we can go somewhere private to have a chat." Makepiece thought you could break ice with the English accent. "Leave the jeep there; no-one will steal it from outside the Guardroom. It's only a hundred yards to Station Headquarters." The Wing Commander host was already turning to guide the way.

There was only time for pleasantries about how fine Kent looked in the June sunlight, despite the unpleasantness of the *Luftwaffe*, when the three men passed through the double swing doors of the headquarters building, turned right along the polished wooden parquet floor to the last office door on the right, which was open. They walked in.

The sergeant at the desk stood to greet the incoming officers. Indoors, he was not wearing headdress and therefore did not salute. A narrow table had been placed along the wall by the door. An unmarked internal door led into a further office.

The aide waved at an open book on the table, "Would you gentlemen please sign the Visitors' Book? The Station Commander is on the telephone at the moment. I'll take you straight in when he has finished. You'd like a drink after your drive, gentlemen." It was not so much a question as an expectation. The sergeant turned to the WAAF seating at the second desk apparently overawed by the arrival of three high ranking officers.

"Four cups of tea, Airwoman Bates. And be sharp about it, these gentlemen are pilots and we don't want to keep the *Luftwaffe* waiting for their attention, do we?"

The sergeant, by some instinct known only to such aides, had hardly turned away from the blushing 18 years old, big breasted WAAF when he announced, "Wing Commander Townsend is off the phone now."

Without further waiting, the sergeant knocked sharply on the internal door and opened it. "The American colonels have arrived, sir. Wing Commander Battel is with them. I have taken the liberty of ordering tea, sir; it is about that time of the morning for a cuppa. Bates, smartly now."

There were introductions, invitations to be comfortable, sipping of tea. The luxury of coffee as a hospitality refreshment was not offered, such was the wartime exigency. Even seated, Makepiece's bearing gave him a presence which his British host recognised. For his part, Makepiece noted the gallantry medal ribbons, for the DSO and AFC with bar beneath the pilot's brevet, on Peter Townsend's jacket. Then the Station Commander spoke.

"Pleased to see you're here gentlemen. The 1574th is very welcome to join us at West Malling on the front line. The engineers have been busy building a lamella hangar for your aircraft, the final earth covering is going on as I speak and they'll be seeding it tomorrow. You won't know it's there in a month."

"That's good, Wing Commander." Speaking with a precise Maryland timbre, Makepiece was pleased that at least there would be somewhere protective for his unique aircraft. Being only 30 miles from the English Channel, he had felt his small force was exposed to enemy interest.

The Station Commander thought his guest's short comment spoke legends for a man he felt he could respect.

"I understand you are bringing some P-38 Lightnings. I did not get a chance to fly one myself when they were being evaluated by the boffins. Probably won't have a chance in one of yours now either. I've just been told I'm on the move again, I only just got six months in with my own station. Fighter Command is putting in Wing Commander T. Heynes as my relief on the 18 June." Looking directly at Makepiece, "You'll have your feet under the table by then. Pity to have to move; I commanded 85 Squadron here while we concentrated on day interception. Now they are shooting down the Hun with night fighting under Cat's Eyes Cunningham, the lucky bastard."

"I am sorry our acquaintance is so brief," said Makepiece. He was thinking, 'Don't these folks look young to be fighting...' Again he glanced at the gallantry awards on his host's uniform under a handsome face.

"West Malling is a happy place, Colonel. Your guys are going to love it here. We all do. I'm sure you'll have lots to talk with Cliff 'The Sprite' Battel here. I'll let him tell you how he got his nickname and don't believe everything he says about his Morgan three-wheeler in Wrotham Forest!"

The colonels sensed the audience was at an end. As they stood to file out, Sprite hung back. Makepiece caught the exchange from Battel, 'Has your foot recovered?... and Townsend's question, 'Are those burns OK now?...' and the visitors were in the aide's office.

Cliff Battel said, "I've booked the Station Conference Room for a chat. We can talk administration and what West Malling can and can't do for us. We'll get across to your new hangar after lunch. Now this way. If you want to ease springs, the Gents is through there."

"Gents?" queried the bemused Makepiece.

"Male rest room," Easy explained. "You'll find they speak a different lingo over here. Just wait until you start talking about female anatomy!"

*   *   *

Lunch in the officers' mess was a first time experience for the American colonels. They were not used to full table service for what they would have expected to be a casual meal. They passed an anteroom with officers reading newspapers, and drinking, presumably coffee, from miniature cups with saucers. Cliff Battel hurried them back to the jeep at the guardroom whence they made their way around the airfield perimeter track to the lamella hangar on the remote, northern side of the field. It looked stark, but the covering of earth for grass camouflage was nearly complete.

'Not quite what I told FDR, I guess. But at least it's nearly finished. Very impressive.' Battel continued the guided tour around the remainder of the RAF airfield pointing out the protective blister hangarettes housing RAF fighters: Spitfire Mk XIVs and twin engine Beaufighters.

The group of officers had not dwelt on the details of the lamella building. 'Time for that later.' It was the cue for Colonel Easy to take his farewell in his vehicle and leave Makepiece in the capable hands of the RAF liaison officer.

"I suggest we make our way to Snodland later," Cliff said to Makepiece, aware that an American staff car was approaching. "That's where your domestic and technical accommodation has been prepared. I hope you will be impressed; we tried to follow every detail of your requirement. It's 5 miles down the road. Our miles are nearly the same as yours, aren't they? We'll need to go back and forth to the lamella hangar and from there we can use our own airfield exit which is nearer to Snodland. It also saves having to cross the runway."

An RAF Police escort jeep had accompanied the replacement US Army vehicle across the airfield and Easy's jeep on its way out.

"By the way, Colonel," opened the British driver, presumably co-opted for the delivery task. "It's time to introduce you to your staff car — er, sorry — military transport. Full colonels are entitled to a Ford V8 Pilot... so... here's yours. It's got a full tank, and the steering wheel is where it ought to be. We can have a few turns around the hangar exterior before we venture on to His Majesty's highway."

"Err..."

"And the colonel is entitled to a staff driver if he wishes."

As they were moving in the car, Cliff continued talking, "RAF Snodland is commanded by a Squadron Leader. He's got a number of lodgers, including a WAAF Barrage Balloon squadron, an ATS Searchlight Regiment, a Royal Military Police guard for the local Italian prisoners of war camp, and an American outfit called the 1574th Special Project Security Group with its ancillary security guard, and American Red Cross element. Your compound, at least the technical part is in an inner compound and has been laid out to look like a hospital from the air."

"Well, Wing Commander, the sooner I see this set up, the better. How the hell do you Limeys cope with driving on the wrong side of the road? And what's with all those abbreviations?"

*   *   *

It was the two days later that Makepiece settled into his office in the technical compound at RAF Snodland. He invited Cliff to come in and shut the door. The air raid all-clear siren had just sounded. Cliff Battel noticed that the safe door was open.

"Now we are alone, call me Makepiece." The hand gesture indicated the 'Sprite' might be seated which meant that he could remove his hat. Although no longer a new sight to Makepiece, he still had difficulty in controlling his reaction to the disfigurement normally hidden.

"That's fine Colonel, er Makepiece, but only when there's just the two of us. You're in charge and that's the way it's going to be seen. Would I be right to assume that you have seen my ABLATIVE clearance?"

"Yes. It's obvious you know about mine. From Air Vice Marshal Charles Medhurst at Air Ministry?"   It was a rhetorical question. Makepiece knew that after Churchill, fewer than ten English names were briefed on objectives of the ABLATIVE mission, including Cliff Battel, Bomber Harris, Chief of the Air Staff Lord Portal, his Vice Chief, and a scientist called R V Jones. Even so, these men knew only that the ABLATIVE mission target was about German 'Vengeance' weapons, about the intention to collect aerial photographic intelligence if possible, and the dissemination of any photographic images that might be made. Makepiece judged that Battel needed to know about further secret intelligence collection methods, and more detailed description of the specific target, intended at least initially for American eyes only. He knew that Roosevelt eventually would share the ABLATIVE product with the British when there was something the Brits had in their unique grasp that he wanted.

"Make yourself comfortable, Cliff. Are you going to be OK with taking off that hat? Tell me something about yourself. Sergeant Greenburg will bring us coffee — if she knows what's good for her. She'll be getting a Level 1 ABLATIVE clearance, by the way."

Cliff had removed his peaked No 1 Service Dress hat. Although four inches shorter than Makepiece, the full extent of the damage to his face and cranium now became apparent to Makepiece for the first time. The man had managed to mask the worst from Makepiece in the officers' mess. Now could be seen the right hand side of his face, from below the jaw line, to above his deformed ear and into the hair line was stretched white skin with streaks of red scaring. His mouth was pulled to the right so that there was a suggestion of visible teeth between his lips. He kept his right hand gloved at all times and used it as little as possible.

Sergeant Julia Greenburg brought in a tray of coffee, creamer and sugar. She could not contain a gasp of surprise when she first glimpsed Cliff Battel's damaged face. She did not delay her departure, closing the office door quietly behind her.

Makepiece waited to gauge Battel's reaction to his aide's sharp intake of breath; none was forthcoming. He noticed Cliff lifted his coffee cup, accepted papers and pointed with his left hand.

"OK. I'm 26, unmarried and not spoken for. That's the sort of reaction, like from your PA, I get from all the tottie around town. Maybe always will with this monika." He was pointing to his face. "Flew Hurricanes out of Biggin Hill, sometimes Duxford, collected four Dorniers and a '109 with a couple of probables thrown in. Caught this when a Junkers 88 blew up when I was too close having a shuftie; set light to my kite and I had a bit of a struggle to get out. Landed near the river at Gravesend and woke up at East Grinstead hospital as a guinea pig."

"I didn't know that RAF drivers-airframe went in for re-incarnation. Guinea pig?"

Cliff grimaced at the memory, then continued: "Oh no! There's a doctor called Archibald McIndoe who fixes up burnt aircrew with a mixture of trial and error sweetened with his brand of torture. He calls it plastic surgery with a bit of psychology stirred in. We christened his patients as 'The Guinea Pig Club' because he was always trying out new treatments. They never found my Hurricane. I got 700 flying hours, 50 at night; 400 in Hurricanes, 100 on Spits. Some Defiants and Blenhiems. I had a couple of hours in a P-38 — we call them Lightnings over here. Impressive machine. I lived through the experience. Never claimed the Junkers that got me!"

Cliff winced as he tried to make his right arm comfortable. Then he continued.

"Medical board won't let me fly because this arm doesn't do all the things it needs to do in a Hurricane. Instructional training is out of the question." His eyes watched Makepiece's face for a reaction to what he was saying. "But Air Marshal Medhurst recognises you can't keep a good chap down so he persuaded me to come and help you operate P-38s on some hush-hush mission, even if they are to carry American markings. Well, we've let some Yanks fly Spits on recce missions at Mount Farm ... oh, I see you know about them already. So here I am. Ask, Colonel Makepiece Ploughman, sir, and Winston Churchill's 'action this day' will work wonders on your behalf."

"I'll try to match that," started Makepiece. "I'm 43, married with four kids; the oldest wants to join the navy. Home, with wife Marybeth, is in Alexandria just outside Washington DC and not too far from the office in Arlington where I was based. I was a staff colonel looking forward to a brand new desk in the Department of Defense's new Pentagon building. I was working the intelligence desk on German future weapons. They insisted that to keep my pilot rating, and the 30% pay hike, I keep my hand in flying. I just happened to go down to Patuxent Airbase and fly a new creature called the P-38. I've got two and bit thousand hours in my log book, mainly on twin engines after initial training. I tried carrier landing a couple of times; not for me, strictly for the fishheads in dark blue. Lockheed have tried to get the RAF to take some P-38s, but your boffins say it's not as fast as the Spitfire, or as agile."

Cliff nodded. One half of his face smiled, the other half did not react. 'This Yank is someone speaking my lingo ... he's someone I can do business with.'

"That maybe your guys' opinion, we didn't offer the P-38M-SP that we'll be getting in the 1574th. Anyway, I put together a paper, which the Joint Chiefs seemed to like." Makepiece was gaining confidence in the man sitting opposite. He had a feeling that they could work together. "It went to the President. FDR said I had to get off my butt and go and find out the truth. So here I am and here you are and the coffee is getting cold."

The two men reached for their cups.

"Hey, that's real coffee; I'm gonna enjoy working here," savoured Battel.

"The Joint Chiefs in Washington have assigned me and my group to the COSSAC invasion planners. It's only nominal really, for show, and in case I need to kick arse in getting support. COSSAC have been told that we are testing a new night sight for pursuit purposes, I don't think they've briefed Ike on the full gambit of the ABLATIVE mission yet. I am pretty much on my own as far as tasking, but we'll need to cooperate with the local fighters and Bomber Command to make sure we don't get shot down by our own folks. The COSSAC line makes some sense since some of what we'll be doing, photographic stuff, will be feeding straight into the targeting planners for the invasion. It helps credibility for the cover story. But there's more to it than that"

Both men were sipping their coffee.

"I think you'll be impressed when we get to look at the aircraft. They are bit special — P-38M-SP dual seat — but not like your production line stuff. The boys at Andrew's Air Force Base have breathed on them more than some. And there are a few Lockheed maintainer crew and some Allison engine fitters all thrown into uniform to help us along. We can also have a look in the strong room in the lamella where the kit from the Georgia workshops will be unboxed for checking."

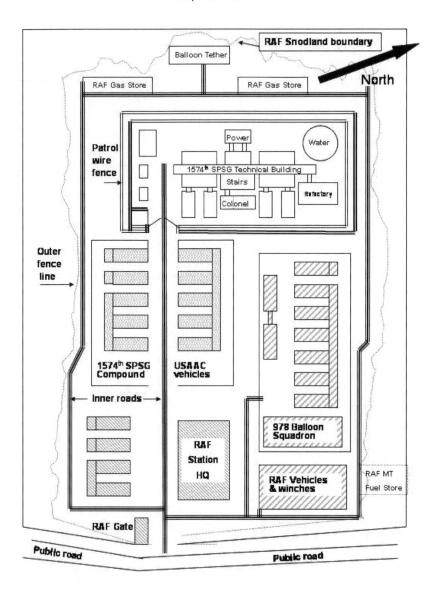

Site Plan of RAF Snodland, Kent, England

Chapter 7
1943 ~ RAF Snodland, Kent, England

Colonel Ploughman had completed his first formal inspection of his compound. His aircraft and maintainers were all due in the next day. Already the US Army Field Security Group, commanded by Captain Jodell Lee Grant, attached to the 1574th SPSG were guarding the inner compound ready for the influx of material and documents essential for their operational mission.

Lines of demarcation with host Station Commander, Squadron Leader Wilburne, had been agreed which allowed for the USAAC team with its ancillary civilians to use the amenities of the RAF compound and they would adhere to RAF security arrangements. The Americans were bringing in a civilian volunteer group from the American Red Cross to provide a little social tenderness for their boys out on the line. The RAF agreed that the local Red Cross from Rochester would be invited to match the American contribution. The Americans would all have access to the British NAFFI provided facilities.

But from the outer of the pair of technical compound's security fences inwards was exclusively the responsibility of the US Army and no unauthorised entry would be tolerated. The US Army was armed with authority to use lethal force.

Now it was time to bring Cliff Battel more fully into the mission of the group. The air-raid alarm had just sounded the all clear. Makepiece had chosen to use his above ground office.

"Come in, Cliff. There's something I want you to read. Only in my office and while I am present, old lad. That's the rules with this stuff."

Makepiece's upstairs office inside the Technical Compound was sparsely furnished. He had an administrative office above ground while being inside 'his' wire where he could deal with the RAF host and other non-operational matters if the need arose. Visitors entered the compound only by invitation. In this room, there were no wall charts, two clean white boards, frosted glass windows with the paper tape anti-shatter cross, a desk, the commanding officer's chair, four other chairs pushed back against the wall. A metal four drawer filing cabinet stood next to a steel, combination lock, safe. Makepiece allowed himself two decorative concessions. Next to his secure telephone was a picture of Marybeth and the four children. Above the safe was hung a wall mounted calendar. The lights were bright and the blackout roller curtain dropped to keep out the June sunshine. A black insecure phone sat on a small desk under the window; security conscious Wing Commander Battel noticed it had been unplugged from its wall socket.

Makepiece also had a second, downstairs, office, close to the functional operations and intelligence areas. It too was sparsely furnished.

Cliff closed the office door to the upstairs office. "A touch austere, Makepiece, if I may say so. A clear desk policy has its limits when there are two rings of armed guards and two fences to keep the bogeymen out."

"We're not horsing around with this shit, Cliff. My butt is for the high jump while they bury the rest of me if any of this stuff gets out. We could be into the end of the world as we know it, Hitler and all, with what we are looking for. Let me give you a résumé, then you can sit there and read it. This paper went to the President and he spoke to Churchill and Makepiece got joed. Simple as that. I have to tell you that FDR did not, as I understand it, tell Winston about the Einstein Engine so you might be the only Brit who knows — for now. It has to stay that way until I, personally, or my replacement, if they shoot me, tells you otherwise. You agree now or this briefing gets heavily curtailed."

"OK. I understand your rules. Me, I'll comply, I guess!"

"None of what I am going to tell you goes out of this room, even to the COSSAC, even to Air Ministry, even to Churchill. Those folks have their sources. We are going to be another source but better. More reliable! Independent, harder evidence."

"I'm all ears, Makepiece. Well, one and half ears." He touched his wounded temple.

"And the crew across the corridor don't know half of it, either. Only Rod and, shortly, you, are getting the full... er... as you might put it... poop."

So Makepiece began his briefing, working with the assumption that the wing commander had the basic knowledge of the search for Hitler's ultimate war-winners. Makepiece began with the Japanese diplomatic telegraph message code which had been intercepted and broken by MAGIC. A Japanese cipher text from their ambassador in Rome had reported an interview with Mussolini held in late 1942. Upset that the

British had not surrendered to Axis overwhelming force, *Il Duce* had boasted that Hitler was preparing a range of vengeance weapons to unleash on the Allies. The telegram had mentioned the ten such devices of which four were well advanced including what Hitler called the V-1 short range flying bomb, a ballistic rocket missile called V-2, a long range smooth bore artillery piece with range to bombard London from France, given the code-number V-3, and an intercontinental rocket capable of reaching New York, which the Germans call the A-9.

London already knew about these weapons, so Makepiece did not dwell on the detail. He presumed that Cliff knew about them before being attached to the 1574th. Makepiece went on to describe known developments on the '*Amerikabomber*' project specifically designed for the return transatlantic mission with four contenders in advanced design. He mentioned developments in advanced weapon systems beyond conventional rocketry.

"Using radar, these surface-to-air unmanned missiles can go bang under your ship before they hit — hence missiles — and you take the ride to St Peter's marble portal high above the clouds."

These were new to Cliff, but a very significant German project had been saved to last.

"Washington is anxious about the Germans getting the atomic bomb."

"What's that?"

Makepiece explained, "If you put a chunk of uranium next to another chunk of the same stuff, the radioactivity compounds away and you get a small sun in your lap. It's what Einstein predicted and a few laboratories have been testing the idea. We are talking lots of energy, possibly hundreds of thousands of tons of high explosive equivalent, all at once. The problem is how to control it and how to make it go bang when you want to. Solve those two and you've got something with the potential to blow down a city the size of London or New York. Some of your scientists had been working the problem and gotten stuck; we co-operated to see if we could do it. Add that and a delivery platform — *Amerikabomber* and or extended range V-2 called A-9 — and Adolf rules the roost. FDR doesn't like it, Churchill isn't too happy at the prospect and, for what it's worth, neither do I."

"You're serious, Colonel?" Sprite Battel was wondering how much of this was known by the Air Ministry staff who had sent him here.

"Never more serious in my cotton-pickin' life." Makepiece was nodding as he spoke and the expression of his face left no room for doubt that was, indeed, serious.

"What does Churchill and the Cabinet think you are up to, with FDR's budget?"

"Churchill's got his own photographic reconnaissance Spitfires. They are good. The P-38M-SP we're putting in the lamella hangar up at West Malling have 350 miles range advantage, each way, will operate at 45000 feet — a mile above the Spits — if they have to, cruise at 465 knots true air speed when necessary and can carry a pilot and a navigator."

"OK, so they knock spots off the Spitfire Mk IX."

"That's not the way to look at it. Try horses for courses. Our P-38M-SPs have been designed to be exceptionally long range photographic reconnaissance aircraft — high altitude ships. Their performance is limited by the sound barrier — the guys at Lockheed are working on that too. These aircraft fly low at their own risk and burn a lot of juice doing it. At altitude, they cruise for hours. We are using the best cameras money can buy, German Lieca lenses actually, and we'll bring back images better than Cecil B de Mille ever dreamed about. So the Spitfires do what they are good at and we help them out when they run out of gas. All our images will go into the RAF processing route for adding to the wider picture. But we'll be mailing copies to Uncle Sam in our own envelopes."

"That's nice. We'll be fighting on the same side next, just like our Navy does."

Makepiece nodded, "But the ace in the hole, Cliff, is that the navigator does not have to be there. We've developed a chassis which slots in the space when we take his seat out. On that chassis we mount some electronics. And we have a choice. Security bites here: at ABLATIVE Level 2 we mount radar monitoring collectors to capture tracking radars, and the like. At ABLATIVE Level 3, we mount communications monitoring and recording gear and bring back the signals that Bletchley Park and Washington only dream about. Radio signals at frequencies that don't carry outside Germany."

"How will you explain your new information if it can't be collected from outside the Axis territories?" He was getting uncomfortable at having to remain seated for so long.

"We don't, I mean 1574th doesn't explain anything. Washington does, describing it as coming from a special source. Oh, we've had guys and gals on the ground penetrating their test ranges for years. Perhaps you Brits have, too? Now's the time that their vulnerability is going to put on the line. They can only see and mail out their reports, their observations. Slow and pretty limited stuff! With 1574th, we are talking about 'same day' material. But, at this level of information those poor devils are... expendable; they explain how we get close enough to collect the raw material. If we can tap what the Germans are saying for their own consumption, or better the telemetry that their test vehicles are sending back for home for analysis, then we're cooking with gas."

"Christ!" exclaimed the RAF officer. "You're serious. You are talking about wasting our agents? To protect your source?"

"Yep," rejoined Makepiece. "We'll know what the Krauts are doing and where they are doing it. Perhaps even before they do! Spaack's B-19s or Harris's Lancasters can go and put a stop to it."

"So we are going to leave the V-1 and V-2 to the regular Spitfires." Sprite contorted facial frown emphasised his surprise.

"Hole in one, my friend."

"And your four Lightnings are going to take on the other eight vengeance weapons?"

"Still shooting par, Wing Commander. Why stop at eight?"

"Jesus H Christ."

"I hope He's navigating on our side. Now you read this paper while I rustle up some coffee. I didn't mention what the Krauts are planning to do about our bombers. You'll find that interesting. I think there may be some questions to answer when you finished reading."

Makepiece stood, but indicated that Cliff should remain seated. His physical discomfort had been subsumed by the scope of the briefing he had just received.

"Tomorrow, when we've welcomed the boys, and not a few girls, to this pleasant spot in the Garden of England, I'll take you out to see the aircraft for yourself. I'll need to be there to check the electronic gear gets put into the strong room. We don't want souvenir hunters making off with that stuff." Makepiece had reached the door when he paused and looked Cliff in the eyes.

"There's just one other thing. I would find it most courteous of you to permit me to read any report you may make to the Air Ministry folks." Makepiece was making light of something he felt most strongly about. Sprite Battel noticed the American's bulk seemed to fill the door frame of his office. "Obviously you will want to justify being paid the King's shilling, or whatever. But I have only accepted a British liaison officer in the ABLATIVE mission so long as our national, which means my US national, security release caveats apply. It is the usual arrangement, for example with the US liaison officers embedded at Bletchley Park and your folks at Arlington Hall. I'll be frank with you, just so long as you play by my rules. *Comprendez?*"

"Your rules, Colonel. *Je suis comprens vous precisement.* But I am glad you didn't test my Spanish!" Cliff Battel seemed to reflect for a moment before asking, "You mentioned ABLATIVE 3. What happened to ABLATIVE 4?"

"Later, Wing Commander, later…"

*   *   *

RAF Snodland provided the home base for the RAF's No 978 Balloon Squadron. Its original compound had been extended into derelict land to encompass space for the American 1574th Special Project Security Group. Within in the Royal Air Force's No 30 Barrage Balloon Group, commanded by Air Commodore W C G Gell, 978 Squadron was scheduled as the smallest squadron of the barrage balloon organisation based in Kent. Its role was to provide barrage along the west side of the River Medway, to cover the west, rearmost, flank of the Royal Navy Chatham dockyard and the RAF Coastal Command Sunderland flying boat facility at Rochester. It would supplement No 952 Balloon Squadron based at Sheerness in protecting the southern coastline of the Thames Estuary giving depth to the barrage protecting the London docks. A similar arrangement covered the northern Estuary coastline from Harwich into the dockland.

Neither Air Officer Commanding No 30 Balloon Group, nor the two RAF squadron leaders on the station, knew the role or mission of the Americans on their station. This was war and strange things happened in this war just as they had in the last.

978 Balloon Squadron was commanded Squadron Leader Percy Davenport, a veteran of World War 1, now too old to fly. Most important to the smooth and effective running of the squadron was Flight Officer Bethany Taverner WAAF, second in command and Operations Officer for No 978 Balloon Squadron. Bethany was a no-nonsense straight talking organiser, keen to get on with this war so that she could marry a farmer and breed. The landbased twenty four balloons which would be assigned to 978 Squadron would be hers to operate, safely and to greatest effect under the direction of Group Headquarters. Waterborne barraging against mine laying aircraft would be the responsibility of 952 Squadron out of Sheerness. 978 Squadron had the use of a big open plan building, in nearby Strood, to repair and test the balloons' envelope.

In June 1943, the squadron was under-manned, having just 30 WAAF and 15 RAF operators; their compliment of balloons was not yet filled following attacks by enemy aircraft. The squadron commander had been told that he would be brought up to strength by mid-October when additional female trainees would be output and the next delivery of balloons was scheduled.

Lines of demarcation between Percy Davenport with host Station Commander, Squadron Leader Wilburne, had been agreed which allowed for 978 Squadron, with its civilian specialist manufacturing personnel, to use the amenities of the RAF compound where they would be accommodated and where they would adhere to RAF security arrangements instituted to protect the Americans. Percy Davenport and Bethany Taverner fully understood the need to keep control over their WAAF component in view of the proximity of potentially hazardous, youthful American soldiers.

Chapter 8
1943 ~ Across Blitzed London

The electric train left Maidstone on time. It would have reached London Victoria as timetabled if it had not enjoyed a 10 minute hold in a tunnel with only emergency, blue, lights and then a consequential backlog through the Clapham Junction interchange. But there was a war on, reasoned Makepiece, and he had the luxury of a First Class compartment, non smoking of course, shared only with a generously proportioned woman of a certain age who wore a hat with a veil covering her forehead and a terrier dog on her lap as a muff glove. The dog just looked at the uniformed Makepiece throughout the 65 minutes they travelled together, not moving, not threatening, just looking.

Makepiece passed under the famous meeting place, the Victoria station clock, where no-one appeared to be waiting and out onto the concourse where he found a taxi standing in the cab rank.

"Where to, Governor?"

Makepiece opened the passenger door, leaned across the open luggage platform to the driver, and gave his destination as Marylebone Station. He did not get a reply. He had no sooner settled onto the well worn leather bench seat than the taxi was moving.

The dividing window was slid aside so that the driver could speak to his passenger.

"First time in London, Governor?" The cabbie was speaking over his left shoulder, his head slightly cocked back, to his passenger in American officers' uniform. His eyes did not leave the road ahead.

"I've only passed through."

"Gerry's trying to knock the old place about. We're having none of his nonsense, Governor. He had a go at Buckingham Palace t'other night. Gave the King and Queen some new windows, but you can't see the damage from this side. Behind that 10 foot wall they lives, with their two girls, like. Nice to see them staying put. Gives Gerry two fingers, like."

The manoeuvrability of the London black taxi was legendary. Makepiece was glad of the passenger handle above his seat.

"Lived out Pimlico way, I did. Got bombed out a year ago last Easter, when they was 'aving their *blitzkrieg*, like. Moved out to Hampstead with me sister. Course me kids have been evacuated to Wales; me Missus won't go, more's the pity, like."

Makepiece hoped the conversation was not diverting the cabbie's attention from London's traffic driving on the wrong side of the road. The approaching Hyde Park Corner roundabout, full of red double deck buses, looked a formidable challenge to an American viewpoint approaching at 30 miles per hour.

"We'll cut up by Hyde Park. There was a coupla of bombs down 'ere last night, but they only dug up the turf. I reckons they was going for the Dorcester Hotel, over there, with that flat front and all the glass papered up. Strongest building in London, they say."

Makepiece did not comment. At least on the dual carriageway of Park Lane all traffic was going one way on this side of the central reservation. He held on to the grab handle as the taxi negotiated Marble Arch and moved onto Oxford Street.

He thought, 'It would be awful to be killed in a taxi when I came over here to fly.'

"Have to go the pretty route, Governor. Down past Selfridges we'll go and up through the back streets. The Army's dealing with a couple of unexploded bombs up Gloucester Place. Have you back on Baker Street in a jiffy."

'I gotta tell Marybeth about this ride when I write.'

The cabbie remained quiet as he negotiated the back streets. Left turn, halt, right turn, inch forward then straight for 50 yards to a right turn, then a left, then halt. More of the same. Finally, onto open road and a clear run to the crossroads at Baker Street underground station.

"Madame Tussauds' waxworks over there on our right. Worth a visit if you've got a coupla' 'ours."

Quiet! A right turn, a left turn, a hairpin outside the station and Makepiece had arrived at Marylebone railway station.

'Thank God that's over,' thought the passenger.

"That'll be seven and six, please, Governor."

Makepiece offered the man a one pound note from his wallet, with a 'keep-the-change' wave.

"Here, Governor, that's too much. I'd lose me licence if the news got out."

"Keep it, please. Buy the wife some nylons."

"Buy me mates a pint, more like. You're a gentleman, Governor, and that's no mistake. Me frien' 'ppreciate a little bit of 'elp from you Yanks, over 'ere, like. Have a safe journey and show that Adolf that we don't like being disturbed when we are tucked up with our lady friends, and all."

A porter pointed to the platform where the 09:45 for High Wycombe was standing. The delays to the train into Victoria had cost him the chance to sample a legendary railways' cup of tea. Makepiece moved along the carriage corridor and settled into a first class compartment, its windows etched 'No Smoking'. He was alone. The four framed pictures of the Lake District were justifiably anonymous. Five minutes late, a guard's double whistle drew a blast from the engine. In clouds of steam and smoke the engine pulled its six coaches into a tunnel and stopped. At least this time the lights stayed on. After two minutes, a train rumbled passed going towards the station. In a further two minutes, Makepiece's carriage jerked into motion, the pungent mix of coal smoke and steam permeating every miniscule gap in the compartment. Through three flashes of daylight where the tunnel breathed fresh air and then the train pulled out into the open.

Makepiece was grateful to be out in the light, away from the tunnel's claustrophic grip. The smell of the engine quickly went away.

The guard, checking the passengers' tickets, assured Makepiece that Burt and his fireman Harry would make up time and get to High Wycombe near as on time as would make no difference. Rail management saw priorities differently, however. The train slowed in Buckinghamshire's verdant countryside, jolted to the left and stopped at Beaconsfield station. Makepiece stood at the window, opened it and leaned through to see several heads looking out of other carriage windows along the deserted platform. The heating in his compartment had just come on. The sun beating on the window made the compartment very warm. Makepiece slid open the corridor door to encourage a circulation of fresh air.

There was the unmistakeable sound of an approaching steam engine. Down the overtaking track came an engine pulling 30 or more box cars and a dozen fuel oil tankers, the whole sealed off with the statutory guard's van with its red lantern safely lit at 10:30 in the morning.

After a short delay, Makepiece's express engine sounded a double whistle blast and the carriage jerked forward. Through another tunnel, then down a long valley of green pasture and woods reminiscent of the Shenandoah Valley. Makepiece was homesick for the first time since leaving Alexandria. On came the brakes and the train juddered to a halt at High Wycombe Station. Behind him, as he dismounted, he was aware of a tall, perhaps 40 feet high, soot-stained brick wall apparently holding up half the town. A ticket collector accepted the offered torn-in-half ticket and Makepiece was in the fresh air.

A military staff car, with a WAAC driver, was waiting. He confirmed his identity and was smoothly whisked through the town and up the steep hill heading south. Within 10 minutes he was signing in for a visitor's pass at the American headquarters Dawes Hill guardroom. The wall clock showed 7 minutes past eleven o'clock. He had been in motion for 237 minutes and had travelled less than 60 miles as the crow flies.

"Welcome to Camp Lynn, Headquarters 8th Bomber Command. The driver will take you down to where Colonel Knapp is expecting you. Have a nice day, Colonel." Makepiece felt he was once more on home territory.

It was a mile farther into the base, down a steeply descending left hand turn to the bunker's entrance, carefully masked from above by high tree foliage. The car stopped at the obvious entry control point. The WAAC driver got out, adjusted her hat and opened the Colonel's door. A smart salute, stretching her uniform jerkin across her ample bosom, was responded to by Makepiece who noticed the straining cloth.

"Thank you," he said. "Very smooth."

"You're welcome, Colonel. You've gotta sign in again, in there. Your escort will take you from there." She had already begun to turn away.

Chapter 9
1943 ~ Dawes Hill, Buckinghamshire, England

"Makepiece!" Colonel Julius Knapp was coming round the desk in his office. "It's great to see you. How was sister, Marybeth, when you left? And the kids?" The two colonels appeared to be genuinely pleased to meet and greet each other albeit in very unwonted circumstances.

"They were fine when I last saw them in Alexandria. The mail hasn't caught up with me yet. And you and yours? I didn't see much of..." Julius' hand was dry, his grip gentle, as he shook Makepiece hand. They were about the same age but the flying, open air life had treated Makepiece's visage more kindly.

"Oh, Antonia never changes. Her letters are always a bit on the vague side. Nigel is flying off carriers somewhere in the Pacific. It's even harder to get any news from him. Perhaps the girls can get together?"

"I think you've gotten an ABLATIVE package for me, Jules." So his brother-in-law was expecting him. Makepiece didn't want small talk.

"Too right! I want to know what's in it."

"Well, you show me yours and I'll show you mine, old son." Makepiece's impatience was getting the better of him, reflected in his body language. There was not even a smile at his weak joke by his wife's brother.

"All in good time. We've got a little admin to do and I guess you'd like something to eat after travelling half the width of the country. We have a passable refectory down here. I'll show you around as we go down for chow. But before I do that, there's a letter addressed to you, marked 'Your Eyes Only' with the seal of the Secretary of War all over it. I don't know what it's all about. Never seen anything like it since I opened my first carton of French letters at the high school prom."

"Where is this missive, Jules? Secretaries of War don't mail prophylactics."

"Not so, Makepiece. Every airman and GI going on furlough has to be issued with a prophylactic pack which has instructions and pictures and Trojan^{tm} in. And Commanders have to give an ethics lecture every year about what not to do with the English rose. Mandatory attendances, old chum, including you!"

"Oh what a lovely war!"

"Right here, brother-in-law. Look, you open your mail," Julius passed Makepiece a paper knife, "while I get us a cup of best java beans. Then we'll go and eat."

When Julius returned with two disposable cups of steaming coffee, Makepiece was sitting in the office armchair. He was fidgeting so much that perhaps he should have been pacing the floor. His face was covered in a furious scowl.

"Who else knows about this letter? It's a bloody insult. I'll quit and go back to tobacco farming. Politicians. I wouldn't give them a bunk in a pig sty. You give half a chance and they rip your balls off without a sniff of opium!"

"Hold on, not so fast." Julius was reaching for the letter which Makepiece was gripping so tensely.

"Read that and I'll have to shoot you."

"No guns in this bunker, Makepiece! Calm down a touch and have a swig of java. Working in a headquarters has its advantages. We get real creamer!"

The phone on Julius's desk rang. He picked it up. As a courtesy, Makepiece moved away to be out of earshot.

"Yes, General," said Julius into the mouthpiece. Then again, "Yes General, Colonel Ploughman is here. Yes, sir, I am sure he would wish to pay his respects to General Spaatz, sir." There was some talking into Julius's earpiece.

"General! If you don't mind, sir, would it be convenient for you to escort General Spaatz to the Intel Briefing Room? This ABLATIVE thing is rather tight. I'm sure that Colonel Ploughman will explain."

A pause while the distant end spoke. Julius' eyes had settled on the wall clock.

"Very well, General, 14:15 in the Intel Briefing Room. We'll be there." Julius returned the phone to its cradle.

"First a letter from Secretary Stimson and now a General I've hardly heard of. Has he gotten an ABLATIVE clearance ticket? And while we are at it, what about your general?" Makepiece's anger carried into his tone of voice.

"Both are strictly kosher, Makepiece. Take it easy, you'll be able to see the register when we get into the Intel Cell. Drink your coffee." He indicated the cup on the table. "Now the letter, from Secretary of War

Stimson? Let me have a look. You haven't upset the old man already? Have you been asking for more P-38s?"

"Read the damn thing, Jules. I have to have a witness sign that I have read it and you have just been elected from a list of one."

MOST SECRET - ULTIMATE - ABLATIVE

From the Office of the Secretary of War
The Pentagon
Washington DC   *June 2nd, 1943*

To: Colonel Makepiece F Ploughman
    Commanding, 1574th Special Projects Security Group.
    c/o   HQ 8th Bomber Command
    High Wycombe, England
    AP0   634

Dear Colonel Ploughman,

The President and Commander-in-Chief has directed me to communicate the following to you.

Now you are in the European Theatre of Operations, the secret intelligence knowledge that you have acquired in project ABLATIVE is at greater risk than hitherto. With immediate effect you are not to expose yourself to any situation where the ABLATIVE source or intelligence product might fall into the hands of our enemies.

To that end you are expressly forbidden to fly or travel or otherwise transit over any part of Occupied Europe or Africa, or the seas bordering such territories, or any ship of any nation allied to the German Axis.

You are to acknowledge receipt of this order by signing and dating a copy of this letter, your signature being witnessed by an officer of equivalent or senior rank. The signed letter is to be returned to my office through ABLATIVE channels.

Signed

Henry L Stimson

"There's no use arguing with the logic, Makepiece. The great white chief, or at least his agent, is calling the shots. You are as good as grounded. At least as far as P-38 operational missions are concerned. If you buck an order like that they hang you out to dry and probably stop your pension as well."

Makepiece did not want any more coffee.

"Let's go and get some food, and then I'll read the pack that's come over from Washington. What's all that about two generals? Do I have to call it all over again? I will admit to being not in the mood."

Julius took the letter away from Makepiece's grasp and slipped it into a combination protected safe. Without asking, he reached for his brother-in-law's elbow and guided him to the office door.

*   *   *

Four men were sitting in the undecorated Intel Briefing Room. The furniture was spartan. There was a plain wooden table with wooden legs. A dozen wooden chairs with minimal cushions were around it. The only wall decoration was a map of Europe showing the west coast of France to Moscow with a pull down projection blind if required. The fluorescent lights could be individually switched to lessen the distracting buzz of the new technology. There was no telephone. A light on the exterior of the door indicated that a briefing was in progress and was not to be interrupted.

"Well, Colonel, you've got some mighty powerful friends on the hill." General Spaatz was reiterating what Makepiece had heard so often before. "You going to tell me what's so special about your mission?"

"Yes, General. I have to tell you this is an ABLATIVE Level 3 briefing. Ten — sorry nine — folks stateside and eleven, including me, in Britain have clearance for what I am about to update you. Some of this briefing does not go to Churchill, or his honchos — not yet any way. When I have finished the technical stuff, I'll show you how seriously Washington takes ABLATIVE. Ask any questions as I go along, I'll try not to repeat what I am sure you already know."

"Let's get on with it, Colonel. Eisenhower wants me to win a war by Friday."

"You may know that from MAGIC sources against Japanese ciphers that Hitler is planning perhaps ten so-called vengeance weapons. The imagery of V-1 and V-2 is commonly circulating in bombing group's targeting circles. You may have heard of Hitler's *Amerikabomber,* currently on Messerschmitt drawing board, being designed to hit New York? You may not have heard that he is testing a V-2 type rocket for a submarine launch off our eastern seaboard. FDR is worried that it would bring down his government if continental USA was struck."

"OK, Colonel, proceed."

"We now know that the V-3 is a long barrel artillery piece with range to reach London from France. We know that V-1, V-2 and V-3 weapons are in full production with thousands of rounds ordered. We know from ULTRA, backed up by human sources, that a so-called intercontinental version of the V-2, they call it the A-9, is being developed and may have already flown to crash in Sweden."

"Where do your P-38s come in?"

"We don't know for sure what V-4 and onwards are, although the big money is on it being a manned rocket aircraft. May the Lord help the pilot if it is! Maybe it was Mussolini mouthing off about ten V-weapons to impress the Japs. One thing the Japs are good at is faithfully reporting ambassador's conversations. But the ABLATIVE paper given to the President lists about 100 development project names from a variety of sources, none of which stand up to the normal test of two or more independent sources of confirmation. So one part of the ABLATIVE mission is to go out and look for it — confirmation."

The generals were giving Makepiece their undivided attention. The colonel remained motionless in his chair while speaking without notes.

"Under responsibility sharing signed up by the Chiefs of Staff between the US and UK, the Brits have responsibility for European and African photo reconnaissance with their Spitfires and for signals intelligence via ULTRA and Bletchley Park." General Spaatz was the senior US officer in the COSSAC group. He was speaking in a most assertive tone. "You know that the Chiefs of Staff to Supreme Allied Commander is Ike's team at Bushy Park, and I am not about to allow anyone to gum up sensible working in Eisenhower's team."

"You know about the atomic bomb, General?" Makepiece pulled the subject his way.

"Careful, Colonel. We don't talk about that in England. No way!"

"What if Hitler was well on the way to his atomic bomb? What if he is sharing his know-how with the Japs?" Spaatz looked concerned, his mouth twitched. Makepiece held his stance to engage the senior general's eyes.

"Go on, Boy, but be careful what you say." Makepiece's confidence was unshakem. He knew the rules about what he could say, and what he couldn't, and would strictly follow them.

"General, we have got to know. If the *Amerikabomber* or the A-9 rocket was mated to an atomic bomb, it would be curtains for the American east coast." Makepiece relaxed slightly; he'd given the reason for his mission to England.

Spaatz's nose lifted to ask, "And how does an aircraft find atomic bombs, Colonel?"

"We fly deeper into Germany, maybe Poland or Czechoslovakia and look with good cameras. Better than that, we take in signals intelligence equipment to collect the frequencies that don't carry to our monitoring stations outside occupied territories. And there are types of radiological sniffers that breathe radioactivity and uranium particles like it's going out of fashion." Now he was talking 'pilot talk' with a general who understood.

"You can do that, Colonel Ploughman?"

Makepiece paused, then nodded. "Yes, Sir. The P-38M-SP has all the capability we need if it's there to collect. And when we bring the intel home then we give the photography to Medmenham and let the RAF do their thing with it. That's sharing photo-intelligence and fits with the cover story. But the signals stuff we send home, wrapped up so that Roosevelt has something to barter with if he believes that Churchill and the British are holding back on the Japanese, or Joe Stalin's, material that we want. We don't know what the Brits are doing privately with nuclear material so we are probably on our own with that stuff."

"These are mighty big stakes, Colonel. You got anymore craps to shoot?" The general's face was now pulled into interrogative mode. But Makepiece had an ace.

"There is one more technical development which could shake the world. It's called the Einstein Engine."

"Am I going to understand this, Colonel. I am only a cotton-pickin' pilot."

Again Makepiece nodded. Julius was admiring his brother-in-law's performance. "It's probably not fair to quote Einstein, but out of his mathematics came the germ of an idea for a propulsion system that doesn't need propellers. The photo guys have seen that the Gerries have been working on ways to shoot down our bombers with high speed surface-to-air missiles — perhaps supersonic craft. But some of our boys, and the RAF too, have been bringing back stories of discs weaving about in their bomber formations giving off coloured aura, especially pale green or blue, typical of electrostatic discharge. Photographs are few and far between. Significantly, these discs' colour is not the red heat of a conventional engine. We want to know more so that we can protect our boys against new technology weapons if they have to go deep against the vengeance weapons."

"Are you talking UFOs and other nonsense, Colonel? So-called foo fighters?" This time Spaatz's body language indicated disbelief.

"Washington does not consider the reports nonsense, General. Pilots and gunners make good observers. All we want is an explanation and we, that is the Office of National Intelligence, thinks the answer lies in test ranges and laboratories way out in western Poland. Only the P-38M-SP can get there and back. If the Germans get wind that we're looking, they could move further away, maybe as far as the Czech-Austria border. If they do that we are screwed for air reconnaissance and the stuff from field agents might take too long to get out."

Spaatz looked at his deputy and said, "So this is what Roosevelt's $15 million was about: vengeance weapons, and atomic bombs and UFOs."

"They are taking it pretty seriously in Washington, General." Julius was speaking for the first time. "Makepiece, show the General the letter you just opened from Secretary Stimson."

Makepiece handed General Spaatz the letter. He read it and handed it back to Makepiece.

"They don't want you letting out our secrets, do they, Colonel?"

Makepiece saw no need to reply. Inside he reached inside the briefing pack by his elbow and extracted a single piece of paper. It carried a circular chart:

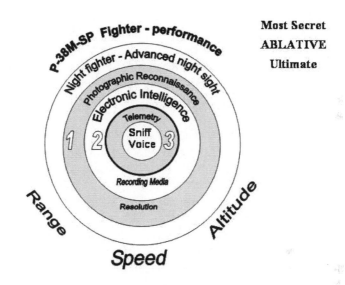

Most Secret
ABLATIVE
Ultimate

Operation ABLATIVE – Secrecy Profile (innermost highest protection required as indicated by the ABLATIVE level numbers shown)

"My pilots will not know it all, General. Only my Intel/Ops officer has ABLATIVE Level 3. He happens to be fluent in German, Polish and Czech; with a name like Chmielewski it comes as no surprise. I picked him myself and he's as American as blueberry pie. All the others in my group are specialists, on strictly need-to-know, who will do their job and keep their mouths zipped shut. Neither will the RAF liaison officer have all the processed material either. He's obviously been put in so the Air Ministry can have a take on what we are up to. He'll see all the photographs the RAF will be getting and those that don't make the grade in quality too; I'll leak the ELINT on radars through Wing Commander Battel so that he can notify the RAF's 192 Squadron and RV Jones for countermeasure planning."

General Spaatz was beginning to fidget indicating to Makepiece that the meeting was about to come to end whether he had finished or not. The movement did not escape Makepiece who had one further matter of moment to talk about.

"General, I think Roosevelt still blames the Brits for not telling him what Bletchley Park knew about the Japanese Pacific Fleet back in '41. When my photo material is fused with the signals and sniffing intel into properly analysed reports back in Washington, the only place in England that will get the reports is this intel office here at Dawes Hill."

"What do you want from me, Colonel Ploughman?"

"Just a clear run at it, General. ABLATIVE could save a lot of Allies' lives. It may help with the invasion; that is up to how your folks use the data when we get it. If we get it. It may help protect the USA and our allies, in the air, at sea, or the civilians on the ground. In the worst case it may prevent nuclear armageddon and the end of the world."

"Send me the specification of what your boys have done to Lockheed's finest. I don't suppose you'll let me fly one, eh!"

"'fraid not, General. But I know a man at Burtonwood who can get you a ride in a regular P-38. Probably not as much fun as ours, though."

"I know the same feller." Spaatz began to move his chair. "You'll get your clear run at your mission, Colonel Ploughman." Spaatz had risen from his chair; the briefing was ended. All four men were now standing. "Just help me win this goddam war, ya hear!"

"I hear you loud and clear, General. Thank you for your time."

General Spaatz, together with his deputy who had not spoken during the briefing, departed the room. Julius closed the door firmly behind the generals.

"Oh my Gawd, as my limey colleagues would say. You gave it to him, straight. I think its time we got another coffee and made arrangements for you to meet the prettiest secret weapon the Brits have got stashed in their barn. We are going to visit Medmenham to work on your cover story. You weren't in a hurry to get back to Snodland, were you?"

"Mmm," grimaced Makepiece.

"There has to be some compensation for being at war," said Julius, "and you are going to meet her."

Makepiece put the disappointment and anger of Stimson's letter behind him for the time being. As the two men made their way through the corridors to leave the bunker, Makepiece spoke.

"One other thing you need to know, Jules. A MAGIC transcript of the Japanese Berlin ambassador quoted Hitler as claiming that he, Hitler, wasn't too interested in the atomic bomb. Too expensive and messy — maybe he was double guessing the Japs, suggesting he can't get enough pure uranium so they can't come knocking on his door for his spare. No siree! He, Hitler, has a secret war winner and it will be ready in just a few months. We don't know what he calls it, or what it looks like, but the President, sure as cherry pie, wants to finds out. This little pearl is not for circulation until Washington puts it out: FDR is worried that Adolf is going to try to blow New York's skyscrapers down! There, now you know what's driving me. I might need a friend in high places, if an office in a buried bunker can be called a high place, brother."

"You're mouthing words like 'beyond the nuclear bomb', Brother?"

"I guess so."

"Oh my Gawd," repeated Julius. "Let's go and meet a flower of English pulchritude called Constance."

Chapter 10
1943 ~ Central Interpretation Unit, RAF Medmenham

It was the same WAAC driver who was waiting as Makepiece and Julius came out of the bunker at Dawes Hill.

"We all going to Medmenham, Colonel?" was the cheerful greeting. Her salute seemed to Makepiece to stretch her uniform jacket even more than this morning.

"That's right, soldier. We'll go down via Marlow, show Colonel Ploughman the Thames River, and then up to Medmenham." Julius Knapp was responding to the salute and giving instructions.

"Ain't no other way to go, Colonel. Views of the river are a bit limited in Marlow, Colonel. If the Colonel wants to see the river we could…"

"Medmenham, via Marlow, soldier. We've gotten a date with the British Royal Air Force and the King of Buckinghamshire don't take kindly to folks being tardy with their promptness. Savvy? Now, cut the chatter and don't spare the horses."

The drive was as comfortable as a military staff car could make it. The WAAC was competent at her job. At a road junction, in Marlow, Julius pointed to a gap in the street furniture.

He said, "They've taken out the milestone to London which must have been there before King Henry was crowned."

"Which King Henry?" Makepiece asked. He knew there were eight from which to choose.

"All of them, I guess. Anyway it pre-dated Jamestown, or Baltimore and Maryland. So it's old. Our fiendish plan is to stop the German tanks finding their way to wherever *Wermacht* tanks want to go if they cross the Thames. The river is down this High Street. Pretty place, isn't it. Marlow, I mean. That pub has got more bars than it's safe to drink at. There is the Thames Bridge. Turn left and right at the end, beyond the church, driver, and we'll go along the bank of the Thames. Pull over when it's convenient."

In the June sunshine, with a full view of the single arch bridge, reflected sunlight sparkling off the river, an old church opposite, and a few small river craft moored at a quay, it would be easy to forget there was a war on. The swans couldn't have cared less. Jules gave them a token one minute to enjoy the view.

"No self respecting tank driver in a German tank — or any tank — would ever risk crossing that narrow bridge." Makepiece's observation was cut short by the other colonel.

"Move out, driver. Medmenham next stop."

*   *   *

"Forgive me for being a bore, gentlemen, but could I see your ID? They get so fussy in here! Good!" Section Officer Constance Babington Smith, Women Auxiliary Air Force was returning the American's identity cards, the single rank ribbon visible around the cuff of her uniform jacket. "Wing Commander Douglas Kendall is out for the afternoon and I know he'd be sorry to miss you. Let's just call and sign the Visitor's Book then we'll go to the conference room where you can tell me how we may be of assistance."

Makepiece could see why Julius was so keen to visit their hostess. In front of them stood an attractive well proportioned twenty-something female officer whose smile would launch a thousand Spitfires. Her short dark hair was swept back clear of her face, a disarming smile showed perfect teeth. She spoke with the confidence of good education and with a conviction of in-depth knowledge of her subject.

The operational buildings complex of the photographic Central Interpretation Unit was a mixture of asbestos sheet clad, single storey, flat roofed huts with all glazing having the paper tape crosses; a big building resembling a Tudor Manor house called Danesfield House, actually built in the mid-1800s, was the principal facility on the site. CIU had outgrown its home in Wembley, where it was known as the Photographic Interpretation Unit, and was renamed on its move in April 1941. The present whole site was engulfed in trees, in full foliage at this time of the year. The atmosphere inside the huts, which were joined together in a maze of corridors of similar construction to the huts, was of a busy energy. Whatever went on behind the closed doors produced an aura of confident busy-ness. A real war was in progress.

"It's good of you to see us. I know you are busy." Julius Knapp was speaking. "I thought you should meet Colonel Makepiece Ploughman, here," Makepiece took the WAAF officer's confident handshake, "while he is in Buckinghamshire."

"Pleased to meet you, Colonel Ploughman." Her smile was certainly contagious and he didn't really want to let her have her hand back.

Julius continued, "Colonel Ploughman has brought in some new photo-reconnaissance P-38s with high altitude capability and his output will be delivered through my office to add to your photograph album, so to speak."

"Oh, that's nice, Colonel Knapp. I like looking at photographs." She turned to Makepiece and said, "Will your tasking be coming out of Bomber Command?"

"Well, not exactly, Miss Babington Smith ..."

"Please call me Babs. It's shorter than Constance Babington Smith, saves time and cuts to the chase — as you Yanks say. Half the Yankee Air Force calls me that, anyway."

'Her voice is so cultured English,' thought Makepiece.

"Babs, then. My tasking comes from Joint Chiefs stateside. I can't explain why, but I will make arrangements for you to be indoctrinated onto a register called the ABLATIVE list. It will become clear then, I promise. But I have to coordinate my mission flying with Bomber and Fighter Commands and with COSSAC at Bushy Park. That way we'll avoid duplication and not get in each other's way. All our take will come from me through Julius Knapp, here, and his team at Dawes Hill."

"I see." She was not sure she was any the wiser. "So your photos will come in here for us to evaluate?"

Julius intervened, "That's right, Babs. No different to the Spitfire's output and anything the bombers bring home. All hardcopy printed stuff, I'm afraid; I'll explain in a moment. And there will be an improved stream of tactical images from the regular P-38s that we'll be sending along from Mount Farm. Roosevelt's son, Elliot, is pushing his reconnaissance group mighty hard and three more outfits will be flying in to form the 7th Photographic Group of American photo/recon squadrons from 7 July 1943. The group will be flying a combination of F-5 — it's what they call their P-38, P-51 and Spitfire IX photo/recon aircraft."

Julius Knapp felt he was preaching to the choir; she already knew this stuff...

"Churchill and Roosevelt have agreed the British will continue to take the lead with targeting and related intelligence for the European Theatre of Operations ahead of the invasion. So all our stuff will come into Medmenham to be merged with the British stuff to make the pile bigger and better."

"It keeps us off the streets," said Babs with another smile.

"But Colonel Ploughman's 1574th Special Project Security Group is out of the mainstream. Their ships will go where no man has gone before, higher and further. They will have to send their negatives to Washington because that's his terms of reference to keep this budget out of the House committees. I know you like to have the negatives, but this time I can't oblige. However, the 1574th has come over with some pretty efficient printing equipment and you'll get positives of the lot, to whatever size you specify. They might have some views of places and things which no one else has seen. So it makes sense that Churchill's Miss Peenemünde has the chance to say what is A-4 rocketry and what isn't."

"That sounds like a challenge, Colonel Knapp. I take it that the 1574th will become a Medmenham customer through your desk?"

"Yes, for selected material, need to know and all that. I'll use the normal channels to set up the feed. I'll also speak with you about how to deal with anything untoward that the 1574th sends to you. There may be a need for restricted distribution of some of the poop that they produce. Makepiece here hopes his brownies might snap a new aircraft type or whatever. Word in our alley is that it is right up your street."

"We prefer to describe such product as secret intelligence or, at its most basic level, simply information." She wrinkled her nose; she was used to dealing with American vernacular. "Poop has a rather derogatory connotation in English as we speak it." She grinned. "We have customers for photos of new aircraft, manned or pilotless. We think they are strapping pilots into rockets as a way of getting rid of their expert bad boys. I particularly like photographs of new aircraft. My collection just grows and grows, but everyone seems to ignore the factories or the test airfields. It does seem a pity."

The movement of her shoulders implied the 'Oh dear!' although she didn't say it.

Makepiece said, "I'll see what I can do, Babs. The word in Washington has it that you Brits have been looking at the Peenemünde airfield. The images I have seen suggest the Germans want to make it bigger yet. Are we sure it's not a feint for something else? "

Julius took up the theme. "I hear that Peenemünde caught a bloody nose the other day."

Babs said, "So I understand." She knew very well that Pennemunde had been severely struck and largely targeted based on her photographic interpretation. "Would you like to see what the boys from Benson brought back? Sort of before and after shots. We don't think it is a spoof. It's nice to know one's work is appreciated. Isn't that a nice English word — spoof? So much more Anglo-Saxon than feint, don't you think? Anyway, after you have seen our interpretation tables, if you have time, we could have a cup of tea in the Officers' Mess and we could walk by the river. It does my eyes good to breath some fresh air, so's to speak. The river is looking good at this time of year. Within reason it's safe to chat out there; I do like to talk with American pilots about jet engines and things like that. There's so little opportunity for a girl to get the real flyer's poop on such things." There was a girlish creasing about her eyes, a satisfaction at having returned their jargon.

"Did you say something about an ablution briefing, Colonel Ploughman?"

"ABLATIVE, Babs. I said ABLATIVE. It's the codename for my mission, which is a touch on the delicate side. It has a control list as short as the edge of a razor blade. What I will do is arrange for Wing Commander Cliff Battel to come and see you."

"You don't mean The Sprite!" Did her eyebrows raise a smidgen?

"I have heard him called that although he has not let on about the reason. He'll come up to Medmenham..."

"Does he still drive that 3-wheel Morgan? He nearly killed me in the blasted thing while I was at Oakington learning to be an officer. Queen Bee, that is top dog WAAF, called it officer experience training. It was more like a knife, fork and spoon course — how to use them in polite company — and how to repel fighter pilots with an urge to undo other people's blouse buttons. I had to restrain my brother Bernard from having a go at him. Did The Sprite tell you about Wrotham forest...? I heard he'd had a rough time thanks to a Dornier."

"He'll come to Medmenham and give you the word on where we'll be taking our pictures and you can tell him what special labels you want us to put on the prints. He'll speak with Wing Commander Kendall too. Cliff — The Sprite if you must — is a member of the Guinea Pig Club; I guess you know what that means. Now, Babs Peenemünde, Ma'am, you show me yours and I'll show you yours. Swops come later."

There was a suggestion of sadness in her, "Oh." These Yanks had come empty handed; perhaps next time?

"Let's go to the picture show," said Jules.

"Let's," mimicked the WAAF officer.

She lifted her left arm to indicate the direction to walk. Makepiece sensed the suggestion of perfume as she moved ahead of the men. Babs Smith was indeed an English rose he would not forget.

*   *   *

Makepiece requested a short stop in Marlow High Street, to buy a newspaper for the journey back to Snodland. He also bought a picture postcard and a high value air mail stamp.

> *June 13th, 1943*   *Marlow, England*
> *Darling Marybeth and the children,*
>   *I have visited your brother, west of London. The good news is that we now have an Army Post Office address for letters and parcels — APO 634. The card will have an English stamp so I don't know how long it will take to reach DC. Julius looks well; I'm fine. I will write when I get back to base.*
>   *All my love*
>   *Makepiece   X X X*
> *PS One for luck X*

Chapter 11
1943 ~ Lockheed P-38M-SP

Colonel Ploughman and his RAF liaison officer, Wing Commander Battel, were being driven by a WAAC driver to their specially constructed lamella hangar on the RAF West Malling airfield. The driver was obviously uncomfortable driving on the left hand side of the roads and, to make matters worse, the roads — country lanes more like — were somewhat narrower than the American highways of Virginia with which she was more familiar. As they passed through the Kent countryside, Cliff Battel recounted some of the folklore about the airfield which was to become a most important part of their lives.

"There was an airfield here before the war, not much more than a flying club by modern standards," opened Cliff. "Come the Battle of Britain, the place became a forward airfield for Biggin Hill and Kendal. It spread the target for the Luftwaffe to aim at and gave greater depth of protection to our airfields guarding London."

Makepiece understood the principle. He was gripping the handle above the door, still uncomfortable about being driven on the left hand side of the road.

"The Germans did not like our good guys shooting down their bad guys, so they decided to be bad guys at night. That gave us a problem because it's difficult enough to find an enemy at night let alone shoot him down. So our boffins dreamt up a radar small enough to get airborne and a cover story to explain why we can now see in the dark. Enter Wing Commander 'Catseyes' Cunningham, credited with eating enormous quantities of carrots, all of which is pure rubbish, but the nickname remained. Number 29 Squadron, flying Beaufighters MkVIs, became a virtually dedicated night fighter outfit and you heard that Peter Townsend, who you met the other day, also flew from here."

"We'll be doing night ops from here," said Makepiece.

"It all happens at night here, Colonel. Daylight is for the birds; this is the owls' nest of Fighter Command. Two months back, on 16 April, the station guard heard a single engine aircraft approaching. It wasn't the distinctive Merlin engine purr of a Hurricane. The said aircraft went round twice and landed. Presuming it to be a Defiant short on fuel, the fire tender and crash crew went out to help. It turned out to be a Focke

Wulf 190. Then, blow me, in comes a second. The first pilot, name of Feldwebel Bechtold, surrendered but the second plane attempted to take off. A trigger happy airman got off a couple of shots which blew the cockpit to smithereens, seriously injuring the pilot. They were taking the second pilot away to hospital in a meat wagon, sorry ambulance, when a third '190 undershot the runway and crashed into the cherry orchard at the lower end of the airfield. Not bad, eh! Three for and none against, and not a drop of AVGAS — sorry aviation gasoline — spent in the process."

The wing commander's head rose with a proud shake. "Just like waiting for a London bus: you wait for ages for one to come along and three come together…" The Sprite's scarred face creased in something approaching a smile.

Makepiece remarked breathed deeply, "That's an interesting tale. Now, let me show you some more interesting tails, two on each aircraft to be precise."

The car pulled up to the side entrance of the hangar, just as the air raid alarm sounded. Makepiece wasn't sure if he'd rather be under an air raid or still being driven on the wrong side of the road. A glance at the driver's anxious face indicated her preference.

"I hope that Hermann Göring has not sent over a welcoming committee for my aircraft. The paint isn't dry on my hangar yet!" His limp joke did nothing for the driver.

The two officers made their way inside the hangar only to be challenged by US Army guards. The driver parked the car under a tree and followed the officers into the building. She was not challenged. The unfortunate guard received the most significant dressing down she had ever heard, or witnessed.

"Take no-one for granted in this outfit, lad. We've got a mission from the President of the United States and you're gonna make sure we do it. Geddit?"

"Yes, Colonel, yes. I sure have gottit, sir, Colonel."

"Is that weapon loaded?" asked the RAF Wing Commander, being somewhat surprised by the exchange he had just witnessed. To his mind, loaded guns and aircraft in hangars was not a happy mix.

"You had better believe it," returned the Colonel.

"Loaded for bear, with the Colonel's permission." The soldier was now pointing the automatic weapon at Cliff's stomach at a rage of about 5 feet.

"That's good, soldier. You guard my ships well and we'll all get along."

"You are taking this seriously, Colonel, sir," said Cliff Battel. He was relieved to have the opportunity to move away and look at some hardware which was more in his specialist field.

* * *

There were five twin boom, twin engine, blue painted fighters parked in the hanger. Their Perspex canopies were covered in tarpaulin protective sheets and there were covers or bung plugs made obvious with dangling red tapes all over the machines. The hangar was echoing quiet. No tools, no maintainers, no intelligence exploitation crew had yet appeared. That tranquillity would soon cease when training, then operations, began. Already the hangar had the unique aroma of an aircraft workshop.

There were no sounds of bombs from outside; the air raid had passed close by. Someone else was the Luftwaffe's target this time. Quite naturally, neither the USAAF colonel nor the RAF liaison officer would show any sign of relief that the warning had passed without incident.

Makepiece was proud to guide the experienced wing commander around his own fleet of aircraft, describing key features as they came across them.

"The P-38M-SP modified aircraft takes the P-38L version 5 airframe and fits a second seat behind the pilot under a lengthened canopy. It keeps the power assisted ailerons and the small under wing flaps to help high Mach number manoeuvring. Because of the extended range we have hung on to the Sperry autopilot."

"I notice that one aircraft has a different nose," commented Cliff. "Are those cannons real?"

"I've gotten four P-38M-SP, a fifth has been held at Andrews for testing further modifications particularly the electronics packages. I brought in a regular P-38L version 5, configured as a pursuit fighter, for training and continuity for the pilots. It will also act as transport to avoid driving on the wrong side."

Cliff's, "You'll soon get used to it!" was ignored by Makepiece.

"These birds are fitted with submerged fuel pumps, with four strengthened under wing (ordinance) points adapted for 125 imperial gallon drop fuel tanks in addition to its 410 imperial gallon internal tanks. The aircraft are fitted with a droop-snoot glazed nose for improved downwards visibility. We use internal, electrically controlled, long focal length cameras — one or three dependent on communications monitoring configuration. The camera lenses are just inside optically flat, clear glass windows with an integral thin gold film electrical heater. The pilot has a vertical view through a prismatic telescope to an eyepiece fitted as a replacement for the gun sight."

"If you've got no gun, I guess you don't need one," observed Cliff.

Makepiece nodded. "These ships are designed to run away from trouble and go for altitude too. For navigation precision missions, a second pilot may be seated behind the pilot. But this second seat and other displays may be removed as a railed chassis to be replaced with a mission configured enclosed and pressurised rack of electronic receivers, recorders and heat dissipaters. When installed for operations, the chassis's hollow frame is filled with high temperature explosive designed to burn and destroy the contents with a 15 second delay from the pilot's command. The aircraft camera bay, main cockpit and everything within it would be disintegrated."

"I still consider you are taking this whole business a mite serious, Colonel." Battel appeared to be chewing the inside of his lower lip for a moment. "I guess that includes the driver?" Makepiece ignored the obvious reference to the vulnerability of the pilot to the disintegration process; RAF aplomb cut no ice with him.

"Within the booms and tailplane there are a series of airframe conformed radio antennae to keep mission sensing equipment at a distance from engine induced interference. Downward looking infra-red detectors are fitted in each wing tip."

"Talking of wing tip," said Cliff, "what are these fins at the wing tips all about. They look too fragile to be stabilizers."

"Lookheed found that small stubs like these help keep the airflow over the wing by reducing the spillage over the wing tip. This gives extra lift with negligible extra drag. They've also fitted stubs at the wing roots to improve airflow — we've gotten another 15 knots airspeed with them.

So we get better takeoff, to you and me that means fuel lift, and higher altitude when we want it."

"Neat," commented the RAF pilot. He was appreciating just how innovative these aircraft were and why Makepiece was going to such lengths to keep them away from prying eyes. He respected that this small fleet was truly advanced aeronautical hardware.

"The cockpit, including the camera bay, is heated and pressurised; the pilot will be at a nominal 22500 feet when cruising at 37500 feet or higher. That's about half normal atmospheric pressure. He will raise cockpit altitude to a precautionary 37000 feet if combat threatens. He will breathe pressurised oxygen throughout the mission."

"I noticed that we have built a very special pilots' preparation area." The RAF officer was comparing what he had seen built with his own experience. "Showers and the like are a luxury we do not normally enjoy on the front line, but a tiled room fit to be a hospital operating theatre is certainly out of the norm."

"It's the oxygen room. We purge the pilot's bloodstream of nitrogen before he flies. That reduces the chance of the bends that sea divers suffer when they change pressure too quickly." Makepiece continued, "We're bringing a specialist flight surgeon with us. We are worried about the effect of breathing pure oxygen under pressure for long flights. We have almost eliminated smoking in our aircrew, we don't allow alcohol 24 hours before a mission and we think that sex will numb the decision making process so that's discouraged too."

"My remark about 'serious' still holds, Colonel." The two were moving about the hangar, admiring the engineering and design of these advance machines.

"The aircraft will cruise with one engine feathered if necessary when the two outer drop tank stations are clear. We use that fuel first anyway and drop the tanks as soon as they're dry. Military boost will give the Allisons 15% emergency power limited to 10 minutes. A water methanol injector into the engine air intake, after the intercooler, is fitted as an extreme boost override in the event of difficulty at heavy takeoff weight. The regular fuel, AVGAS 130, is supplemented by an additive to allow for safe over-boost and extreme low fuel temperature at altitude. We'll bring that stuff in direct from America."

Cliff wished he could have a ride in one of these aircraft. Maybe he would be allowed to ride the second pilot's seat on a training sortie? He ran his ungloved left hand along a tail boom surface and marvelled at its smooth finish.

"And the final feature in our special aircraft, invisibility paint — well at least —camouflage. Lockheed has been working a new deep-blue, base coat, over-painted with a thin layer of absorbent white particles suspended in synthetic enamel. They've made it darker underneath and lighter on top, but you have to look carefully to see the difference. They tell me that at altitude you have to touch the skin to see it."

"I've heard of pushing the flight envelope, but this kite pushes the pilot envelope too."

"Sure as hell does. The only ship — err... kite — that gets as high as us is the German's rocket fighter, but they rarely land in one piece. They are not too popular with the Kraut pilots, I hear. We've got a stable platform for super-dooper Kodak brownies to take photos and we can bring the snaps home for moma — well Auntie Constance anyway. You like it?"

"At the risk of repeating myself, Colonel, and mixing my metaphors, 'You've got some serious shit here'. Constance, you say? That wouldn't be longhand for one Section Officer 'Babs' Babington Smith by any chance? This war is about to get much more interesting." There was a gleam in the Sprite's eyes which Makepiece could not fail to notice.

"I have to tell you, Colonel, that I am deeply impressed by these kites... err ...ships and I feel honoured to be attached to your outfit."

"I'm pleased to have you aboard, Wing Commander. Now, let's find our driver and do something really adventurous ... drive home for tea!"

Chapter 12
1943 ~ Familiarisation and Training

It was the eighteenth of June, a Friday. The three American transport aircraft had landed at West Malling with little ceremony. The first transport had included a ground handling crew. With a little help by a few willing RAF groundcrew, the five P-38s which had landed two days earlier were under cover in the lamella hangar before their engines were cool. Today, within three hours, the transport aircraft had emptied their holds, their passengers had disembarked into the hangar, and everyone waited to see what would happen next.

The transports did not delay their departure, their crews anxious to get more miles from the Kent coast and possible attention from enemy aircraft.

Next was the arrival of the Salvation Army field refreshment van at the fence gate. The cry 'Sally Up' rang out. Soldiers with automatic weapons appeared from nowhere and made their way to the van held at the gate. The queue of 75 officers, enlisted men and some civilians uncertain of what they were, took 35 minutes to clear.

Two old hands, they had 2 days and 3 hours each on site, approached the assembled men standing around with assorted kit bags, tools boxes and spares' cases. They had in common wonderment of the delights of urn tea and the chicory variety of coffee. They had been flown in separately as the handling crew for the five P-38 delivery. With everything inside the hangar and its doors closed, adjutant Major Clarke McKing organised a pile of crates upon which to stand and attempted to bring the 1574th Special Project Security Group to order.

"Men and women of the 1574th SPSG. Now hear this. Welcome to RAF West Malling, Kent, England, Europe. We are the wrong side of the Atlantic Ocean from the U S of A. Hitler is out there and he is trying to kill you. And me! The British don't want lots of bodies to bury, so they tell you Hitler's hordes are coming by sounding an air raid warning. When that happens: you get under cover in a shelter, unless you're with an aircraft when you get it under cover, or get the hell into the sky pretty damn quick depending on your skill set. You'll know it's safe to come out when the 'all clear' sounds."

The attitude on many of the faces was that they would rather be in the bar, drinking Coors^{tm}. But the Adjutant had not yet finished, "You all know Colonel Roddy Chmielewski, he is our Operations Officer here in the 1574th. The Colonel tells him what to do and you all do it. It's real easy. I'll pay you, and bed you down and make sure you get chow on time. From now on forget dollars and cents; from today you'll want pounds, shillings and pence; it's four dollars to the pound and two cents to the penny. Some Americans on other airbases get the delight of kosher greenbacks in their wallets; you've volunteered to share a base with the King of England's finest and you'll use their quids and copper." There was some shuffling of disquiet at the news.

"You'll get the hang of it before you go home. Anyway, administration and bunktime happens three miles away at a little place called... Snodland... you heard it here first and there is lots of fun down there. The officers will detail you into shifts and tell you where to go, and timings, once we have settled in. Now I have to introduce you to Captain Jodell Lee Grant, one of the US Army star performers. He is charge of ground guns. He has pokies around the hangar here and around our fence in Snodland. When his pokies say 'Halt', you halt. Rank, age, gender, colour of your skin, or your mother's marital status at the time of your birth, gets no privileges in Colonel Ploughman's 1574th. Same goes for the British Royal Air Force Police. And they've gotten dogs, practised on German Alsatians, bred to kill at the throat or - for the men - worse. You'd better believe it."

Clarke McKing actually stopped for 5 seconds, prompting more shuffling of disquiet, allowing him to breathe and swallow before: "There's one difference between this outfit and the other man's army. Not only have we got WAAC, but we have lots of 'No Smoking' signs about the place. This hanger is a 'Smoking Verboten' zone, totally, for everyone. You want a Chesterfield™ you go outside in the 'sin bin'. It's the same down at Snodland, where there's some areas down there where smoking and chemicals don't mix. Where we've got aviation gasoline and oxygen up here, they've gotten hydrogen for balloons and arc lights. The rules are easy: obey the signs or be prepared to carry a load of bricks around the perimeter fence."

He paused for breath again. "The Sally wagon will not be visiting again for your delectation." There was a groan. "That's a Brits only treat." More groans.

Captain McKing knew he had a captive audience and allowed himself to place his hands on his hips, nodding his head. "But the good news is that we've learned that the air corps fights better on lubricated gullets. Our secret weapon is the American Red Cross and they have begged, borrowed or stolen a Sally wagon lookalike. If you hear a 'Sally up' call it's the British wagon at the front gate, where it came today, and it's driver is lost. If you hear 'Red Cross wagon's ho', it means our mobile chow is at the back door, by the 'sin bin'. You'll soon catch on. Now, the Colonel wants a few words."

McKing climbed off his crates and Makepiece climbed up.

"My name is Colonel Makepiece Ploughman. I am your commanding officer. Some of you I have met, for others it is only a matter of time. We are here to do a mission which I will tell you about tomorrow. We will have a commanding officer's parade in this hangar tomorrow at 11:00 hours when the 1574th really gets underway. Until then it's time to make yourselves at home. The natives are friendly, the beer is warm, and this team is as good as the Army can put together. There are more soldiers on their way to join us. They took off from Prestwick, Scotland 20 minutes ago." He started to turn away then checked himself. "Oh! Keep your mouths shut. The British don't know too much about us and I want to keep it that way. Now ..." Makepiece looked at his adjutant and nodded.

"1574th Group. Attention! Commanding Officer on parade. To the centre doors — dismiss!" The saluting Adjutant, as was often the case, had the last word.

A determined looking colonel left the gathering first. A background murmur grew. The group was going to war.

*   *   *

Lieutenant Colonel Roddy 'The Rod' Chmielewski had assembled the group's pilots in the aircrew briefing room. "Gentlemen, today we start flying. When we are ready, and the Colonel says 'Go', then we go and photograph Germans. You're old enough and ugly enough to know this outfit is something real special. Each of you will get to fly a part of the overall mission, but only a part. When we've got 12 pilots on the board the team will know it all, but individuals will only know their part. In this outfit you either fly or you write reports. Colonel Ploughman reckons you all would rather fly. Am I right?"

There was a general chorus of, "You are right, Colonel," or words to that effect.

"Good. First we've got to learn what Europe looks like from 35000 feet. We've got the meanest reconnaissance aircraft that man has built. You are privileged to fly it in this theatre of operations. You are going to need every ounce of mother-loving skill you've got and then some. These Lockheed kites ain't gonna know they could look after their pilot's so well. But they'll learn and so will you. You know you won't have guns, but you will have speed, altitude and American know-how on your side."

The Rod's nickname came from his ramrod stature, his spine was always straight. His short haircut would have done justice to a three days old unshaved beard. His bearing defied any attempt to guess his age. He turned to his covered briefing map wall and drew back the curtains. There was a wall covered in an aeronautical map of the British Isles.

"You pilots know where this is? Don't groan at me." Roddy was using a long pointer to indicate West Malling.

"You are going to fly around this island to cream every ounce out the P-38M-SP until it's second nature. Here you can push your kite to its limits, up there where the daytime sky begins turn dark blue, where the night time sky has stars as bright as Cadillac™ headlights, where there are no contrails and where it's so cold that a polar bear's dick would fall off."

The pointer had circumvented mainland Great Britain on the wall map. He had settled with his body square on to the seated pilots, feet apart, assertive in his delivery. "You are going to learn what endurance flying is, heavy fuel uplift, flying on one engine, getting home on empty tanks with a wing and a prayer. You'll take pictures that Life™ magazine would die for and how to use some real special kit that some Georgia rebs have laced up to make Marconi turn in his grave. And when that's done, then you'll use our Kodaks™ on Adolf and his cronies.

Uncle Sam wants the best. Colonel Ploughman's 1574th is gonna give it to him. Right?"

Rod's hands, one still grasping the pointer, had settled on his hips.

"Right, sir!" came the response in unison.

The training route was marked on the map extending from West Malling to beyond the outer isles north of Scotland, then down the west coast beyond Wales to turn back into Kent. While holding his posture, the speaker's whole body rotated, as if made of a single solid piece of wood, to survey the wall map and then to face his audience.

"Get to know it, fellas, this training route. The turning points are identified; the practice photo targets are listed." His free hand jerked a thumb over his shoulder. "The example opportunity targets of our reconnaissance tradecraft are listed in the route briefing packs. Your safety callsigns and radio procedures are in the packs. You'll all get your turn as quickly as the maintainers can get the ships together. You'll do at least two day and one night missions each, as per your packs. You'll fly a rating mission with operational fuel uplift when I say you are ready. The good news is the basic P-38L will let you keep your pursuit fighter eye in with some real Junkers or Dorniers to discourage from our skies if you are lucky. Planned combat pursuit missions will be separately briefed and those of you who the gods choose will join one of the regular P-38 pursuit groups at its base as briefed by HQ Fighter Command at Bushey Hall. You'll also get some local familiarisation flying in the -38L so the British air traffic can get to understand American drawl. Hell, you may even get a sqwirt at a *Luftwaffe* turkey if they come a-callin'."

"Yes, sir!"

"With real cannon for bigger, better holes."

"Yes, sir!" with greater enthusiasm egged on by Rod's uncharacteristic nod and smile.

Roddy Chmielewski moved across the front of his audience, "The guys and gals are putting the real map of Germany together next door. The next time we meet together we'll be talking about the real show. The RAF flyers have a saying, 'Happy landings'. I have another for the jockies in 1574th, 'Smile for the camera please!' OK, that's it. Collect your named packs, and let's get ready to fly. You first, Major Guthrie. You have been elected to take point. You are in the oxygen tank in two hours."

The assembled aircrew began to rise from their chairs. Pilot chatter was inevitable. Their real flying was about to begin and most felt it had not come soon enough. Only the experienced Guthrie was concerned that they were pushing the flight envelope too far. He was about to find out.

*　　　*　　　*

Major Patrick "Supershot" Guthrie had earned his name flying the regular P-38 photo-reconnaissance variant designated F-5B, out of the airfield at RAF Mount Farm, Oxfordshire. It was a dedicated photo-reconnaissance base and located close to the principal RAF equivalent at RAF Benson. There was friendly rivalry between the two bases, and plenty of social mixing, not least in competition for the girls of Oxford.

Supershot gained his nickname for coming home with a photograph of a naked soldier, judging by his discarded German uniform, mounted on a presumably naked Danish female near Esbjerg, Denmark. The vertical photograph taken from an altitude of 150 feet had remarkable clarity and was popular in the crewroom. The success of his operational images was not so publicly acknowledged.

Guthrie knew his way around British skies and, with 250 flying hours on P-38s, he was the logical pilot to test the training route and the P-38M-SP for European conditions. With reference to the 1574th mission, particular attention was required to air navigation at these latitudes and high altitudes. The photographic interpreters wanted to know the effects of latitude and oceanic air masses on image exploitation, particularly clarity of shadows using 36 inch focal length cameras. Lockheed wanted to know how well the cabin pressurisation and camera bay heating systems performed. Allison was concerned that long duration flights were protected by effective glycol coolant flow and sufficient engine oil lubrication. The flight surgeon's team was aware that the pilots were being taken beyond previous single seat limits of endurance. The pilots wanted to know the navigational issues arising from high altitude transatlantic airflow.

Every P-38M-SP mission started in what the pilots called the 'oxygen tank'. In a clean environment, the pilot breathed pure, unpressurised oxygen for two hours before take off. He carried a portable oxygen set to visit the toilet and ate a light meal with lots of fluid. The oxygen tank would clear his blood stream of nitrogen and avoid the potentially lethal phenomenon of the bends. This period could be used by the pilot to review his briefing notes, check his maps and planned navigation calculations. For the last hour, if takeoff was to be at night, the crewroom lights were dimmed to a low intensity red to accustom the pilot's eyes to night vision. As he dressed in flying clothing, he fitted himself with an adult diaper in case the need arose during his long period strapped to his pilot's seat.

The training went smoothly. The only mishap was on the final night evaluation by Lieutenant Hank Gregson. After flying north over the Scottish border, the cloud cover progressively thickened. He flew dead reckoning around his route, but found no holes in the cloud to take photographs or check his navigation. Gregson had been airborne 5¼ hours when a photographic opportunity occurred. Gregson continued south until it was time for a radio call to request descent clearance. He was unable to make contact. So he began a gentle descent and eventually broke cloud over what he recognised to be the English Channel. He radioed again, identified himself to the partial satisfaction of the RAF West Prawle radar controllers, who scrambled a fighter escort of a pair of RAF Hurricanes to see him back to West Malling. Gregson had the pilot's shame of drinks all round in the Officer's Club and having to fly the mission again. His photograph turned out to be of Dublin, Eire but there were no diplomatic channel complaints by the Irish government.

Makepiece was satisfied that his aircraft and aircrew were ready, and declared his group operational on 28th June. Now the real work could begin.

*   *   *

APO 634   *Letter #3*
June 22, 1943

My Dearest Marybeth,
    We are still waiting for our first mail delivery now we have an APO. Perhaps the censors are having a great time reading love letters... You will see I am numbering my letters so you will know if any have gone astray.

All my group have now arrived and are settling in well. It is strange to be alongside men and women of Britain's fighting services. They all look so young, barely older than our own children. I never cease to be amazed how they cope with food rationing. Of course we are looked after from home, and the Red Cross does wonders for morale. The Brits have a similar arrangement based on the Salvation Army, but I have to say that their version of tea or coffee is not for me. You will be pleased to know that we are based a long way from the German air force's targets so although there are frequent alarms, we remain safe.

I hope you will be able to get away from Washington's unpleasant summer months. I envy you a holiday on the Bay, with feet dipping in the water at the Rocks.

Please write and let me know your plans.

All my love and cuddles for the children,

    Makepiece   X X X

PS   One for luck X

Typical grass covered Lamella type hangar

Chapter 13
1943 ~ Lamella Hangar, RAF West Malling, Kent, England

On the last day of June, tomorrow Guthrie would fly the first operational mission, Makepiece took time to reflect on his situation. Makepiece reviewed on the accommodation that had been constructed for his fleet of five P-38s. It was a unique construction at RAF West Malling although its basic outline was widely used elsewhere. Its actual clearance from the ground at the doors was masked by the roof curvature down to ground level. When it was covered in earth, its form was indistinguishable from a natural feature unless viewed from square on to the doors at either end. The main doors, painted in camouflage green, were normally closed with people and trolley entrance being via side doors concealed along its length. The 1574th version had the whole building surrounded by a steel fence 95 feet clear of the structure; it was five feet high with roll back gates to allow aircraft manoeuvring and road lorry or fuel tanker approach. The grass was kept to a height of about 12 inches and the perimeter was continuously surveyed by armed US Army guards. People on foot entered the fenced area via a remotely controlled gate and were identity checked by the guard.

A standby electricity generating power plant was built into one corner with transformers to provide the US standard 110 volt, 60 cycles per second supply.

Cars and other vehicles were parked under trees so as to be not visible to overflying aircraft. Six weeks after the roof was grassed, no one would know there was a building there unless the lightproof hangar doors were open. RAF West Malling was once more a small airfield with one J-type hangar and 16 single aircraft blister hangarettes.

Notwithstanding the American Adjutant's assertion to the contrary, the British Salvation Army tea wagon was allowed once a day to approach the lamella car park area. The nearest US Army guard would announce "Sally Up" and there would be an exodus for hot beverages and sandwiches. At other times, the evening hours, at the weekend, and usually about 03:00 each night for the night shift, an equivalent American Red Cross vehicle would appear, having driven out of Snodland with American coffee and national favourites. It was greeted by the announcement, "Red Cross wagons ho," but the effect was the same.

There was an area of the lamella compound where four air raid shelters had been dug. They were deeper than usual for such structures, to allow for the roof line to be nearly flush with the ground between the hangar and the fence and thereby retain clear line of sight for security. They were earth covered and sown for grass to match their surroundings.

Aircraft refuelling, which for safety was an outdoor activity, was invariably conducted at night. Non-fuel delivery lorries were moved as quickly as possible inside the hangar to a curtained-off area, until they were ready to move away from site. The RAF police escorted all non-US Army delivery vehicles across the airfield up to the security fence when the US Army took over. Invited Army vehicles came in via the airfield north gate.

Makepiece believed in adhering to the leader's axiom that an officer should be seen and recognized by his men and that he, in turn, should know as many names as possible. Everyone in this group had his part to play in the overall success and Makepiece's aim was to keep the various cogs well oiled. Today, one aircraft was receiving special attention.

"Hallo Colonel. Come to check up on us?" The maintenance crew-chief wiped his oily hands on a rag.

"Uhm. You do the best for my ships, Chief, and we'll get along fine."

"You could climb into the cockpit, Colonel. We're clear of all we need to do. All the safeties are in position."

"Yeah. These ships are rather special. Give me a coupla minutes."

"Take as long as you need, Colonel." Out of sight of his commanding officer, the crew-chief ushered the other maintainers away.

Aircraft were started and closed down, in the open, outside closed hanger doors as quickly as possible consistent with safety.

Inside the hangar, the open plan floor area was more than adequate for the five P-38s. Along one side of internal edges of the maintenance area was lined with the storerooms, locker rooms, component workshops and a ground crew room. The other, northern most side away from the active airfield, side was dedicated to the aircrew with accommodation for flying clothing, safety equipment, briefing rooms, aircrew room and senior staff's office accommodation. This side also include the operations room where the individual flight missions were released and recovered. This was where the secure communications back to Snodland terminated.

The maintenance floor was well lit from above and benefited from roof mounted, radiant panel heating. The hangar was a windowless structure and a number of special measures had to be taken to ensure sufficient ventilation. The running of internal combustion engines for aircraft maintenance plant was actively discouraged by day, when the main doors could be slid open. At night the practice was only allowed in desperate circumstances. Most tools were pneumatically powered to reduce the chances of a spark. Close lighting was provided by flameproof lights. Wander lights were not allowed, torches had to substituted in difficult areas.

Aircraft jacks, access ladders, hoists and trolleys were neatly parked along the walls, behind a safety yellow line. Each aircraft in the hangar had its nosewheel chocked and a towing arm fitted in case of emergency evacuation. Two spare Allison engines were stored in delivery boxes stowed close to the hangar wall beneath a spare propeller.

An unusual room next to the operations room was the clean tiled area where the aircrew were purged of nitrogen. The room was equipped with a number of oxygen outlets for the day's mission pilot to relax while breathing pure oxygen through a lightweight mask. This room ventilated through an exit filter direct to atmosphere to avoid potentially explosive oxygen enrichment on the hangar floor. Outside the room, under weather protection, a wire cage accommodated the high pressure oxygen bottles which supplied the internal distribution system.

The accommodation on both sides of the main floor each had big strong rooms with entrance only through a manned area. On the maintenance side, the room was dedicated to the electronic role equipment and its mounting racks designed to replace the second pilot seat. On the aircrew side was the ABLATIVE intelligence briefing cell where the last minute knowledge of the specific mission route was available to the pilot. It was here that the latest meteorological information was laid out for the pilot's detailed planning.

"Colonel, may I say something?" The crew-chief greeted Makepiece once the colonel had returned to the hangar floor.

"Go ahead, Chief."

"Well, sir. We're obviously something special… with these civilians attached and such."

"The best you can get for your dollar, Soldier."

"Yes, sir. But we don't know nothing about what these aircraft do, or where they go. We know that they take photographs and have all sorts of secret gear…"

"We're fighting a clever Hun, son. We go to find out how clever so that Uncle Sam's finest can knock five bales of shit out of them. You'd like me to arrange some sort of group briefing so you all know where you fit in?"

"That would be just great, Colonel."

Makepiece realised he was making a rod for his own back. ABLATIVE security would make any such briefing difficult. Rod? Just the man for the job…

Outside the hangar structure, within the fence line was a small store for explosives.

On either side of the main doors, at each end of the lamella structure, there were lookout offices. These had been internally sandbagged by the Army guard and would provide firing points if an intruder should try to approach the main hangar entrance.

While back in Washington, Makepiece had been anxious that there might not be enough space for all the activities necessary in the lamella hangar. The restrictions on usable floor area caused by the sloping roof particularly worried him. In the event, there was more than enough accommodation. At least the security demands of his mission would prevent anyone trying to move in with him or — as he put it — 'rain on my parade'.

He smiled at the private thought.

*　　　*　　　*

Post card to Marybeth:

Dearest Marybeth,　　　　　　　30th June, 1943
I came across this picture during an outing in Kent County. The old church is at Snodland and I guess it's where G G G'father Bernard came from. All my group's equipment and personnel have arrived so now we can get down to business. I'm well. I can't wait for your first letter, you are always in my thoughts.
All my love,　Makepiece　　　X X X
PS　One for luck　X

Chapter 14
1943 ~ Marybeth Returns to Maryland

It was well into July that Marybeth had made all the necessary arrangements to move home. The house in Annapolis had to be opened and aired. The backyard needed some seasonal attention and she arranged for some domestic assistance. Since Makepiece had left, she had felt much more tired, but she didn't want to worry him when it would probably wear off.

'Letters can be so worrisome; it's the waiting for them is the problem. Perhaps it's my age. The years catch up with us all! I'll go and see the doctor when we've settled in. There's no need to worry.' So Marybeth kept her concerns to herself. Anyway, Makepiece's postcard and first letter had arrived from so far away. So he was settling in and was not in direct danger, thank Heaven. But his letters made her feel much more lonely. Oh how she missed her lovely, broad shouldered, considerate, easy going lover.

At the earliest opportunity, the family drove north out of Annapolis, through Wilmington around the Chesapeake Bay, and made arrangements to open up their holiday home on the Eastern Shore. The grandparents were, of course, pleased to see the family and to learn all the news. Rosetta's Rocks' stables and outhouses had to be prepared and riding ponies correctly stabled. Cheerful youthful sound filled the family's principal Homestead plantation throughout the summer and the ferries plying between Kent Island and the Annapolis shore did good trade courtesy of the Ploughman family and its friends. Makepiece's letters would need to be redirected and the family had to ensure the children wrote to their father at least once per week. But at least the first postcard had arrived. How sensible to have used something which would not have a problem with the censors.

**Rosetta's Rocks Plantation House on
Chesapeake Bay Eastern Shore**

The original plantation house had been adapted by the fourth generation immigrant Ploughman who gave it her name. It was a lifetime gift by her father to Rosetta who, in the 1780s, developed it with personal funds derived from trading in South Carolina. Subsequent generations improved the property so that was suitable as a fulltime home or a holiday escape as the incumbent chose.

The day came when eldest son, Bernard, had to apply to join the navy and what could be more natural than to lodge his papers with the US Naval Academy? When later, Marybeth learned that her son had volunteered for the submarine service, she had had a few reservations, but there was nothing she could do. However, she did persuade Bernard to write a personal letter to Makepiece to tell his father the news.

So the summer was spent, between the happy times, obtaining college places for the youngest three children. She was delighted to receive the picture postcards as they came through; somehow it seemed they brought another dimension, a reality, to their enforced separation.

It wasn't until mid-September that Marybeth had time for herself. It was high time she made that appointment with her doctor.

Chapter 15
1943 ~ Jenny Plowman

Throughout the spring of 1943, Jenny Plowman had been watching the construction work on West Malling airfield. It was a 40 minute cycle ride back to Rochester. She enjoyed being in the open air, sometimes watching the brave young RAF airmen flying their fighters off the airfield. The romance of the Hurricane's Merlin engine, often in fours, sometimes in squadron strength, made her tingle all over. 'Why should men be the ones to fly? Because they fight up there, of course. I wouldn't want to fight. But watching their formations and their contrails dance in the sky is almost balletic, perhaps not so when you could hear their guns and knew their dogfights were real.' Jenny had once seen an aircraft come down silently trailing white smoke for, it seemed, minutes. Although she did not see the crash, she did see the fireball.

"I hope he was a Gerry, not one of our boys," she had said out loud.

She stopped by a thinning of the airfield hedge. The army pattern sweater over dark slacks, with her hair pinned up under a flowery headscarf, was not complimentary to the young lady. She was hoping she would see some more of the new building, so large it had to be a hangar, through the gap in the fence where the Focke-Wulf had crashed last month. It was getting difficult to pick out if you did not know where it was. Then two pairs of strange aircraft passed overhead to land on the airfield. She had never seen anything like these before. Or heard such engine noise, so sweet and yet so confident in their rhythm. Each aircraft looked like two aircraft glued together onto one pair of wings. Most peculiar, they were moving towards the new building, surely confirmation that they were going into a new hangar.

An RAF Policeman rode up, inside the airfield hedge, on a BSA motorcycle.

"Here, what you doing there?" He was waving his arms in a most officious manner, but Jenny thought he was scarcely a day older than her. His manner was threatening even though he remained astride the motorcycle.

"I wasn't doing no harm, Constable Airman, or whatever you are called. I was just catching my breath and those funny aeroplanes nearly knocked me over."

"Not a good place to stop, Miss. If I was you I would be up on my bike and pedalling away and being about my own business."

Jenny was persuaded. Without delay she rode away and was pleased to hear the motorcycle rev up and be driven away on the other side of the protective hedge.

"Why should they have all the fun? I'll do it. I'll join up tomorrow and stop digging carrots." With a determined nod, "Move over, you WAAFs, Jenny Plowman is a-coming in."

The recruiting office at Chatham gave her a railway warrant with which to purchase a ticket to Gloucester 'where you'll be met by the RTO who'll put you on the garry to Innsworth... don't forget to change at Waterloo and Swindon... and don't talk to strangers or soldiers.'

'What's a garry? Or RTO, come to that?' she thought. 'I suppose I'll find out. I should've asked.'

It came as a shock to join 59 other recruits and be put through six weeks basic training. Being kitted out in uniforms with its emphasis on functionality not glamour, sharing dormitories, ablutions, drill parades and medical 'free from scabies, babies and rabies' inspection, combined to produce a camaraderie which Jenny enjoyed. Even wearing her hair at the standard one inch above the collar became acceptable.

The accommodation was basic. It was 15 girls in an open plan, corrugated iron hut with one central stove for warmth. The ablutions block served six such huts with chemical 'elsan' buckets behind curtains for the necessaries. There were showers, but the hot water was unreliable. Canteen food, four meals per day, was unappetising. The only hot drink on offer was urn tea which had a unique flavour and which Jenny would loathe for the remainder of her WAAF career.

She did learn that the Royal Air Force, females included, spoke its own language. So she found 'garry' meant a motor transport, often a four ton lorry with a canvas awning. An 'RTO' was a rail transport officer, located at main mainline railway junctions to assist with military passengers or freight. Soon she had slipped into the jargon usage discovering it was not worth asking was the word meant because she'd soon find out or be in trouble — often both.

There was no time to be miserable. Activity was proscribed from reveille to lights-out involving, in addition to attempts to retain a modicum of personal hygiene, stripping the bed, cleaning the bedspace, cleaning uniform and polishing buttons, cleaning and polishing anything that didn't move, cleaning anything that did (move), eating, laundry, pressing uniform, making up bed and collapsing into the same before lights-out. When they were not in their huts, they were on the drill square or in lessons learning the basics about the RAF and WAAF, fundamentals about service discipline and facing the rigours of physical education.

Once a week there was a 'bull night' when everything that was polished was repolished, personal kit — with buttons and shoes polished of course, shirts and underwear neatly folded, not a button missing — was laid out on the bed according to the prescribed layout shown in a poster on the notice board at the end of the room. The room had to be dust free ready for a white glove inspection. At the nominated time, in came the section officer and, attended by the sergeant with clipboard, a minute detailed examination of the hut, its contents and its occupants was conducted. On the infrequent occasion when the hut 'passed', the occupants trooped off to the NAFFI for a cup of tea (better than the cookhouse's — made in a real teapot!) and a bun before scurrying back to the hut to remake their beds ready for lights-out. If the room failed the inspection, the process was repeated the following night.

Jenny did not recall a trade evaluation test. 30 girls were in a classroom when a WAAF officer entered. She was wearing the 2½ rings of a squadron officer WAAF on her jacket sleeves. Everyone stood up.

"Sit down! I am Squadron Officer Piquet-Berkeley of Balloon Command. Our fighting airmen need to fight and that leaves holes in our balloons barrage which need filling. You have been selected. Because we are the fairer sex, it will take 15 of you to replace 10 of them. The work is hard, but I know you will not let the side down. You 15 on that side of the room have volunteered for Inverness, you on that side for Snodland. That's in Kent. If any of you smoke, you'll need to know our balloons are filled with hydrogen which burns at the first excuse. Zepplins have got nothing on our fires. So stop smoking. You will have your jabs at 15:00 in case you need to go overseas; the inoculation nurse has been specially trained at Wroughton, is credited with good aim, and has a sufficient supply of needles. Fainting is not permitted."

Delivered without any sense of emotion, the officer continued, "Sergeant Bart here will issue you with travel warrants and your coach leaves for the station at 06:00 tomorrow morning. You will be leaving before breakfast so I have arranged for packed lunches for you all; pick them up on the lorry to the station. You will leave your huts in an orderly condition for the next recruits who arrive at 15:00. Since there are no questions, I'll leave you in the capable hands of Sergeant Bart."

Sergeant Bart leapt to her feet, tipping over her chair in the process. It was time to exercise her authority. Well, not quite yet.

"One moment Sergeant! I have not finished." Jenny had not noticed the officer flinch an eyelid. "When you have joined your squadrons, airwomen, you will be sent to RAF Cardington in Bedfordshire for some trade training. Cardington is very busy at the moment so you may have to wait a while until your course comes in. You will get there by train, naturally. There you will learn what hard work it is to be a balloon operator. The course will take six weeks. You will learn how to operate the winches which are used to fly the balloons and also to keep the winches in good working order. You will learn how to fill a balloon and how to discharge it. You will also need to know how to repair the winches in case they fail at night and how to fix their engines. The instructors will show you how to do a daily and weekly inspection."

The squadron officer permitted her eyes to look each individual recruit directly in the eyes as she concluded, "If there is time at your squadron before embarking for Cardington, learn to drive and get yourselves RAF Form MT20 diving licence. Now, Sergeant."

"Thank you, ma'am! Section! Attention!" Thirty chairs scrapped the wooden floor; three girls stumbled as chair backs fell against their shins. One WAAF fell backwards and rolled over showing her 'passion killer' knickers. Everyone laughed except the sergeant, who was saluting, and the officer who grimaced at the ceiling as she departed too shocked to acknowledge the salute.

"I have never witnessed such a dog's breakfast. Call yourselves defenders of the realm. Thank the Lord we've got an ARP to catch the bombs when Hitler sends his black shirts."

"They're brown," piped a hidden voice from the floor, stifling laughter in the process. "Their shirts are brown, Sergeant."

"Black, brown!" The sergeant was not going to be out done. "When you lot launch your balloons, you'll be slicing the balls off those filthy Hun with your cables and mailing them back to the Führer. Now pick yourselves up and get fell in for a kit inspection."

Thirty voices, in unison, shouted, "Yes, Sergeant."

Jenny turned to her chum, "I joined this mob to get away from the Medway. And where do they send me? The River ruddy Medway. And what's all that about inoculations for overseas? I know that Snodland is in Kent, and Inverness is in Scotland. Neither is overseas in my atlas…"

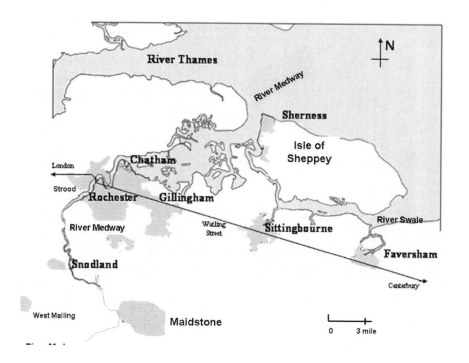

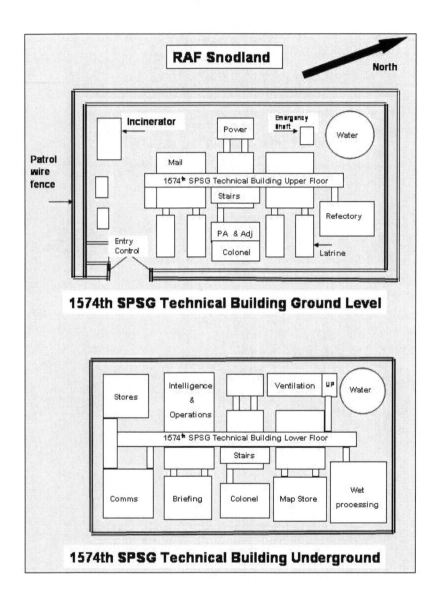

Floor Layout of the Surface and Underground
Accommodation in the 1574th SPSG Technical Compound

Chapter 16
1943 ~ Technical Building, HQ 1574th SPSG, RAF Snodland, Kent

With the RAF Snodland compound edging a public road, well set back within its own wire enclosure, the 1574th SPSG Technical Building appeared to comprise a clutch of wartime temporary, asbestos sheet walled, windowless huts linked off a central corridor. A minimum of windows along this corridor was the only daylight for the occupants; all the working spaces were built without windows and the latrine area's ventilation was by extracted air with its windows thickly blacked out. The refectory had frosted glass windows with external shutters. At night, light tight shutters covered even the corridor windows. The corridor entrance passed through a light tight system of double doors.

This overt building was constructed on a level floor within a double close mesh fence, topped with barbed wire. The 220 yards long, by 170 yards wide, compound was patrolled by pairs of armed military police along all four lengths of fence. At night the patrol relied on natural light since there was no perimeter fence lighting. A pedestrian entrance to the compound, through a turnstile control, was placed next to a vehicle access for essential deliveries. To the casual observer from the public road, the compound did not appear to be anything special.

If the observer from the road had time, he would perhaps remark that there appeared to be an inner fenced compound within the RAF Snodland boundary — a compound within a compound. It was obvious there were Americans about, riding bicycles up to RAF West Malling, but they probably had something to do with the Balloon Squadron — you couldn't ask them, could you? Not in war time, anyway. Perhaps a military hospital? You did see the occasional American Red Cross vehicle.... You'd expect that at a hospital.

However, below the inner compound's surface, 40 feet below the surface corridor and its on-the-surface administrative wings, lay buried the operational areas of 1574th SPSG. This was where the ABLATIVE intelligence work was undertaken. Off the lower central corridor, affectionately known as the cloisters, behind closed doors were several areas each 400 feet square, constructed in reinforced concrete with the only obstruction to a clear floor being one central, load bearing pillar from floor to ceiling. Each room had its dedicated purpose with appropriate apparatus and reference aids: photographic analysis, signal intelligence analysis, radio-nuclides and sniffer filter processing, operations mission briefing and route planning. The fifth area was subdivided into offices for report preparation and communications. Such was the security that a specialist from one area only entered another by invitation and under escort.

The post-mission processing began with the arrival of the latest mission's material, by hand of a courier, from the airfield. After being logged in, the photographic and electronic recording films were passed downstairs to be chemically processed and dried before duplication and analysis. The technical material could now be coupled with the pilot's intelligence debrief report. Specialist staff would extract as much intelligence as they could without reference to their colleagues, thereby protecting the integrity of the source data. A first level specialist report would be prepared. The material would then be passed for in-depth, cross sensor consolidation by an experienced intelligence officer; his role was to prepare a post-mission report for distribution to authorised recipients in England and America. After verification that the images were not compromising the security of the ABLATIVE mission's capability, duplicate photographic material was prepared for Medmenham. All other mission product was bagged for couriering to Dawes Hill for onwards passage to Washington.

Meanwhile, through every day and night, the 1574th SPSG was receiving a seemingly unending flow of intelligence product from the photographic interpreters at Medmenham, from the signal intelligence processing at Bletchley Park released via the American cut-out at Bushey Hall in North London, from human intelligence sources through the Dawes Hill, and from the Washington based Office of National Intelligence.

With so much material, waste management became a major concern for the commander. Colonel Makepiece Ploughman had commissioned an incinerator within the compound in which all waste which could burn was burned; any metallic waste which would not incinerate was physically broken up and boxed for return to the USA. Makepiece took no chance that security of his mission might be compromised.

Chapter 17
1943 ~ Outing to Maidstone, Kent, England

One Sunday afternoon in September, Makepiece decided he needed to go to church. Where better than the village church in Snodland, just over the railway track, and by the River Medway? There he found the ancient building of All Saints, resplendent in the afternoon sunshine, looking as though it had been standing on the spot for 700 years. It had.

While he waited for the service to begin, Makepiece made his way along a footpath beside the graveyard wall, down to the Medway where the river was shallow and flat stones suggested a ford existed on the spot.

After the service, Makepiece, wearing uniform, introduced himself the rector.

"Colonel Makepiece Ploughman. Well, there is a name to conjure with. Have you seen the brass in the tile? Hang on a minute while I say goodbye to these good parishioners and I'll be right with you."

Within 10 minutes, the rector was showing Makepiece the features of the 13th century church, probably founded on a former Anglo-Saxon site going back to the 850s. A window had been blown out when, on 21 February 1941, a land mine had exploded in the nearby gas works. A temporary patch would have to do until things calmed down. The air raid siren sounded but the rector ignored it so Makepiece followed his lead.

"They won't be coming for us today. They'll be going for London to catch the poor folks coming out of church and on the street." The rector's summary of the *Luftwaffe's* tactical air bombardment had a great deal to commend it.

"We have a Ploughman grave in the cemetery, out by the east wall. Would you like to see it? It may be rather overgrown. We don't give the graveyard the attention we ought these days. War has its victims. Come with me, young man." The colonel, not much younger than the rector, followed the lead.

After a little kicking away of the weeds and pulling out the long grass, there, exposed, was the cracked horizontal gravestone of 'Susannah Catteral Ploughman died MLCXV' next to a similar gravestone inscribed, but barely legible, 'William Ploughman'.

All Saints Church, Snodland, Kent

"Now that is interesting," said the rector with the glee of discovery in his voice. Just what he had discovered intrigued Makepiece, but he did not comment.

"Our parish records have been deposited in the Bishop of Rochester's custody down in Rochester Cathedral. Anything he did not want went to the county archives office in Maidstone. Once we could have looked up the provenance of the dead Christians, their marriage and their births. Now we have to go somewhere else."

The rector sighed; the world was changing and he was not sure it was for the better.

"I can't tell you anything about the Ploughman family except there are none round here these days. There used to be a hall occupied by the family, but it went into decay after owner, a Mrs Ada Ploughman Long — a widow I believe — died without issue. You can't see the place now because it was taken down as being unsafe about 50 years ago. There's a military camp up there now; we see some of the boys and girls down here sometimes. Got something to do with balloons and a hospital they say. I don't go up there, I don't want to interfere."

Before Makepiece could invite the rector up to his Officers' Club, the rector began speaking again.

"You can't identify where the Hall was. There used to be five old oak trees up there, but one blew down in a storm and the others quickly followed. There's a picture of the damage somewhere. So where there were four old oak trees, in a line, well that's where the old Hall stood. I don't know when the four oaks were felled, probably during the Great War." He shrugged his lack of knowledge of the insignificant detail.

Makepiece's technical site was built on the very spot. This Ploughman had, in a manner of speaking, come home with the very roots being described being excavated to make space for his underground offices forty feet below the ground.

"If you want to know more, young man, try a visit to Maidstone. I have done a bit of family history myself. I have to warn you that they, the old folks, weren't too good at spelling let alone reading and writing. So you have to be ready for all sorts of ways to spell your name and place names and everything else. But with patience you get their drift and a different world opens up to you. You never know, William and Susannah here may just be your kith and kin."

"I already know the answer to that one, Rector. The grandson of this couple lies buried, under a cracked gravestone, in the family plot in our backyard in Maryland, USA. His name was Bernard and he died in 1675."

*   *   *

Makepiece approached the counter of the Kent County Archives Department in Maidstone. A spectacled, grey-haired man was seated studying a card index and did not look up. A mature lady was fussing with papers under the counter. But Makepiece's attention was caught by the attractive third assistant, reaching high to place a book on a reference shelf above the central desk. Makepiece's concentration was diverted by the female figure in front of him. He must have been staring.

There was a cough which brought Makepiece out of his trance.

"How may I be of assistance, Colonel?" A spectacled face was staring into his. "Is that correct, er… Colonel?

"Yes, Ma'am. Yes, colonel. United States Army Air Corps, Ma'am. I'm enquiring… no… to be honest I don't know where to begin. The rector at Snodland advised me to come to see you in the county archives. You see, my family back in Maryland had its origins hereabouts in Snodland, Kent County and I thought I would see if there was anything in the archives which would help me and my wife with our family history."

The young woman had stopped reaching and had turned to look towards the American accent. Her face was round, her skin clear, her lips slightly rouged. She wore her dark hair away in a rolled bun off the neck. Makepiece was having difficulty paying attention to the clerk speaking to him.

"If you wish to make an enquiry, or to use our records, you have to fill in this application form. And provide proof of identity. Colonel …?"

The young woman's eyes had a suggestion of a smile. She had turned full front on to him. Now she paused and then picked up another book to read its cover. Turning into profile, her flat stomach in a tight office suit, emphasised her slender build surmounted by a pleasing bust. Her knee length skirt seemed to float on a pair of legs which would be the envy of any Hollywood star.

"Er... I guess my military identity card says who I am." Makepiece reached to his inside pocket for his wallet; for a moment he did not find it. For some reason it was on the other side of his jacket today. "Will that do? A form, you said, may I borrow a pen?"

The form and pen were placed in front of Makepiece. Now he had to pay attention to what he was doing. The clerk took the opportunity to look at the young woman while the colonel's mind was otherwise distracted.

'All the portents of a free dinner and a pair nylons here, you lucky girl,' she thought.

"Thank you, Colonel... Ploughman. Older records about Snodland, you say. Well, we have an archivist who has been reviewing those records and it may save some time if I get her for you. Please take a seat over at one of those empty tables and Mrs Aynette Bates will join you shortly." The clerk went to the seated man, mumbled something in his ear and received a nod of approval. She moved towards the young woman who was still looking at the spine of the same book she had picked up while Makepiece was watching.

Within three minutes Makepiece was standing to acknowledge the arrival of the young woman. He offered a handshake which was gently returned. Her hand was warm and dry — he would never forget that first touch. There was a faint aroma of rosemary. They sat on opposite sides of the bare table. Makepiece noticed the gold wedding ring on the third finger of her left hand.

"Colonel Ploughman, hello. My name is Aynette Lyon Bates. Mrs Clarke tells me you are interested in Snodland. It just so happens that I came across an old folder of Ploughman family history closed a century ago and recently given to the archive. I wonder if that will help. And I have come across the surname Ploughman in some research I have been doing for a book. Perhaps you can help join the strands together."

"Mmm." Makepiece was captivated by Aynette's eyes. He allowed himself the luxury of looking at her mouth as she talked. Did her lipstick make her lips more attractive? Blurred, off his line of focus, her hands were holding something. He glanced down to notice that her fingers were long, thin, sensuous. 'Be sensible, Makepiece. You're old enough to be her father.'

"Colonel?"

"Yes. Call me Makepiece, please." Makepiece cleared his throat, not for the first time. "May I call you Aynette? Old family documents, did you say? There was a story about my great, great Aunt Ada who kept what the family called a heritage volume. It was rumoured to carry a curse or some such nonsense. The family, stateside, lost knowledge of it when she — that's Ada — came to England in about 1828. After the War Between the States, back in the 1860s, no-one paid too much attention. There were more pressing matters."

Aynette said, "Very interesting. Now we normally keep the old and valuable material in a locked strongroom. We don't want any accidents with bombs or fires, do we? But most of the records are irreplaceable and so they have been sent off to Wales to keep them out of harm's way. Ooh, I got that the wrong way round, didn't I? They're not in Wales most of the time... Ooh! Bombs and war and... It would take a week to get something back if it was needed urgently, always assuming it's catalogued accurately and the stored shelving information is accurate."

Makepiece was smiling at the verbal slip the archivist had made. 'She is drop dead gorgeous,' he thought. Every word she uttered washed over him like a balm. 'I've heard of knee tremblers, but this really is one ... and she's gotten an English accent!'

"We have a copy of the catalogue here. It is half an hour well spent to be sure to get the right material out, even if the material was here, and the door was open, which it isn't."

"Oh." Makepiece could not think of anything sensible to say. He had not yet learned of the tenacity of the lady in front of him.

Customers were few in these troubled days and Aynette was not going to let this one off the hook. What a coincidence that this Ploughman might just gel with a character in her historical novel. 'Will he have any more details of the family that I can add to make the whole more plausible?'

"But," said Aynette, "if you fill in this interest questionnaire and let me know when you can come and see me again, then I will extract the relevant pack and any maps or pictures that we have. We ought to allow at least 10 days."

Her brain was racing, 'There is something about this man,' she thought. 'A mature, upstanding man he is, wearing a pilot's badge. I like the way his eyes let out what he is thinking. Is he thinking about me? And he speaks so American!'

"That sounds excellent service." Makepiece decided to chance his luck.

After a short pause, Makepiece cleared his throat. "Look," he said. "Uncle Sam keeps me busy with this war. Why don't you give me your phone number, and I'll call you when I can get away?"

"I couldn't do that, Colonel." Her response disappointed Makepiece. It must have showed. "But I can give the number here and you could call and leave a message. My name is Aynette Lyon Bates, er... Mrs Lyon Bates. My husband was killed a few months ago. Here, I'll write it down."

"I would have to make the journey 'specially for the purpose." Makepiece's eyes gave trace of smile coupled with embarrassment, almost shyness. "Would you care to take a bite to eat and catch a movie when I come? It would be my sort of way of saying thank you for your support."

Makepiece was wondering, 'Why do I feel this way? It's like taking a first date to an ice cream parlour.'

"That would be nice, Makepiece. As they say in your movies, let's make it a date." Her smile lingered. As she stood to move away, she said, "I'll look forward to that very much."

Then she thought about what she was doing, 'What will he think of me, being forward like that. Watch it, Aynette, my girl. War plays strange tricks with the emotions. But he is attractive, in a masculine sort of way.' With her face hidden from the American, her cheeks blushed with the ease with which she had conceded a date with a much older man.

Chapter 18
1943/44 ~ Rosetta's Rocks, Eastern Shore, Maryland, USA

Marybeth decided that the children's education would be better served by attendance at the colleges in Annapolis rather than the smaller and less accessible establishments across the Chesapeake Bay. She decided that the family automobile should remain on the Eastern Shore, at Rosetta's Rocks, since most places were easily reached from their home in Annapolis. So the family settled to the pattern of residence on what they called the 'mainland' with occasional weekends on the Rocks. With naval training now fully occupying Frisby, and the other three in college, and with 'paid help' as Bernard called the lady who came and cleaned for them, Marybeth was able to volunteer for the Nursing Service.

Marybeth decided that she should not even consider one of the armed services' nursing corps. She was probably too old anyway, but more important was the need to be able to control where she was sent while she had parental responsibilities. A little research and she found the American Red Cross was a lead civilian agency working closely with the military services. She did not know that by 1943 there were 40,000 employees of the American Red Cross who directed the efforts of 7.5 million civilian volunteers, serving the Armed Forces both overseas and at home. This was exactly what she was looking for and the children agreed.

In her letter to Makepiece, Marybeth wrote:

> *... I just had to do something for the war effort and for our boys and girls. So the Red Cross signed me up and Sue Ellen says the uniform suits me. And the Red Cross makes me feel closer to you and your friends over there. Bernard wants me to send you a photograph. I think he is secretly proud that his mother can look as smart as any starlet in a recruiting poster...*

"Sue Ellen, my darling. Do you think I should get a photo for your father?"

The younger son joined in with, "Awh, Mom. You'll make all Dad's pilots jealous that he's gotten a film star waitin' fer him at home."

"Waiting ... it's gotten... whoops... has a 'g', my darling Bernard. And it's 'for' not 'fer'. Just because Judy Garland doesn't say her words properly in the movies doesn't mean you are excused." Secretly she felt honoured that her son should compare her with a movie star. "This is Maryland where we do things just right. Savvy?"

"Mother! Where did you get an expression like 'savvy'?" Eldest daughter Antonia was attempting to look stern but she couldn't control her grin. In a feigned imitation of Englishwoman Vivien Leigh doing her Atlanta accent in *Gone With the Wind*, she continued, "You bin talkin' to too many 'gyrines'."

"The United States Marine Corps is well represented around her, daughter. And I don't want you getting too free with any of them until after you've finished in college — if then." Then matching her daughter's accent, "Ya hear, ya all?" Now it was Mother Marybeth's turn to be pretending to be stern.

"Changing the subject," Bernard was bored with this exchange, "I reckon Dad would be proud to know his little woman was doin' her bit — just like the President says we all should. We're all in this together."

"Hey, hey. Not so much of the little woman, my son. Just you remember who you are talking to. Now then, it's time for chores, then you can…"

ENROLL TODAY AS A RED CROSS VOLUNTEER NURSE'S AIDE
YOUR HELP CAN SAVE MANY LIVES … FIND THE TIME … GIVE IT NOW
Call Your Red Cross Chapter or Local Civilian Defense Volunteer Office

Marybeth joined the thousands of women who participated in the Red Cross Volunteer Nurse's Aide Corps; they each pledged a minimum of 150 hours annually to perform non-technical nursing services at civilian and military hospitals in the United States. Women in the *Gray Lady Corps,* as it was affectionately known, provided recreational services at military and veterans' hospitals. Their terms of service were no less stringent than those for the regular forces. They had their own manual which provided information such as hospital ethics, assignments, hours of service, deportment on duty, uniforms and authorized duties. They were each especially trained and were awarded the American National Red Cross Volunteer Services Certificate for completion of Nurse's Aide Corps course which Marybeth duly framed and hung prominently by her front door.

*   *   *

Marybeth's nagging ache in her lower abdomen sometimes eased and sometimes became worryingly uncomfortable. It was something she felt she should talk to her doctor about and duly made an appointment.

Doctor Myer had been the family practitioner for more years than Marybeth would choose to remember. He had delivered two of her children out at Rosetta's Rocks and so she made arrangements for a consultation one winter's weekend while they were on the Eastern Shore. This was a situation where she really wanted Makepiece to be with her, to hold and comfort her. But it was clear from the radio reports that he had his own worries in England and she did not want to add to all the pressures he had. After all, there was nothing he could do from the other side of the Atlantic. Her work in the Red Cross, dealing with other military wives who had domestic situations beyond the help of their husbands, taught her that lesson.

Just as Marybeth expected, her doctor was very straightforward with his client. "It can be very difficult for doctors to decide who may have a suspected tumour and who may have something much more minor that will go away on its own. We hate to talk about possible cancer because it is a frightening word to use. And with certain ladies of ... let's say certain age ... their body begins to change. Look, with many symptoms which individually may mean nothing, what I do is to ask you to wait to see if they get better or respond to treatment. We've got new potions which we call antibiotics and they can often make nasty symptoms go away. And while we wait, there are good painkillers — a bit stronger than aspirin — to help. Now I don't want you to worry. I'll give you a prescription and let's see how you are doing in three months."

Doctor Meyer was well aware that if he referred everyone who came to see them to a specialist immediately, the system would get jammed and those needing urgent appointments wouldn't be able to get them.

"And just before you go, Marybeth, I want you to pay a little attention to looking after yourself. Now I know that Makepiece is away and the children are well into their teens, but you must find time for you. The best advice I can give you is to diet high in green vegetables, particularly cabbage, broccoli, brussels sprouts or cauliflower. I know … I know they are not everyone's favourite. But, it's what the posters are saying and it makes good sense. I want you keep down on red meat and certainly anything excessively cooked. Now you look good, your body weight is normal and that job of yours will do for taking regular exercise."

"I bicycle from our house to the hospital."

"That's good. Keep it up — leave the automobile in the garage."

"Thank you, Doctor Meyer."

"You take it easy now. I'll see you in three months. Bowel symptoms are very common. Usually, they are related to a something less serious than cancer. But let's be sure … I'll see you in three months."

Chapter 19
1943 ~ Hospitality in Cleeve Lyon Cottage, Kent, England

Makepiece and Aynette had enjoyed his second visit to the archives. He had told her the date and time when he would be able to return and he was prompt. She had extracted all the relevant material from the vault including the most significant documentation which was the Ploughman Family Heritage Volume, donated to the archive by the lawyer to a certain Ada Ploughman Long, whose firm had held the material since 1845. When Makepiece first saw the item in a porter's basket, it was tied with a ribbon which had been retied by Aynette. There were a number of other folios, some rolled scrolls, some leather bound books and two maps.

"Welcome back, Colonel Ploughman," she had said. Aynette would always remember that special date: the 23rd of September 1943. "We have a treasure of old documentation here. Before you touch it, you must put on these cotton gloves to protect the parchments against you body oils. We all do it."

A momentary frisson was exchanged as she delivered the white gloves into big, American hands.

Aynette had placed the basket on a table. The room had only one other researcher at a distant table; behind the counter, just as before, the spectacled man was seated studying a card index and a mature lady was fussing with papers at the counter. They paid no attention to what Mrs Bates might be doing with the American.

Aynette had said, "We'll have to speak quietly, so as not to disturb the others. I'll come round to your side of the table to help with the old texts. Some have faded with age, some are written in old script which may not be familiar to you." She had pulled out a chair next to Makepiece. There, again, was that smell of rosemary; her warmth seemed to radiate so as to be almost tangible.

Makepiece had been captivated by the family treasure trove. He had in his hands Grandmother Susannah's Catterall own words, reproduced of course but as good as the original in his mind. 'Best evidence' they would call it at court martial. There on the first page of the volume was Susannah's granddaughter's own hand:

From Abigail Ploughman
This chest was given to me and within was the parchment and
Grandmother Susannah Catterall's scarlet petticoat which did
not keep well. The best of the material was used by me for the
lining as you see it. She charged me to open the chest only on the
day of my marriage upon pain of natural peril if I broke the trust.
I opened the casket two days before I wedded Mister Pendleton.
We have not been blessed by children. I was to close the chest
only once, at any date of my choosing, when I had added the
details of the Heritage as I understand them to be.
Chest held open on 5ᵗʰ day of November 1639.

Added Note by Abigale Pendleton (born to Oswalde Ploughman)
The casket remained open in a dark corner of my closet whilst I
added heritage to Grandmother's original. We remain unblessed
by children. Now it is time to donate the casket to brother
Bernard's daughter Maria on the occasion of their emigration to
the Maryland Colony. I seal this in trust:
First day in August of the year 1661, King Charles Second
reigning.

Makepiece had become quite excited. "There it is: the reference to the heritage casket. I knew it wasn't a myth. The damn thing actually existed. Well I'll be damned. What happened to it? Do you suppose the answer lies in these pages, Aynette?"

"I don't know. Half the fun is finding out." She had been delighted to be with this man; to him the day was an interest or maybe a family hobby. "Shh! This place is supposed to be quiet..." To her, archive research had become her life's interest even extending into her non-office hours when she applied her skills to her writing. Now she was sharing it with a real life American hero ... he even sounds like an American ... maybe a special American? Her cheeks began to flush at her thoughts. He's so broad shouldered and good looking...

"Look, Makepiece," Aynette had trodden a research path a number of times, "look and ye shall find, as they say. You will have to look through the book and find the answers. It could take some time and I will help you where the old fashioned ways are not our own. You must be patient.

A lot of history lies within those covers. I'll show you one other remarkable passage, which goes to help determine the manuscript's authenticity."

She controlled her display of emotion by adopting a professional posture. She had previously searched through a number of folios in the volume and found what she was looking for. She opened the volume for Makepiece:

> *'This chest is given in trust to the most likely matriarch concerned*
> *with upholding the Family Ploughman heritage.*
> *To be opened only on the day of the wedding of the trustee.'*

She was really impressed that her American customer was so obviously 'over the moon' as the American movies might say.

"Before you ask, there is no chest in the archives vault," she said. "No, I do not know where it is. Somewhere in this book may lay a clue. The only hint is that the volume and the chest must have been separated before 1845 when your Ada Ploughman died — or at least stopped writing in it. Let us get looking."

"Mmm," said Makepiece, feeling keen to start. Was he imagining the warmth of her body bridging the gap which separated them? Would their legs touch under the table? He was fascinated by the way her words crept out of her mouth ... so effortlessly English.

"Before we move on, just look at Abigale's letter. Do you notice that she has not been consistent with spelling her own name; see, she's spelled it '...ail'. That's typical of what we shall find. Remember that, in the old days, the folks could barely read or write and spelling was something of a black art. And, for good measure, what you are calling a casket, Abigail is calling a chest."

"OK. But let's get on with it. Where is the darned casket?"

"Patience! Who knows, all may be revealed..."

For an hour the pair had scanned every page in the volume. They did not allow themselves time to absorb much of the detail. Many sheets were covered in tree charts of families born, married and died, most of who had lived in colonial America. There were trees for pre-colonial times in England also. Most treasured to Makepiece was the tree for Bernard and Charity Ploughman and their daughter Maria who emigrated in 1661.

"This is the very Bernard who lies in our family plot in Maryland," said Makepiece. "Did you know his grandmother, that's Susannah, has a stone at Snodland Church? Next to her hubby William?" Aynette just enjoyed the thrill of pleasure in 'her' American; she knew she did not need to reply. She watched his face as he scanned the folios on the table. He seemed to be devouring every detail.

Then he had come across the writings of Rosetta. He told Aynette, "We live in the house built by this Rosetta out in Maryland. She is buried close to the Bernard we spoke of earlier. She married a Colonel Alexander Makepiece after the Great Revolutionary War. Don't know of any offspring though. That's where I get my name, Makepiece."

Aynette was smiling. Makepiece had the appearance of being as happy as if he had found the cask at the end of the rainbow. He seemed to have shed some of his worries, to be more comfortable than before.

"I'll leave you to catch up on your kith and kin. There is a staff canteen we could go to, it opens at 12:15. The offerings are a bit war like and limited. But it will give your eyes a rest and we could talk about something else I have found with your name on it. I'll collect you later. There is no hurry." Aynette had pulled her chair away from the table, stood and returned the chair to its rightful place under the table. She turned, perhaps flirtingly slowly, and smiled an *au revoir*.

As she walked away, Makepiece thought, 'Those legs do it for me every time…'

*   *   *

True to his offer, Makepiece took Aynette to eat at a hotel in town. Even there, the menu's fare was not very exciting. Makepiece had not commented. She had been concerned about getting home in the winter's gloom. The last bus had gone and she did not want to be out on her bicycle in an air raid. So Makepiece had taken her back to Cleeve Lyon in his car.

This had been the home she was going to make for David and their children. It occupied the gate guardian position off the main road, inside the gate as part of, yet fenced from, the greater estate. But David had been killed in a stupid road accident on the night of the wedding. Her marriage had been cut short before it had even begun. For 18 months she had hardly spoken to a man: Mr Evans in the office, the postman, a shopkeeper and her father. Her brother was in submarines somewhere in the world. She must not forget she did exchange pleasantries with the vicar too. Now into her life had come this tall American, who she wanted to snuggle up with, to feel protected by his arms. It wasn't fair if he was married. He hadn't said. She would have to know!

Aynette put a match to the prepared fire.

"I don't mind if you smoke, Makepiece."

"Thank you, but I don't. Before I venture back into the wild blue yonder, as we airmen call it, do you think we could manage a hot drink? I'll even drink tea if you gotten the making. My wife likes the stuff, but I never really enjoyed it."

"I think there is something stronger under the sink. David put in a stock of whiskey before the pubs ran out. I don't entertain much so it's still there."

'There, now,' she thought, 'he has a wife. Perhaps I should have thought of tea?"

"Tea will do just fine, Aynette. Are you going to show me over this old cottage? These beams look as if they've been here since Pontius was a Pilate. And you've got a fine collection of horse brasses hanging on the walls."

Aynette had smiled at the airman's joke about Pontius. David had used the same expression. Strange how she had thought about David so often today when there was another man around her. 'Tragedy is that this man is spoken for,' she thought. 'I don't know how old he is.'

"There is paperwork that shows a cottage here in 1575, Good Queen Bess and all that." By changing her thoughts, Aynette wanted to engross the American in the story she was writing. "The murdered body of the widowed mother of the landowner was found here, according to the Shire's Constable's records, three days after Guy Fawkes was caught on 5 November 1605. She had been stabbed in the throat and lay here, I think on these very same slate floor tiles, until she was found by her servant. I've had the tiles checked — they are originals."

"That's too creepy for me. What else do you have to show me? My Rosetta's Rocks out on the Chesapeake is a little modern by your standards. I know Rosetta was living in it when she was first married to Reuben Johnson in 1770. She made some alterations to it over the years, but the two wars on the continent bypassed our lands, so it still stands pretty much as Rosetta built it."

"You tell me about it as we go round. Where we are now is the kitchen cum parlour. It's warm from the stove and fire is nice and cosy too. The old walls keep the winter out. In recent times an indoor toilet — you call it a rest room, I think — has been added and the plumbing allowed for an upstairs bathroom and facilities for the two bedrooms."

"It's got everything you need," had commented Makepiece. "I like the homely feel to the place. We've gotten indoors plumbing too." He smiled. "It is what I would call a woman's home. It's all soft and frilly and laced and nice. It is a home for a lady who wears rosemary."

"Well thank you kindly, sir." Aynette feigned curtsey. "Fancy you noticing…"

"Aynette. Is it possible to borrow the heritage volume? What I would like to do is photocopy it so that I can study it while I am waiting the long hours while I am stuck in Snodland."

"The photocopying process takes a long time and is costly. If I was to somehow get the book to you, do you have the facilities to do the job properly at your base?"

Makepiece had said, "Mrs Bates, Ma'am. You'd better believe it. I have gotten the best there is in photocopying. And the folks who know how to use the kit. And we have shelf expired materials which are good as new, but the military is not of a mind to declare so. Yes siree, Ma'am!" Makepiece was chuckling as he delivered his self-praise. "But seriously, there is far too much to copy out by hand, and too many opportunities to make mistakes in a rush. If I had a copy, there would be no rush and Ada's and Rosetta's and Susannah's work would come back to life. Isn't that what archives are for?"

"That is mighty persuasive, Colonel." Aynette promised to look into the matter. When Makepiece called her to set up his next visit she would have answer for him.

"Very well, Mrs Bates. The colonel here will be celebrating his birthday on 5 November and he requests the pleasure of your company."

"Why, Colonel Ploughman!" Aynette had fluttered her eyelids in the manner of the film star in the film *'Gone with the Wind'*. "I do declare," her accent was not quite 'southern belle', but it was passable, "I am mighty obliged, I am sure. I do declare that the Fifth of November shall hereafter be known as 'Ploughman Coincidence Day' and all calendars be suitably annotated. I am pleased to accept the Colonel's company. But the Colonel is advised that Mrs Bates insists on a condition. Very firmly insists."

"Very well, Mrs Bates. I am all ears. And just what condition do you impose upon this war weary aviator of the United States Army Air Corps?"

"After we have paid our respects to the parchments and scrolls of the strong room, I shall require the said colonel to repair, with due haste and in good order, to the Cleeve Lyon Cottage, where he shall partake of the said lady's company in a birthday celebration appropriate to the prosecution of war rationing and coincidencing."

"This here Colonel will comply with the condition imposed, but will add a codicil to the effect that he will bring such rations as he may reasonably liberate from his chow hall."

"We'll shake hands on that, sir."

And that was how Colonel Makepiece Ploughman came to be in Cleeve Lyon Cottage on the evening of 5th November 1943 and a letter home was finding its way across the Atlantic:

1574th SPSG
APO 634

October 28th, 1943   *Letter #11*
Mrs Marybeth Ploughman
Rosetta's Rocks
Kent County
Maryland, USA

My Dearest Wife Marybeth,

I have some really good news. I have met the local British Rector at Church last weekend and he tells me that Army office accommodation has been constructed on the site that once G.G.G....Father Bernard's relative's once owned. I have seen some papers in the County Archives which mention Grandmother Susannah Catterall's casket and so much more. I just wonder if

G.G....Aunt Rosetta is turning in her grave. When you read her confessional letter you may wish to abscond from the Ploughman dynasty. The papers stop with G.G. ...Aunt Ada in about 1845 when a family heritage volume was placed in the hands of some legal firm. I am trying to arrange a photocopy so that we can study the history ourselves. The archivist who has helped me is really knowledgeable and I have high hopes of success.

I am sorry I cannot tell you where I am based. But my group gets its allotted flying done and I am sure that the authorities here are pleased with our contribution. We are able to get most of the things we need, especially clothes to keep out the English cold and damp. We are made very welcome by the locals. I am hoping I shall be able to repay their kindness when we celebrate Thanksgiving next month. We get a good supply of movies and now there is AFN on the radio. And I have met with your brother Julius who seems in good spirits but missing home.

Please write soon and tell me the family news. I would like to hear how big son Frisby is enjoying being in uniform. And the others as well. And how are you coping with Red Cross uniform, starch and all? Have you got Rosetta's Rocks looking the way you want it yet? Christmas is coming and I know you'll be making a family home for the festival. I shall not be there in person, but my love will cross the ocean to be with you all around the tree.

I love you and miss all of you,

Makepiece   X X X
PS   One for luck X

Aynette's Cottage in Cleeve Lyon, Kent

Chapter 20
November 5th, 1943 ~ Moonlight Becomes You

"Happy Birthday, Makepiece. Within my cottage, I can guarantee we shall not be disturbed. Nearly everything is ready at the table. Now I shall try to do justice to these luxuries you have brought in. I seem to remember they call it food. Now you relax. Take off that coat."

Aynette had borrowed the Heritage Volume — 'to study at home' while the blackout was drawn to help her forget about the bombing while she was writing her book. She was prepared to loan the heritage folios to Makepiece provided he returned the originals next week. If he should happen to make for her a duplicate photocopy, Aynette could promise it would go to good use allowing the preservation of the original for another 100 years.

The personal warmth and rosemary scent bridged the self-conscious gap as she went to hang up his coat.

"This food will take me about half an hour to cook. You have been so generous with these vegetables and the steak. Ah me, the luxury of unrationed steak... I'll carve some off and it will feed me and the Home Guard for the next three weeks."

"I hope it's not too much trouble. I brought a couple of bottles of California wine too. Do you drink wine? They are in the car."

Makepiece was not sure he should be doing this considering him being married and being a military officer with an example to set.

"You get the wine." She thumbed over her shoulder to the door and reached for a kitchen pinafore hanging on a kitchen hook. "I'll get out the book I am writing. It follows a long tradition of telling tales to travellers on the Pilgrim's Way — it's just north of here. I see by your nod that you know already. The part which concerns Henry Ploughman is finished. You can read it while I am cooking."

Aynette was making small talk to cover her nerves. Was this a proper thing to be doing — a man she hardly knew? And married too?

"It's a deal, Aynette." To Makepiece's eyes she had never looked lovelier, but that was no excuse.

'What a way to spend your 43rd birthday,' he thought. 'Wow ... she's a stunner. Just remember you're married, my lad. And you've got 4 children. And you're old enough to be her father.'

"The book is on the table, by the couch, by the fire. Help yourself when you are ready. I hope you like it. It's more of the length of a novella, actually. Take a wine glass off the table." Being busy in the kitchen was a relief.

Makepiece settled to read the typed manuscript:

> *"It is good of you to see me, Father Garnet," said Don Juan de Tassis, envoy from the King of Spain to the court of James Stuart, King of England and Scotland ...*
>
> *... was quick to show the unsigned letter to the Secretary of State Lord Cecil. The King was informed on his return from a hunting party at Royston. After receiving all the necessary undertaking about the safety of the monarch, it was decided that there would be no further delay to State Opening of Parliament....*

"Come on, Makepiece. Take your nose out that manuscript. What is it they say in the westerns? Chow's up, come and get it." Aynette gently lifted the text out of Makepiece's grip and guided him to the dining table.

The touch of her hand on his was their first contact after the handshake in the Archives Centre. They both felt again the frisson, but who would take the next step?

Half an hour later, and the guest spoke, "Aynette, that meal was superb. The thing a soldier misses most when he's away from home — well, second most, — is home cooking. A mighty fine way to celebrate a birthday. A fifth of November to remember!"

"Thank you kindly, sir." There was the mock Georgia accent again, maybe a little the worse for three glasses of wine. Then she abandoned the pretence. Her refined English accent was much more acceptable to Makepiece's ears. "I am so pleased you enjoyed it. I shall not ask what a soldier misses most. I think I already know the answer."

'Was that a wink that I detected in Aynette's eye? She is a pleasure to be with,' he thought, 'and a charming hostess too.'

He said, "Let me help with the chores, and then you can put your feet up while I finish the tale. In some respects historical novels are a fraud because you think you know how they end. I mean; this Guy Fawkes is going to get burned at the stake and this Spanish chap is going to make a run for it. Am I right?"

"After the chores, as you put it, and with some real coffee, you'll find out. One thing about any historical piece is that the parts and the players have to have been written as realistically as possible. Just remember where you are putting your feet, Makepiece, there's history under them there tiles. Would you like to slip those shoes off and warm your toes by the fire? You're very welcome. And they didn't burn traitors, they chopped them up. Burning was saved for wicked priests and witches."

"I stand corrected, ma'am. I am looking forward to what happens to Henry Ploughman. We can look him up in the Heritage Volume. Oh, I guess you've already done that?" His question went unanswered as he picked up the text with one hand and a cup of coffee with the other:

...Late on the evening of 4 November 1605, a careful search of parliamentary premises was undertaken led by Sir Thomas Knevett. In a cellar beneath the Parliament buildings, Fawkes was caught with the 36 barrels of gunpowder....

...Those who bothered to count the new heads on the pikestaffs along London Bridge would have noticed that there was one too many to be accounted by the 'Powder Plot' executions.

"You have an interesting imagination, Aynette. You say it happened on these very slates? Knife wound in the throat ... that would make a nasty mess!" Makepiece's socked feet rubbed across their surface. Was it an accident his feet stopped in contact with her stockinged feet? Makepiece found it exciting to touch in this way. Not perhaps the most intimate of touches, but she did not withdraw from it.

"The very spot, in front of this fireplace. Do you find it intriguing to be so close to history?" Her feet seemed to respond to his gentle contact.

"So close to murder," responded Makepiece. "Do you know what became of Henry Ploughman in Barbados?"

"I would like to think that he married and produced his own line. Perhaps he used his real name out there. Maybe you'll be able to visit the West Indies after the war and find out. It would be intriguing to know."

Aynette was looking enthusiastic as she added details.

There really was a Henry Ploughman, a second son; it is a long stretch of the imagination to believe he would have been caught up in the biggest conspiracy of the time. You be the judge. Have you finished your coffee? There is something I would like you to see. Come on."

Makepiece handed the manuscript to Aynette who promptly put it on the table. She said, "It is blend of fact and fiction. But now you know a little more of our history, it's your pre-colonial history and has a spice of family history too." She pulled the man to his socked feet. This was a rather more positive contact than hitherto and this time without release.

"Come on. We'll leave the radio on. They sometimes broadcast nice mood music at this time of the evening."

Aynette led Makepiece through an internal door, closing it carefully behind her to contain the lights of the room they were leaving, and up the narrow staircase. The war time blackout was an unforgiving routine. They took their time to allow their night vision to adjust. The music on the radio could still be heard. She still had hold of his hand.

"I sometimes do my writing in there. It's the spare bedroom." She was indicating a partially closed door off one side of the landing. He had no time to look inside. She continued to lead Makepiece away from the top of the stairs. "It's a bit chilly in there in the winter…"

She led him through a dark bedroom, which smelled mildly of rosemary, and up to a window where the blackout was not drawn. The full moonlight illuminated the view across the estate. The grass glistened in heavy dew where it was free of fallen leaves. It was a very special view, silver in this light, one to be savoured.

"We call that a bomber's moon," said Makepiece. He was aware that Aynette was standing in front of him at the window, and that he was pressing in to her or was it she was pressing back into him? The scent of her hair was in his nose. He wanted to embrace her. He sensed she wanted him to embrace her. Standing 8 inches shorter than he in their stockinged feet, Aynette turned inside the man's embrace, pushed up on tiptoe and kissed him. Makepiece hesitated before responding to the kiss. It became mutually warm, tender and yet searching for the prompt for the next move.

Downstairs, in the background, the lyrics of Sammy Fain and Irving Kahal's song with Bing Crosby's crooning set the mood…

> *I'll find you in the morning sun*
> *And when the night is new*
> *I'll be looking at the moon*
> *But I'll be seeing you.*

"Makepiece," Aynette whispered. "I was married for six hours only. David and I did not wait so I know something about men and war and their needs."

"You don't have to do this." He was being excited by the warmth of the breasts pressing against his shirt front.

"I want you to make love to me, Makepiece. Here in the moonlight. As two passing lovers, uncertain of what the future may bring. There will be, there can be, no commitment. It will be a night when a man and a woman, with a loneliness worsened by danger, surrender to inevitable desire in order to escape and forget for a few short hours."

Their coupling was too hurried to be a success. Each was too anxious to draw pleasure from a simple bodily function and yet too contrived so that the needs of the partner was not sufficiently observed.

*   *   *

Later, as Aynette closed the door on his departure, leaning back on its ancient wood, she realised that her soldier had not totally surrendered to her body. She resolved to get Makepiece back to her cottage and to do the job properly next time.

"I can wait for my soldier boy. I've got the Moon to remind me." She drew her dressing gown tightly around her body.

When Makepiece left the cottage, he was not sure that he could live with his first infidelity. He was grateful that he had a war to return to, something tangible, something demanding of all his energies. Under his arm was the cloth wrapped Heritage Volume which he had solemnly promised to return, undamaged, within as soon as Uncle Sam would allow.

He looked at the Moon, so cold and white and distant. The last two lines of the refrain kept repeating in his head:

> *I'll be looking at the moon*
> *But I'll be seeing you.*

That clear sky warned of a cold autumnal night. A shiver ran down his back. One of his group would be flying tonight.

'Is Marybeth looking at the moon? Will I ever be able to explain what I've done to her? Will she understand, will she ever forgive me... ?''

113

Chapter 21
1943 ~ Festive Season for Some

The RAF was intending to make Christmas as traditional as possible, given the wartime shortages. RAF Snodland had the advantage of a resident American presence which might be persuaded to make a generous contribution if they were invited. Squadron Leader Adrian L Wilburne, the Station Commander, set out to persuade Makepiece's group's adjutant, Major Clarke McKing, of the merit of Anglo-American harmony in the challenging conditions of war torn Kent.

He need not have worried because the Americans were thinking along similar lines. When Adrian called on Clarke 'for a chat' he was pleasantly surprised.

"I am only a part time airman," Adrian began, "doing my bit for King and Country, but I do like to do things the proper way."

"Us full time Yanks see it pretty much the same way, Squadron Leader. What's your problem? Can Uncle Sam fix it with some coffee and doughnuts? There's only one proper way to do things in this man's army. Gee, I guess I should have said men and women's army. They're wanting to give our WAACs carbines, but the Colonel thinks there's enough guns about the place as it is."

"What I had in mind does not concern guns." Adrian did not yet feel at ease with what he was about to propose. But he did have to make his point.

"Although we give our WAAFs experience in using a rifle on a range, we believe it is a man's business to shoot at an enemy except in self defence. Anyway, to matters more seasonal. It can't have escaped your notice that Christmas is coming. It happens every year."

"True," supportively remarked the American, wondering what truism this Limey old-timer was going to deliver next. The Brits take their time coming to the point. "I read it in the newspaper, so it must be true."

"Quite so. The RAF tries to ease the distress, which our other ranks have, in being removed from their loved ones, and sweethearts, and kids and so on. Naturally the officers are expected to grin and bear it, what?"

"Well, that list seems to embrace everyone except Old Nick, Squadron Leader."

"Please call me Adrian. I'll address you as Clarke, when we are in informal situations such as this — if that's alright with you?"

"Wilco, Adrian. Heh, are you worried that Santa ain't going to recognise the stockings hanging on the bedpost? Have the same problem myself if I entertain a WAAC in my bunk." An American eye winked.

Attempting to disguise the horror at the disclosed misdemeanour between an officer and another rank, something the RAF would never countenance, Adrian said, "I thought that we might celebrate the festive day together. By the nature of our units, work will continue throughout the holiday, day and night. I am presuming you may be flying, I wouldn't know, it's not my business. But the guards and balloon girls and the communications staffs will have to work through. And the cooks, too! Precious few will be able to take leave of absence."

"I read you, loud and clear, Adrian. Our enlisted men might want to take a London furlough, but there will be better than 90% of them on the base some time during Christmas Day. What do you have in mind?"

Adrian Wilburne relaxed; the conversation was going his way. He allowed himself to sip the black coffee and to nibble an edge out of a doughnut balanced on his cup's saucer. The American host looked so young and clean.

"I had thought about a combined Christmas Lunch, but I don't think we have a mess hall big enough. If we did it in two shifts, how would we decide who went first? And with catering on that scale, where and who would do the cooking? And what about the shift at work? So many questions and no answers! Do you eat Brussels sprouts?"

"Questions I don't like. Answers I do. Down in Texas we make room for parties like this one. A tent is the thing we need and a barrage balloon has all the making. I think that one of your balloons is about to have an accident, Adrian old son."

Clark pretended to scratch his beard. Adrian thought he might be too young to shave.

"We'll make your enlisted men's hall bigger with a tent extension and all the guys and gals can chow down together. Well, separate but together if you get my drift." The American winked.

He gestured at his guest's cup. "Is that coffee OK? Then the American Red Cross hut will throw a ball. We've gotten 600 kids here between us and surely we can muster a dance band out them. May not be

Benny Goodman but we'll give Glen Miller a run for his money. Maybe ENSA will have a show in town that we can get in for a stage show. Bing Crosby would be nice, but I guess we are a bit small for him."

Adrian liked the way this was going. "Our experience on RAF units is that there would be at least a quarter of the staff having to be at their place of work while the traditional turkey and brussels sprouts are being served. They can have their meal later."

The older dog was teaching the blade new tricks.

"So the problems have shrunk. Now that's positive thinking, Texan style. So our 600 has dropped down to 380 to 400 excluding the officers. There's about 25 of them, officers, in their special clubs, so we budget on 350 mouths for the big show down."

Adrian still approved of the drift of the conversation. Even with a smile on his face he was shaking his head negatively. Now had to raise an even more delicate matter: "Clarke, old chap, you do know the RAF tradition is that the commissioned officers serve the airmen their Xmas lunch?"

"Wow ee! The Colonel's gonna love that. When in Rome… as they say."

"Quite," said Adrian. "The Romans were here about 1900 years ago, but left in a bit of a hurry. Anyway, the SNCOs invite the officers to a drink before going to feed the men — and women — to sort of fortify them for the tribulations ahead."

"It gets better." Then with a worried look, "Just a moment, who feeds the cooks?"

"Never did find the answer to that, Clarke, old lad." His wagging head inexplicably became a nod. "I think it's what we have SNCOs for — to decide the answer to conundrums such as that."

"If there's 15 cooks a-cooking then they're not a-sittin' for us to be a-servin'."

"Your point is presumably that we've dropped the head-count to 335 maximum at the main sitting. Good thinking, if I may say so."

Clarke McKing pondered for moment then he came out with, "What is a gentleman such as yourself doing dressed in military uniform in this man's war, out here on the front line and scarcely outta the trenches?"

"Second born of twins, I was. He came out 20 minutes before me." The head had stopped moving and the shoulder slouched a little.

"Therefore my brother got the title, a commission in the Guards, and eventually the estate in Derbyshire. Second son went to one of the smaller redbrick colleges at Manchester, had to join the University Air Squadron to pay his way through college only to find too late that I was colour blind and unfit aircrew, so I was put into the Administrative Branch. All I shall inherit is a box of old photographs and the second set of wine glasses with the broken decanter."

"It's a hard life," commiserated the American.

"Sure as hell is," responded Adrian, ungrammatically. The smile returned. "Do you just happen to have anymore doughnuts?"

*   *   *

Elsewhere in RAF Snodland compound sat No 978 Balloon Squadron's commander Squadron Leader Percy Davenport RAF and his Operations Officer Flight Officer Bethany Taverner WAAF. No 1 Balloon Group commander, Air Commodore W Gell, had been on the telephone to his squadron commanders about the requirements for the Christmas period.

"Fighter Command's met men say the weather is expected to be foggy with light winds to blow it away. Balloon Command's line is that, although the *Luftwaffe* may plan a break in their operations, it is essential that London's defence remains at readiness. In short, Squadron Leader Davenport, that means balloon flying will continue without respite. Phone in your stats when you are ready."

Bethany told her commanding officer what she thought would be a reasonable declaration of status. "We have 14 of the 16 balloons serviceable and 11 winches to launch them. There are 10 launched at the moment, sir. Two have minor tears where guy cable damaged the lower surface, straightforward to patch repair. There are no replacement balloons due before Christmas. We have adequate MTGAS for the vehicles and winches and sufficient hydrogen stocks. I'll order a delivery for the 28th, just in case. If spares arrive by the 23rd, we should make 14 winches for 14 balloons. Assuming no accidents or unforeseen sickness we will have 3 WAAF Section officers, 16 SNCO operator/drivers and 190 WAAF operator/drivers. The squadron Operation Room will not be affected, we would be working through anyway. I will pull in the cable workers from the Strood workshop; the repair team at balloon centre

Kidbrooke will be open throughout the break. Given 12 hours on and 12 hours off, we should be able to keep 12 balloons flying between 12:00 on 23rd to 12:00 on 27th with two more stood by for contingency gap filling if we get away without fabric ruptures. You will wish to reassess our serviceability before declaring assets to Group HQ in time for the New Year time period."

The situation report was delivered, without hesitation or notes, while seated across her squadron commander's desk.

"Thank you, Bethany." Davenport was not surprised that his Operations Officer was abreast of the job, delivering her status report without reference to any notes. She was efficient and he would be recommending her for promotion in the current round of officer assessments. He admired her knack of maintaining her femininity in a man's war. He would regret her leaving if his recommendation was accepted, but such was the nature of Air Force life. But he had been approached by the Station Commander about the Christmas Day arrangements and these needed to be included in the planning so that their boys and girls got a fair crack of the festive whip.

"Adrian Wilburne has told me that the Station and the Yanks are planning a traditional lunch, drinks with the sergeants and all that. He has asked me for an old balloon to make a tent extension to the Dining Hall. He expects 350 other ranks to sit down for lunch. But we will have half the squadron in the field and many of the others will be asleep."

"I suggest, sir," opened Bethany, "that you advise the Station Commander that we will be needing to feed lunch to 150 at lunchtime, and another 150 at the evening meal, after shift change. The Yanks are bound to keep going with whatever it is that they do. I think the Catering Officer needs to do some realistic head counting with the workers so that the front offices are properly briefed on numbers. There would an outcry if we over catered, sir. The Daily Herald would wreak havoc if it ever got out that we had wasted good food." She had not changed her composure.

"I entirely agree, Bethany. And while the bean counting is going on, do the same for whatever the social planners are dreaming up. I hope we are not going to have a problem with rampant WAAFs chasing the American Army all over Kent. God forbid! I think the RAF Police are going to have to stay off the hooch on Christmas Day. Sort that out, will you. They can have a party on another day, when the excuse to overdo it is removed."

"I'll fix that, sir. Will you be staying on camp over Christmas?" Did he detect that she had relaxed a little? She was an attractive woman who would make some lucky man happy after this war madness was sorted out.

"I'll stay until after the Sergeants' Mess drinks and the Airmen's lunch. I'm not sure how the rest of the day will go. It's too far to try to get home in Lancashire."

"Perhaps you would care to join us in the Ops Room, sir? We'll have some American coffee on the go. I thought we might invite the ATS officers over from Rochester; they'd be close enough here to be able to get back to their searchlights if a flap breaks. If it's quiet, we might even have a rubber of bridge."

"I'll certainly bear it mind, Bethany. Thank you for the idea. I might even rustle up some mince pies and a spot of malt to lace them with." He allowed himself the opportunity to survey the retiring curves as Bethany left his office.

Chapter 22
1943 ~ Maximum Effort

From his office in the Technical Building, Makepiece was on the secure telephone to Julius Knapp at Dawes Hill.

"I've an idea to try and catch them unaware. In a few days it will be Christmas. The Krauts will expect us to shut down and be off guard. The weather forecast is none too bright either. *Pax-yuletide* may be true for others but not the 1574th. It's just the time when they are likely to be testing their new kit, while they think we're not watching."

Julius had caught the concept. He said. "If you go out there you'll stand out like a dog's whatsits. They'll throw everything they can at you because there is no other game in town."

"Precisely. The difference is that if they are more relaxed than usual, ideally half- cut or better on Rhine wine, then they are more likely to miss what they are shooting at and very much more likely to make mistakes. It's the mistakes that tell the boffins more than regular operations; it's the evidence they cry out for." Makepiece had thought this plan through and he wanted to sow the seed in his contact to get staff clearance for his intended maximum effort.

"How much detail have you worked on this idea, Makepiece?"

Makepiece replied, "Full targets, routes, timing, probable photographic conditions and the electronic payload. If staff give the go ahead, I'll negotiate fuel delivery with the RAF throughout the holiday. They'll have contingency staff on, anyway, and air traffic will be manned just in case the *Luftwaffe* decides to do the dirty on us."

"Define maximum effort, Makepiece."

The prepared reply was, "Four ships on 25th and 26th each, with single pilot and full electronics 'though I might put a navigator in one to get better details from south-east of Berlin. Maximum fuel uplift."

"That sounds as if you are pushing it, Makepiece," commented his brother-in-law. "OK! To sell it to the staff I'll need two signal messages. The ABLATIVE targets as clearly spelled out as you are best able at that level. Obviously I'll keep that text within channels. The other needs to be a proposal for your routes with key photo targets for each. This second open circulation text will need to have timings so that our boys don't get in your way, and vice versa. We won't want Fighter Command getting trigger happy when you come home."

"That's good. The messages are already drafted. I'll release them shortly."

"Makepiece," cautioned Julius. "Are you sure you can launch all four P-38M-SP ships on two consecutive nights?"

"I am gonna give it my best shot, Jules," replied Makepiece. "It is what I was sent out here to do and I'm sure as hell gonna try." He was quietly confident, but the thrust and pressure, of his real mission, which had been sanctioned by FDR, communicated to his fellow officer.

Julius Knapp wondered if the conversation was over. It was not.

"Jules, what would be your reaction if I was to ask you to recommend to me that I should use the services of a specialist scientific officer for the extreme end of ABLATIVE level 3, radio nuclides and such."

"You playing politics here, Makepiece?" Out of sight of his brother, Julius leaned back in his office chair.

"Playing ain't the name of this game, Jules. And," went on Makepiece, "I really do need an experienced high altitude meteorologist, one who understands winds in the stratosphere and top troposphere, say 32000 feet plus. We are being blown about with groundspeeds in excess of 550 mph up there. I think there is similar effect in the top squadrons of B-17s and B-19s which is screwing their bombsights. That's not my concern. I need to know how far east my ships can go so they can get back."

"It sure seems a good idea, Makepiece. For information, Eleanor Roosevelt keeps a special watch over all P-38 reconnaissance pilots now her son is here running a reconnaissance group out of Mount Farm. 8th Fight Command moved his group out of Steeple Morden; before you ask, it's 40 miles north of London, out Cambridge way. She got lost looking for the place."

Makepiece was not interested in the antics of the President's family. He knew Julius was stalling, for a moment, while he reflected on the requested being made.

"About the time I was leaving Washington, Headquarters Army Air Forces activated a new outfit called the Weather Wing. Jules, buddie, it seems to me it's about time they won their spurs! That's more important than Mrs FDR!"

"You want me to arrange that Dawes Hill is seen to impose this meteorological high priced help on you photo-jockeys out there in glorious Kent county?"

"Right." Makepiece had made his point. Now, what was the reaction? "Kent county, England, that is — not Kent County, Maryland. I'd hate for the expensive help to wind up supporting the wrong war. It's happened before!"

"Why don't you ask for them straight out?" queried Jules.

"You will have the clout in DC, Jules. I am only a humble field commander. There'll be an easier ride through COSSAC too, not that they interfere with me. But expensive civilians can attract a lot of flak."

"When do you want them, Makepiece? Is this going to ruin some stateside kid's Christmas?"

"New Year's Day would be OK, Jules. I have the heaters on in their bunks right now." He smiled. He'd made his point and was confident of success.

*　　　*　　　*

Makepiece's adjutant, Major Clarke McKing, was let in to the 1574th commander's administrative office by Sergeant Julia Greenburg.

"The Adjutant wishes to speak with you, Colonel. I believe it is about the Christmas arrangements with the British."

"Thank you, Julia. Would you please have Wing Commander Battel and Colonel Chmielewski meet me in my office in the Technical Block in 30 minutes."

The aide closed the door as she left.

"Now, Adrian, what can I do for you?"

The adjutant explained the idea for Christmas festivities he had hatched with the RAF. Makepiece gave the matter some thought and then he gave his reaction.

"I like the idea very much and you have my full support. But I am expecting to be tasked over Christmas and so there will be no relaxation in the readiness status for the officers or the men. We need to be particularly careful about the use of alcohol. And not to put too fine a point on it, I have a duty of care to the women under my command. I shall want the Military Police to be particularly vigilant to protect my girls from the unwanted attention of Brits or Yanks. Same goes for controlling our lads from getting too keen with the WAAFs. I'm not a prude, but I do not need a Senate Investigating Committee rattling my cage out here in Snodland. Do everything you can to encourage them to work off their energy on the dance floor. Are my wishes entirely clear, Major?"

"Protection will be issued, Colonel."

"That is not what I said, and you damn well know it." Makepiece rose and came round his desk to emphasise his point. "The party is a good idea. Don't let some sex-crazed GI spoil it. Same goes for the WAACs too, make sure Lieutenant O'Grady is aware of my requirement to keep her girls under a semblance of good order. You had better make sure there is an adequate supply of non-alcoholic liquid about the place. There may be quite a demand by those who have a war to fight, even if it is the period of goodwill to all men."

"Yes, Colonel."

Makepiece had not yet finished, "One final thing, Major. Life around here might get busy up at the hangar over Christmas. Check with Sergeant Greenburg before committing me to be anywhere between now and after New Year's Day. She'll know where I am at all times. I was hoping to have a 48 hour furlough, myself, over the period."

*   *   *

In the technical building, in Makepiece's office, three men were pouring over a map of Germany and the occupied countries to its east.

"I have explained the concept of catching them with their knickers down. Here are the targets I have declared to Dawes Hill: 4 routes on the 25th and 4 more on 26th. It's maximum effort. I want to make it happen. You are going to tell me how."

Rod Chmielewski, the 1574th SPSG Senior Operation Officer and Senior Intelligence Officer, rubbed his chin. Chmielewski was an ex-Pole, fluent in Polish, Czechoslovakian, German and English. His English was delivered with clarity although there was a hint of Europe in his accent. Makepiece thought he would recognise Rod's upright stance, even on the darkest night.

Cliff Battel waited for the American to speak. Makepiece's deputy, of indeterminate age, was clearly under pressure from the boss. Cliff's professional interest lay in how Rod would handle this situation. He was overly surprised when the answer came.

"We'll have to give the maintainers a chance. Limit flying to one mission per day for the 18th to 23rd and no mission flying on 24th. We could put the P-38L on a navigation exercise or combat practice with the P-38 groups up the coast. Just in case someone is watching us!" Rod grinned at the thought of the German Y-service monitoring the 1574th just as we monitored them. Then he added, "It is some time away yet, but the weather looks set for a cold, damp, light winds period of high pressure. That adds up to fog. Fog and flying are not a happy mix; fog and photography are a no-no!"

Makepiece's reaction surprised the two other men, both experienced pilots, "Take-off at night with limited visibility is not too bad, provided the aircraft flies. If it doesn't, engine failure or something, you'll hit the deck and be dead whether you can see or not. Coming back is a bit more testing if you can't see, but fog tends to burn off during daylight hours so we'll do our timings to suit. I will only cancel out if it's a real English pea-soup and it's not safe to ride a bike! Fog is no problem to the signals intelligence gear the P-38 will be carrying."

Makepiece nodded his satisfaction at his putdown of the objection. He directed his operations officer to ensure that the established meteorological officer, Hastings Palmer, begin to assemble comprehensive data to support flying operations over the period required.

Then Makepiece addressed the RAF Liaison Officer. "Cliff, find out what the RAF are doing with the airfield over the period. I hope they'll keep it open for normal fighter defence, just in case. While I don't want to broadcast what we will be doing, I do want to use the runway on the 25th and the 26th. And find out what are their arrangements if it should snow? The 1574th ships have got to get their material back here for first level processing. More so the first wave on the 25th so that we know how to milk the best out of the missions on the 26th when Gerry has got a hangover."

Cliff said, "I understand. I don't anticipate you'll have any problems. I'll go and talk nicely to our boys in blue. You'll need aviation fuel and oxygen on the 25th when the first lot get back. That will be unusual, but I will sweet talk the RAF Supply Officer at West Malling. I flew with her dad."

"Right, Cliff, make it so. Rod, you select the seven pilots who will do the routes, 4 on the first night, one navigating the Berlin mission, and three on the second. No-one is to fly on two consecutive nights. I shall be flying route 4 here," he pointed at the map, "myself, on the 26th. It'll give one of the regular joes a rest."

Cliff was about to cough his surprise but, before he could, Makepiece continued, "I need a refresher trainer. I know that before either of you say anything. So, Rod, set me up with the long route around UK on say 21st. Tell me timings so I can put them in the diary with Julia."

Rod nodded. Makepiece had not told his deputy about Secretary Stimson's letter. Nevertheless, this would be the colonel's first flight, training or operational, over Germany.

"I don't want anyone to know it's me on Route 4. I have my reasons. Colonel Ploughman will be in the lamella hangar, out of touch, while the aircraft are airborne. For movement notification purposes, a hot-shot, Captain Bates drafted in from the States, will be at the P-38 controls around Route 4 on the 26th. But I don't see why I shouldn't have some seasonal fun too. Absolute secrecy on this, gentlemen! Do I have your assurance of my requirement? Cliff? Rod?" Both men nodded. "Good!"

After a brief pause, Makepiece said, "Cliff, could you give me a minute with Rod, please. Then I'd like to talk about an RAF Christmas with you."

Cliff Battel closed the door behind him.

"What's this all about, Makepiece? You sure picked an odd ball night to loose your virginity over Germany. It isn't any picnic out there, you know."

"Rod, I want you to arrange for a sniffer on my P-38. Stateside wants to know if the Germans are messing about with radioactive weapons and we are the only outfit that can find out. But it's so secret that even the ABLATIVE level 3 does not open this door. Cliff does not need to know. Only the Lockheed maintainers who fit the canister will know I've got it, tell them Washington wants to trial the kit, and when I bring it back it will be mailed to a special place through my old desk in

125

Washington. Not even Dawes Hill will know. I need to do this one myself."

"OK, Makepiece, I get the picture. You'll get your mission only if you complete your trainer flight. That's not too easy either."

"Thank you, Rod. Would you please ask 'The Sprite' to come in? I hope I can understand what the Limeys make of Kris Kringle. And one other thing, try and find out why he's called 'The Sprite', please. I don't sleep worrying about it."

"You do understand that the whole outfit will know we're on operations on both nights? And you won't keep it away from the British either. Their steely eyed killers will think we've gone mad."

Makepiece decided to confide in Rod Chmielewski about his calling for high grade scientific specialist help. The Operations Officer understood his commander's thinking. But he remained ignorant that his commanding officer was planning to disobey a written order — about the worst crime in the book.

"I'll need to sell the idea gently to Hastings Palmer. He'll see it as overriding his skill set. I'll tell him it's Washington's idea to get a second view on the safety of our boys out there in deepest Bavaria, or wherever. Even Ploughman's special ships don't have unlimited fuel range. They'll be citing me for the shrink next!" Rod was making to rise from his chair.

Makepiece commented, "If I find what I am being sent to find, then madness may be the least of their problems."

Chapter 23
1943 ~ Fortune Favours the Bold

"Colonel, it would help if you could say where you were heading at that moment. The image is not helpful. Local snow clouds and all!" In the colonel's operational office, the intelligence officer had a communications intercept transcript in her hand. She knew that her commanding officer had flown the mission under discussion.

"OK. Let's work this chart. I had a positive waypoint here," Makepiece stabbed his navigation chart, "at Nordhausen, an unpleasant place even from seven miles up!" Airspeed 295 knots was giving a groundspeed over 400 mph. I was heading 090. Pretty much downwind I'd say. So 20 minutes later I'd be here." Makepiece lifted a pencil off the table and drew an ellipse 20 miles long by 10 miles wide at its extremes.

"There, give or take a Christmas brussels sprout induced fart." Makepiece was satisfied with his effort. "I was in clear skies. Pretty much 10/10th cloud cover over the ground. ELINT was quiet except for a couple of air space sweepers probably covering Berlin. It was supposed to be Christmas and all quiet, after all; Father Xmas had parked his sleigh for the duration. No hope of decent ground photos out there, shame because the sun was just the right angle for shadows. I reckon, at 05:40, I was close by this turning point, southwest of Halle hoping to capture this airfield at Laucha and the buildings at Freyberg. Failed on both counts! Too much cloud, dammit. My fuel plot put it as my furthest east for my planned route. COMINT was quiet up to that time, but as I turned onto heading 195 degrees, I must have entered either a sidelobe off a radio link or an overshoot on a point-to-point link; VHF often extends over the radio horizon. So I flew a tight orbit until I had to move on for fuel reasons. Based on time and speed, I would say I was 9 miles west of Gera. My mission priority was Bavaria."

"That's good, Colonel." Her calm extraction of vital details helped enormously. "The sound on the film recorders gives the time. Pity there is no collateral positional fix. Would you care to read the draft transcript, sir?" Makepiece accepted the offered sheaf of papers from the young woman's hand.

'A wise, capable head on young shoulders,' thought Makepiece.

He noticed the pilot's name was shown as 'Captain Bates' not his, that is not Ploughman, for his protection against his breach of Secretary Stimson's written instruction. Sarah Johannson had noticed the pilot's name discrepancy and, assuming that it was something to do with ABLATIVE security about which she did not need to know, had not corrected it. She was concerned that there was still so much italic in the first draft indicating uninterpretable material on the recordings.

The formatted report read:

MOST SECRET ABLATIVE 3 -- ULTIMATE -- DRAFT
Partial transcription of 1574th SPSG Mission 431226/41 dated December 27, 1943

Pilot: Captain Peter Bates USAAC
Transcribed: Lieutenant Sarah Johannson US Army Intelligence Corps
Media references: Sound Film: 431226/41 Channel: 5 LSB and HSB
Cross references: ELINT: 431226/41 E12 thru E18
                     Photographic: 440101/01 frames 09 thru 20
                     Other: none
Time Zone: All time datums are GMT. Times in text (if any) are verbatim
Caution: DRAFT: This is a first level analysis and is subject to reassessment.

Datum		*<comment: technical chatter, awaits further work>*
05:54	Man A	Yes, General Kammler. There are 17 in the mine. There are six scientists with me in the safety cavern. We have power from the *<water?>*. Shall I trigger the sequence?
05:55	Man B	Get on with it.
05:55	Man A	Yes Herr General. *<unreadable>* two, one, fire. *<comment: whirring noise like machine operating>* done, Herr General. Very big flash *<unreadable>*. *<pause>* Roof in cavern *<collapsed?>* *<unreadable>* *<name ... ?>* burned on face, hair scorched off, blood from nose and mouth. Four scientists here vomiting. *<All Jews?>* in cavern dead, all significant blistering on exposed *<skin?>*. I can see cavern wall tiles glowing green, General

		Kammler. *<pause>* Another scientist has just died.
05:59	Man B	Are you hurt, Manteufle?
06:00	Man A	I was behind the *<chassis?>* when flash *<unreadable>* *<pause>*. Four of our scientists are dead. Protective clothing did not *<operate as planned?>*. *<unreadable>* get more Jews to collect the bodies from the cavern and *<to>* take readings.
06:03	Man B	*<comment: after a pause>* What were the power readings?
06:05	Man A	*<comment: voice trembling as if anxious>* 2500 volts shock, 150 kilowatts. Gravity meter 0.73 I repeat 0.73. Congratulations Herr General. Do you have *<any instructions?>*
06:06	Man B	Get those corpses out and bagged. *<name?>* will want to *<forensic?>* *<unreadable>* *<comment: unknown technical terms>*. Check radiation level and report. Prepare another cavern. Block the tunnel to the test cavern, build door to*<contain?* or p*rotect?>* evidence. I will send *<name>* Ninestein to inspect. He will leave Görlitz within the hour.
06:10	Man A	*<comment: voice anxious/stressed more than before>* My right hand has blistered like a burn, General. My throat is dry. I feel *<sound of vomit>* *<silence>*.
06:12	Man B	Manteufle! Are you there? Manteufle? Shit! *<change to radio background noise suggests link closed>*
06:13	Woman A	I'm sorry General. The link with Ludwigsdorf has been interrupted. Shall I try to re-establish it for you?
06:13	Man B	Yes. Do that. Call me immediately you make contact. And make haste about it.
06:13	Woman A	I shall do my best for the general and the Fatherland.
06:15		*<comment: intercept ceased at this point>*

Makepiece returned the transcript sheaf to the intelligence office. He noticed the absence of wedding jewellery on her left hand. Had he taken to looking at female left hands for wedding bands?

"Thank you, Sarah." After a pause, Makepiece said, "Find out what you can about this General Kammler. Go through Dawes Hill, personal to Colonel Knapp from me. Make it 'Exclusive' handling caveat. Knapp will protect our source. That must have been one hell of a bang to wipe out the Kraut scientists. They'll take better precautions next time! Check the preamble, see if you can get more names or place references. I think we'll be taking another look at friend Krammler."

"Kammler, Colonel. It's Kammler." Her colonel nodded at the correction.

"And Sarah, check the film to see if they are taking exceptional security measures. Codenames, extra guards, that sort of thing. It will help confirm that they are 'upping the anti', treating this project as something special."

"Will do, Colonel."

As the intelligence WAAC officer turned to leave, Makepiece said to her, "Ask Julia to get hold of Colonel Chmielewski, please Sarah. I would like to discuss the results of our maximum effort. Oh, by the way. Thank you for showing me that text. Keep up the good work."

"We'll do our best, Colonel."

"I never doubted it. Did you do the transcription?"

"Yes, sir. I am sorry there are so many gaps. We will get the transcript better before we issue a report. We'll take a best guess that the ship was at Freyberg for starters."

"Watch for the ABLATIVE level 3 rules, Sarah. We cannot afford to blow our source yet. And remember, Captain Bates was the pilot!"

"That's OK, Colonel. I'll have Colonel Chmielewski check the text before it leaves the 1574th."

"Well done, Sarah. Now, I'd like to speak with Rod Chmielewski myself. Time for a good intel officer to bug out."

"Good evening, Colonel. And would the Colonel object if I was to advise a good night shut-eye…"

"Bug out, Sarah. And thanks for the advice…"

She left Makepiece Ploughman, at his office desk, reflecting on a successful mission. How many other P-38s had brought in some cream? Rod Chmielewski was in for a grilling.

*   *   *

"I'm pleased to see you back in one piece, Colonel. The place seemed mighty lonesome without you."

"Bull!" responded Makepiece who was pacing his office beyond the desk from the seated Rod. "Have you seen Sarah Johansson's transcript? There are too many gaps to let it go yet, especially in absence of decent photographs."

"This Görlitz place, it could be a headquarters or research group. I'd like to know more." Rod Chmielewski was looking satisfied with the two days work. "It's tucked right up against the former Polish border, say 50 miles east of Dresden. That's got to be a contender for where this General Kammler parks his Mercedes. His is not a branding that I recognise. Interesting remark about a gravity meter in that transcript. Does it ring any bells with you, Makepiece?"

"Einstein, Rod, Einstein. He did two things in my copy of the almanac: he said there would be an atomic bomb when we split the atom; I'm not so sure about that. The other thing he said was that there was a null point where gravity as a form of energy cancels out time and space. He did some clever sums to prove it. Ever since, the bright boys have been putting the long money on someone pulling it off. The prediction says the universe is full of this gravity energy in infinite quantity: tap that source and the universe is yours, stars and all."

Rod thought for less than a second, then, "I'll have a word with Allison to put some in your supercharger next time you fly a P-38. It would do wonders for your endurance record! I'll meet you on the Moon!"

"Ok, wise guy," came back Makepiece with a smile. He had ceased his pacing — as though he was more relaxed than hitherto. "This could be it, Hitler's ultimate weapon and the true war winner. Directly that report hits DC the fan will be distributing the excreta on a liberal scale. This is one angle we keep out of the Sprite's way. FDR can trade widely with this hot poop! But he will want to know it's kosher."

"I get the picture, Colonel. It's a pity that a rookie pilot called Bates will get the credit."

"That's just what I want you to get, Rod. I think this intercept calls for more. For the next mission, let's have one of the pilots concentrate on the extended line between Dresden and Görlitz, both east and west. My guess is we're gonna find something in the mountains on the Polish/Czech border, maybe out as far as Katowice and as far from Allied eyes as it's sensible to be. My chart does not show any Ludwigsdorf. Perhaps Sarah Johannson has the spelling adrift. You check it for me Rod and see if you can find it in a gazetter. We don't even know which country to look in: Germany, Poland or even Czechoslovakia?"

"You're the boss."

"Factually correct, Colonel Chmielewski. I want you to get me more facts so we can all sleep better at night."

"Talking of which, sleep that is, I know one colonel who needs sleep now. If you don't want a mutiny on your hands, you had better get your cotton pickin' head on a pillow. No-one will be sending out any reports about gravity energy until you have second sighted it. Now sweet dreams, Colonel, sir. That's not a subject for further discussion."

Makepiece had remained standing and was about to move around his desk, "One final question, my last tonight I promise."

"Yeah, yeah! I heard that before! OK, Colonel, one question, then shut eye!"

"Did they all come back?"

"You all came back, including a new boy on the block called Bates. We're doing the first level processing of the take right now. Maximum effort! There'll be something for the Colonel to see in the morning. Now…"

"Night, Rod." He would sleep easy tonight.

"Night, Makepiece."

*   *   *

Colonel Ploughman was approaching his office in the administrative area of the camp. Already seated at her desk was his aide Sergeant Julia Greenburg WAAC. Standing waiting for his arrival was the group's adjutant, Major Clarke McKing and Captain Jodell Lee Grant in charge of the US Army Field Security Group for the protection of No 1574 SPSG. The aide rose as he entered the outer office to his own.

Without pausing, Makepiece entered his office, knowing not to close the door since Julia would be bringing in a coffee.

"Major McKing and Captain Grant wish to speak with the Colonel," she said.

"Bit early for a mutiny, Julia. What's up?"

"I don't think the Colonel will be offering doughnuts this morning. Should I show the officers in?"

"Let's get on with it. Hold my calls unless it's FDR or Hitler giving up. Right, ask the gentlemen to come in."

Makepiece acknowledged the salutes and waited until Grant had closed the office door with uncustomary gentleness. The young officers looked anxious. Even so, the colonel did not invite them to sit.

"Bit early for a mutiny, gentlemen. Oh, I already said that! What's up?" Original thought was not Makepiece's strong point at this hour of the morning.

The Adjutant spoke, "There has been an incident in the town, Rochester, Colonel, and we think you need to know before there's trouble at the gate."

Makepiece responded, "Well, let's have it."

The Adjutant nodded at Captain Grant. He was reluctant to start.

Makepiece was beginning to lose his patience. "Well, Grant? What kind of trouble?"

"Girl trouble, Colonel. One of my grunts got caught by a 14 year old hooker in downtown Rochester. Underage hereabouts! Her father was non-too-pleased with Private McMahon and chased him out of the house with a poker. That's a rod of tyre iron they use for stirring the coals in the fire."

"Yes, yes." He sucked in air as his grimace emphasised the need to get on with the bad news.

"Was McMahon aware he was doing wrong, I mean, was there any doubt about the tender years of this young lady?"

"Who can tell in the blackout, Colonel? McMahon told the duty officer when he got back to camp and I immediately put him behind bars for his own protection. Anyway, he heralds from blue grass country where anything is legal, even home grown hooch…"

Major McKing intervened, "May I suggest to the Colonel that we get McMahon outta here pretty damn quick. We don't want trouble at the gate with the New Year coming. I could have the man in Scotland within

8 hours or stateside in two days. That'll give time for the storm to blow over."

"Was any money being offered or taken?"

Grant replied, "McMahon says he offered the girl two pounds which she accepted. I think her Pa wanted a slice of the takings. I think she knew what she was doing, Colonel. There's plenty of limey soldiers and sailors about; a Yank would be easy picking."

"Major McKing. Get this idiot off my patch quickly. Get a report into COSSAC to keep the administrators in line. That'll leave us with a hole in our defence lines so get a replacement with all haste. I don't want to hear any more about this."

"Yes, Colonel." The Adjutant was grateful that Ploughman had taken the matter so calmly.

"As for your privates, Captain Grant. You'd better get a grip on your troops before there's another War of Independence between the Brits and the Yanks. And Major McKing, give my compliments to Squadron Leader Wilburne — the Station Commander — and give him the outline in case the Mayor of Rochester or the Bishop decides to visit."

The junior officers saluted, Makepiece responded from the seated position. He was pleased to see them go. He had other matters to prepare for his own New Year celebration.

Chapter 24
1943 ~ Wartime Desire

Makepiece had driven to Aynette's cottage, having previously arranged that he might spend two nights at Cleeve Lyon. Aynette was waiting for him as his tyres crunched to a halt. She did not leave the entrance porch as he climbed out of his vehicle, slammed the door and moved towards her. His towering frame enveloped the beautiful woman he had come to be with.

"I've given myself a 48 hour furlough over the New Year. I'd like to spend it with you, Aynette. My number two is a capable officer and would not recall me unless Hitler himself was parachuting into West Malling."

"Makepiece, my lover, I would be pleased to have you stay here." She emphasised her welcome by pressing herself against Makepiece's still uniformed bulk.

"Tomorrow, we can walk about the park if you would like some fresh air from those noisy aeroplanes of yours. And you know how secluded it is, we would be very private here. Father was wounded in World War One; he lives in the big house, it's the former manor house, which is now used as billets for British Army officers of Maidstone garrison. Mother died in 1931. If we could disguise your uniform with one of David's coats then no-one would guess that a there was a 'Yankee in the Court of Queen Aynette' to paraphrase Mark Twain." Makepiece noticed the reference to Aynette's dead husband and chose not to remark on it.

"Have you been reading American literature, mistress?" He was attempting to unbutton his topcoat while Aynette maintained her proximity.

"Why no, kind sir." Aynette double blinked her eyelids. "But I have seen the Bing Crosby movie. I like that — 'mistress'. Do you think it suits me? Will you be my gallant knight in shining amour?"

"My thoughts about you, mistress, are neither gallant nor pure." He drew Aynette closer. "Now, lift those delicious lips to me. I have a need to kiss them before my chain mail rusts over."

"Ohh!"

Further conversation was impossible from that moment on.

*　　　*　　　*

Aynette's preparations for Christmas and the New Year's Eve in Cleeve Lyon Cottage had been as traditional as wartime rationing would allow. A decorated Christmas fir tree stood in a corner, a dozen cards stood on various shelves, a couple of hanging streamers made of paper were pinned to the wall. There was some holly strewn along the tops of picture frames. A sprig of mistletoe dangled above the entrance door. Makepiece had brought in some treasure only available on American bases, or through the black market. In addition he had persuaded his catering staff to prepare a lunch box for him to carry off-base on his furlough; the cookhouse had done him proud with a hamper to rival any that pre-war Kensington might have prepared.

The couple spent much of the afternoon pouring over the copies of Grandmother Susannah's volume. Some of the copying was rather faint and needed to be rewritten with care. But they made good progress and were able to reconstruct 11 generations in England and America onto one family tree. They had broken their studies for a meal, but both had had quite enough old writing by the mid evening. The two sat together on a fireside couch, touching each other tenderly until, quite naturally, Aynette lifted her legs onto the couch and relaxed against Makepiece's body. The couple just sat, watching the log fire. There seemed no need to speak. The radio was making pleasant music somewhere in the cottage.

With about an hour of the old year remaining, Makepiece was still sitting on the long couch in front of the log fire with Aynette lying on her side with her head resting on his lap. Their faces were towards the fire. Makepiece was upright with his back firmly against the cushion. Aynette had positioned her back along the cushion, her legs bent so that the soles of her stockinged feet were against the back cushion.

The couple were comfortable and warm and, for the time being, at peace.

"Makepiece?" Aynette broke the silence.

"Yes, Aynette."

"Do you have a wish for the New Year? I don't mind if you tell me. They say it brings bad luck if you tell about your wish, but that is nonsense, isn't it? And anyway, I can keep any secret that my gallant knight shares with me."

"If I tell you mine, will you me tell yours?" Makepiece was teasing. Neither felt the need to engage eye contact. Their physical contact was sufficient for the time being.

"I promise," she replied.

"I wish this war will be over soon. I want to get home to my Rosetta's Rocks, to be with my family, and to enjoy all the pleasures of sailing on the bay — the Chesapeake — once more. I've seen too many men and women being hurt or killed and I want to be at peace. In a manner of speaking, peace is my profession. I don't want to go to war, but I recognise that someone has got to stop it. At the moment it's my turn. But Maryland is waiting. You have seen from Grandmother Susannah's Heritage Volume just how dear the family is to us Ploughmans. Rosetta's Rocks and the Homestead is where I shall find peace."

"Ooh!" There was a hint of dismay in her voice.

"You asked me, and I've told you, Aynette." Makepiece's left hand reached around her head to touch Aynette's cheek. "You know that we can only be friends, very close friends, temporary wartime lovers. One day we must go our separate ways, just two more victims of war."

"Am I a wartime fling to you?" Her eyes searched his. He noticed Aynette's were showing the first signs of tears which she tried to blink away.

Makepiece thought about how best to frame his reply. "You opened your love to me in the moonlight, upstairs in this cottage. We were two lonely people seeking respite from this angry world. You have always known about Marybeth and our four children, stateside. I cannot forget the 20 years she has stood by me, in hard times and the good. Marybeth might understand our friendship, here in distant England in these circumstances. She might even forgive me. I don't want to hurt her or the family."

Makepiece's index finger was gently caressing Aynette's cheek which remained dry.

"But I don't want to hurt you either so I have always been honest with you. You are a delicious dream and when I wake up you will be gone. Your memory will be with me for the rest of my life, but I can't take you with the other half of my life."

"Ooh!" Aynette's head moved slightly on his lap but she did not move away. Deep within, she already knew the essence of what he had said. She accepted the transience of the situation. This man she courted was almost old enough to be her father; no long term relationship was possible. He was honest when he spoke of his love for his wife at home. Without David, she needed the arms and protection of a man until the right one came along. She would not go headlong into marriage with a fighting man again. Next time she would choose carefully. Time was on her side. She felt herself to be a very lucky woman to have this wonderful man sharing her life, however temporarily it might be.

"Are you alright about what I have said?" Makepiece's left hand remained close at her cheek, his right had settled flat on her stomach.

Aynette breathed deeply and there was a suggestion of a sigh as she replied. "My gallant knight, I need you to defend me against the rigours of the world." She could feel the warmth of his palm on her midriff. "I need you to teach me how to be strong so that, when it is time for you to leave, I can accept the parting with sweet sorrow." Her head pressed down on his legs as if it was a substitute for a comforting touch on the arm. "I know I can't compete with your Marybeth. Neither do I want to. We do not know if we are going to be alive tomorrow, we have to live life for today. Tomorrow must look after itself."

Aynette turned her head so that she was looking straight up to Makepiece's face glowing in the firelight. When her head was settled, she manoeuvred her body so that her back lay flat to her hips along the seat of the couch. Her legs remained so that her stockinged feet were still against the back cushion. The movement had lifted the hem of her dress to her knees. She let her head become heavy on his legs as if prompting a reply. His right hand settled stationary on her flat stomach.

She waited. She longed for his hand to move. She could feel its warmth through the dress material. She longed for its caress, but the hand did not move. The heat of its palm, with the gentlest of pressure was calming while she waited for his reaction to what she had said. Was there a suggestion of movement in his fingers? She knew she must be patient. Her body wanted this man. Did he feel the same about her?

He knew exactly where his right hand lay with its warmth reflected off her clothed body. He knew his left hand was waiting to stroke her hair, to lift her face to his, to enable the kiss which must lead to embrace, to satisfaction of his desire, to temporary escape from the madness which surrounded his daily life. He could feel the hand of her free left arm entwined about his right leg, touching the skin above his ankle sock, holding it firm as though it had a mind to run away. He did not move other than to let his hand on her stomach rest more heavily.

He said, "You made me a promise, my mistress. What is your wish?" He pursed his lips in feigned impatience for her answer. "Madam, your knight at the Court of Queen Aynette awaits disclosure of your wish."

"Well…"

"Just a moment," commanded Makepiece, with a chuckle. "If this is a long wish then I have a request."

"Go on."

"It's the hairclip. Aynette, I love your hair just as I love every other part of you. But right now that is difficult. Your clip is pressing into my thigh muscle and it's putting my leg to sleep. It's got to go."

Aynette laughed. He felt her stomach muscles tightened as she lifted her head off his lap and for two minutes there was fiddling at the back of her head as she allowed the clip to be freed and removed. By allowing Makepiece to help to do the task, he was touching her hair, caressing her head, and she enjoyed it.

"There." Makepiece held the ornamental piece with its RAF wings motif.

"A present from David," volunteered Aynette without being asked. "He was a fighter pilot, you know." Her head had settled back on Makepiece's lap with her dark hair, its touch of auburn emphasised in the firelight, spilling across the cushion of his thighs.

Makepiece placed the hairclip on the arm of the couch and he smiled at the eyes looking deeply into his. He did not want to move; indeed the only part of him that could move was his head, but their eye-contact took priority. His peripheral vision took due note of those legs, the very same legs that had caught his attention in Maidstone 8 weeks ago.

'Strange,' he thought, 'I've the best looking girl in the county on my lap and I am fighting her off. How can her grip on my ankle be sexy? What is this pleasure I get from the curves on this woman? There is no way of getting inside this dress from the front; it must button up at the back. She's lying on the buttons!'

Aynette was speaking, "As I was saying … I have a wish. I am a 25 years old woman who knows little or nothing about being a woman. My marriage lasted 6 hours. We didn't even make it to the honeymoon hotel.

My knowledge of men is what I call 'bicycle shed experience', all about Oxford, where student urgency did not give a girl a chance. Our moonlight encounter together was fantastic, but over too quickly to be other than a dream such as we spoke about earlier. I want to understand being a woman, with woman's needs, in this world of men. I need a tutor, a man with experience who will have me for what I am and will one day give me freedom to move to select my mate. I am not asking for a baby; there is time for that later, and not during this war anyway. Makepiece, I want you to be my master and tutor and my knight. I want to share you, without commitment, until we know that I have mastered what there is to learn."

Makepiece was not at all sure what to say. Whereas he was expecting sex to be a part of the New Year's night, the context in which it was put here was a revelation to him. He had hardly any experience of a direct approach by women, and those that had thrust their wares towards him were usually the hangers-on that attach themselves to military bases. He had firmly resisted any such temptation. This time he wanted this woman, this warm flesh and blood who sent his blood coursing round his veins, whose eyes held his in word-free communication, whose body he urgently needed to fondle.

His thoughts were interrupted as the air raid siren sounded in the distance. It was 15 minutes before midnight.

"We can ignore that," said Aynette. "The *Luftwaffe* hasn't got this address. I'll tune the wireless in a minute, to catch Big Ben's chimes for 12 o'clock. Then we'll know it's official." Her ear was nudging his groin from his lap. "What do you think of my wish?"

Makepiece sat in silence, watching the flickering in the fire. Aynette's body moved under his grip. He leaned forward to kiss her mouth but contact was not made until she lifted her head off his lap. The discomfort of the position for both stopped the pleasure before it had begun.

There was a crump of an explosion outside.

"They missed! I told you they did not know we live here," she said. Makepiece smiled. He hoped that West Malling had not been hit. One of the group was taking off at 03:15 this morning. The duty officer knew how to contact him in an emergency.

The all clear siren sounded.

Aynette rolled away from the couch and moved to the radio. She tuned to the BBC Home Service. She moved a draught screen behind the couch, between the door and the couch where they had been sitting, away from the fire.

"Why don't you take your shoes off and enjoy the carpet and the fire warmth?" Aynette was moving towards the door. "I'll go and get some more logs for the fire. Pour us some drinks, Makepiece, please. I'll have a small sherry, help yourself."

She was gone from the room before he could reply.

Makepiece went to the fireplace to rebuild the fire. There were plenty of logs in the basket, so why did she need to get more? He went to the sideboard and poured two drinks. The radio commentator was getting excited about the approaching chimes. Makepiece returned to the couch, now cosier with the draught protection in place. He removed his tie and eased off his shoes.

'I haven't given Aynette a reply to her wish,' he thought.

Chapter 25
1944 ~ Cottage Comfort for the New Year

In Cleeve Lyon Cottage, the wireless was sounding Big Ben's chimes beginning as the room's ceiling light was switched off. Makepiece could sense that Aynette was back in the room. He heard a door close. There was a suggestion of rosemary scent in the air. Aynette appeared.

She stood between Makepiece and the fire. She was wearing a satin dressing gown. Her hair was tidily brushed, her face without makeup. She had no shoes, but her stockings showed over her feet and up into the privacy of her gown. She hesitated, standing quite still for 15 seconds, then her hands moved to her waist and slipped the belt so that the gown parted. She was naked beneath the gown except for her stockings reaching to her upper thighs. Aynette shrugged off the gown and let it fall to the floor. She kicked it clear of any possible spark which might be thrown by the logs on the fire. She raised her arms as a beckoning to the amazed Makepiece.

Makepiece stood. The radio began to relay a Scottish Hogmanay programme.

He said, "Do you mind if I turn that off. Better, let me find the American Services Broadcasting in Europe programme. They usually put out quieter music at this hour although I suppose tonight is special."

While Makepiece was attending to the radio, Aynette moved to the couch, collecting the drinks on the way. She placed the drinks on the floor and kneeled on the couch. The warmth of the fire helped avoid anxious shivering. Makepiece returned and approached the kneeling Aynette. He leant forward to kiss her and was greeted with her arms stretched up around his neck, pulling him forward and nearly off balance.

"Let's get those clothes off you. I want to feel your skin against mine." Aynette undressed Makepiece until he now was naked.

"Come kneel on the couch, in front of me. The queen is all yours. Be gentle with me, my knight. You need no protection for my month is right for your pleasure tonight." The radio had settled into a sequence of Glen Miller tunes.

The couple were kneeling 12 inches apart, their hands exploring each other bodies, giving and experiencing pleasure with each touch, each caress and each kiss. The stocking tops directed Makepiece's attention to the tuft of hair at her pubic mound. His palms caressed every curve, tenderly roving above all the wondrous parts to prepare her to receive the ultimate male accolade.

Makepiece was aware that the pressure within him was rising and he attempted to move the pace along with firmer caresses. He made as if to lift her. He realised that Aynette's arms were round his neck, that her mouth was seeking out his and there was a look of sheer delight on her face.

"No, no! Not yet!"

Makepiece was finding it difficult to relax. He did not want to burden his total weight on this frail woman beneath him. But there was no denying that she was encouraging him as his whole physique lay along hers, in total contact, from mouths to groins and down to most of their legs. With care he rolled her above him, care because the couch was less than 30 inches wide without the 4 inch thick back rest.

Within minutes, Aynette took the initiative with controlling movements until it was time for them to climax.

Makepiece withdrew, stood and collected the dressing gown. He put two more logs on the fire. Aynette had rolled so that her back was against the couch's upright cushion and Makepiece lay alongside, deliciously containing her, their chests, stomachs, groins and legs in intimate immovable contact. It was as though they were bound together in the gentlest of bonds, neither being able nor wishing to move for fear of denying pleasure to the other. Aynette had not found the opportunity, or desire, to remove — or have removed for her — her stockings. He placed his lower arm under her head as a cushion.

The radio was playing Frank Sinatra singing,

'Fly me to the Moon; let me play among the stars ...'

Makepiece manoeuvred the dressing gown over their glowing bodies and they went together into dreamless sleep.

*   *   *

It was Aynette who woke first. She thought the mantle clock indicated something near three o'clock, but the room lighting was too dim to be sure. The log fire was in its final throws, its duty done. The wireless was still playing; it must have been the GMT pips that woke her.

'I can't move. I don't want to move.' Aynette was reflecting on her changed situation. 'This gorgeous hunk of manhood has shown me how to be woman. I don't want this moment to end. There he is, pressed against me, his eyes closed; he's at rest, momentarily at peace. I did that for him. I gave him a moment away from war, from danger, from responsibility. For an hour he was mine and only mine. He was totally absorbed in me, my mind and my body — as I was in his. We have made physical love in a sense and perhaps without the emotional baggage. But I could love this man if I allowed myself, if he was free. He isn't. He has given me the gift of understanding my body and I shall always be grateful to this man.'

Makepiece did not stir. Their noses were so close that she could feel his breath. Her head, cushioned on his arm could not be moved without waking the man. Her breasts were crushed against his hairy chest.

'I'll try to synchronise my diaphragm to his breathing.' Aynette found that task impossible. 'His maleness is asleep against me. I'm glad he liked my legs. I could move this right leg to caress his thigh. There, he has not stirred. I don't mind losing the dressing gown; the man radiates enough warmth for both us. I always thought this couch was uncomfortable; it's amazing how this man makes me change my mind. His back is so close to the edge, how can he comfortable? I am the meat in the sandwich, between the cushion and my man, just like the proper way but now on our sides. He is controlling freedom except for this hand and this leg and I love him for it. Just a little further up his thigh with this leg. My skin above the stocking top is touching his hip.'

Makepiece's eyes opened. It took a moment to realise that Aynette's eyes were watching his at very close range. Her eyes told him she was smiling. He could only see her eyes looking deep into his.

"You are looking into my eyes."

"It's what eyes are for."

Her hand was doing marvellous things. Her head moved a fraction on his arm and brought their lips into a warm, tender, sweet kiss of surface contact which of itself demanded nothing but which forecast delight to come. Her warm breath demanded they kiss. Her hand was becoming more insistent. The wonderful leg was caressing his, inviting his attention at its top; its foot was hooked behind his buttock and between his legs. He could not roll way even if there was spare width on the couch. She had him engaged to her purpose, deliciously wanting.

Her response was to search his eyes more deeply, to allow their noses to brush before taking another, more searching kiss.

Makepiece thought he would explode. There was no controlling the next ten seconds. Masculine sexual energy burst forth. The air was drawn out of his body in a shuddering cry seated deep inside his being.

Aynette was carried over the edge also. Her man's sudden sexual release developed her own peak. She wanted to scream, to laugh, to cry, to let go every emotion she had ever known. Instead she started to laugh. She laughed at her reaction to her man and at her reaction to the reflex reaction of her body. She laughed at the general pleasure she felt and at the pleasure she could see deep in her man's eyes. She laughed because she could not kiss. She laughed because Makepiece was laughing too.

Aynette lifted her right leg away from Makepiece to give him more room on the narrow couch. For a moment Makepiece forgot his back was unsupported. As he rolled away from Aynette, he fell off the couch. He fell on the floor in a flurry of arms and legs. Aynette could not help but laugh some more which helped Makepiece recover his composure before rising to his knees in order to kiss his woman properly.

"Oh, Makepiece," she blubbed. "I've laughed so much that it hurts."

Makepiece wrapped Aynette in her dressing gown. He picked her up under her legs and shoulders, still naked himself, and began to move towards the staircase and bedroom.

"Are you going to say something?"

"Switch off the light, Makepiece. And carry me over to the fireplace first so that we can put up the fireguard. Then take me to the bed where we may sleep the true sleep of lovers. And when we wake, I will be your Scheherazade and tell you stories of old Kent and older England"

The radio announced a time check of half past three in the morning. The next piece of music was Benny Goodman and vibraphonist Lionel Hampton playing '*Moonglow*'.

*   *   *

It was twenty minutes past three in the afternoon. The sky was just dimming when the phone rang. The manual telephone exchange was ringing Aynette's bell in a way that could not be ignored.

"Cleeve Lyon Cottage," answered Aynette.

An American voice said, "Howdy, Ma'am. Happy New Year to you and yours. You happen to know the whereabouts of a certain Colonel Ploughman? It is mighty important that I have a word in his shell-like, if you'll excuse the expression, Ma'am."

The exchange was crisp and to the point. The knight in shining armour was being recalled to his castle.

"How soon do you want me in?" asked Makepiece.

Whatever the answer was, Makepiece was already stripping off David's dressing gown and looking for his uniform.

"Do we have ten minutes? Once round the orchard and then off you go to your war?"

At that very moment Makepiece was stark naked. He grabbed hold of Aynette's gown and within seconds she was naked too.

Aynette was delivered of her request, at least to the fulfilment of her knight, if rather too quickly for her. "Whow! You could have given your queen a moment's notice. That was reminiscent of the Oxford bike sheds, but none the less welcome for it. I suppose there isn't any more?"

"Shame on you, Madam. You've had your ration today. I don't know if I'll be able to walk after what you've done to my body." Makepiece was now reaching for his uniform. This time he would not be distracted, even by the still naked Aynette.

"It is something important. I don't know when I'll be able to see you again, but I promise I won't stay away any longer than is necessary. I will call you at home, during the evening, when I can get away for the next lesson. You get three gold stars so far."

"You weren't counting, sir knight. I made it four before being saddled on the chair."

"Oh, alright, your majesty. I'll make it 4 gold stars and a meritorious conduct medal. But that's my final offer!"

"You must come again, dear knight, my lover. Keep yourself safe for me. Farewell." Aynette gave and received a full kiss on her mouth and then her colonel was gone into the gathering Kentish mist.

As Aynette secured the door, she leant against the wall. 'O what a gorgeous man. I don't want to share him, but I have to. Marybeth, I wonder if you know how lucky you are...'

Chapter 26
1944 ~ One of Our Balloons is Missing

"I can't just walk into the village and buy them. I'd be too embarrassed?"

"Come on Jenny Plowman. You can do it. All you have to say is 'two packets please' and it's all over." Janice was nagging.

"If it's so easy," shrugged Jenny, "then why don't you do it?"

"Because I'm Catholic, that's why. I ain't allowed to touch them."

"But you've been talking about hanging them out to dry if I buy them?"

"Jenny, if they're yours then they ain't mine, so it don't count."

"Oh." Jenny could not think immediately of a put down to that logic so she tried a new tack: "We'll ask Corporal. She don't look like a virgin to me."

"What does a virgin look like then?" queried Janice.

"I don't know, but... err... not like her. Go on, Miss Knowall; you go along and ask the corporal or the whole deal is off!" Jenny looked determined.

Jenny was about to say something about seeing a virgin whenever she looked in a mirror, but already Janice Lockyer was making for the distant end of the WAAF accommodation hut where Corporal Linda Bates sat on her bed reading.

"Corporal," opened Janice, "as tradeswomen, we're all balloon operators or combined operator/drivers, aren't we?"

"For someone who's shared this hut for two months, I'd say that is a correct assumption."

"If we're all the same, then is it OK for someone to be nominated to go to the village to purchase essential supplies? Something the Air Force don't give us?"

"That something isn't small, and comes individually wrapped, and you get it from behind the counter at a chemist?"

"I guess," replied Janice. Jenny was keenly interested in what was to happen next. Sound travelled well inside a nissen hut. "You see, Corporal, Jenny — that's Jenny Plowman — and me was wondering if we needed such a commodity from the chemist then perhaps you, with your experience like, would get them."

"You talking about johnnies, Janice Lockyer? You are a mite embarrassed about going into a chemist and asking for men's appliances? We'll I never. You'll be telling me you haven't used one yet. You've never done it?"

"I haven't. Neither's Jenny. And I don't reckon the other girls on our team have, neither. Except Crotchet that is, and I am not so sure about her, neither. She's all talk and no action. So we're asking you if you'll do it. We'll help out in the field, where it's dark and private, but I just could not put a packet, worse two packets, in my pocket. You do understand, Corporal, it would be a sin."

*   *   *

Two nights later, the last day of the 1943, in a field midway between RAF Snodland and the American gate on to RAF West Malling airfield, a detachment of B Flight No 978 Balloon Squadron stood collected to watch the off-going shift depart on their way by bicycle back to camp for the New Year's party. The detachment comprised two trailer mounted balloon winches, one ten ton lorry with eight full high pressure bottles of hydrogen gas and four gerry-cans of fuel, a second lorry with a deflated balloon on its open flatbed, a wooden shelter and a group of one Corporal WAAF with five airwomen. They had travelled with the replacement balloon. A 4 feet square tent contained a chemical toilet. Each woman wore a greatcoat, gloves and boots. Ahead of them was a long, dark, cold night. Each woman carried a torch and had an emergency torch in her greatcoat pocket.

The only concession to being in an open field was the entrance gate, an area around the hut and toilet and the lorry parking area each of which had been laid with perforated steel plate to lessen the risk of boot or tyre sinking into mud. The chill had not fallen to ground frost level.

The Corporal was outlining the task for the night. "It's now 21:00 hours. We've got to launch the new balloon and get it to 6000 feet soon. The one that's up there is leaking like a sieve and we've got to retire it. So action one is to get it down to 500 feet, lay out the new one, fill it and get it up. It's not too windy so it won't take us long. Crotchet, you're driving the winches tonight. When we've done then we can see what we can do with the thingees?"

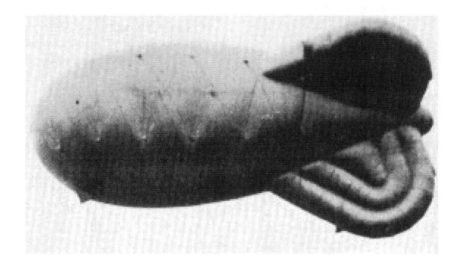

A British 65 foot tethered barrage

An option to suspend lengths of steel rope, some with attached explosive devices, was available. The attachment points are visible on the balloon's envelope. Their purpose was to provide additional snags, to the guying ropes, to aircraft attempting to underfly the balloon.

"What's thingees, Corporal?" whimpered Crotchet.

"We'll find out in due time. And just so as you know, the ATS girls up on the hill are game. The Air Traffic will give us a bell if the air raid alarm goes, but I reckon we can hear the siren from here. They say they have no planned RAF or USAAC movements tonight — at least not before midnight. They say that their intel says the Germans are quiet so we should have it all our own way."

In 55 minutes, making no concessions to New Year's Eve, the practised team had their new 65 foot long balloon, inflated with 19000 cubic feet of hydrogen, high in the sky and the defective envelope tethered at 500 feet. It had been hard work manoeuvring the cumbersome gas filled envelopes into their correct positions to be tied to the prepositioned tethering blocks. The girls' heavy overcoats, vital protection for nights in the open, made the work seem harder. One of their normal crew was off work, in sick quarters, with a suspected stretched stomach muscle from the last shift's duties so they were working one woman light. Now, however, it was done.

"Right, girls," said Corporal Bates, "before we put the kettle on, we had better check out the thingees." She reached into her coat pocket and withdrew six individually wrapped, American issue, Trojan™ condoms.

"Crikey!" swore one of the girls. "Where did you get those?" Linda Bates ignored the question coming back with her own.

"Not very big, are they?" whimpered a voice in the darkness.

"So you know what these are? I wonder how. Been flirting with Yank soldiers, eh? All virgins? Bah!" Linda was taking control before any squeamish airwoman fainted when the seals on the packets were broken.

The corporal surveyed her command, comprising four young women, none over twenty-one, individually lacking physical strength yet when combined as a team, fully capable of doing the job at had. She instructed, "Alice and Janice, you go and test these johnnies with water to see they don't leak. Fill them up to full stretch so we have some idea what we have to play with. Then fill them with hydrogen — not too full, mind — we don't want them blowing up when we launch them. They'll get bigger with the excitement when they rise to their job." Her joke fell on deaf, or rather inexperienced, ears. "And Jenny, you assemble that washing line with passion killers ready for hooking onto the wheezing bag over there." Her thumb was gesturing at the porous balloon, looking deflated and sad, hanging a few hundred feet above their heads. The gentle wind was making the stabilising guys and the fabric sing gently and discordantly in the night air.

The fourth girl, having asked what she was to do, was assigned to the task of replenishing the leaking balloon envelope.

"Crotchet," so called because she read music for the trumpet so badly, "you tie the thingees' ends off when they are filled and secure them in the latrine so they don't blow away. Come on, girl, now's not the time to be squeamish!"

By 23:30, Corporal was satisfied that the necessary arrangements and attachments had been made. The lower balloon was adequately replenished for the task at hand. Crotchet had winched it down for Jenny to attach her fixture and then had it returned to its tethered 2500 feet altitude; with its nose into wind it was oriented exactly pointed to the south east, its long side at right angles to the searchlight site on the opposite hill across the river. The ATS girls said they could shine up an aircraft at 20000 feet so 3½ miles to the WAAF's field would be no problem. The inflated Trojans had been tied into two pairs resembling the index and middle fingers of the human hand; the couplets had been secured to the ends of a thin bamboo cane. One condom had burst in inexpert hands; the sixth was slipped into the Corporal's pocket under the reasoning that she never knew when she might need it. The site was tidy with no uncoiled cables strewn to cause a trip in the dark. The upper balloon was correctly tethered, a silent invisible sentinel in the near cloudless sky. Beneath it, about 3500 feet below, the modified envelope floated motionless. Corporal Bates looked at her luminous watch and pronounced it was time for tea.

At 23:45 the air raid alarm in the village sounded, and within minutes a field telephone rang when air traffic repeated what the WAAFs already knew. It was too late to stop it now.

"Check your tin hats," ordered the corporal. "This is not the time to worry about your hairdos."

*   *   *

At 1500 metres altitude, Luftwaffe Hauptman Erik Strachen was aware that he was approaching the outer edge of the balloon barrage protecting London. He was confident that the enemy night fighters would not find him on this dark night. Up here, this close to the Medway line, RAF fighters would leave him to their ack-ack. He glanced at his cockpit clock which displayed 23:50. It was nearly one o'clock back in the homeland, already into 1944 over there. He would rather be in the arms of a French mademoiselle than up here on New Year's night.

Without warning a searchlight beam hit him. His reflexes suggested the aircraft juddered with an impact, but of course it did not. The cockpit was brighter than daylight. His immediate reaction was to throw the Heinkel into a violent avoiding turn and dive, but the beam stayed with him. Within a few moments British anti-aircraft fire was exploding outside his aircraft, much too close for comfort. He pushed his aircraft nose down and dived for the ground. He knew his safe altitude was 250 metres. British heavy anti-aircraft would not reach that low.

In front of him a second searchlight beam appeared. This was not seeking his Heinkel. It was pointing the same way that he was flying until it illuminated a barrage balloon at his altitude, almost in his path. He was flying straight at a British balloon.

Strachen was well below the ack-ack and now the searchlight on his aircraft began to wander. He guessed its radar had lost him at his low altitude. It was too good an opportunity to miss, a British balloon in his sights with plenty of airspace above to recover his original track. The British searchlight continued to illuminate the balloon. Was it his imagination or was the searchlight actually beaming below the horizontal?

'They must be mad,' he thought. "What is that painting on the side, on the balloon, in the spotlight?'

On the side of the balloon was cast a shadow. Strachen could clearly make out two 'V for Victory' shadows and between them, surely, that is a pair of ladies underwear. Just hanging there. The flying gap was closing at 300 km per hour. His attention was absorbed for the critical final two seconds of his approach. The shadow of his Heinkel filled the upper half of the balloon.

"Shoot it down, Hans!" Strachen commanded the bombardier in the aircraft nose. "Shoot!"

The Heinkel was 200 yards away from the balloon when it burst into flames. A bright reddish yellow fireball erupted out of the top of the envelope and it began to fall to the ground. Strachen pulled his control column into his stomach to climb clear of the flame. His port wing hit the tethering cable of the upper balloon, setting off two incendiary devices which separated the cable from both the ground and the balloon simultaneously deploying two parachutes. The port wing was wrenched off and the Heinkel crashed vertically in flames within 15 seconds.

The hilltop ATS troop, satisfied with their night's work having watched the whole episode through binoculars, had switched off their light. On the ground the WAAFs began to scatter from the descending mass of incandescent gas and burning fabric. They had temporarily lost their night vision. Suddenly, it was quiet except for the distant crackling of flames from the crash and occasional pop-pop of its exploding ammunition. There was a pattering of ack-ack shrapnel hitting their vehicles and the winches. The girls scrambled to get under cover.

Then the shock of what had just happened hit them. Somewhere in the distance a church clock chimed 12 midnight for the New Year. To Jenny, elated with her searchlight show less than 5 minutes ago, the monotone of the clock bell sounded like a toll for the dead aircrew. The 19 years old began to cry.

A searchlight pierced the darkness above the girls' heads. Lit by the thrusting tight beam, a grey balloon with its tethers ruptured floated silently away on the wind. It seemed to slowly climb towards the heavens as though that was its rightful place. It floated in the searchlight's glare for 10 minutes then disappeared. The powerful radar laid searchlight went out. Total darkness returned.

*   *   *

Racing engines, low overhead, had brought out the celebrants from the village pub. Having ignored the air raid warning, what next? They saw the brightly lit balloon with its defiant shadows, searchlights sweeping the skies in the manner of 20th Century Fox™, and a *Luftwaffe* bomber bent on destruction. After the burst of gunfire they witnessed the apparent immolation of the Heinkel followed by the flash of its impact.

Reaction to the spectacle ranged from gasped silence, through awe, to some cheering. War was seldom this close. The chiming village clock soon reminded the villagers that their priorities lay nearer the bar. They hurried indoors for Big Ben's chimes on the BBC Home Service.

*   *   *

Corporal Linda Bates, Leading Aircraft Woman Plowman and four others were stood to attention in the office of their commanding officer, Squadron Leader Percy Davenport RAF, who was seated behind his cleared desk with his hat on. Behind him stood Flight Officer Bethany Taverner WAAF, the senior WAAF officer of No 978 Balloon Squadron. The ninth person in the room was the Sergeant WAAF Administration, responsible for WAAF discipline on the squadron. The tense atmosphere was that of a disciplinary hearing, but no charges had been laid and was the reason why the offenders were still wearing their headdresses.

"Misuse of RAF equipment is a court martial offence. You lot would be for the high jump if your officer had not spoken up for you. Right now some unfortunate Army ATS girls are getting dressed down for a silly prank. I have asked their commanding officer not to be too hard on them in view of the outcome."

The five airwomen were straining to contain their nerves; the corporal had to be brave whatever punishment might be handed down.

"You may think that flying two balloons from a small site is fun, it was downright dangerous and you could have been killed, or worse."

The squadron commander was trying his hardest to look stern and serious; the WAAF officer held eye contact with the sergeant ... she dare not engage with any of the girls standing rigidly to attention.

"The squadron counts itself lucky that it received only one complaint — from the primary school headmistress as it happens. An unsavoury display of adult accoutrements is unseemly and uncalled for in a well kept village. She was beside herself with anxiety about the reaction your stupidity would draw from young children out for the New Year's midnight with their parents. You five have to be made aware that display of unauthorised and irresponsible actions is something with which the Air Force will not put up." The squadron commander realised that his words had not come out as he had wished. He swallowed before continuing.

"As for killing Germans, that's man's business. You are here to frighten them onto our guns, not to entice them with lewd displays more appropriate to Soho than to Snodland. I am told the downed balloon was beyond repair and that seems to be a fair exchange for a frontline Luftwaffe bomber. I have not been advised of the serviceability of the item of women's uniform! Thank goodness none of you was hurt, or no vehicle was damaged."

Crotchet was choking back tears. Jenny thought this was worse than waiting for the needle for overseas' jabs.

"It would have meant so much paperwork," continued the squadron leader. "Balloon Command would have been on my back for ages! And, there was nothing to recover from what was probably a Heinkel so you saved the Station Commander some paperwork, too." He waited for the implication for this workload avoided to sink in. In silence he looked each WAAF in the eye to keep the tension high. "And for good measure, the farmer was fortunate to have had his cows under cover so their udders didn't curdle in the explosion, neither!"

Was the Plowman girl about to cry? The spotty girl on the end of the line looked to be about to have an attack of facial pox.

"The Air Officer Commanding the group has authorised me not to charge you. But I can't have my girls taking the war into their hands. You five airwomen will each do one week's extra fire piquet as a reminder to treat His Majesty's fighting equipment, and issued items of uniform, in an appropriate manner. As for you, Corporal Bates: you set a bad example of leadership and discipline to your colleague NCOs and airwomen alike. Since you conveniently collected another Kraut for our honours board, the AOC has agreed that I shall not have your corporal stripes removed. Arrangements have been made for you to be posted to No 913 Balloon Squadron, RAF Sutton Coldfield out near Birmingham and may heaven have mercy on your soul!" The squadron leader had finished his reprimand. He nodded at the sergeant standing behind the line of girls.

As with all such situations the next command was routine, "March out, Sergeant!"

"Airwomen, left turn! Quick march! ... Halt. Right turn! Stand out ease!" The door closed behind the girls. Percy Davenport smiled and reached into the lower drawer of his desk while removing his hat.

Through the closed door came the sergeant's instructions for the corridor, "Stand still, I haven't given you permission to speak. Stand tall … chests out … wait 'til I tells yer to do something … Yer ain't got nothing to blubber about, yet …"

In the office, Bethany removed her hat and placed it alongside the squadron leader's, on the desk. He nodded. Bethany went over to the door.

"March them in, if you please, Sergeant. The squadron leader wishes to speak with the girls. You may leave them to me when they are inside."

"Airwomen, attention! Left turn! Quick march! Halt … Left turn! Hats off!" Her duty done, the SNCO saluted, retired and closed the door.

"Relax, ladies, relax." Davenport was smiling. "Bloody good show, I am really proud of you. Inter service cooperation, good … good! Cost me a bottle of best whisky to calm down the army. Whole new definition of a Trojan horse, what? You showed the Krauts our women have got some spunk, eh!"

The airwomen did not know how to react to their commanding officer's enthusiasm.

Bethany Taverner cleared her throat and translated, without being invited, for the sake of female decorum, "The Squadron Commander is very pleased you have brought down an enemy aircraft, although he is perhaps surprised at the way you did it. He would be pleased if you would join us for a well deserved noggin of the best we can extract from the American's O'club. I should tell you that more than one Yank pilot watching the goings on from here was, as he put it, 'mighty impressed by the little ladies of the 978th, and wished they could have been out there to help'."

The airwomen visibly relaxed.

"I say 'Knickers to the hun!' Come now, Squadron Leader, a poured noggin measures two fingers on anyone's glass, especially for a WAAF of 978 Balloon Squadron. Cheers, or should I say, bottoms up!"

Chapter 27
1944 ~ Operation ABLATIVE Producing Results

"Hi, Colonel. Happy New Year. Jesus, Makepiece, you look like you was dragged through a hedge backward — and then again for the practice. Too much bed and not enough sleep?"

"You mind yours and I'll mind mine. This had better be good, Rod. I was enjoying a lie in."

"I know you don't have good German," opened Lieutenant Colonel Roddy Chmielewski, the Operations Officer for No 1574th SPSG. "But this transcription has just been translated and I have had a second go at it. You need to read this."

"Anyone else seen it yet?" asked Makepiece.

"Nope!" came the cheerful reply. "I reckon you'll want The Sprite to read it though and get it on the road to Bletchley Park."

"The Brits don't know we're carrying communications intelligence... err COMINT... gear, and The Sprite is not going to tell them how effective it is while I have any say about it; electronic intelligence data on radars is another matter, though. I don't know enough about Bletchley Park to know if they appreciate ELINT on its own. Any images to back this up?"

"Please read the text, Makepiece. Captain 'Edge' Cryshaw flew a P-38 a long way to get the raw stuff onto the film recorders. He's a good pilot for his age. You'll get the gist of his take pretty damn quick, I'd say. Then you can decide how you want to play it. I'll get you a coffee."

The Special Project Security Group Commander took the offered sheaf of papers from his deputy and settled in a chair to read the formatted typed text.

MOST SECRET ABLATIVE 3 -- ULTIMATE
Partial transcription of 1574th SPSG Mission 440101/01 dated January 01, 1944
Pilot: Captain Edward Cryshaw USAAC
Transcribed: Lieutenant Lorne Amhurst US Army Intelligence Corps
Media references: Sound Film: 440101/01 Channel: 5 LSB and HSB
Cross references: ELINT: 440101/01 E27 thru E53
                              Photographic: 440101/01 frames 103 thru 126
                              Other: Telemetry: 440101/01 (6) upper sideband
Time Zone: All time datums are GMT. Times in text, if any, are verbatim

Caution: This is a first level analysis and is subject to reassessment.

09:37	Man A	*<unreadable>* ready and primed.
09:37	Man B	Berlin will want the results quickly. Are the recording systems operating correctly and have they been calibrated in accordance with my directions?
09:38	Man A	Four channels are showing. Calibration *<nominal?>*
09:38	Man B	Are you using a target?
09:40	Man A	*<unreadable>* failed engine test. Deep snow at take off field *<digested ?>* *<unreadable>* intake. We will simulate a *<unreadable>* bomber type at 11000 metres. Warhead envelope set up for 100 metres radial *<unreadable>* command signal.
09:41	Man B	If there is no actual target you may shoot at your discretion.
09:42	Man A	Understood. I'll go on the 15 minutes before the hour mark. Our plot shows clear skies for 40 kilometre radius.
09:45	Man A	The firing sequence has initiated. *<pause background noise>* The weapon is flying. *<comment. Two other male voices in background, unintelligible.>*
09:47	Man B	Time to target height?
09:48	Man A	105 seconds from *<initial boost?>*. Allow 40 more for sloping range. Four channels being received, recording pens tracking as expected *<unreadable possibly a system name>* is plotting flight on both screens.
09:50	Man A	*<pause>* time to detonation 10 seconds *<pause>* plot shows detonation.
09:51	Man B	Is all in order?
09:51	Man A	Yes Herr Doktor. Visual sighting shows effective dispersal of destructors *<unreadable same name as before>* plots detonation at planned altitude under controlled climb and simulated target angle. Telemetry downlink has ceased.
09:53	Man B	Give me your assessment. Was the test a success as I

		predicted?
09:53	Man A	Nothing could have survived that burst, Herr Doktor. You may report a success and we are ready to test *<unreadable, name different from previous>* against real machine when we have reloaded. The pen traces of the telemetry are of high quality. Congratulations Herr Doktor.

Rod Chmielewski had returned with the coffee to find his commanding officer smiling. "It gets better, Colonel. See the next page!"

09:55	Man B	Herr Göring will be pleased with your work, Fundnabel.
09:55	Man A	Thank you Doktor Düren. I would wish to test the proximity device against a real target before the weapon is put to service.
09:56	Man B	That is not your *<decision?>* Fundnabel. Berlin judges what we give them. Be satisfied the test went well < *unreadable>* Göring will < *unreadable, some fading>* make arrangements for a further test against high flying bomber machines. Now listen carefully to my instructions, Fundnabel. Use the tethered balloon to drop a test warhead from 200 metres to test the proximity device. Set the detonation range to 66 metres and film the warhead as it drops from the balloon. I shall want *<to see the statistics of the warhead?>* shrapnel scatters after detonation. Change the destructors rods; steel is alright for cutting, I am looking for a magnetic induced pulse to knock out the target's electrics. *<substitute?>* copper alloy for pure steel and monitor wideband radio interference at around 20 megacycles. *<Jssel probable person's name?>* has just brought in paper traces of your test's telemetry. They will do me for now until you can get the originals through the snow. Prepare copies for yourself at the range.
09:57	Man A	My team will be working on the tasks immediately,

		Herr Doktor.
09:57	Man B	Good *<pleasantries about families>*
10:01		*<link shuts down>*
		Transcription ends.

Makepiece commented, "So The Edge caught a missile test." He was tidying the paper sheaf as he spoke.

Chmielewski replied, "It looks like it on that evidence alone. But there is more. As it says in the reference table at the top of the transcript there were six data channels, typical of telegraph or maybe missile telemetry with time coding. We don't have the kit here to exploit it but the egg-heads in Washington sure do. They'll love it."

Makepiece was happy that his ambition for the 1574th SPSG was bearing fruit. It had been a steep learning curve. "Have you finished?"

"As you can see, we got ELINT on the tracking radars: an area sweeper and a missile guidance system. It seems they steer the missile from the ground onto a target tracking through their airspace. I reckon those beauties alone justified flying in Santa's airspace. But I have an ace. The Edge's recordings show a continuous radio frequency, not pulsed like normal radar, which came on halfway through the missile flight. It was very low power and easy to miss. It could be the proximity fuse radiating from the warhead before it went bang."

"What's this reference to photographs? Are you going to make my day having, I might say, nearly ruined it? I could be sitting in front of a log fire, now, learning about pre-colonial England where my twelve greats grand papa came from."

"The Edge just happened to turn on his oblique camera to document where he was. The snow on the ground was making navigation difficult was his excuse! There he is, minding his own business, when he sees this missile exhaust plume climbing like a P-51 with flak up its arse. So he lets the Kodak[tm] keep snapping and he records the bang. He says it was probably 20 to 30 km away but the flash was unmistakable; 'biggest he's seen,' he says. 'It was bigger and brighter in daylight than any he had seen at night.' There was a bluish hue to the explosion ball, reminiscent of copper, he thought. It is in the intel debrief. The sun glinted on large shrapnel, he was not sure if the camera caught the glint. He guesses it was 10000 feet below him, but he had no good point of reference to judge. He says he was 37850 feet indicated at the time."

Makepiece knew he had to get this intelligence up the chain. "Have you got someone putting together a first level fused report? Dawes Hill will be very interested. They will probably want to see the raw, unassessed data too."

"Already underway, Colonel. Two versions, actually, with all the photography: one with the COMINT from Herr Doktor and company for the Yanks, the other all the ELINT excepting telemetry for the British which I will get The Sprite to run his finger over. He might ask us to anglicise it a bit, but I shall control his enthusiasm. Both will go to Dawes Hill, in different courier bags of course. I'll ask Dawes Hill to get Medmenham to give precise coordinates of where the detonation happened so that we can go get some more of German very private, unprotected communications."

"It will be interesting to see if the Brits come up with the same position as us."

"Right," acknowledged Chmielewski.

"In this case, have Edge Cryshaw read the Washington text. A little bit of feedback will do him good. Maybe something will trigger another morsel of data. Get a receipt from him that he has read it, for the records. Warn him to keep his mouth closed, the fewer who know the source the better. That includes unnecessary cross feed between the pilots."

Chmielewski knew Colonel Ploughmans' leadership style. He admired his commanding officer greatly and would move heaven and earth to see that his wishes were carried through.

Makepiece directed his deputy, "I would like to see both versions before they go out, Rod. The ABLATIVE level 3 stuff is a political hot potato in the White House. I need to protect my vitals from FDR and Secretary for War Henry Stimson if they should foul up relations with Churchill on our operations. You understand?"

"Goddit, Colonel." Chmielewski was reliable, and loyal, and Makepiece knew the material would be well prepared. "It'll be here on your desk at 22:00 British Summer Time. How the limeys can call this summer time defeats me. First of January! I'll quiz The Sprite, he's sure to know. He can spin me the yarn and then I'll hook him for his tale about being called 'The Sprite'. Word on the street is that he likes to give

WAAF officers a ride in that death trap he calls a Morgan three wheeler. Prefer four wheels and a roof myself. I don't see how he can get his leg over in that contraption."

"Don't be too hard on the lad. Perhaps he doesn't try! The Sprite strikes me as more of the 'four poster bed' type. Now, Rod, what news of the stateside experts? Have they arrived?" Makepiece was expecting his two specialist advisers before the New Year, but the recent poor weather had delayed their crossing.

Rod answered, "They were routed directly here, rather than through Bushy Park or Dawes Hill. Neither were happy bunnies when they were picked up at Rochester Station. But then, would you be, arriving after dark in a wartime Medway town, in winter?"

Makepiece's head nodded in understanding, allowing Chmielewski to continue while he chewed the inside of his cheek to conceal a smile.

"The Adjutant, Clarke McKing, went down to greet them on your behalf. He had to be hauled out of the O'Club at 20:00 last night which probably saved a WAAC from a fate worse than death." Rod grinned at Makepiece, who knew what the other man was talking about. "Clarke saw them to their bunks, the arriving men I'm talking about now, and suggested they join in the party for the New Year. That went down like the proverbial lead balloon until near midnight when one of the guards told us about the real balloon up near West Malling with the knickers. By coincidence, the air raid siren got them out of bed pretty damn quick."

"Oh, God!" Makepiece could sense the portent of trouble.

Rod continued, "Not WAAC pantyhose, WAAF knickers. At least that's what I was told, but I don't know how to tell them apart. Not until the voice above them starts to speak! Anyway, there was an air raid, an ATS searchlight, four Trojan[tm] french letters, a British balloon, an inglorious example of commodious underwear and a Heinkel bomber all in the same slice of sky. Oh, and a mess of ignited hydrogen, Hindenburg style. I've always said that knickers and flying don't mix. So the 978 Balloon Squadron collected another trophy and lost a pair of cremated knickers, WAAF, one pair, issued, for the use of. In the blackout too! Our WAACs are running a collection for the destitute maidens of Kent."

"I heard it hit the deck, last night. The Heinkel not the garment! Have Clarke McKing draft me a letter of congratulations to the WAAF's commander. Send him a bottle of best scotch with my compliments."

"Will do, Makepiece."

"Now, the new arrivals?"

Chmielewski gave himself a moment to collect his thoughts. The conversation had taken a turn to more serious matters. "The meteorological man is still trying to work out what year it is. It turns out that our resident met man, Hastings 'Wishful' Palmer, knows Michael 'Way Blue Yonder' Ryman from old days. He speaks highly of Ryman's understanding of stratospheric skies, but is less praiseworthy about what it means to him to look out of the window and see it raining... I guess most met men have that problem. I think 'Wishful' and 'Way Blue Yonder' will work wonders with their synoptic charts and our poor jockeys will just have to make the best of it — as always. We're lucky that our briefing rooms don't have windows!" Rod was pleased with joke.

"And, are you saving the best for last? 'Never trust a man in intel,' they say. It's a dishonourable activity only one step up from prostitution. I have a feeling the fan is about to be distributing excreta!"

"You might say that things have not got off to a good start for Doctor Bernard Weiss, graduate of MIT and a specialist scientific officer lifted by Donovan's OSS out of a project called MANHATTAN for duties in downtown Kent, England. You requested someone who knows about radio nuclides, whatever that is when it's at home, and we get a weirdo who would rather be building snowmen in New Hampshire. Not to put too fine a point on it, his face makes Popeye look positively handsome. He did not take kindly to being stuck in Reykjavik for Christmas Day, without a phone call home allowed either. Then he found the snow in Scotland is a lot wetter and has more soot in it than in the Vermont mountains; worse, that skiing is off the menu until we liberate the Alps. And there is milk in his coffee, not creamer. And the money! And that 'easy over' is what the Piccadilly commandos offer for 50 dollars in Leicester Square and not a way of cooking hens' eggs. He needs an explanation of why this war needs him, at least our side does."

"I get the picture. Has his ABLATIVE clearance come through yet?"

"It was on the wire from Washington while you were on furlough."

"And the 'Blue Yonder' chap?"

"Same!"

"Have Julia book them in to see me tomorrow morning, after met briefing. In my Tech Block office, of course. Have Hastings and Cliff Battel with Ryman when he comes in. Weather is all about pilots' stuff and it will give The Sprite a chance to be involved in how we do what we do. Tell Julia to book me 30 minutes with Ryman, we won't need that long, but you never know. Tell Julia I want an hour with Weiss. I am going to have to be fully frank with him about how we intend to crack Hitler's nut and I need him to tell me how to recognise the shell around the nuclear kernel. You had better be there too, so that Weiss can see how we do things in the 1574th SPSG and who would run the show if I got caught by a WAAF with a balloon."

"Did you have a nice New Year, Makepiece?"

"It's so long ago I can't remember. Something about a phone call, I remember, to interrupt my peace. I think I left a glass of pre-war malt on the table. I will have to try to get back to finish it off. Let's go to the Club and celebrate Edge Cryshaw winning our spurs for us."

As he reached for his hat, Makepiece said, "Rod, what's the name of the American Cross woman, the one who likes to mother the homesick soldiers?"

"The troops call her 'Frau Noir Net' on account of her penchant for black net stockings. Her real name — er — Cherrylinda Gildenstern, or some such typical Bronx handle. Why?"

"I think that 'Frau Noir Net' and Herr Doctor Weiss are going to have to meet. Black and white could set the dice rolling. What do you think?"

"It sounds to me as though Lieutenant Vivian O'Grady, queen bee for the WAACs of 1574th SPSG, has just volunteered for a war mission of some challenge — introduction-wise."

"My thoughts precisely, Rod. What an excellent deputy commander you are!"

"Strange you should say that, Makepiece. I was thinking exactly the same thoughts. Next you'll be telling me that you think the first round is on me."

"It had crossed my mind. Let's get outta here," said Makepiece. "And sometime I'm gonna have to teach you about radio-nuclides. Oh, by the way... happy New Year, Rod."

Chapter 28
1944 ~ One of Our Aircraft is Missing

Lieutenant Hank Gregson, at age 25, was the youngest pilot on 1574th SPSG. He had been chosen for his navigation skills. He had the knack of flying to a place with uncanny accuracy for time and location. He provided the benchmark for others to seek. Few achieved the standard. He could also handle combat aircraft with a proficiency that placed him top of any assessment. The P-38 and Hank Gregson fused into a fighting entity. When he was selected for the most challenging flying environment of solo fighter reconnaissance, none of his mentors was surprised.

Hank Gregson sat in the oxygen room, reading his briefing notes, checking his navigation maps and waypoints, recalculating his fuel and time tolerances. The Colonel had personally briefed him about this mission. It was being timed to catch a test of a new missile type on a test range about 150 miles south of Braunschweig. But first there was some routine reconnaissance gap filling to complete beyond Berlin in the Polish/German hinterland. There was still considerable snow cover over central Europe to make navigation more difficult, there might be cloud cover over the target. There was always the problem of flying too close to Berlin and its flak protective belt. But he would be flying the best aircraft of its type; they were all lovingly looked after by experienced maintainers. Nothing mechanical was left to chance. The chips were stacked in his favour if he used his common sense.

In 20 minutes it would be time to mount up. The groundcrew would have warmed the engines, checked all the systems, refuelled. 'I'll be carrying four drop tanks, got a long way to go today,' he thought. Starting to put on his personal survival equipment, Gregson reflected about the snap ring at his waist.

'That's the bit I don't like about Ploughman's specials — being hooked to explosives designed to destroy the cockpit and the role equipment. Rod Chmielewski says we've got 15 seconds before it blows, the aircraft would be a mile away if the fuse starts as I get out. In fact it's never been tried; no-one has done it for real... '.

'Last minute checks. One deep breath. Kneel for a prayer. OK. Let's get this show into the sky.'

Ten minutes later, Gregson had set his autopilot to fly cruise climb through the dark Kent skies to rendezvous with the back squadron of British Lancasters leaving for the Ruhr. They were expecting him. A single blue light from a tail gunner ahead provided just a bit of company in these hostile Dutch skies. Radio silence of course. The east sky, the way he was going, was totally black obscuring the horizon although the starlight made the ground snow glisten. His night accustomed eyes could make out the shapes of friendly bombers, mainly due to glowing engine exhausts. The outside air temperature was -25 degrees centigrade, his cockpit temperature and his role equipment was being held at +15 degrees — chilly, but bearable.

The front aircraft in the formation were bounced by German night fighters. There was plenty of air-to-air tracer and radio traffic, but no aircraft burned in the night sky. No sooner had the fighters moved away than German anti-aircraft flak began reaching for the bomber stream. Gregson was grateful to see three flashes of blue signal lamp from his escort 400 yards ahead.

His first waypoint.

Check all fuel has been used from the drop tanks. Jettison the now dead weight. Rock the wings to salute the bombers... 'If they can see me with this camouflage...' and away in cruise climb, above the wave of Lancasters silhouetted against the snow. Soon they were behind him as he climbed to 38000 feet for optimum tailwind and the Polish border. 'It will get colder out there... down to -50 degrees perhaps...' Was his P-38 more comfortable now those external tanks were absent? The outside air temperature gauge was indeed reading -52 degrees centigrade, but his cabin conditioning was well up to the job of protecting man and equipment for the task they had to do.

It was relatively easy to pick out Leipzig to his left and to keep well south of the city and its anti-aircraft protection. There was now enough daylight on the ground for his oblique cameras to work; the electronics packages were busy also. To Gregson's knowledge, the ELINT was getting nothing unexpected. 10 miles to the east of Leipzig, the River Mulde glinted in the low angle daylight. Just as he turned to head south along the east bank of the river, on his second waypoint, Gregson saw the lights of Colditz Castle to his right go out. Confirmation, if any was needed, that there was good lighting at ground level. 'That's worth an oblique image for the record,' he thought. He followed the Mulde south until he flew over a river junction just 2 miles north of the town of Chemnitz.

'Way point 3 coming up.'

Gregson made another right turn and over the airfield of Burgstadt, his vertical camera recording the ground below. Light was getting better all the time.

'Excellent!' Gregson moved as much as was possible within his seat straps. This was where he was expected to be busy with his cameras and his electronics. Trouble could find him from here — if anywhere — until he crossed the Dutch coast again.

Aloud, Gregson said to no-one in particular, "This is why you've come, Hank. Let's hope the Krauts want to show off for us this New Year. Smile for Uncle Hank, *bitte!*"

* * *

The *Luftwaffe* radar had been tracking a high altitude intruder for some minutes. Their intelligence knew the Americans called these 'ferret' flights. The duty controller assessed this to be an intelligence collecting ferret, most probably photographic reconnaissance. The radar plot indicated he was alone in the skies but at extreme altitude for a Spitfire, perhaps 11850 metres.

"Get the commander in here and call the duty officer at Erfurt airfield. Tell him he is about to have high altitude company. Tell him the present track suggests overhead in 40 minutes at a Spitfire's maximum of 38000 feet or 11850 metres. And tell him the ferret will be at his maximum fuel endurance for good measure."

Oberlieutenant Wendt was not happy at being called in. When he realised it was his opportunity to a make a decision, his attitude changed.

"Call the duty officer at Erfurt airfield," Wendt commanded. "Tell him he is about to have high altitude ferret photographing his airfield. Tell him the ferret's present track puts it overhead Erfurt in 35 minutes at the Spitfire's ceiling of 11850 metres."

"Yes, Oberlieutenant."

"Tell him to have one Me 163 Komet rocket fighter brought to immediate readiness."

"Yes, Oberlieutenant."

"I will issue the launch command, personally. Get the Berlin controller on the line immediately. I will inform him that I am engaging a ferret under my command."

"Yes, Oberlieutenant. Does the Oberlieutenant not think… "

"Do it."

"Yes, Oberlieutenant."

*   *   *

On the Orhdruf test range, in the Thuringer region, Doktor Düren was visiting his missile test team headed by Scientist Engineer Fundnabel.

"Your tests on the proximity device have been satisfactory, Fundnabel?" It really was an unnecessary question because Düren had read the test reports. In ground tests, the fuse was triggering warhead explosion at 60 metres range while travelling at 225 metres per second. This was the design performance required for the warhead type, an expanding rod and blast design with embedded electromagnetic properties. A test at altitude was now required.

"Have you organised a test target, Fundnabel?"

"I have, Herr Doktor. It is due to overfly at 10:00. The range director has already indicated that the mothership is airborne and that separation of the target drone should experience no problem."

"Very well, Fundnabel. It will be acceptable for you to initiate the missile launch. I shall be outside watching the performance through a binocular telescope."

"Very good, Herr Doktor Düren. I will double check our ground monitors and our electromagnetic pulse detector. The supplying company told me that the electromagnetic pulse detector is their very latest model used to protect overhead power pylons from lightning storms."

"I shall be outside, Fundnabel. This will be the first time a test EMP device has been detonated in the atmosphere. I wish to view the results for myself."

The telephone beside Fundnabel rang. "*Ya… Ya…* I'll ask. Wait! Herr Doktor, there is a live hostile single target flying towards the range. There is time to abort the dummy target and engage the actual enemy."

There was something said down the telephone. Fundnabel continued to tell the Doktor what was happening. "Our tracking radar indicates that the enemy will be overhead in 9 minutes. Our guidance *Wurzburg* radar is showing the target at 11850 metres altitude, but this is at *Wurzburg's* maximum operating range. We shall have a more accurate altitude in two minutes when the *Wurzburg* radar is operating at closer range. If we launch in four minutes the enemy will be within the missile range and altitude engagement parameters. Our missile is primed and ready to engage. May I have your permission to shoot the enemy down?"

"Proceed. Berlin will think highly of our success and I shall be honoured by the Führer personally. Confirm the *Wurzburg* missile tracking and command guidance systems are warmed up?

"They have been, Herr Doktor Düren. We are ready to engage the enemy."

"Shoot the enemy down, Fundnabel. I shall be watching your success."

"Very good, Herr Doktor Düren." Then Fundnabel spoke into the telephone, "We shall engage the hostile aircraft. Switch over control to this facility. We have all recorders on all four channels running. I have control. Remain in your bunker until the weapon has flown clear. You will be able to monitor progress as I provide a commentary to design headquarters. Out!"

Fundnabel turned to an assistant. He snapped his fingers to emphasise the urgency of his directive, "Command the target mothership to abort its launch and return to base. We shall not need her target today."

Fundnabel began his commentary to a remote authority. "The time is 09:42. Test site 54 is engaging a single, high-altitude, hostile passing close to the Orhdruf test range. This is Scientist Engineer Fundnabel reporting on behalf of Doktor Düren who has authorised the live engagement of the enemy. On my command the Missile, Serial Number 013 will launch with a pattern 7 warhead. Proximity fusing has been set at 60 metres. Launch will be on my mark... *drei, zwei, einer*, mark. Our sensors are showing missile launch, boosters correctly functioning. Boosters separating... the missile is climbing as planned... the control radars are functioning correctly... the missile is responding correctly to follow the target. The target has not made any corrective alterations to his flight track. The time is 09:44 and the missile continues to engage the enemy. We have a second aircraft visible on our plotting radar... range 20 kilometres... unidentified. I will investigate. He is closing on our target..."

In a development Messerschmitt Me-163 Komet rocket-powered fighter, Capitan Enrich Müller was not enjoying the ride. The machine had climbed to 12300 metres in 3½ minutes and he had throttled back. Nevertheless he was flying — strapped inside a machine moving through the air under very little control from its pilot — showing 660 km per hour airspeed. The safety pins were out of his cannons. Müller would get just one chance to engage the enemy target as he flew by, assuming he could see the Spitfire. He used his radio to call for instructions.

"Control. Give me a vector and target height. There are no condensation trails at this altitude."

"Komet, Komet. Your target is 12 km ahead and below you. You are closing down sun at 190 km per hour. Your target is now 10 km ahead and 800 metres below you. Your target is now 8 km ahead and 600 metres below you. Komet, Komet. Respond."

"Control. I hear your instructions. I am throttling back to close more slowly. I cannot see him yet. There is a ground rocket, smoking, climbing up. I have visual contact on the target. It's not a Spitfire, it's a twin boom American P-38. I am engaging... he has broken right and is climbing. My machine will not respond to the controls. I have passed the target. And will throttle up for a second pass. I have three minutes fuel left. The engine is burning again, the ground rocket is ..."

*　　　*　　　*

Doktor Düren, looking through his telescope, watched as his missile flew straight at the Führer's latest secret weapon — the Me 163 Komet rocket fighter. The proximity fuse functioned perfectly. The Komet disintegrated in a blue ball as the warhead rods cut their target to pieces and the larger pieces pulled themselves apart under the pressure of 600 kph airspeed. The American aircraft, not a Spitfire as he had expected, had pulled away from the passing Komet but had caught fire. The pilot was trying to escape but his machine blew apart, before the Doktor's eyes, in a series of four sequential explosions presumably from internal ordinance. Düren guessed the American was at least 1500 metres away from the missile's warhead detonation, maybe much more. He had no explanation of why the P-38 should have ignited.

On the ground both the radars had failed. The motor generators had rundown. All the lights were out, some alarms were ringing for no obvious reason. One of the ground technicians lay on the ground, quivering characteristically of severe electric shock; he had been holding a film recording tripod at the instant of explosion. The motorised cameras had all fried under internal combustion. A technician who wore a hearing aid had the device blown clear through his head taking the side of his face with it. Was this an unexpected effect of the high altitude electro-magnetic pulse burst he had so carefully designed into the warhead?

Düren tried the telephone to the control room. He needed to speak with Fundnabel. The phone did not work; the insulation on the wires looked to have burned through. As he approached the control building he noticed that a portion of the metal roof had blown away. The paint on the metal entrance door was heavily burnt although the concrete structure looked intact. There had been no sound from the detonation, no shockwave, no heat. Some distance away, a transport aircraft he recognised as the type used to ferry his targets was in a vertical crash dive.

Inside the range building the main equipment chassis looked as though a madman had attacked it with an axe. All the lamp bulbs had exploded. Four operators were slumped over their desks. A fifth had his hands to where his ears would have been; the earphones had exploded presumably killing the man instantly not allowing him time to fall out of his chair. The pen recorders were burning, unattended, their records irrecoverably lost.

Düren did not know that 50 km away telephone switchboards were experiencing electrical fires in the connecting frames. Two power stations were automatically shutting down. The Nordhausen manufacturing and assembly underground factory resorted to emergency lighting only. Insulation was falling away from many long distance communications centres' copper connections. An over ground electricity pylon and cabling had collapsed with a transformer sub-station erupting in a fireball 700 metres tall. There was chaos. There was no explanation to the frantic officers trying to recover the situation.

*　　　*　　　*

In the sky above Hamm, a lone American P-51 Mustang had, with others scattered around the bomber stream, been escorting a wave of American B-17 raining death on a German munitions factory in a daylight raid. He was 20 miles to the south of the main force, out wide to protect the flank. He was at high altitude and alert. For no obvious reason his engine stuttered and his electrics went haywire for just a few seconds then settled down, except for his radios which had all kicked out. In the far distance, to the south of east, he guessed 30 miles away, there was a small blue cloud with a white smoke and fireball above it. His guess of range was not reliable, but he did think the altitude of the event was about the same as his own — above 35000 feet. This was no foo fighter UFO. Something out there had blown up — maybe there were two fireballs? He'd tell his intel officer when he debriefed. The time, check the time, his watch indicated 07:47 GMT — that would be nearly 10 minutes short of 10 o'clock German local time. The electric clock on his dashboard seemed to have frozen at that time.

Chapter 29
1944 ~ Escape to Cleeve Lyon Cottage

It was Flight Surgeon David McFallis who insisted that Makepiece took a 48 hour pass. If he would not take a regular furlough of perhaps seven days, at least he should allow himself two nights away from Snodland. It would re-energise the commander's batteries for the challenges ahead. Accordingly, Makepiece cleared his desk, cut orders nominating Lt Col Roddy Chmielewski — his deputy — as acting Commanding Officer for the period Friday February 4th and Saturday and closed the door to his office, handing his aide WAAC Sergeant Julia Greenburg a 'shopping list' of things he must have within four hours.

The list read:

(1) A list of the official British rations allowances for food,

(2) A suitable food parcel, befitting a 'bird' colonel, to donate to the family hostess where he would be staying, including a white loaf, three rolls of toilet tissue and a tin of pineapple rings,

(3) A personal gift of six pairs of stockings for the lady of the house,

(4) A bottle of Jack Daniels[tm] for the man of the house,

(5) A carton of chewing gum for the children of the family.

At the bottom of the list the colonel had put his contact phone number: Cleeve Lyon 421 — 'just in case the President wants me back in DC'.

"Is the colonel going to give me a name or address?" she asked.

"No time to, Sergeant. You've gotten some ass to kick to have that list in the trunk of my Ford in four hours. Now, hit the dirt. Make sure its gas tank is full. And, while I'm over the hill and far away, look after The Rod so that I've gotten a group to come back to. Savvy?"

"*Ich savvy beintot, mon gruppenfurher,*" had come the saucy reply. She was already reaching for her hat and there was no disguising her smile at corrupting so many languages in so few words.

"All I can say about that is: 'Thank you, Lord, for giving me some real linguists in my group'. Three hours and 59 minutes, Sergeant." He had winked at the WAAC. She knew better than to wink back.

*   *   *

Makepiece had checked there appeared to be a generous offering positioned in the tail boot of his car. The false trail of a visit to a hosting family, albeit with a valid telephone contact which had been used at the New Year, had been laid. On top of the goodies, held in position by the liquor bottle, was a recent official leaflet:

Rationed

The fixed rations cover milk, sugar, tea, cheese, bacon, butter, margarine, lard, meat.

Milk	.. ½ pint per day for each adult. 1½ pints per day for each child under 5 years of age. School children may also obtain milk at school.
Tea	.. 2 ozs. per week per person. Children under the age of five receive no tea ration ; men and women over the age of 70 receive an amount additional to the normal.
Cheese	.. 3 ozs. per week. Miners and heavy industrial workers receive an additional amount.
Bacon	.. 4 ozs. per week per person.
Butter	.. 2 ozs. ,, ,, ,, ,,
Margarine	.. 4 ozs. ,, ,, ,, ,,
Lard	.. 2 ozs. ,, ,, ,, ,,
Shell Eggs	.. Approximately 3 eggs per person per month. Often no eggs are available, especially in the large cities. There is plenty of egg powder on the market.
Meat	.. ½d. worth per week.

Copy of food rations published in most British newspapers in 1944

Now he was parking the staff car off the track from the estate road to the big house and out of sight from casual observers. Even with daylight saving time, it had been dark for nearly two hours and the cottage was blacked out. With a torch pointing to the ground Makepiece found his way to the front door. He checked his luminous watch; it showed precisely the time Aynette had said she would be ready. It was half past seven when he knocked on the cottage's old wooden door. It was opened quickly, as though she had been waiting for him.

"They say an Englishman is always a polite 10 minutes late, a German is usually an awkward 10 minutes early and an American is always on time." Aynette was reaching for his sleeve to pull him into the dark hallway. "Come in, so that I can fix the blackout curtain and switch on the light. Take off that coat, Makepiece, and hang it up."

With the curtain correctly fitted, Aynette turned to the living room door and opened it to allow its light to spill into the dark of the hall.

"You are most welcome in my cottage, my dear Colonel. Will you be able to stay for long? Slip your tie over your coat on the hall stand." He was already undoing the knot while looking at her from top to toe. Her slim frame, narrow waist, those legs standing in high heels, was just as he remembered. He wanted to touch this woman but he was reluctant to start down the uncontrollable slope.

"I've brought enough provisions to stock a chuck wagon heading west across the prairie. I hope we might have two days together. I know that getting food onto the table in time of war is a demanding business, but we Yanks have so much when you have, or are allowed to have, so little. And I have brought over some of our American goodies such as a white loaf, absorbent toilet tissue, and deodorant, and stockings, and soft soap and tinned fruit. Of course some real coffee, I don't get on with chicory! In no particular order of preference you understand. It's my way of saying thank you for opening your home to me. Should I go and get the box from…?"

Makepiece could not speak more with Aynette's mouth pressed against his. Her kiss was searching, warm and suggestive of more devoted loving later. In very high heels, Aynette's lips could comfortably reach Makepiece's. With her whole body she pushed the man against a wall and moved one leg between his, lifting her foot clear of the ground. Her hip bone was applying gentle pressure to his groin. His hands felt the curvature of her hips before reaching round to apply pressure to her buttocks. As he moved her body against his, he could make out the silhouette of her hair against the spilled kitchen light, presumably restrained by that RAF hairclip.

Her tongue was caressing his lips as he rolled Aynette so that her back was pressed to the wall pushing both feet to the ground. He withdrew his head seeking to look deep into her eyes before reaching for her breasts with both hands. He pulled at the blouse's front buttons which parted easily to reveal a nakedness that Makepiece found irresistible. He noted the surprise in her eyes at the firmness of his touch. He gripped both her hands and lifted them above her head; with one hand he held her hands against the wall, with the other he lifted one of her legs so that its thigh was at his hip. The leg remained high as he began to hitch her skirt so that the material was held, behind her, exposing nakedness from waist to shoe.

Makepiece placed both his hands behind her knees and lifted her, her arms settling around his neck. He carried Aynette up the stairs to her room and placed her standing with her back to the bed. He noticed the counterpane and blankets were folded back as though to air the mattress, the lower sheet had not been smoothed flat.

Makepiece peeled the open blouse from Aynette's shoulders and undid the clasp holding her skirt at her waist. He pushed the material away from her, and then lifted her on to the mattress. She was naked except for her high heeled shoes. After undoing his sleeve cuffs, without undoing all the buttons, he pulled his shirt over his head. He was now naked except for his stockinged feet. He leant over Aynette, gripped to separate her knees, and knelt between her thighs. In a single movement he lifted her hips onto his haunches. His face began to change colour and contort as Aynette reacted with a spontaneous cry as her body shook in response to the spasms in his belly.

Makepiece's head settled on her shoulder, his face buried in her neck. He was relaxing, both on her and inside her. His breathing calmed. She assumed he had gone to sleep; he did not move. They had not uttered a word since he had picked her up in the hall. A lot of his weight was being taken by his folded haunches underneath her hips. He could stay where he was, at least for a while.

Aynette felt behind him and found Makepiece's back to be a pool of perspiration. She reached under a pillow and brought a pyjama piece which she spread along his spine.

They remained immobile for approximately 10 minutes, until Makepiece began to stir. Aynette was not upset by these events since Makepiece's arrival. But neither could she understand how this, the man she regarded as so considerate, not least in sex, should have used her this way. She had a moment to reflect that she had been taken by her man — her wonderful, lovely man — a man she must share for a short time — her man with who she shared the most intimate parts of her being — her lover... His face had now withdrawn from her neck causing greater weight of his torso along hers, her breasts under pressure from his chest. She was unable to breath as deeply as she would normally; she accepted the temporary discomfort from his weight while she whispered in his ear.

"What was that all about, Makepiece?"

"I have no answer. I didn't mean to hurt you. I didn't hurt you, did I?" Aynette rocked her head to indicate she was alright. "You were... are... the avenue to escape. Sometimes it gets very heavy being in charge. It's lonely. You are never free of problems. Everything from budgets, personnel and personal problems, war, politics, the sex drive of the GI, the list goes on. One of my pilots is MIA — 'missing in action' — which puts a special strain on a small professional group such as mine; writing to his folks is not easy when he is a personal chum. When I'm with you, all those clouds float away; you are my sanity in a mad world. You become my sunshine for a few short hours."

"There you are, my lover. Queen Aynette is here to give her pilot knight some respite in this wicked world, to assuage your woes. I am here for you, my knight, tonight and for as many days and nights as you need me. I make no demand on you; I do not look for long term commitment. I have the relief, the cure and the salve which will wash away your troubles for a few blessed hours or days. Relax, Makepiece, relax."

Makepiece rolled off his woman, allowing her to bring her thighs together. Their naked torsos remained in full contact. Aynette's breathing settled to its regular rhythm. She had her heels, he had his socks. It was February outside; their warmth came from human energy. They kissed, and relaxed under a coverlet and slept in each other's arms.

177

Chapter 30
1944 ~ Tip of the Iceberg

Having made a light supper, and after Aynette excused herself to make a couple of essential telephone calls, Makepiece and Aynette were sitting in front of the log fire, on the couch, with the draught screen behind them. The provisions box had been brought in from the car and its contents now lay scattered across the delighted Aynette's kitchen table. She had settled into her favourite position, with her body along the couch and her back against the upright; her head was resting on his lap looking towards the fire. Makepiece had taken the precaution of removing Aynette's RAF wings hairclip before she settled. The fingers of his left hand were combing her hair behind her neck; his right hand was rested on her uppermost hip.

"Aynette. Would you be offended if I asked you a question?" They were both naked under dressing gowns each with the tie belt bow-knotted at the waist.

"It is very unlikely that you could offend me. We have been lovers and we shall be again. Ask away."

"Well... I was wondering... how is it... I mean... you seem to know a lot... you know... ?"

"Come on, Makepiece, what do I seem to know a lot about?" Aynette's head rolled on his lap so that she was looking up into his face. Shortly after she had settled her head and shoulders, she moved her body so that she was now lying on her back. She stretched her legs straight; they just reached the end of the couch. Makepiece was hesitant.

"Men. Well, this one in particular." He seemed reluctant to engage in eye contact.

'Is he being shy?' she wondered.

"I mean, I am a normal sort of guy, if a colonel in the Army is ever normal. But, I mean... our moments together... our intimate moments... well, any moments together actually... you seem to know how to give me so much and enjoy yourself at the same time."

"Are you telling me that I am a satisfactory lover, my knight?"

Makepiece paused, then, "Mmm... You see... it is hard to understand... to accept that 'experience behind the bike shed' gels with an expertise that would put Cleopatra in the shade." With his point made, he could now look at the face looking up at him from his lap. If anyone could rival his Marybeth then surely this was her. But he didn't want to think such thoughts.

"I was up at Oxford. You know that. The bike shed is a metaphor for the circulation of certain volumes of literature that some don't see as fitting for English folk to read. We had copies of such masterpieces as *'Kama Sutra'* and *'Lady Chatterley'* — just to name two. Well thumbed copies, printed in Egypt, they were. I am not saying that I liked that sort of stuff, but some of it rubs off. Mind-blowing stuff and nothing like the real thing... a bit like 'how to manuals' without the tools. And so, my lover, it is on you where the magic dust has settled. You have come out of the wide blue yonder and unlocked the treasures closed inside this body of mine. Like the Sleeping Beauty and her Prince Charming..."

"Yes... but..."

"Yes... but... nothing, my lover." Aynette's left hand was reaching upward for Makepiece's cheek. Did his eyes tell her that he accepted her explanation? It was pretty-much true. Her movement had the effect of pulling her gown hem to mid thigh exposing her legs to her lover's eager gaze.

"You are a most satisfactory lover to me, my lover. Your masculinity fulfils my dreams, calms my desires and relaxes my innermost needs. From head to toe I would have you no other way, and yet, I would have you any and every way this body can."

Makepiece's hand was exploring the opening of her gown at her chest. Her smile, visible as his gaze transferred to watch his handicraft, assured him that his fondling was welcome while she talked.

She continued, "And you know I am a writer, so I have to have an imagination. Being a writer means reading a lot and library books have a habit of falling open at the juicy bits. So I put it all together. In the real world of my cottage, my pilot knight navigates his way to the land of milk and honey that this eager body offers. You need no passport or licence to have me, my love. We escape our mortal coil together."

"That was a pretty deep, 'Yes... but... nothing, my lover' as you call it. OK, no more questions! Shall I put another log on the fire?"

Aynette replied, "That would be nice." She began the movements to rise to her feet. "I have to do something that girls have to do. I shan't be long, my love. Make yourself a drink and a small sherry for me. Perhaps we could pretend that you are Don Juan de Tassis, envoy from the King of Spain to the court of James Stuart, King of England and Scotland escaping from London and dallying with his Kentish lady in front of the fire."

"Your imagination…"

"… knows no bounds," she caught his theme. They exchanged a smile. He stood to embrace her, mutually enjoyable for sure, but she had other things to do.

There were domestic sounds in the distance as Makepiece renovated the fire, poured the drinks, and reflected on his recent exchange with Aynette. His thoughts were soon interrupted by her return. She was carrying a small bowl and a linen towel which she placed near the fire hearth.

"I read somewhere that the ladies of Japan wash their menfolk to keep their love alive. It seems to be a good idea to me. No arguing now. Come, kneel on the rug in front of the fire…" Aynette led him to the hearth rug, allowed him a taste of his drink while she reached for his dressing gown tie. In a single sweep his gown had fallen away and its tie removed from its waist hoops.

Makepiece was surprised by the unexpected disrobing. He offered no resistance as Aynette collected his two hands, palms together, and bound his wrists with the tie.

"Don't be afraid, my love. Aynette will tell you everything — all the details of the story shall be revealed. There is no need to talk. It's a woman's prerogative to talk and it's her knight's duty to obey. Just let Queen Aynette be the storyteller."

Aynette manoeuvred to support Makepiece's head as she laid him flat on the rug. "I am going to secure this tie to the leg of the couch so that your busy hands don't have to do any work. There, it's not too tight? Oh, you've still got you socks on. Never mind. Queen Aynette will make sure those feet are comfortable by binding them together. There, her gown tie is just the right length to reach the leg of the sideboard. Oh, my stretched out knight is taller than I thought and I see he is preparing to defend my honour. Now don't wiggle while I put this cushion under your bum, or whatever you Yanks call it; your hips will be more comfortable off the hard stone floor. Just imagine how uncomfortable it must have been for the lady under Don Juan de Tassis."

Aynette wriggled out of her dressing gown.

Makepiece's eyes followed her anxiously, wondering what the woman was going to do. 'Surely she not going to stick me with a dagger, like in her book?'

"This flannel is perhaps cooler than one is used to... but... with a little consideration it is no different to having a cold splash to waken up after a dream. That's better. Oh, my knight's instrument has retired now it is spic and span. The queen will dry her knight and perhaps he'll come out to play again."

'My God, that was cold. There's no sign of a weapon...'

"I must turn round to see my knight's face as he delights his queen. That's nice. My knight's tummy is strong enough for my little weight and I can reach to reward his lips with a regal kiss... so sweet a kiss... I think that a queen's kiss is much friendlier than being dubbed by a sword. There is no need to be anxious, my knight. Queen Aynette will keep all the bad spells at bay. If I rock forward you can kiss my breast... not for too long now... and the other. There. That was pleasureful, wasn't it? My nipples have come out to see what the fuss is about. You may caress my nipples with your tongue, first one... ooh... now the other. Did you enjoy that? Your queen did, my knight. Don't speak. Shh! There's lots more."

She lifted her body away from Makepiece to look into his eyes. "Shh!" An index finger pressed against his lips, through his lips into his mouth. His face reflected wonder about what might come next.

"I hope that was not too bad, my dragging down across your erection like that. But now I am comfortable astride these soldierly thighs. I think it is time to wake up other dreaming parts of my knight's body. This ice cube will freshen those lips, and this throat, and these hairy nipples. Why do men have nipples? A circuit with the ice cube makes them stand up, ready to be kissed. But my cube wants to explore down here, to this button where life was given, and beyond into the dark reaches where the future holds so much promise. I know my knight wants to be free to use the ice on my body, but he can't. So Aynette will do it for him, round these breasts all eager for his attention, across her stomach and into her waiting sex. There, I've said it — sex."

Makepiece was mesmerised by the transit of the ice cube which had come to rest where their pubic mounds touched.

"The queen and her knight are going to have sex. Fulfilling, unqualified, unequalled sex. It is going to be quite soon now. I need to move forward so that I may introduce you... I nearly forgot... you have already met. That is why you entered so easily, so comprehensively filled a yearning for your company. I can see these movements are to your pleasure, dear knight. I can tell you that they are greatly to your queen's pleasure too. Just be a little patient, my love. Your queen will help you if you are patient. I need some more of this lovely ice... to cool my hand to calm the hurry out of these balls... that's good. Now some more cubes... that's two hands and a scoop full... if I put them here on your stomach... whee!"

Makepiece had lost all restraint with the shock of the chill to his solar plexus. Masculine strength coupled with reflex contraction combined to bring forth a powerful seminal flow matched by contractions in Aynette's vagina.

Makepiece could not contain an uncharacteristic expletive, "Jesus H Christ!"

Aynette let out another, "Whee!" and flopped her body onto Makepiece's chest.

They both laughed, producing unexpected feelings in their still engaged sex.

Aynette moved to bring together her thighs, held tightly closed by the restrained man's legs and thereby holding Makepiece's declining phallus within her. 'This time,' she thought, 'my body will not kick him out.'

"Makepiece," she whispered in his ear, "Makepiece, as Lady Chatterley didn't say — I feel well and truly fucked."

His face creased into a smile. His body wanted to laugh but the stretched layout somehow prevented it. He had to be content with a smile. He was at a loss for words.

She reached for his cheeks, pulling his flushed face round to hers for a lingering kiss before she succumbed to the need to relax her back. Her face settled into his neck, her hair caressing any skin it touched. Within its conformal fit, her relaxing vagina accepted and embraced the unfamiliar soft penis. In this position, prone along her bound man serving as her mattress and her warmth, Aynette went into near sleep.

"Be at rest, my love. You won't have to endure the indignity much longer. It's time to do something for Aynette." Aynette's face remained buried under Makepiece's jaw so that he could not turn to face her. Her body lay unmoving along his. "I shall be the commentator and you the audience, I the principal and you the support... the beautiful supporting actor."

An index finger ran across his lips.

"If there was an observer, he would see two naked bodies, apart from a pair of socks, lying on a damp rug in front of the fire. We know that they are lovers in intimate hold in the afterglow of great energy. But Queen Aynette is looking towards the future, when her Knight Makepiece has flown away to war and his family. Aynette will have only memories then, memories to endure to her last breath. And so she has to prepare for the solitude she knows must come. But be not anxious, my love. What has gone before and what is yet to come will all help."

Only Aynette's lips were moving. Every muscle in both partners were still in anticipation.

"First I must waken the sleeping man. If I roll my muscles this way and back, your manhood will be aware that Aynette needs his company. Our observer will see nothing move because it's all inside me, in private. That's better, the life giver returns. I can encourage him and I will. Think hard and long, my Makepiece. This is no time to be shy or reserved. I will help as these loving muscles caress you and accept you ever deeper in my body. All the love we have made, and all the loving to come — when you have me against the oak tree, or take me in the back of your car, or ravish my body while tied to my writing chair, or when we share the bath, or when we join in bed in the manner of the animals — these are but happy episodes contributing to this one moment. Now is when Aynette's memory is to be formed — a memory to be cherished for the rest of her days. I notice that your manhood thinks highly of these opportunities for the hours to come, to have me again. That helps me feel you as if I were gripping you with a sliding hand. This private, unseen and unseeable ecstasy is what I shall remember when I am writing, when I am riding on the bus past the gas works, on the train, in my bed watching the fields in the moonlight, sitting under a tree surrounded by bluebells. In my private innermost being, no-one will know of forces exploding inside me unless my face betrays my joy. In my waking moments, and in my most personal dreams, I shall treasure most dear this special loving when we awoke together from sexual nothingness and rose to the ultimate peak. My womanly muscles will remember their embrace of this moment and they will dance for more."

Restrained Makepiece could make no physical contribution to this intercourse. He did not need to speak, his woman was having him her way.

"In just a few seconds, my Makepiece, ooh... it feels like a volcano is going to explode within me... I can feel your shape as I help you reach... ooh... now, my angel... oh yes... just one more pull you in and then a push... ooh... you can breath, ooh... did you feel the ground tremor? ... ooh."

She had lifted her head to look into his eyes.

"There now. I can feel you have finished. And you have completely fulfilled my need. My Makepiece has done his duty by his Aynette. That silly observer will wonder what all that heavy breathing was about. He could not know how deliciously served I feel. So, I will undo those lovely hands so that you may lift Aynette's head to kiss you. There."

Makepiece eased the numbness in his stretched arms, in his wrists. He reached to hold her head by cupping her ears.

"Madam," began Makepiece, "I doubt you have left me the wherewithal," a kiss, "to, as you put it, have you again. You have taken my adultery beyond any reasonable bounds," a longer and more persistent kiss, "and you know darned well that I shall not forget the experience. I have but one request before you do with me what you will."

"So?"

"Please could we move away from these ice cubes? The cold and damp are getting to my water works."

Makepiece was now able to lift his hips, and her body, clear of the floor.

"No sooner asked than agreed, my love. Pass me that piece of linen, dear one. You may withdraw when you are ready, but I want one more kiss before you go. Ooh... you can't be coming up for more already... that wasn't part of the plan... I suppose... look, if we roll this way you will be on top..."

"Quiet wench, your master speaks now..."

"... and your back can... ooh... it must be something you ate... ooh..."

Chapter 31
1944 ~ A Visit to Dawes Hill

"Sergeant Greenburg. Will you come in here please?" The colonel was summoning his aide, having just replaced the telephone. "I have to go to Dawes Hill tomorrow. I shall need a driver. Do you fancy an outing — I presume you've gotten a permit to drive in UK?"

"I'd like to drive the Colonel to headquarters. Will there be anyone else?"

"The Sprite?"

"If the Colonel insists!" In the too quick response, there was more than a little reluctance in the aide's voice which surprised Makepiece.

"The Sprite has some photographs to deliver to Medmenham, which is just along the road from Dawes Hill. In a manner of speaking, you could kill two birds with one stone and see how the other half lives all in one." The Colonel was making friendly banter of a serious matter. He had been left in no doubt that his presence, face to face was required at Headquarters. Colonel Knapp had given him no alternative.

"Why the reluctance to drive The Sprite as a passenger, Julia?"

"Wandering hands, Colonel," said with a sigh of resignation.

"If I make him promise to be on his best behaviour? When he gets to Medmenham, I might say he knows the way without the British roadsigns, he will meet with a load of RAF chums of the female variety. Perhaps they'll find a way of cooling his ardour. Anyway, I shall be with you for most of the way there and back."

"OK, Colonel. I'll do it." Julia was none too confident that tomorrow would be a wholly enjoyable experience. But a day away from the Medway, in February, had to be an opportunity not to be lightly dismissed. The 1574th was still mourning the loss of Hank Gregson, missing without explanation.

"What's the timing on this mission, Colonel?"

*   *   *

It was after 10:00 that Colonel Julius "Jules" Knapp, Makepiece's brother-in-law, of the USAAC in Europe intelligence staff was greeting shaking hands for his first meeting with RAF Wing Commander Cliff

'The Sprite' Battel outside the entrance to the bunker at Dawes Hill. Makepiece had forewarned Jules so that the latter did not show his reaction to the burn disfigurement on the RAF officer's face and hands.

Makepiece was doing the introductions, "Jules — meet the 'The Sprite' who the RAF has seen fit to assign to the 1574th as liaison to keep our P-38s flying straight by their rules. Cliff — meet Julius Knapp who is my link with the real world and reads all my mail going back to DC. This is not the place to talk missions, but you both have the same ABLATIVE tickets."

This was not strictly true. Battel had not been fully indoctrinated about the nuclides target of the SPSG mission. Jules knew this. But it was the nature of ABLATIVE security that Battel believed he was party to the complete story.

"Jules — The Sprite is taking some photographs down to Medmenham in my car for Babs and her cohort interpreters to pore over and admire for their artistry; Babs and the Sprite are sparing partners of old! I've brought your pack of the same pictures which I will explain when we get inside."

Then addressing Julia Greenburg who was holding the rear door open for the Wing Commander to be driven away, "Sergeant, be back here at 15:30. I expect we shall be going straight back to Snodland." She saluted her colonel and made it plain that she wanted the RAF officer to get in where he could do least damage — the back seat.

The two colonels did not delay in going into the bunker and moving into the intelligence area.

*   *   *

"While I am doing the coffee, read this. A P-51 Mustang jockey filed this report four days back. Note the time." Jules handed Makepiece the incident report about the strange explosion over the Thuringen area of central Germany. Makepiece noticed that the American pilot had used the place description as 'the Harz mountains area'.

"Now see this." This second report had been filed by a specially modified B-17 equipped for ELINT collection. This was an unpopular mission with the bomber crews because the weight and space occupied by the sensor with its operator cost payload, or fuel and a mid-fuselage gun station. But the airborne electronics had captured the signals of two radars associated with a surface to air missile engagement in addition to heightened activity in the normal *Luftwaffe* airspace management when a bombing raid was in progress.

Again Jules said, "Note the time. Because our airborne sensor was moving, the ELINT got cross bearings so we can get some idea of the ground radars' location. But this time our operator said his equipment failed a few moments later. The maintenance report attached to the intel summary, which they would not normally send although sensibly they have attached it to this one, says that some of the B-17's kit had fried beyond recovery."

"You are suggesting a link with Hank Gregson...?"

"Makepiece, in the words of the bard, you ain't seen nothing yet! I'll just tell you that the B-17 continued flying home OK. The spooks normally keep this next stuff out of our aircrew's hands in case they meet an unfriendly SS interrogator if they have to walk home. But this set of clippings is the expurgated version out of Bletchley Park concerning the day's events. It doesn't get more secret than this!"

Knapp passed his brother-in-law a sheaf of papers marked 'MOST SECRET ULTRA' in red. Makepiece was quite used to handling this security classification level of paperwork; it would have to be rather special to cut much ice with him. He knew of no process whereby material more sensitive than ULTRA would be handled, but he would not expect to have been told of such a mechanism without a special briefing and it was likely to be marked 'UK Eyes Only'.

"It seems that Hitler's mob suffered a major communications blackout timed around this explosion. The damage reports seem to radiate out to 50 km from a place called Ohrdruf, where there is tank testing range and some other funny goings on. It happens to coincide with the ELINT fix. Seems that the hun went berserk and blamed everyone for anything worse than halitosis! So, when they found out that a Kraut missile had shot down a Kraut Me-163 Komet, denying Göring of one of his finest test pilots, instead of a visiting ferret, then it was curtains for lots of folks. There is even a report of a special order of piano wire by one SS execution crew."

"And...?" Makepiece, grateful he was seated, was wondering if there could possibly be more. There was.

"Enter the boffins: RV Jones and his lads in the Air Ministry in uptown London. They say that there has been concern that if anyone ever set off an atomic bomb, an electro-magnetic pulse — they call it EMP for short — would be triggered. What EMP does is what lightning does to any adjacent wires. It makes them get hot, melting hot. But an EMP event is a spherical radiation, not straight like lightning. So any electrical conductor, not having a proper shielding or an earth, would act like an aerial and shoot the pulse along to the nearest electrical earth — which could be your nearest telephone exchange, or radio set, or radar, or whatever. Power lines and pylons are especially vulnerable, with enough energy in the pulse to blow the sub-stations to Valhalla. It's not selective, this EMP stuff. It just fries copper, and steel, and iron and anything else. Your wrist watch, your dental fillings, your spectacles, anything. 'Nearest' is manner of speaking; EMPs ain't discriminatory like Alabama. They goes any which way they damn well like and are nasty over oodles of miles — radiation-wise. Nearby aeroplanes are particularly attractive to it; railway lines too. That's London's theory, anyway, and it seems they may have found the proof for this hypothetical brand of pudding."

"Are you saying that someone is saying that the Krauts were testing an atomic weapon against my Hank?" Makepiece had completely forgotten about his coffee.

"No. The boffins don't think so. Bletchley Park swears there is no evidence to support a nuclear event. But since no-one has done it, let off an atomic bomb, who knows what to look for? The smart money is that the EMP was an unexpected side effect from an exceptional hot burn with an unusual chemical mix."

Makepiece said, "I'm no chemist. You know there will be no hope of getting anything back from the P-38. If anything had gone wrong, Gregson would have done the honourable thing and there were built in certain automatic features to keep the P-38 and its kit out of enemy hands. Even his dog tags would have melted!" Shaking his head negatively, he offered, "But our tests of the destructors, stateside, didn't mention EMP or anything close."

"Spare me the details, Makepiece." Jules heaved a sigh. "We're saying it was a Kraut effect, not Makepiece's fault! You and I are going to spend a couple of hours working out how to sanitize this pile of reports so that your pilots can have a briefing pack within the ABLATIVE rules. Then I want to talk with you about a report out of the Vatican, well our man working near the Bishop of Rome anyway, which indicates that Hitler may be building a pair of alternative Chancellery bunkers well removed from Berlin … spare funk holes if you will. This news will have double special interest to you since one area concerns this very same Ohrdruf in Thuringen mountains that we have been chatting about. The other is out Poland way, round about Katowice where your man Bates got some unusual signals and DC have spent lots of manhours exploiting the COMINT recording film he brought back."

"And? Is there any more?" Makepiece recognised the symptoms in an intelligence officer who had the bit between his teeth, an interested audience, and most important knew something he wanted to say but had not yet got around to.

"Oh! Yes! There is ALSOS."

Glancing towards the ceiling, "Am I going to like this, Jules? I just have the feeling that…"

"First things first, Makepiece! Let's have a go at the briefing pack for your crew so that my guys can type up a draft before you leave. You might want to leave early when I've told you about ALSOS, a certain general name of Donovan, and your Dr. Bernard Weiss, Specialist Scientific Officer, requested by the Commander 1574th SPSG for expertise in radio nuclides."

"And? Is there any more?"

"'fraid so, brother. Your coffee has gone cold. Shall I get you another cup? You're gonna need it."

Chapter 32
1944 ~ Hunt for a Nuclear Weapon

It was two and a half hours later that the two colonels reached the subject of Bernard Weiss and ALSOS.

"OK Jules, break the ice. What is ALSOS and what about Donovan?"

"I am gonna assume you remember what the MANHATTAN Project is about." Jules got a nod from Makepiece but it did not interrupt what he had to say. "Roughly speaking, no-one is gonna beat us to the atomic bomb. FDR has said so, so it must be true. Out here on the front line, we don't need to know much more! Well, with Henry Stimson's agreement, there is going to be a separate intelligence operation, under the MANHATTAN Project and with men chosen by the project's Brig Gen Leslie R Groves. What they are going to do is look at all the evidence and assess how far the Germans have got with atomic bomb research. Right out of your book, ain't it? But these ALSOS troops have gotten clout. They are headed up by a Lieutenant Colonel Boris T Pash…"

"Never heard of him!" offered Makepiece with a shrug.

"…who's a school teacher turned Army intelligence officer, who took a lead in the security investigation of MANHATTAN's top honcho scientist called Robert Oppenheimer. These guys report into MANHATTAN channels only, information fed to them is a one way ride, zilch feedback! Now the plan is that Pash's crew will be going in with the front line Tommys and GIs and may be going into no man's land — or even behind enemy lines — in search of information and top scientists. They are not being told any details of the MANHATTAN Project. This way, if they were captured, they could reveal nothing of use to the Germans. They're going into Italy behind the Allied armies as they push deeper into Europe and, ultimately, into Germany itself. Paper, designs, hardware, stockpiles, people and anything else remotely connected with atomic capability is going to be lifted out for our benefit. We're keeping it out of the Soviets hands too."

"So that is ALSOS." Makepiece paused then queried, "What does ALSOS mean?"

"It's so secret no-one knows. At least, I haven't seen any expansion if it is indeed an acronym. Now the general who runs MANHATTAN, and is therefore Colonel Pash's one star, is one Brigadier General Leslie Groves and the Greek word for grove is *alsos*. Coincidence?"

"OK, Jules. This presumably doesn't alter the way we work. If you want a particular target covered, you tell us. Right? If your customer is Pash, that is not my concern, right?"

"Hole in one, Brother. But the one to watch is Donovan. He's the big cheese in the cupboard. During the First World War, Donovan joined the United States Army and as a colonel in the 69th Infantry Regiment won the Medal of Honor and three Purple Hearts.

"You'd have thought he would have learned when to duck!"

"Shh, brother. While in Europe he visited Russia and spent time with Alexander Kolchak and the White Army. He ran unsuccessfully as lieutenant governor in 1922, but was appointed by President Calvin Coolidge as his assistant attorney general. In 1932, he was the Republican candidate for the post of governor of New York. So he has a political track record on the Hill. Enter Franklin D. Roosevelt, elected president in 1932, and by now this man Donovan is a millionaire Wall Street lawyer. He announces he shares the President's concern about political developments in Nazi Germany and so, in 1940, Donovan gets picked to take part in several secret fact-finding missions in Europe. You could argue that Donovan was, at least in part, responsible for our being ready to help Churchill when asked. Come July 1941, Roosevelt appoints Donovan as his Coordinator of Information. A year later, Donovan gets appointed Head of the Office of Strategic Services (OSS), an organisation that was given the responsibility for espionage and for helping the resistance movement in Europe."

Makepiece was nodding to encourage his brother to continue.

"Along the way, chummie Donovan seems to have struck up a friendly relationship with Britain's MI6 chief, Stewart Menzies. Anyway, Donovan was given the rank of major general and is building a team of more than 10,000 agents to operate behind enemy lines. The means: Germany, Austria, Italy, Denmark, France; you name it and Donovan will be opening a store. This rapid growth of the OSS has done him no favours with John Edgar Hoover who sees it as a rival to the Federal Bureau of Investigation. Of course it isn't, the FBI is strictly US mainland, the OSS strictly offshore. But that's Washington politics for you."

Makepiece's eyebrows rose with concern. "Are you thinking that Donovan will make a play for the 1574th?" Makepiece queried.

"I don't rightly know, Makepiece. But he plays with the big boys. The word here is that Donovan wants his own air force to drop his agents behind the lines. He may even be making a play for his own airfield near the RAF special agents' ferry port at RAF Tempsford."

Makepiece's body language displayed his belief that anything was possible in this man's air corps. "Thanks for that heads-up, as the RAF keep saying. Anything else while we're face to face?"

"I've been saving the best for last, Makepiece."

The guest's eyes rolled into his head in anticipation.

"The wraps on this are so tight that it's not written down here. Bletchley Park got a day's code break into the Russian spy network in the former Poland feeding Moscow. And, guess what: the Soviet agent was reporting a major project in the former Wenceslas Mines, on the former Polish/Czech border and Katowice is close enough to send their kids to school. Apparently these mines were once good for silver and other ore, but are now mainly worked out. But the Germans like holes in the ground and our chum, Agent Ivan, just happened to be reporting on a significant bang and lots of dead bodies and smoke coming out of one particular entrance where he just happened to be."

Once again, Julius held Makepiece's full attention.

He continued, "Sounds familiar? It should. So now we have a Russian interest in the place where there are underground explosions quite similar to the one your guy brought back in that sniffer sample. Well, I've seen the report. DC are very interested and want more sniffs."

The staff colonel noticed that Makepiece was becoming agitated. Nevertheless, he continued.

"I said it was too risky to fly at that range, fuel usage and such, but they say they need to know. And they want the sniffer at low altitude for maximum particle collection. So, somehow, you've got the challenge of making your P-38 go further than ever before ... and lower too. Call in at an autobahn diner and refuel, perhaps?"

There was a twinkle in Jules' eyes which did nothing to calm his colleague.

"Do you want some more coffee?" Jules offered.

Shaking his head in disbelief, Makepiece moaned, "Do you know what you are asking? We already stretch..."

"I know, I know. But the powers, that be, want! He who pays the piper calls the tune."

Makepiece replied, "I'll work on it with my guys and see what we can come up with." His head was shaking negatively. "But we can't risk an aircraft falling into German hands."

"Enough said, Makepiece. I'll let you chew on it. You haven't asked me about your man — your Dr. Bernard Weiss."

"Am I going to like this?" His question brought a shrug of Jules' shoulders.

"ALSOS want your man... to work in London. There is no point in arguing. If he goes to work with Pash, he's got to be cut off the ABLATIVE source, directly at least. Will you object?"

"The aim of the game is to beat the Germans, not to defend my team." Makepiece could recognise the needs of the bigger picture; it was part of his character. He shrugged at the inevitability. "All I ask is that staff delays his reassignment to look as if I have no choice and neither does he. He kicked up a rumpus the night he arrived at the 1574th in an air raid. He'll find things rather noisier in London."

"Lunch?" suggested Julius Knapp.

"Just before we move, Weiss has told me that our P-38 sniffer filters have to get in closer to pick up any particles in a dust or smoke plume. That means low flying and that costs fuel. So I need him near while we work out an optimum collection pattern. I'll get him to check in his channels of communication about this EMP thing and magnetic anomaly detection. The big question is: 'With our magnetic detector in the tailplane, are we carrying an attractor of trouble?' We don't want it inducing high currents inside our airframes."

"Uhm!" responded Jules.

"Jules, buy me 10 more days of Weiss's time. Ike ain't gonna invade while there's snow in Europe. ALSOS can wait 10 days more."

"Lunch." As he stood, Makepiece said, "Should we look in on your team to see how they are doing with that draft?"

"Uhm! OK, Makepiece, I'll do my best. Sit down, I've gotten a final snippet before I die of hunger. Kammler."

Colonel Knapp immediately had Ploughman's full attention.

"Your team telegraphed a query about a top hun nasty called General Kammler. Do you want the poop now or later?"

"I'll have it now, brother Jules," replied Makepiece. His smile indicated he would rather have some goodish news now to settle what had gone on before. He suddenly, for no obvious reason, wondered about The Sprite. 'Has Julia abandoned him? Had Babs revolted at the return of this man into her sphere of influence? Problems for later…? I hope not!'

"He's a bit elusive is Hans Kammler — Doktor Hans Friederick Karl Franz Kammler, Engineer, born 26 August 1901 and made a senior officer in the SS by Himmler. He's so behind the scenes that we don't even have a photograph. Kammler is a go-getter with ambition. Sources say he is ruthless to the point of paranoia. Peenemünde test range owes a lot to his efforts and a source close to the Swiss Red Cross says he's instrumental in enlargement of the concentration camps. We believe there is friction between Himmler and Speer about the way that Kammler has cast his net over the Germany's high technology weapons such as their rocket programmes. Kammler's forte is construction and organisation."

Makepiece was again nodding encouragement as his brother-in-law continued. Now there was heightened interest in every word said. Makepiece had believed for some time, that the solution to his mission was to get a firm hold on Kammler's activities.

"I would not be surprised if he was instrumental in the underground factories in the Harz Mountains, Hitler's alternate bunkers, maybe their atomic bomb or even the 'war winning weapon' we're all trying to find. Follow Kammler, just like King Wenceslas's footprints in the Polish Christmas snow, and my money is that you'll find your ultimate killing machine."

Their thinking was aligned. "Wenceslas is the name of a hole in the ground, not a regal lyricist," said Makepiece.

"Uhm!"

"Lunch?" prompted Makepiece. "Your team first?"

"Give them a bit longer. Lunch!" beckoned Jules with a sideways nod of his head.

*   *   *

194

Adjutant Major Clarke McKing had been summoned to the Colonel's office the following morning. His instructions were quite clear: he was to organise a wake for the memory of Hank Gregson, in the O'Club, beginning at 18:30. All officers except those on duty were expected to attend; of course civilian contractors with officer status would wish to pay their respects. The adjutant was to arrange a funeral parade for tomorrow, adjacent to the lamella hangar, where a suitable interment ceremony was to be held. The adjutant was to beg, borrow or kidnap a military chaplain, preferably American, to officiate. The duty pilot, returning from his mission would conduct a solo flypast in keeping with the traditions of saluting lost colleagues.

The RAF could certainly join the wake. The Sprite would advise the RAF air traffic control that a special American air event was to take place over West Malling airfield at 14:00 the next day. The funeral parade would have full military honours; a firing party of 12 GIs from Captain Jodell L Grant's security group would be trained using blank ammunition.

Chapter 33
1944 ~ A Wake

The wake had been going well. The O'club had adopted, and adapted, a 40 foot long nissen hut. The bar was set halfway along one wall, otherwise the walls were adorned with travel advertisements of American scenery. Nice things were being said about Hank Gregson, and his excellence as a pilot, and what a charming officer he was, and how popular he was with the ladies of Chatham. The station's officer cadre, American and British, had assembled with most standing near the bar. The only absentee was Major Cuthill, scheduled to fly tomorrow's mission taking off at 03:45: no alcohol and hopefully a decent sleep were his orders.

Makepiece had selected the corner where the bar joined a wall. From this vantage point he could judge if the party was getting out of hand. This wake was an opportunity for the tensions of war to momentarily relax. The floor was uncarpeted linoleum, a sensible precaution in a room where spillage was common. A well-worn upright piano stood against a distant wall.

It was at 19:30 that the adjutant appeared with a 2 foot cube cardboard box, of strong construction. Its lid was under the box, but the contents were hidden from view by a folded Stars and Stripes ensign. Clarke McKing stood on a bar chair and called for silence.

"Ladies and Gentlemen. Tomorrow we shall inter, with due military ceremony, the worldly remains of Lieutenant Hank Gregson, United States Army Air Corps, renowned pilot of the 1574th Special Projects Security Group. In this representational casket I have assembled the remains to be buried in a corner of an English airfield which will always be America. Those that wish may view the remains. I have protected the accidental viewing by those who may be distressed by covering the contents in our national flag."

Clarke climbed off the chair and went to get himself another can of Budweiser[tm]. It allowed him the opportunity to exchange nods with his commanding officer; evidently so far so good.

Someone gingerly lifted the flag off the box. Within it was laid an officer's best field cap, a baseball glove, a belt with a two piece clasp representing the coital joining of human genitalia and two copies of

196

Razzle^{tm} magazine. A US five dollar bill lay in the upturned cap; clipped to it was a note which read: 'To tip the cabbie for the final taxi ride'. A cellophane sleeve contained a US Pilot's wings badge, a standard issue prophylactic pack and a pair of Lieutenant's epaulette rank bars.

The usual bar banter was a little subdued. It was time for the pilot's tall stories to begin. Their exaggeration deepened as the alcohol flowed. It was entirely appropriate that, initially, the stories concerned Hank.

Patrick 'Supershot' Guthrie, at age 29, some 4 years older than Hank, had trained with Hank as 'Americans in Canadian uniform' flying for the RAF. The RAF had dispatched them to Rhodesia in southern Africa to earn their wings. Hank Gregson had been sent on a long distance navigation exercise where a navigation turning point was a settler's farmstead.

'Supershot' Guthrie set the scene, "Hank had stopped off for lunch, done a spot of game shooting — as you do — and had the head of a gazelle mounted to be sent back to the States."

"Yeh! Yeh!"

"Don't know why the Brits sent him training." The American was waving generally at the RAF officers sporting wings brevets on the uniforms. "The boy was a real natural aviator." Supershot was warming to his theme. "Born in a biplane, he was, out Idaho way where they do things right. His father wanted to call him Orville but his mother would have none of it. So Hank learned to fly before he could walk, instead, and he had more flying hours upside down in the dark than the limey instructors had got right way up."

"A natural," announced a voice in the audience.

"Are you going to tell how you got the nickname 'Supershot'?" came another voice from somewhere near the bar.

"He won't, he's too bashful," chimed in Rod Chmielewski. "He and Hank were flying Hurricanes with the Brits in France, in 1940, before Dunkirk and all that. The Krauts christened him *'der sargfüllstoff'*. Now that's quite a load for the British to say, even when they're sober, or for a Yank to say when he ain't, so they changed it to 'Supershot'. It turns out that the Gerrys didn't want to fly their Stukas in France when they heard that Patrick *der sargfüllstoff* Guthrie was flying. Oh no siree!"

All eyes were on Rod telling his tale. Even Makepiece wondered how tall this tale would go?

"It seems our Patrick got a reputation for collecting parts off Stukas he shot down, six I heard at the last count, before it was time to walk away. Story has it that Patrick didn't fancy German hospitality after Dunkirk so he decided to swim the Channel and was picked up by an Air-Sea Rescue launch which happened to be passing."

"Are you going to tell us what '*der sargfüllstoff*' means in German speak?"

"Well," Chmielewski adopted his most thoughtful visage. "The shame of it is that there is no real English equivalent. I guess '*the coffin filler*' is a pretty good approximation."

"Close enough for government work?" There was a general uproar at the tale.

"It's all rubbish." Lieutenant Lorne Amhurst from the intelligence processing staff gave his interpretation. "All that coffin stuff is a cover story for the truth. Fact is that 'Supershot' Guthrie is a dab hand at pointing his F26 camera. When he was briefed out on the training route, he was told that he had to take a vertical shot over a certain Scottish farmhouse up near Thurso. When he came back, his vertical was so vertical that we could see down the chimney and count the number of pieces of peat on the hearth."

Patrick Guthrie with feigned bashfulness came in with, "I thought we were here to talk about Hank. I wonder how many of you know that he was the first fighter pilot to carry out a solo leaflet raid over a German airfield. While we were in France, he went to the squadron orderly room and had 100 notices printed on the Roneo^{tm} duplicating machine. The next time we scrambled on an airfield strafing run, he broke away from the pack and went over low. He turned his Hurricane upside down with the cockpit open and let the leaflets fall out telling the *Luftwaffe* that the RAF had enjoyed the party. Story has it that the Germans forgot to close the hangar doors while they were picking up their letters from Hank. He did another pass so low that he flew through their hangar, bagging another couple of Junkers on the way."

There was considerable whooping and roaring at that tale. Someone managed to order another half-dozen Budweisers^{tm} from the barman.

Edward 'Edge' Cryshaw joined in with, "It's a real shame that 'Whiffenpoof' isn't here. He drew the colonel's short straw and has to fly tomorrow." Makepiece waved his beer-can in acknowledgement of the reference to him.

No-one knew why he was called 'Whiffenpoof' Cuthill; of course there were rumours. He could not sing nor had he any known association with the Whiffenpoofs of Yale University. It certainly was not the name Mr and Mrs Cuthill wanted for their son. Military aviation rarely respects parental choice when nicknaming the characters in a unit.

'Edge' continued, "While we are telling the truth…" Uproar. "…I have heard it said that 'Whiffenpoof' does not like the smell of unwashed socks. He claims that the *Luftwaffe* are particularly unhygienic with regard to their feet since they rarely have time to take their boots off before they have to march the goose step for Göring. So their feet get whiffy. And Major Cuthill can whiff these feet coming before the siren sounds so he scrambles into the sky and 'poof' — another nasty German bites the dust." Laughter and cheers.

"You're exaggerating again," came a voice from the back of the room. The room turned to look at the speaker, a relatively older man than the remainder of the group who was waving a beer-can at the 'Edge'. The speaker was assigned to intelligence duties in the group.

"Whiffenpoof has no fear of flying over water. He says that it's a scandal that the War Department has to buy him a Mae West life preserver in case he ditches in the Channel or wherever. He says that he's related by marriage through the female line to one of the aunts of Mary — you know that Mary…" the speaker was pointing upwards in the hushed room and nodding at the ceiling, "…that Mary. So if he ditches in the drink, all he needs to do is to get out and walk."

The near blasphemy silenced the room, until, "It's not fair to disparage a pilot who's not here to defend himself." It was Rod Chmielewski again. "You're going on about the only person I've seen fly an aeroplane backwards."

There were various comments about bovine excreta and the like. The Americans understood the British accepted that '*bull shit*' was Yankee humour. But Rod was not about to be diverted from his line shoot. Makepiece hadn't heard this one…

"It's true, I tell you. I saw him fly a Havard out west. He had been throwing the ship about the skies when he put the nose up and stopped. Now most pilots would let the aeroplane roll to one side and pull it through. At the very most a pilot might set up a tail slide. But with his engine going at max chat, Whiffenpoof controlled that Havard hanging on its engine as the damned machine moved backwards in the skies. He's never let on how he did it. It wasn't an illusion. I'm telling you that he flew the aeroplane backwards."

There was silence, that hanging silence of professional disbelief. Then someone started to make a noise which resembled singing. It was a sort of hymn to 'Whiffenpoof' and quite popular with different words on the bomber groups' stations:

> *"I'm a solo pilot who has lost his way.*
> *Baa! Baa! Baa!*
> *My P-38 has gone astray.*
> *Baa! Baa! Baa!*
> *Ploughman's pilots over Germany.*
> *Doomed from here to Eternity,*
> *Lord have mercy on such as we.*
> *Baa! Baa! Baa!"*

Sarah Johansson whispered in WAAF officer Bethany Taverner's ear, "Can you persuade your old man to give us a tale from the other war?"

"I'll try, but I don't hold too much hope."

Five minutes later, Squadron Leader Percy Davenport who by now was ruddy about the cheeks under the influence of copious Jack Daniels[tm], was standing insecurely on a chair. Rod Chmielewski banged his glass on the bar for quiet.

"I think it's about time to hear an old-timer's line-shoot. Come-on Percy, tell us about real pursuit pilots."

The reluctant First World War pilot was regaled with the clubroom chants:

> *"Tell us another one,*
> *Just like the other one,*
> *Tell us another one, do…"*

"Fighter pilots, Colonel, that's what we call them. You jonnie-come-lately colonists may…" a Brit addressing Yanks in this manner was sure to draw some reaction, which it did, "...I say again, may, care to hear about Ludwig."

"Tell us a Ludwig one,
Just like the other one,
Tell us a Ludwig one, do..."

"Ludwig joined our squadron in June '16. We were operating Bristols behind Ypres. Ludwig wasn't his real name. From memory that was *Hans orf Klosterkeller von Schitzundshovelven*. He lived to make Captain rank. Trouble was that the adjutant ran out of chalk every time his name went up on the Operations Board so he had to be rechristened."

"What was a name like that doing in the British Air Force?" questioned Makepiece from near the piano. He was pleased to see how morale was holding up in these circumstances.

"In those days it was the Royal Flying Corps, old lad. They say he was trying to emigrate to Baltimore, but the porter lied when he asked if the boat had docked at New York. He got off at Portsmouth before the liner had started its crossing to America. So he joined the army for its food and the King said he could go and visit the Kaiser for payment." Percy Davenport was warming to his theme.

"Anyway, *Schitzund*... whatever, our secret weapon against the Red Baron, was related to Beethoven through his uncle's second cousin twice removed. So we had a cue. Then, one day, his flight commander noticed chummie, *Schitzund*... whatever, got lots of shoot-downs with economical use of his guns. He said using ammunition made him deaf, like his relative. Seems chummie, *Schitzund*... whatever, like to fire in bursts, like: 'Dah, Dah, Dah, Daaah' — the Morse code for V for Victory."

Percy's clenched fists were raised in front of his cheeks, juddering in mock gun recoil. It was unfortunate that one fist was holding a half-filled glass which did not remain contained in the squadron leader's hand.

"You all being music lovers will notice resemblance to a certain 5th Symphony, thereby anticipating chummie *Schitzund*... whatever, flying over the trenches, and the BBC using it in his memory. So *Schitzund*... whatever, got christened Ludwig. I heard it said that Churchill couldn't get the 'Dah, Dah, Dah, Daaah' out of his head, and that's where his two fingers V-sign comes from. Ludwig's story has a sad ending though."

The audience was spellbound and silent.

"Ludwig bought it out there and was buried alongside his comrades. Formation flying to the very end, you might say, in true Corps tradition. But no-one knew how to spell his real name; so *Schitzund*... whatever, is the guy who will forever rest in the grave of the 'Unknown Warrior'."

The silence lasted fully ten seconds. Then:

> *"That was a horrible one,*
> *Worse than the other one,*
> *Tell us another one, do..."*

But Percy Davenport had had his moment and was already dismounting his chair.

*   *   *

RAF liaison officer Sprite Battel had been standing quietly in the corner listening to this banter. He had heard many tall tales in his career and had no doubt contributed to some. To his mind there had been too many wakes for colleagues who 'bought it' and this one followed the pattern. It was an interesting variation on the theme to bring in a box of assembled remains from the man's locker. But Battel's fighter pilot's eyes missed little in the room. In particular, he noticed the reaction on the young intelligence WAAC Lieutenant's face when she looked under the American flag. It must have been the belt buckle that triggered some memory because her eyes saddened until she noticeably got control of her emotions and acted in a soldierly manner. Her moistened eyes blinked, her shoulders squared and she stood in a soldierly manner. She had said her goodbye to Hank Gregson.

The Sprite was not too sure that women and fighter pilots' drinking institutions were a good mix. However, they had chosen to join the men's world albeit without having an inkling of the goings on. So it seemed to Cliff Battel that, since the assembled American officers were actually inside an English boundary fence, it was only appropriate that Hank Gregson should be honoured in the RAF manner — his name written large on the ceiling. No matter that the curvature of the nissen hut took the ceiling 14 feet above ground level, that was, after all, part of the challenge and part of the honour.

Cliff Battel whispered something in the Colonel's ear and got a nod of approval.

"Nothing lewd now, Cliff! Remember that she is still of tender years. A good-looker and a reliable intel officer to be sure, but still of tender years. No disrobing while ladies are about and, if it goes too far, you'll be standing on the bar telling the assembled 1574th just how you came by the name 'Sprite'."

"Roger, wilco, over and out," jested the wing commander. "I say, chaps, if this was an RAF mess, we'd write Hank's name on the ceiling."

"Can't be done, old lad. We ain't got no ladders."

"RAF's got sky hooks," was another remark.

"We know where there are some WAAFs with a spare balloon and some extracurricular uses for Trojans[tm]."

"Listen to him, we're using grown up words now. Extracurricular indeed!"

"We don't need ladders when we've got pilots." Cliff was moving towards RAF Squadron Leader Adrian Wilburne, technically the host nation's station commander for RAF Snodland's lodger units. Wilburne could sense trouble coming.

"Need some RAF types to show these Yanks how it's done. Do you think old timer Percy Davenport of Balloon Squadron fame is game for it?" Wilburne was grateful because he wasn't alone in being co-opted.

"Bound to be, sir," replied Adrian to his superior officer. "Percy was probably writing words in the sky when Pontius was a Pilate."

"And you were his navigator!" retorted Battel.

The Station Commander continued unimpressed, "You might even get his Queen Bee to show her muscles. Mighty proud of her gels was Flight Officer Bethany Taverner WAAF, and with some justification. I'd love to have a got a Heinkel of my own!"

"Plenty of war left yet, old son. But for the moment let's round up all the light blue jobs and get the pyramid in the sky."

"I say, sir," said Percy. "I suppose we've got a candle and someone who can write?"

"No sooner asked than solved, old son." Cliff leaned over the bar and lifted two emergency lighting candles and a box of matches. He thumped the bar top with the side of his ungloved fist in order to get some quiet. "They teach girls to read and write in schools these days..."

"With the Colonel's permission," he started, "we have to build a pyramid. Simple rules: rule one: the heaviest on the bottom, lightest on the top. Ladies may remove their shoes and anything else to lessen the weight. Eight of you blokes at the base, four stacked on their shoulders and two lightweights at the top. By presidential decree the pinnacle of our pyramid shall be shared by Bethany Taverner (enemy bomber downer of repute) in the British corner, and by Sarah Johansson (intel officer and motivator for photographing the most difficult targets in the Third Reich) in the American corner. Rule two: gentleman shall avert their upwards glances while the ladies are performing their scribing duties and will give no guidance on how to spell 'Hank Gregson.' I shall be standing on the bar to ensure adherence to the rules. Chocks away, switches on, start."

The confusion developed into a melee as the middle layer began to climb and stabilise on the shoulders of the lower rank. Then came the turn of the ladies to climb the tower. There were the inevitable cat whistles, and bawdy comments, and there was little dignity as the ladies rose to the top. One whispered to the other and off came the ladies' jackets.

"More, more!"

"You aren't supposed to see what the ladies are doing, you dirty young man," scoffed The Sprite. A foot in the face stopped a disgusting reply from the base support.

"Oh damn," swore The Sprite. "I forgot to light the candles. Girls, you'll have to come down and get them. Careful now, we don't want any injured pilots. And we don't want any hot wax treatment while you are up there."

It did not take long for the ladies to get back to the summit and, writing in candle smoke, to trail 'Hank Gregson' in soot across the white ceiling.

"Right," said The Sprite. "That's a job well executed. The ladies may dismount and the gentlemen may study the work of art."

The American judgement was that the job had indeed been well done and the ladies ought to be rewarded. The Edge, never slow in coming forward, announced, "We have a tradition in San Antonio which requires that a lady who performs a service shall receive her due deserts." So saying, he picked a soda water siphon off the bar and, with fizzy soda water, dowsed the blouses of the two lady climbers.

"Not so fast," said Bethany, well aware that the men's view while she was at the summit had been rather more flash of her flesh than was customary and wet linen blouses tend to cling to their contents. "There is also an RAF tradition which says that any male officer who takes advantage of a lady in the bar shall be debagged. Gentlemen, I believe that Sarah and I have been taken advantage of by that officer." A condemning finger was pointing at Wing Commander Battel. "Accordingly, it is the wish of the WAAF Queen Bee that the drones present shall do their duty by the Sprite's trousers."

Seeing the piles of arms and legs and bodies of masculinity on the floor, the ladies decided it was expedient to leave. All the ladies, that is, except Cherrylinda 'Frau Noir Net' Gildenstern of the American Red Cross; she would later say that she had never seen anything like it and was really pleased to be at the bottom of the pile. She had no idea who had removed one of her black net stockings, but had a vague memory of enjoying the experience.

Chapter 34
1944 ~ A Pilot's Salute

Sergeant Hannah Black sat at the visual Air Traffic Control console in the glass canopy on the roof of the ATC tower. Her role as duty 'Local Controller' gave 360° all round visibility of the West Malling airfield. She was paying particular attention, through her field glasses, to the American parade in front of their lamella hangar, on the other side of the grass airfield.

Their RAF Liaison Officer had telephoned the Senior ATC Officer advising that the 1574th would be doing an honorary flypast in the traditions of their service to a lost pilot. The event was timed for 14:00.

'This could be something different — break up the routine,' she mused. 'Life here was seldom boring, but the Yanks scarcely caused any bother, so…'

The sky was clear of aircraft. Sergeant Black had noted that the Senior Air Traffic Control Officer (SATCO), on the ATC Tower's balcony, had been joined by 'The Wing Co' as the Station Commander was known. Both RAF officers had field glasses also. Wing Commander J A O'Neil had been in command of RAF West Malling since 1 February 1944 and had little experience of the exuberances of the outfits along the road at RAF Snodland, especially the American SPSG. The only thing untoward in sight was the balloon, presumably flown by the Snodland girls, which tethered at a low 500 feet. But it was 2 miles outside the airfield flying pattern and today the visibility was excellent. There was no cause for concern over safety today.

It was 13:57 when the radio in her console came to life. She nodded at her clerk to instruct him to note the time in the log. It was routine procedure.

"Securité, Securité, Securité."

A pilot was calling on the West Malling local control radio frequency using the call word to indicate that he was experiencing some aeronautical difficulty short of actual risk to aircraft or life. But a 'Securité' call demanded priority attention. Sergeant Black's training cut in.

"This is West Malling tower, Securité, what is your callsign and status?" She snapped her fingers at the clerk to jack the line into the loudspeaker so that SATCO and the Station Commander could hear the radio exchange, outside, on the balcony.

"Securité, Securité, Securité. This is Two Screws ploughing a furrow across Kent and requesting landing clearance, over." The voice was certainly American, recognisable even through the radio distortion.

"Use correct procedures, Securité, what is your callsign and what is the nature of your problem? Over."

"This is Securité, just need to put this ship on Mother Earth." The accent was certainly American.

"Securité, correct procedures please!" Sergeant Black, unflustered, knew she had to remain calm. "I have planned traffic in two minutes, please state your callsign and status."

"Your fence in one minute. Securité. Two Screws here requesting clearance for final approach and landing." From outside SATCO looked in through the window to see how his sergeant controller was coping. She appeared very much under control; naturally, she had been a good student while he was an instructor at the ATC school.

Across the airfield the Americans had lined up 12 carbine-armed soldiers.

SATCO had a thought, 'Oh God, they're not going to execute someone!'

The field glasses were now scouring the skies looking for an aircraft in some kind of trouble. The eyes in the runway control cabin, at the landing end of the runway saw him first. The P-38 was at 10 feet altitude with his undercarriage still retracted. The runway controller's immediate reaction was to fire a double red Very pistol signal — the usual warning to the pilot break off the landing. The P-38 kept coming. Sergeant Black hit the red alarm button on her console to alert the fire and crash crews. The alarm repeated throughout the RAF station as the alert reached the distributed Tannoy speakers.

At that very moment, the balloon beyond the lamella hangar displayed two boot-black dyed sheets hanging from its underside tether.

"Securité, Two Screws requests permission for a fast taxi to lamella." The time was 13:59. The American voice sounded very relaxed. He had been strapped to his seat for more than 8 hours, talking to himself to relieve the boredom between sessions of intense activity.

"Aircraft over Malling runway. Go round, I repeat go round again! Your wheels are not down!" The clerk had fired two red Very pistol flares from the balcony and returned inside while Hannah Black was flashing a red Aldis lamp in the direction of the incoming P-38.

The way the pilot was manoeuvring the P-38 made it clear that he intended to do things his way. Sergeant Black's voice remained calm, but this was, after all, an American. Some allowance had to be made.

"You are cleared to join for taxi, if you can land! Use correct procedures, Securité."

At the controls of the P-38, 'Whiffenpoof' Cuthill pressed the transmit button on his control column. A single blip sounded on the radio speaker in the tower. He knew it was incorrect procedure, but it saved talking while he was busy. He was flying at 140 mph and so low the blades of grass parted to let him pass.

"Be advised, Securité, the runway in use is 06 and the wind is blowing steady at 8 knots from 070. We are flying right hand circuits today. Altimeter setting is 1012. There is a hydrogen obstruction north of the circuit."

The P-38 was now halfway across the airfield, 20 seconds short of the lamella hangar. Its engines were throttled back making its flight almost silent. Even this close the camouflaged P-38 was nearly invisible unless silhouetted against a cloud.

At precisely 14:00, the armed guard fired its first of three volleys over the open 'grave'. The P-38's engines were throttled up to full take-off power as its nose pointed towards the sky and the 12 ton machine came to an apparent stop in the sky. A Stars and Strips fluttered open halfway up a tethering guy beneath the balloon, its colours contrasting against the black mourning sheet.

Behind the lamella, the Salvation Army van appeared through the trees, its klaxon sounding. Its lady operator was delighted with the view of a waiting American queue for her trade and for an instant was unaware of a dozen tons of aircraft above her head. She hadn't been advised they were doing rifle practice today, but they were soldiers…

The P-38's twin Allison V-1710s, heavily uprated for the 1574th SPSG role, let out a banshee shriek at the unusual demands being made of them. Their parent aircraft had its nose pointed very high as the airframe hung on its propellers. 'Whiffenpoof' Cuthill had stabilised the aircraft nearly empty of fuel, for an instant, at 500 feet above the lamella security fence. The observing professionals watched in disbelief as the aircraft began to creep backwards against the forward thrust demands of the overboosted Allisons. The P-38 dipped its nose, as the water methanol injection did its trick, to sacrifice altitude in order to accelerate forwards towards safe flight speed.

The P-38 banked to its right to remain inside the airfield boundary, climbing and accelerating all the while, until it was flying downwind along the runway at 500 feet.

"Twin Screws for an upward charlie. They like it straight up — as the actress said to the bishop."

"Twin sc… Securité. Whatever. Correct procedures, ladies present."

The radio gave another blip as the P-38 climbed to 1000 feet and manoeuvred into normal flying attitude, with the cockpit uppermost, at the peak of its climb.

"Roll off the top — as the bishop said to the actress," announced the American radio transmission. SATCO and his wing commander watched with airmen's awe as the agile fighter was pulled around to be aligned into wind along the runway line. It was now in controlled descent.

"Two Screws for approach."

"Proceed, Two Screws. We have no additional traffic … call three greens…" It was her way of reminding the pilot to check his undercarriage was lowered and locked.

The radio gave another single blip. The P-38's nose was eased above the horizon as 'Whiffenpoof' pulled up for a loop under full engine power. When the P-38 was in the vertical climb the undercarriage doors began to open; while it was upside down the main landing gear locked into position; while it was in the vertical descent the aircraft's radio announced, "Two Screws, three greens for finals."

The aircraft's engines quietened as it settled for landing.

"You are clear to land, Two Screws. The wind is 070 at 8 knots." That calm, reassuring, female voice in his headphones was a very welcome return to normality.

"Two Screws for the fast taxi previously requested. Thanks for the pretty fireworks."

"Malling tower. You are clear to proceed. Understand you intend full stop this time?"

The radio gave single blip.

"We appreciate correct procedures, Two Screws,"

The radio gave two blips.

"Good afternoon, Two Screws. Be advised that our new three ringer and the SATCO are proceeding in your general direction. Suggest you switch off your radio as the interview might be a bit one sided."

The radio sounded a single blip.

Sergeant Hannah Black, at her console in the glass canopy on the roof of the ATC tower, pressed her radio transmit button to give the P-38 pilot a single blip. She looked at the clock and ran the palm of her hand over her hair. The time was 14:03. Her nod at her clerk instructed him to note the time in the log. It was routine procedure. The distant barrage balloon, with its appendages, had disappeared. The lamella hangar doors were already opening to accept the recently landed P-38.

Sergeant Hannah Black instructed her clerk, "Stand down the emergency crews; incident concluded at 14:04 local time."

Wartime calm settled over the RAF airfield — except for an RAF staff car, sporting the Commanding Officer's pennant, making a fast transit towards the American compound.

Sprite Battel looked at his colonel. "Blimey, Colonel, you Yanks do it in style! Looks like you've got visitors."

"No other way, Wing Commander. When you've gotta go, you've gotta go! Now, what do you think your man is gonna say when I invite him for coffee?" Sprite noticed Makepiece's chewing the inside of his cheek could not conceal his satisfaction of having witnessed one of the most impressive flying displays ever in a combat machine.

Chapter 35
March 1944 ~ Miracle in London Town

It was the Monday, 6th of March. A clock chimed the three quarters past nine o'clock. In the London morning mist, the already limited view from the steps of the British Museum was lessened by the hanging moisture. Makepiece could just make out the wall where the railing had been cut away for war metal. There were few people moving about. He was waiting for Aynette.

She had told him that she had an 8:30 appointment in Harley Street — nothing to worry about, women's business — and she would stay in town overnight to avoid difficulties with early morning travel. Makepiece discovered what she meant: the crowded trains pouring in the London termini were uncomfortable, sweaty, unventilated and, before daylight, had their window blackout pulled down. As his mud-flecked, green, Southern Region, electric train moved gingerly through the south east outskirts of London, towards his destination at Charing Cross, the fog restricted visibility to 100 yards.

He had arranged a 48 hour furlough, 2 nights in London. Yes, he would call the duty officer when he had checked into his hotel.

"Catch a couple of shows, I guess. Just relax. Nothing planned."

"That's good, Colonel. We'll all be here when you all get back. Keep your umbrella up. If it's not raining, the Krauts will do their best to catch you out with their nasty bits of metal. It's what *Luftwaffes* do!"

Makepiece had made his way past the book shops of Charing Cross Road and on towards the museum. Shop windows that were not shuttered had crosses of adhesive paper glued against glass shattering. London was miserable, dark and dank in the late winter, dirty, drifting mist, and unwelcoming. Everyone he passed appeared downcast in these cold conditions with scarves seeking to retain the last vestige of bodily warmth. His abiding impression was lack of colour and plenty of damp grime. The chill seemed to penetrate right through to his spine. Even the many military uniforms moving through the shops appeared dark, some even soaked. He hoped that Aynette would not be delayed from lighting his world. She had said that she would make all the arrangements. There was nothing else to do but wait.

"About 9:45," she had said, "assuming I can get a cab. Don't worry, Makepeice, I'll walk if I have to. If I say the steps of the British Museum, we can't possibly miss each other."

The mist stirred at the last chime of the clock. A black London taxi drew up at the gate, its hooded headlights hardly showing in this light. A beam of bright sunlight came from nowhere and picked out a smartly dressed female climbing out of the rear door. A leg came out first, then a hat and finally a body. A dark coat with fashionable big shoulder pads was surmounted by a hat set not squarely on her neatly bunned hair.

'Even at this distance, I'd know those legs anywhere.' The woman was reaching into the cabbie to pay the fare, her stretched back was eye-catching even at so great a distance. Already the sun was breaking through as Aynette reached the steps and hurried up to her waiting colonel. She went one step above him, without speaking, threw her arms around his neck and kissed him.

"I hope you haven't been waiting long. It's too cold to hang about. Let's find a cup of something hot." She kissed him again and this time Makepiece responded.

"Is everything alright in Harley Street?" asked Makepiece, fully aware that it was the centre of medical excellence in England. "You look incredible…"

"Couldn't be better, my own knight. I'll tell you later. Now, tea. And on the way I'll buy you a hat so that you can pretend to be a civilian for 48 hours."

"My raincoat will give me away."

"More like the starch in your back, and that haircut, my knight. Take those bird colonel's eagles off and you'd pass for a spiv anywhere."

"What's a spiv?" The American colonel looked quite perturbed by the Britishism. He was far from sure that it was complementary. The chill in his back had disappeared. The answer, when it came, did little to set his mind at rest.

"A colonel without his eagles. Now let's walk. I've planned a London treat for you — a special Ploughman excursion. I'm pleased you like my coat…"

*　　　*　　　*

Morning tea was to be taken in Aynette's hotel.

"We shall stay here tonight. It's a bit old fashioned but we are right in the middle, convenient for the shows and everything else London has to offer. Let's take your bag up to the room."

"I have to check in with the base. Let them know how to contact me. It won't take a moment. Just in case… " He paused for a moment, "Am I using my real name?"

"I'm going to stand here while you make your call, so that you don't get trapped. Yes, I am a widow and this is war."

Then to the receptionist, "Colonel Ploughman is on my bill…" Makepiece wished she had not been so quick with his name; he was… is… a married man although the chance disclosure of his public association with this woman was very remote.

Aynette was speaking to Makepiece, "The concierge will give you a card with the hotel name and telephone number. We are in Room 204." It became clear to Makepiece that this was where she had stayed the previous night.

While Makepiece was making his call, Aynette was ordering a tray of tea from room service. Then it was into the lift, "…you mean we're taking the elevator… and surely this is the third floor…" and up to their room where they could be alone.

Fifteen minutes later, the couple were again in the foyer. Makepiece had a white silk scarf concealing his tie and military jacket. With his rank badges removed, his coat could have come from any army surplus store. The trilby felt unfamiliar to the American, but it fitted.

Aynette had offered no explanation for her rejection of his advances other than, "Later, my urgent knight, later."

She directed the cab to St Paul's Cathedral via Lincoln's Inn Fields, "Go right around the park once so that my friend can see the architecture… then along Holborn to drop us at Wood Street". As they passed through London, noticeably more damaged by bombing as they moved east, Aynette told Makepiece of her project.

"I am going to base my next novel on the Ploughman family history, just as it is recorded in Grandmother Susannah's heritage volume. I'll have to change some of the names, I suppose, but her heritage is documented through 250 years and I have access to all the history and records I could possibly need. Today we can visit where it all began, at least the emigration part anyway. Are you excited, my knight?"

Aynette's body had moved across the cab seat so that they were as close as could be, her arm under his, conveying enthusiasm for her project. She could sense his physical warmth through their touching thighs. The mildest hint of rosemary fragrance floated in the air.

"As we go around Lincoln's Inn — this is where good colonial lawyers came to learn their trade in the first decades of the 18th century. I can have some fun with Bernard the emigrant's grandson getting caught up in the London night life." She giggled at the prospect. "He'd turn in his grave if he knew what his descendents were going to be doing." Her thigh pressed against his.

"Well, an author may exaggerate a little. I am sorry they have taken away the railings here, too. But the park is there and the lawyers can have a romp on the grass..."

"Aynette," whispered Makepiece, turning to plant a kiss on her glowing cheek. "It's quite an undertaking writing a novel. But I would love to read how you fictionalise some of the most tumultuous times of the last 300 years. I would be pleased to help if I can. Are you going to put you and me...?"

"All in good time, my pilot man, all in good time."

The taxi dropped them behind St Paul's, standing resplendent and resilient against the worst the *Luftwaffe* could throw at it. All around the cathedral, the buildings were either flattened or severely damaged. The scene was familiar to Makepiece from the newsreels, even though it was the first time he had seen the ancient structure. A police barrier prevented access to Wood Street.

Aynette spoke, "In a manner of speaking that's where your roots are." She was pointing down what was left of the street. "It's a shame we can't get closer. But it would be different now from Grandmother Susannah's son Oswalde's time in the 1620s. In those years, they had a minor plague and a fire before the great troubles of 1665 and '66. But your Bernard, the emigrant, was probably conceived hereabouts and wisely moved out before it all got serious. Come on, there's lots to see. I hope those are your walking shoes..."

With Aynette's arm under his, welcomely pulling their hips together so they walked as one, their closeness enabled her to steer Makepiece east along Cheapside towards the bomb damaged Cannon Street railway station.

"Oh dear! There's not much left here either. I wanted to show you where St Mary's Bothaw church once stood. And a very special jeweller too. What a shame. It was mentioned in Susannah's papers. It all went in the Great Fire too. Never mind, a hundred yards or so up here, turn left and there should be a very special place."

Makepiece let her lead. He thought it was a tragedy that so much devastation was being wrought on these old streets. Turning left into Abchurch Lane, he could feel joy exuding through her body as she strode forward. The church known as St Mary's Abchurch, a little war

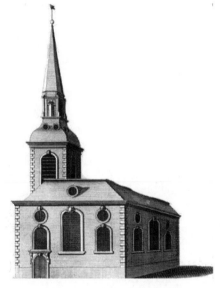

St Mary's Abchurch, London

blemished but still recognisable as a religious building, stood hemmed in by office buildings in a quiet backstreet off the busy Cannon Street.

"If there is a Ploughman's own church in London, this has got to be it. Can't you feel Oswalde and Elizabeth walking the aisle here, baby Bernard being christened here and then his marriage? It was rebuilt by Wren after the Great Fire, and Hitler has knocked it about a bit. But it's still here, open to all despite this horrible war. Outside is where Oswalde's daughter Abigale says her father and his two wives were buried, side by side. How romantic!"

"You really are enjoying this, aren't you?"

"Oh, Makepiece." The pull on his arm communicated her enthusiasm. "This is real history, not something out of a musty old book. Real blood and sinew, real bricks and mortar, real families and lives. Ploughman stuff. Come inside, sit for just a moment and savour the atmosphere. I don't know if you are a religious man... it doesn't matter now."

The screen behind the altar had been badly damaged and that wall looked rather bare. But a temporary altar had been set in place and some early spring flowers had been found to give a hint of colour to the otherwise grey blankness. It was a token of defiance against the desecration. Much of the roof was intact, although the painted dome had suffered, and had been made weatherproof with a tarpaulin. Makepiece was content to be with Aynette, sitting on an ancient pew, enjoying the moment and the place. In later years, his memory of this ancient place would be triggered again whenever he smelled the scent of rosemary, her fragrance. Deep within his essence, Aynette had become an element of his core, a guilty secret, which would never leave him.

"This is a place where memories are made," she whispered. "I can feel you are making memories here too." Her arm pulled his closer to her side. "Do you know — these pews are mostly originals from the Wren restoration and were once fitted with small kennels for the benefit of parishioners' pets in church!"

Makepiece found this detail unbelievable, but she was so positive with her story.

"If you are ready," Aynette said, "I'd like to move you on. We are going to see the Tower of London. I'll explain why when we get there. Why don't you sign the Visitor's Book?" She had to drag a reluctant bulk out of his seat and away from 'his' church.

Past the tall Monument to the Great Fire of London in 1666, 'Closed to Visitors' said the notice with the graffiti 'keeper's lost the key' added, and along Thames Street to the north bank of London's river. A short diversion into a newsagent's shop to purchase a post card and an overseas stamp, then onwards. Just beyond Tower Pier, with the great Tower Bridge spanning the river in full view, Aynette brought Makepiece to a stop. She leant him against the riverbank wall. In the March sunlight, marginally brightened by reflection off the Tower's century's old ramparts, she was glad to have her man's frame protecting her from the river's cold draught.

'Damn the consequences!' thought Makepiece. A squadron of *Luftwaffe* Stukas and a tsunami up the Thames would not have prised him away from his Aynette at that moment. He watched her delicious mouth as it began to speak.

"This is the spot I have chosen for second wife Elizabeth to tell Oswalde that he's going to be a father. With the sails and yardarms of the East Indiamen rocking on the Thames tide, providing their serenade, she'll tell him she's working on it being a boy and he, one day, will sail down the Thames and be a brave colonist trader in the New World of the Americas. Here they will kiss, in public, not caring what reaction they are drawing, and then they will hurry back home and make long, sweet, romantic, enduring, love."

"You've got it all mapped out, my comely author queen. You've gotten barrage balloons instead of ocean freighters."

"You bet I have! Now it's time you bought me lunch. All this walking and talking has given me an appetite. Comely, eh? We'll have to see about that."

Aynette smiled at her lover and reached up to give him a kiss.

"Just practising. I've got my memory to keep me warm." She smiled and he smiled back. "You'll have got to wait, my love. But they do say that all the best things come to he who waits."

She pressed herself against Makepiece who was unwilling and unable to move against the waist high wall. Her kiss was full of sweetness and warmth and promise.

Chapter 36
March 1944 ~ Russell Square, London

Eleven hours later, Makepiece was cleaning his teeth while Aynette was getting ready for bed on the other side of the closed door. He was reflecting on the day: the early start, the London walk, lunch, the river ride to Greenwich past the historic wharves and dockland and the double-deck bus ride (his first) back to the centre. With the postcard written and lodged with the concierge, they had caught a movie in the West End: *'Now, Voyager'* seemed to mirror their relationship with Bette Davis's memorable, *'Oh Jerry, don't let's ask for the moon. We have the stars.'* which when delivered to Paul Henreid drew tears from every female in the house. They had completed the evening with a light meal in Southampton Row before returning, through the unlit streets, to Russell Square for their hotel at 11:30.

A few searchlights were penetrating the dark London blackout sky although there was no air raid warning in progress. Occasionally, the narrow beam would illuminate a cloud before moving on in its apparently random search. Arm in arm, the couple hurried into the protection and, within stringent blackout, brightness of their hotel.

As he looked at his reflection, Makepiece thought about her surprise announcement — that the Harley Street specialist had warned her against penetrative sex for 24 hours.

"That means half past nine tomorrow, my darling," she had said. She had come out with it in such a matter of fact way, as if it was a normal topic of conversation. His 'Oh!' seemed woefully inadequate and made him wonder what was going to happen in the next 10 hours. One room, one bed, two craving lovers each with one urge. His undershorts were hardly the effective passion killers of choice.

'It sure as hell beats fighting Germans in the interest stakes,' he thought. He dried his face, tidied the bathroom and turned to open the door, switching off the light at the same time.

The bedroom was dimly lit and the blackout curtain effectively closed. The room struck a touch cooler than the bathroom against his bare torso. Aynette had switched off the ceiling light and one bedside standard lamp. The other had been set on the floor to shed only a soft illumination about the room. The electric fire threw redness into the white sheets where the bed had been turned back. She turned to face him as he entered the room from the bathroom darkness.

As his eyes accustomed to the light, Makepiece saw the barefoot Aynette on his side of the double bed silhouetted against the floor lamp. She was wrapped in a bath towel modestly covering breast to mid thigh. Her hair was loose, her arms outstretched in invitation.

"Come over here, in front of the fire," she invited while patting the bed. "You're not cold, are you?"

Before Makepiece could reply, she continued, "Tonight I have a special request of my loving knight."

"We're hardly dressed for a night at the Grosvenor. And you've declared what, to a military man, some would call challenging rules of engagement."

"No, no, silly. I want to learn about men at war and a woman's reaction to it. I want to write a special episode in my book where a man of courage seeks escape in the company of a passing stranger. To him she may seem like an upmarket whore; in fact she is secretly one of the good guys reporting on what's going on — a sort of horizontal Mata Hari with a conscience. There won't be intercourse, but there will be sexual tension in the liaison. When they part, she'll have only an enduring memory of the encounter including whatever he said. The man will ride away, before dawn, to his war and their paths will never cross again."

She led Makepiece to the bed and sat him down. "Authors have to write about what they know… from personal experience."

"Has this something to do with half past nine in the morning?" asked Makepiece. He was unsure of where the conversation was heading. It crossed his mind that Aynette might just try to inveigle secrets out of him. After all, you could hardly move about without seeing a poster warning of the perils of loose talk. But no! She'd had plenty of opportunity before. He'd never had this problem with Marybeth!

'I'll go along with her game, just for the ride! It's never dull with an archivist,' he thought.

"In a manner of speaking," she answered, "the time provides the excuse for your storyteller queen to deny love to her lover knight." She had not yet let go of his hand.

There was a hint of concern in Makepiece's voice, "Stir some Scheherazade with Mata Hari if you will. What do you want me to do?"

Aynette detected his tension. She reached to touch his cheek in a gesture of reassurance.

"I want you to protect me through the night. I want you to protect me from disobeying doctor's orders. And I want you to protect me from this war. My knight's two part mission for tonight, the queen needs protection on two counts."

"Are you going to tell me how?"

"I am," replied Aynette. She had inched forward to stand between his knees and now reached out for both his hands. Makepiece noticed the absence of radiant heat off the single bar fire as she was now shadowing him from it.

Aynette whispered her instructions, "For tonight your favourite places, when you need to think about something different to your Aynette's love, are going to be your home at Rosetta's Rocks, your aircraft cockpit and a lone cactus in a sun-drenched desert."

"Why those, my queen?" the intrigued Makepiece asked, trying to follow instructions. His mind was really set on getting that towel wrap off her delicious body and he knew that, if he followed his urge, he would not be able to control himself. Maybe her strategy was beginning to work with controlling his thoughts.

"Because, my knight in shorts, when you think of those places your mind will move from worrying about your manhood and the agony will ease. Right now your eyes want to take this towel away. But it will be alright if you accept and concentrate on your favourite places... try thinking about the desert." Aynette's hands had released Makepiece's, while her eyes sought out his innermost thoughts. Her fingers were now at the tuck holding the material around her body.

Makepiece remained silent. She knew she had control because he allowed it. His eyes told her that he would do what she wanted. This opportunity should give her the experience to construct a telling characteristic of one of the female principals in the novel she was shaping. She would not let this moment pass.

She pulled at the towel. It fell across Makepiece's bare feet. Her nakedness seemed to Makepiece to light the room. He was grateful for the image of the lonely, ugly desert vegetable as she pulled him to his feet and pushed off his shorts.

The shadow of the firelight was no longer an issue.

*   *   *

The luminous dial of his watch showed half past three. On the towel spread on the bed, both lay on their right sides so that they were facing the still glowing electric fire and under a sheet and single blanket, Makepiece lay around Aynette. From the soles of her feet to the nape of her neck he was in contact, their skins holding warmth and perspiration between them. His relaxed penis lay along the cleft between her buttocks offering no threat to her womanhood. His uppermost left arm was tucked under hers, leaving her limb free to move as the only means she had to ease any cramp; the length of his arm was holding her tightly back against his torso. His elbow was pressed into her groin and his wrist lay between her breasts. The slightest move she made was resisted by just the necessary pressure so that she had to lie where she was put. Her upper leg was contained at its knee by the weight of his left leg ensuring she did not get leverage to roll away from his grasp. His right arm was passed under her neck and held her right arm outstretched across the bed. They were warm, comfortable and content. She felt protected and safe in the arms of her man.

Once settled, they had not spoken. Both dozed in their mutual comfort, neither crossed completely into oblivion.

She had told Makepiece that the Harley Street specialist had insisted his nurse shave Aynette's pubis for the examination. Now her knight could enjoy the totality of her nakedness and, with a little private chuckle between them, she was glad of it. It was the comely queen's token to her knight on this special night of nights.

'It was feeling her curves that I meant by comely. I had no idea...'

As he thought about her naked mound of Venus, his manhood began to stir. Aynette was awake and noticed the change of pressure at her back. She reached behind her hip to separate her buttocks, but that had the effect of opening room for his testicles to move forward to be trapped by her cheeks. She did not speak, he did not complain but his forearm applied pressure to her stomach to prevent her moving further. He was fully awake. He held himself quite still. Neither spoke until the silence was disturbed by the urgent bells of an ambulance passing close by.

"Are you awake, my knight?" Aynette knew the answer.

221

"I reckon."

"Oh. I feel surrounded and contained. No harm can come to me now. Just think of all those dials in your cockpit…"

Makepiece resisted the temptation to urge the woman to shush.

Aynette was calculating how far she could push this experience. She might never get another chance, certainly with such a simple excuse as the time on the clock! It wasn't as if she was in mortal danger, but there was no doubt in her mind that she could get the man to talk, just as she wanted her heroine to do. She had to try.

"What do you think about when you are flying those aeroplanes? You don't have to kill people, do you? I'd hate it — you having to do that."

"Shush. No, I don't have to kill anyone. I leave that to others. I don't fly as much as I wish I could, I have to leave it to my men. I have been put here to help Churchill rid the world of fascism. My part in the grand design is to take photographs."

Makepiece's innermost thoughts turned to the need for care about what he told this woman — to err on the cautious side!

"Oh." She was glad that he was not a professional killer. She could not imagine what it would be like knowing your lover had just shot someone. But now her man of courage was talking and he needed a little push along her path.

"But what is it like being in one of those machines, flying like a bird?" She tried to push down with her legs, to straighten the angles in which her thighs were held. There was immediate resistance, immovable beyond the merest fraction. The elbow ball pressed against her mound as if to remind her who was in charge. Aynette expected nothing less and she admitted to herself that she quite liked having the sustained presence of his elbow at her clitoris.

"A pilot is firmly strapped into his seat. Twice actually, once to his parachute which would come away with him if he baled out and then to the seat straps attached to the frame of the aircraft. The tighter the straps the safer you are."

"Just like me."

"I reckon," answered Makepiece.

"Have you ever baled out?"

"No need. While the engine is working it's the safest place to stay — the cockpit. The pursuit pilot, the Brits call him a fighter pilot… Your

David… is surrounded by a clear Perspex cockpit hood so he can see all round. He's gotten a rear view mirror just like an automobile. And some armour to protect the vitals. It's a busy place, lots of levers, and switches and dials. The main one is the control column which you hold to climb, dive, turn left or right and use some thumb switches like the radio or the armament. Your feet rest on pedals which you use to make the ship swing left or right."

Makepiece braced his insteps upwards against Aynette's soles. This time she resisted the movement. He could not see the tremor of a smile move over her mouth.

"There are the throttles for the engines, forward and you go faster and back to slow down."

Aynette sensed that Makepiece was relaxed. She could not move any part of her other than her outside arm, but there was no tension in any area of contact.

Makepiece continued, "After the excitement of take-off, the ship will settle down. There are small adjustments which allow the pilot to relax in three dimensions. If there is fuel for the engines, a well set up airplane will go straight and level for ever."

"What happens if you want to turn or the wind blows from the wrong direction?"

"The very gentlest of pressures will ease the plane around the sky. She'll dance to your every wish and if you don't overdo do it, she'll recover back to where she was stable in her new direction. You don't feel a thing. Only the view has changed, the sun will have gone round, the track over the ground will be different and some of the dashboard dials will be reading new numbers."

Aynette moved her free hand to Makepiece's to lift his wrist lying along her cleavage to place his hand to her left breast. She placed her hand on his cheek stretching her breast open for his attention. The restraining pressure across her stomach came on immediately and there was a suggestion of life between her buttocks.

"Show me the pilot's gentle pressure, my knight."

Makepiece gripped her breast beneath his cupped palm. His insteps under her soles gently lifted, but the elbow at her groin held the angles of her thighs in place. Her hardening nipple was caught between two fingers with a squeezing sensation as her flesh was fondled by his fingertips. These sensations across her whole body were not static as he applied his muscular tension to one or more areas of her skin in gentle but positive sensory caress. She moved her hand to behind his back, changing her breast beneath a grip which quickly rearranged its pressure points to his satisfaction. She was trying to bring Makepiece closer to her back, to apply her own pressure to his now flooding penis tip against her lower spine. Her effort was unnecessary as Makepiece's forearm pressured her torso back onto his. She pinched her buttocks together to apply some feeling to his encased testicles; his intake of breath told her of her success and there was a reaction in the hardening of his manhood along her cleft.

"The pilot has to watch all his instruments; he has a pattern for checking them all to ensure the machine is running properly. Keeping straight and level can only be left to the aircraft in perfect conditions. As the fuel gets used, or the track over the ground is not quite what you want, you have to make gentle adjustments. And your eyes never stop searching the skies, looking for the one going the other way."

Her spine was not moving against his penis, she could not move such was his control, but the pressure she was applying was relentless.

"When you take-off before dawn, it's the most wonderful experience. It starts with the sky chimney soot black, but with the stars so close you could touch the millions you can see. Then the east turns purple and never settles until it has turned blue with the cloud tops like a snow field stretching hundreds of miles ahead. Slowly the sun pushes its way out of its bed, first peeping over the horizon then, when all is clear, it climbs to flood the earth in its light. If there is no cloud the dark earth suddenly comes out of its shade with its greens and browns and towns and cities all welcoming a new day. A Canadian pilot wrote the best description I have seen:

Oh! I have slipped the surely bonds of Earth
and danced the skies on laughter-silvered wings;
Sunward I've climbed and joined the tumbling mirth of sun split
clouds...

Then his last lines are:

... I've trod the high untrespassed sanctity of space,
Put out my hand and touched the face of God.

I've never heard it put better. Some call it the 'Pilot's Prayer'."

He could not relax his restraining hold because he suspected Aynette would turn towards him and that could only lead to one thing.

"That's beautiful," she whispered.

Makepiece's need for distraction meant he had to keep talking, "Sometimes you have to talk to the ground or to colleagues in your formation. If you have been ordered to operate in radio silence, all commands are given by hand signal so you have to watch the leader."

Aynette had collected his hand from her breast and opened his palm so that she could place two of his fingers on her mouth. His pleasure and this mock kiss caused him temporarily to lessen the pressure by his elbow and her hips moved a fraction. He was quick to return the ball of his elbow against her clitoris, a move which drew a gasp of pleasure from the mouth just recently vacated.

The mental picture he tried to conjure was of the veranda at Rosetta's Rocks. He continued to talk about flying — anything to divert his attention from his prick.

"Of course you can't stay airborne for ever. The fuel is limited and you have to land. That is when the pilot earns his rations." He returned his hand to her breast, firmly pulling at her now fully erect nipple until she moaned in reaction to his fingers. She tried in vain to move his outstretched arm so that his hand could reach her naked femininity, but she could not overcome his masculine strength.

"Now is the time to make sure your straps are tight."

Pulling against her, his hand moved to her lower right breast, partially trapped against the mattress and, with gentle finesse, he pulled her flesh so that he could fondle that side.

"There are pilot's checks to complete before landing, the vital fuel, the instrument settings, the air traffic radio, the state of the runway and the airspace for other aircraft, while the aircraft is descending. You have to get the air speed right and the undercarriage down and make sure your straps are still tight."

The fluctuating pressure on his balls was giving him problems and she seemed to be making her stomach contract away from his arm but heightening the feeling from her back. He sensed he was going to loose control.

He reached for her shoulder just below his chin, released the elbow pressure to rest against her stomach below her navel. He sensed that she was flexing her internal muscles in her own rhythm. Aynette's uppermost hip eased forward and she tried to pass her hand down her back, to reach the man, to help relieve the stress.

"You line up with the runway in sight, its lights emphasising the edge between the tarmac and the grass."

She so much wanted to hold the man and take him out of his agony. But the necessary gap did not open. His hand slipped back to her breast, but his elbow was now outside her hip.

"The white lines marking the runway threshold are very clear now…"

Her free hand pulled his fingers onto her groin where she encouraged him to explore.

"Then the ground starts rushing towards you; it's the great test that everything you've done is right. And across the threshold… and, oh… the main wheels on the ground … oh… you're down… ooh, ooh… and you can throttle back to let your ship slow down."

Makepiece had ejaculated along Aynette's back in five superhuman spasms. She shook with matching pleasure. She had delivered her own release with a flood of warmth passing from her hips down to her vagina and out to her whole body.

"I'm so sorry," whispered Makepiece. "That should not have happened." He strained to reach to kiss her ear and relaxed the restraint of his arm to lie at natural rest along her body.

As she moved to hold his elbow to her groin, Aynette said, "It's alright, my lover knight. Don't move. You stay just there. You go to sleep if you want to. You are still protecting your queen." She moved his hand back to her breast, but now there was no tightness in his grip. More, it was a gentle warm containing of a vulnerable part of his woman.

She sensed he had relaxed into sleep. Her memory had worked for her. There would be time enough to think about what had happened as her man was taken beyond the point of control. He had continued talking. Her fictional heroine would certainly be able to exploit her feminine prowess on the mattress.

Behind her, Aynette felt Makepiece twitch. Reflex? Something in a dream? She smiled at her thought — while at Oxford she had once read: '*get him by the balls and his heart and mind will follow*'. She passed into sleep, content.

Chapter 37
1944 ~ Recall

Makepiece and Aynette took an unrushed breakfast. There was an unspoken agreement that they would not breach the 9:30 timeline. Neither did they speak of the events of the night, except for a mumbled, 'Thank goodness for the foresight...' by Aynette as she cleared away the towelling from their mattress. Both had taken a bath before dressing and their kisses before leaving the room were those of understanding lovers in no hurry to anticipate the pleasure of the day to come.

"Beggin' your pardon, Colonel," said the waiter at their table. "Reception asks if you would be so good as to pass by there as they have a message for you." Makepiece noticed that his watch showed five minutes to nine.

The 'Please call the base' message turned out to be a recall to duty, prompting a hurry upstairs to pack his things and a too-brief farewell kiss to his lover.

"I have to go. Reception has called me a cab. I'll call you when I know what's going on. No need to worry, I shall not be going to any danger."

Tears were welling in her eyes at his sudden change of plan. She had not yet told him her special news. She had decided to wait until they were away from Oswalde's wall at the Tower; now... Makepiece could not be persuaded to stay, even for five minutes. He did not want her to come down to the station; railway goodbyes were always painful. A final kiss and he was gone, the finality of the door closing bringing on full crying which she was glad her pilot knight did not witness.

'I am a lucky woman,' she thought while trying to hold back her sobbing. 'I have my memory. I have last night to record my feelings when protected by my man. They can't take that away from me.' From that moment, however, Aynette's tears flowed with a deep foreboding that she had seen Makepiece for the last time.

*   *   *

"Sorry to do this, Colonel," welcomed Rod Chmielewski. "Colonel Knapp is coming down from Dawes Hill. He said I was to get you back for a face-to-face. Either you are up to your arse in alligators or Bomber Command is hatching some weirdo mission for the 1574th. He said noon. I'll have Julia organise some sandwiches in your Tech Block office — and plenty of coffee. I'll hang around Snodland in case you need me. The guys can look after Whiffenpoof when he lands."

"Yeah. I'll go and rinse the train grime off my face and go on straight to the Tech Block. Is there any reading I should do before Jules Knapp arrives?"

"I can't say as I know, Colonel. I don't rightly know. No hint. We've had nothing special. But it's got to be good to spring a bird colonel from his eagle nest." Makepiece nodded at Rod's description of getting a senior officer out of his headquarters. This time, this colonel's chewing of his inner cheek was not accompanied by a smile.

"And, Colonel, we've got a new hot shot pilot drafted in to replace Hank Gregson. He beat his file to the gate, but his orders check out. Dawes Hill has confirmed his ABLATIVE ticket. He's picked up some P-38 flying hours out of Mount Farm. He'll be going round the training route tomorrow. I'll get Julia to set up an appointment for you when Colonel Knapp has cleared. Hastings "Wishful" Palmer, the Met man, says the weather will be just fine, tomorrow, for a long haul to the Hebrides and back."

"Does this pilot have a name?" asked Makepiece. He knew that Rod was not concealing anything from him, but he was intrigued as to why Rod had not been immediately forthcoming.

"Sure does. Says you trained together in Georgia. His handle is Major Howard Edison and he looks as he's been round the block a coupla of times. Touch of grey, huh!"

"Like me, I suppose?" The chewing had stopped.

"I couldn't rightly say." Rod's smile was barely concealed. "I'll go and find Sergeant Greenburg."

*   *   *

Visiting Julius Knapp was smoking. It was an unfamiliar habit in the 1574th, certainly indoors. The aircrew were actively discouraged by the flight surgeon but then, he discouraged everything including heterosexual sex.

"Riding in an RAF Anson is one thing. Holy Mother! I was nearly converted, but to be bounced by 16 Typhoons without juice just ain't for the sinners. Those poor Bosch sons of bitches at the receiving end of those mothers... And... and... a woman delivery pilot, in a Spitfire, on radio silence, too!"

"Jules," said his brother-in-law, holding up his hand and with a chuckle in his voice, "you're at the front line here. West Malling gets a whole load of shot-up ships and kites low on gas. Gerry is 60 clicks that way." Makepiece was jerking his thumb over his shoulder. "Until Ike does something about it, life around here is going to stay mighty hairy. And the host nation lady ferry pilots rival Peter Pan's Tinker Bell in aerobatics. You gotta believe it!"

"OK, OK!" Another deep drag and the fag end dropped into the half drunk coffee. "Shit!" Jules stood to pour himself a fresh cup.

"I hope you've called me back from sin city to do more than swear at me... And no more smoking down here, please, brother-in-law. There's too much chemical stuff which might go bang! We get kinda anxious..."

"OK! Forget the ABLATIVE and ULTRA crap, Makepiece, old son. This is 'burn before reading' stuff and they're not telling FDR or Winnie about it. Geddit?"

Both brothers had served in the Office of National Information in Washington — the Sealed Room Brigade someone had christened it — where folks and information went in and seldom came out.

"Any paper lists to sign on it?" Makepiece was already reaching for his pen.

"Nope! Only you, and I, and an untouchable in the Embassy know about this. I can't answer for the Brits though. You've got to go and get the corroborative horseshit that will let it out on regular channels. That's why I'm here."

"No chance of Rod Chmielewski sitting in on the act?" Makepiece was easing his inner tension by opening and closing his right fist on his desktop. Julius noticed the anxiety.

"No chance! We'll construct something so he gets what he needs to know then it's up to you. Look, for security, even in this windowless construct you call an office, let's move away from the phones and the door. I know... I know... we're 50 feet underground! This is hotter than Eva Braun's panthose."

"Shoot, and don't hold the horses," invited Makepiece. He stilled his hand and tried to convey relaxation to his brother-in-law. Jules was not fooled.

"You've gotta believe this source. Her husband was in the Wenceslas Mine when the Krauts tested their kit they call CHRONOS — literally time — but we'll leave that to one side. The fourth dimension always escaped me at college. Apparently her hubbie got fried in the test, literally; his brain boiled through 200 metres of solid rock says the source. Whatever exaggeration by the poor biddy, he snuffed it. Naturally, she's pissed off and wants the allies to avenge Hubbie. I didn't say that Hubbie and Mrs Hubbie are — were — scientists working on this CHRONOS thingee."

Makepiece just knew that Jules was giving him the background to an extreme mission's tasking. Perhaps his language was somewhat removed from formal staff briefing, but…

"We already know that Herr General Kammler thought the tests were the bees' knees; now we can give his pet project a name. Better, although we don't know if Kammler has actually been to the site, we do know from Mrs Hubbie that SS Gruppenführer und Generalleutnant der Polizei Jakob Sporrenberg has been told to get his butt to the mine on March 13th for the next test."

A frown by Makepiece prompted reply to the unasked question.

"I see, Brother, that the name Sporrenberg is unfamiliar. He's one of Himmler's up-and-comings in the SS order of battle. Wrong, he's at their most senior rank now. Christ! He's got more pips than a lemon. We know that he was appointed top police dog for Poland on 16 August 1943 and we reckon this test must be something big to order him about. Remember, Kammler is Himmler's chief engineer. So when Kammler says jump, he jumps. And Sporrenberg has direct access to Himmler in his new job."

"Got the picture, Jules." Makepiece was reaching for an open sandwich. "Help yourself to chow! You're talking about high priced help." Makepiece's description of key German personalities produced a confirmatory nod.

"Remember I told you that Bletchley Park had cracked a soviet agent's code from the area? Well, they've done it again. If Uncle Joe Stalin was ever to get wind that we know, boy wonder with the Russian code is in for one hell of a headache when he gets his retirement interview with the Red secret police... or NKVD... or whatever."

Makepiece smiled and offered an open hand to the lunch tray on his desk. Jules shook his head in polite refusal.

"I thought we didn't do intelligence against our allies. It's not gentlemanly..." Makepiece's aside about collecting intelligence against Russia was ignored by Julius.

"Bletchley Park says bad boy agent chummy says he has seen test reports mentioning 17 dead, a church bell floating on mercury, massive electrical power switches and an underground test chamber 50 metres across and 30 metres high. Mrs Hubbie had already told us that that the underground complex is built like a car muffler, lots of interconnected side tunnels and expansion chambers so that the expanded hot air can gallop around to lose its pressure and doesn't escape by blowing the top off the mountain. This soviets' report says all sorts of oddball materials were mentioned, including uranium, thorium, and a radioactive gas called radon. Oh... and ... err... antinomy? Washington wants some samples to play with, but we haven't — hadn't — gotten anyone with the wherewithal to get it out. Not, that is, unless Mrs Hubbie is allowed in — or the 1574th sniffer can get there and back."

Makepiece was already shaking his head.

"I told you it's 125 miles too far, each way, for realistic fuel uplift. I've been working the problem with my Lockheed and Allison guys and we reckon we may knock off half the deficit, but still not enough to get back. We'd have to take in the full range of sensor kit for a mission like that."

"I hear you. Don't confuse me with the facts! But Mrs Hubbie says the guards have gotten the place sewn up. You can thank Kraut Sporrenberg for that! At the mine's entrance, they change clothes down to naked going in and are stripped, hosed down, body searched, hosed down again and then dress in their own clothes before passing through metal detector, x-ray and geiger counter screens on the way out. There's no way she can bring out samples. Worse, once they've done a test all the rubbish is moved into a side cavern, incinerated with flame throwers then the ashes stirred, the roof blown down and the tunnel sealed with two metres of concrete. Mr Hubbie is in one such cavern."

"No wonder she's... as you say... pissed..." Makepiece's face was screwed with a 'so-what?' look and his shoulders were raised. The open sandwiches on his desk looked attractive and breakfast seemed a long time ago...

"I didn't mention body cavity search..."

"I get the picture." Makepiece relaxed his usually upright stance; his shoulders hunched and forehead creased in anticipation. His brother was leading up to tasking the impossible mission. "Are we talking to Mrs Hubbie?"

"We have a tame Swede..."

"Oh," grunted Makepiece.

"Mrs Hubbie says they've done five tests so far. She does not have the words to explain what the CHRONOS gear is supposed to do. But you and I have both put money on this being the 'Einstein Engine' prediction coming to fruition in test hardware."

"You know that even, I say EVEN underscored, if I got a P-38 sniffer in there, unless the mine leaked at just the right time in the test sequence, we'd not collect any sample. How do we know the mineshaft will leak? Look at our success so far in trying to find radio-nuclides. Zilch!"

"I was coming to that. One of your sniffers over Heidelberg — I've gotten the details in my briefcase — according to boffins in Washington found the wrong type of uranium, wrong type of caesium and the wrong type of strontium to prevent the eggheads in DC going to sleep well." Jules Knapp was speaking with earnest emphasis.

"Are you saying the German's have gotten a working nuclear pile?"

"Seems just possible, Brother, at least in a laboratory! And we know about it because they are careless how they incinerate their waste. That crap doesn't burn."

"So our sniffers are playing in trumps?" Makepiece, whose idea it had been to fit the P-38M-SP with the capability to take air samples, displayed obvious delight. His pleasure was to be short lived.

"That's the good news. The bad news is that your sniffers have gotten up the nose of Wild Bill Donovan. He says if the USAAC P-38s can't get the Hitler nuclear stuff out, OSS P-38s can. He's already making a play for Heidleberg and every German speaking university on the planet."

"Bullshit!"

"He's seen the report that P-38s of 55th Fighter Group based at Nuthampstead, Cambridge became the first American fighter unit to penetrate the Berlin skies on 3 March 1944. I told you he would latch onto anything labelled intelligence collector and 1574th SPSG has that branding. He's rumoured to be going shopping for his own air force — to deliver his own ground agents, for Christ's sake! The only way to keep him out of the ball-game is for one of your ships to do what Mrs Hubbie can't."

Jules' head was shaking side-to-side to emphasise his point. "I don't have any evidence that Donovan knows about Wenceslas, but equally I don't have any evidence that he doesn't. He's gotten friends in high places."

Makepiece pointed his index finger at his guest. "I'll just say again that Wenceslas is one flying hour out beyond Berlin with a howling gale up your fanny, and more than one hour back fighting against that same wind on your nose. That's another 400 pounds weight of fuel to lift at take-off, added to an already stretched total." Makepiece would brook no argument that any other P-38 variant could be better than his. "And another detail, regular P-38Ls of the Nuthampstead variety, don't fly as high, as fast, or as long as P-38M-SPs. OK, they do carry guns instead of sensors. Anyway, Berlin is a mighty big airspace for the 55th, or anyone else, to cross — geography-wise. You didn't say which part of Berlin or how far across those guys went."

Jules' eyebrows went up in mock despair. "That's classified, Brother!"

Makepiece showed disgust at the unnecessary putdown delivered by his brother.

Julius Knapp knew the politics of the situation. He respected Makepiece's knowledge of the P-38 machinery. But over-riding was the need to understand what the Germans were doing. He waited for Makepiece to speak. But Makepiece was deep in thought, contemplating a half eaten sandwich and a cup of black coffee. So Jules Knapp broke the silence.

"You're thinking."

"It happens… just occasionally. Getting to Wenceslas needs an hour's extra fuel uplift compared with even our standard P-38-SP with long-range tanks — that's two hours better'n a standard P-38 pursuit ship with their drop tanks. We could borrow some bigger RAF drop tanks and have my guys fit them in lieu of Yankee's best. But will the ship leave the ground? You're saying we've gotta try?"

"Right," Jules shrugged. "Have another coffee and we'll chat over how much of all this we can tell Rod Chmielewski. You've gotten the best aircraft and engines specialists industry can cobble together. I know you've got the cream of the pilots. For this mission, he's got to be the best. He's looking for Hitler's war winner and perhaps this CHRONOS thing is it. He's gonna fly the most difficult mission of the war and he's only gonna know half of the why — and maybe run out of gas as well."

"Jules. We absolutely have to protect the ABLATIVE capability. How about getting the photo-recce group at Chalgrove to take some medium altitude, high resolution pictures of Heidelberg? Then you'll have a hook to hang that info on... contamination of the cabin air intake filters, or something. It'll be an Air Corps plus and hold Donovan off."

"Good thinking, Brother. Except that Donovan thinks it was your outfit 'wot dunnit!'" Jules was not wholly persuaded.

"Wenceslas is four hundred miles further east than Heidelberg is south." Makepiece's comment could be a show-stopper.

Nonplussed, Jules suggested, "OK, now let's think of a similar get out for Wenceslas — always assuming you manage to find a petrol pump in the sky! Perhaps we could leak the soviet agent to the SS... through the Japs in Geneva has a nice ring to it. We might have to stop short at disclosing the potential of CHRONOS having more crunch beyond the atom bomb though. Uhm!"

Makepiece's face was again screwed with a concerned look, but this time his shoulders expressed disbelief in the line his brother-in-law was taking. He was still trying to come to terms with the requirement for an impossible fuel uplift. Was it reasonable to ask any man to take such a risk?

Chapter 38
1944 ~ Meteorological Briefing

In the SPSG Technical Building at Snodland, the following morning's mission meteorological briefing was in progress.

"Good evening, Colonel. Gentlemen. Err... ladies and gentlemen." The senior met officer stumbled over his introduction. Makepiece was patient. The naturalised American, former British, meteorologist Michael 'Way Blue Yonder' Ryman often stumbled at this point with the pleasantries. But, when the real briefing of weather, synoptic charts and forecasts began, then it was his ground and his confidence in his particular blend of art and science that shone through any initial hesitation.

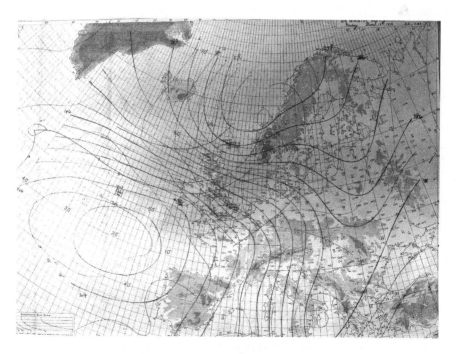

**Air Ministry Meteorological Office 300 millibar Chart for
00:00 hours on Monday 13 March 1944**
reproduced courtesy of the Meteorological Office archive

235

"This is the synoptic for 00:00 GMT on 13 March 1944 released by the Meteorological Office at 23:15. The jet stream at 300 millibars, that is 39000 feet altitude, has a ground speed over the central North Sea and central Germany to beyond Berlin of 175 miles per hour. It will persist for the next 24 hours taking a cold front over South-east England at about noon. A front will pass on a generally easterly drift to pass south of Berlin at approximately 04:30 GMT and will cause moderate to full cloud cover for a band of 100 miles. However, ahead of the front, we anticipate precipitation falling as snow particularly over high ground well into Poland. We are predicting broken cloud with light snow over the Sudeten Mountains to clear about dawn until probably midday local time — that is 10:00 GMT."

'Way Blue Yonder' turned away from his high altitude jet stream chart.

"Take off conditions, at 02:30, at West Malling will be a cold mist, visibility more than 1000 yards with a light wind. The weather at midday, tomorrow, at West Malling is expected to be a light wind from the east with a temperature of 40 degrees Fahrenheit."

"Do you have any figure for the cloud tops over Poland?"

"'fraid not, Colonel. Our team at Dunstable says the Germans' weather people are showing the jet stream at 200 miles per hour, orientated generally south to north over Prague and up to the Baltic. They do their measurements at about 45,000 feet."

"And low altitude conditions over, say, western Poland?"

"Nothing current, Colonel. The Germans' weather people say that snow cover east of the Rhine is patchy. We assess conditions as suggesting minimal fresh snowfall over eastern Europe during the next 24 hours except where the cold front crosses the Harz and Sudeten high ground. Cloud cover beyond the Rhine is predicted to be patchy except on the weather front.

"Thank you, Mister Ryman. Please leave a copy of the chart on the table. I'll call you if I need more details." The met officer did not need to know any more about the mission specifics. Colonel Ploughman had effectively dismissed his metrological adviser, who now left the room. He knew the UK intelligence source for the German weather was an outstation of Bletchley Park near Dunstable.

Other intelligence briefings could now begin.

*　　　　*　　　　*

Behind the Snodland Village Hall, Jenny Plowman and T/Sgt Delaney J. Openshaw were locked in an embrace. Their regular roller skating sessions at the Chatham rink usually ended here, allowing Jenny to judge the walking time necessary to get to RAF Snodland Guardroom to sign in before her leave of absence pass expired. Mutual warmth kept out the March evening chill, her top coat open so that his embrace could fondle bare buttocks under a lifted skirt hem. The brick wall clinging to her hair was no discomfort as he pressed his lips to hers.

Jenny knew she had stirred her man. Now, as their mouths searched the other's and his strong hands swept over her flesh, she wanted more. She brought his hands around to reach her breasts, which remained enclosed in a buttonless top over a strong utility brassiere. His reaction was to lean away slightly with a change of breathing as he caressed these wonderous shapes beneath his grasp.

"That's nice, Delaney. You do love me, don't you?"

"You know you're the only one for me, Honey."

All too soon, "If you are ready," Delaney said, "we ought to make a move back to the base." He was taking masculine control. "We don't want to spoil a perfect evening by being late in. I've pulled a midnight shift, we've gotten a busy day tomorrow."

"We're relieving the crew at Hoo at 06:00. The garry leaves at 04:30 and we have to eat before that."

Jenny decided not to hitch up her panties. It would be fun to walk into the guardroom, at the main gate, with all those airmen milling around, not knowing her bum was bare.

Chapter 39
1944 ~ A Wing and a Prayer

Captain David McFallis, flight surgeon for 1574th SPSG, had looked in at the Oxygen Room in the lamella hangar. He was aware that a mission was to be flown this morning, departing at about a quarter before three. It was special because Makepiece Ploughman was flying it himself. Seated, as he had been for 30 minutes of his 2 hour pre-flight preparation, having glanced at the Meteorological Chart prepared for him, Colonel Makepiece had his eyes closed. His weekly family letter had been written and posted; his 'goodbye' letter to Marybeth lay on his desk... just in case he didn't come back. McFallis approached his commanding officer and sat on the bench next to him. Makepiece looked to be as calm as any group pilot at this stage of the mission.

"Everything OK, Colonel?"

"Right as rain, Squire," replied Makepiece, "as the locals might say."

"You've been listening to too much BBC, Colonel."

Makepiece opened his eyes. "Something worrying you, Doc?"

"Matter of fact, yes, sir. You! You look mighty tired. Are you sure you should fly this mission, Colonel? It's hard, this pattern of flying, on the young blades of the outfit. 10 hours is a long time to fly solo, especially when there's a whole nation anxious to gun you out of the skies. And you're no spring chicken! Give it to someone younger."

"No chance, Doc. Lockheed and the Lord cooperated with Allison to make my ship. Today the bird flies and I take the ride. A pilot has to use his wings, Doc. What could go wrong? Only angels do it better."

"If I were to advise you not to go, to give it to someone else?" The flight surgeon knew he was wasting his breath, but he felt he had to go through the motions.

"I'm already briefed in for this one, Doc. It's the biggest for the group so far. 'Lead from the front' has always been my motto."

"Just thought I'd ask, Colonel. Let me put it another way. Is there something worrying you, away from the group, perhaps? You've looked off-colour for awhile and I don't reckon it was losing Hank Gregson. You've been that close to others who didn't come back."

"Since you ask, and I know you'll keep on until I tell you — Doctor's secrets mind, not even Rod Chmielewski knows this — I've been visiting. Keen widow, she is, local, what you might call an 'enthusiastic amateur'. We had a party for two about six weeks ago. No protection. It's worrying me that she may have been carrying and given me a dose."

"If that's what the issue is, there are fixes these days for most problems down there. I won't give you a shot as you are flying, but then there is no great rush either. Why don't you come and see me when you land? We'll have a check and a precautionary treatment. No records, if you like. Call it peace of mind."

"Thanks, Doc. I'll do that. Now, I've got 1700 miles to fly before 13:00 and I'd sure as hell appreciate a little time to myself. Good of you to look in, losing your beauty sleep and the like."

"Happy landing, Colonel. We appreciate having you around."

"Bye-bye, Doc. Buzz off!" Makepiece smiled his appreciation at the doctor. The doctor's closure of the Oxygen Room door prompted Makepiece to reflect on the letter to Aynette he had left next to Marybeth's. He felt he had to offer closure, somehow, should he not come back. His text had to have been carefully chosen so as not to distress the family in Maryland if it was ever delivered:

To: Mrs Aynette Bates   March 12th, 1944
Cleeve Lyon
Maidstone , Kent

Dear Aynette,
I would like to thank you for your friendship and hospitality through these winter months. Your assistance in researching my Kentish family history is greatly appreciated and I wish you every success with your forthcoming novel based on the Ploughman experience. I would have wished to see a bound and published version of the manuscript, perhaps there'll be a copy in the great archive in the sky.
Have a long and happy life,
Makepiece Ploughman

*   *   *

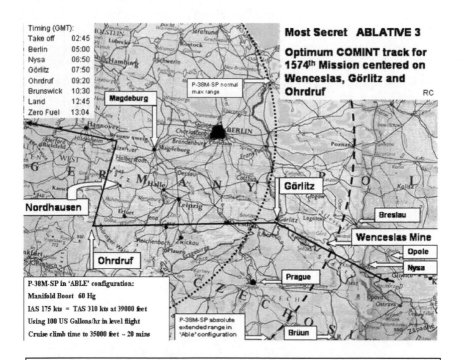

Makepiece's *ABLE* configuration maximum safe range superimposed on map of Europe with return route shown to fly in target communications radio links

This was the time when the pilots checked their maps, their fuel calculations, their emergency procedures, their thoughts of family and friends. Tonight, Makepiece's mind was considering the discussion with Rod Chmielewski about the optimum route for communications intercept. His Operations Officer had produced a map which showed the best track to remain in the most likely point-to-point radio communications path between south west Poland and Orhdruf. It was based on a copy out of an atlas to make handling easier in the confines of the Oxygen Room, a single navigation chart would not show the whole route without being laid out on the resting couch...' A real air-navigation chart was already folded for ease of use in the confined cockpit.

Makepiece knew the German SS radio channels were productive to the ABLATIVE mission, now he wanted to add another dimension. If the Germans did a test at 10:00 local time, that's 08:00 GMT, while he was about, the P-38's sniffer could be put in the plume.

'That'll make Weiss earn his keep and we may get lucky with something we don't expect,' thought Makepiece. 'How typical of Rod to sketch in maximum ranges, including one for my ship in its *Able* configuration — special fuel uplift and all the gizmos. He said I could possibly push his *Able* line out 25 miles if I fly out with the high altitude jet stream up my six o'clock and the wicks turned down on the Allisons. It's getting back that's the problem, he had said. The understatement of the century... *'You might try flying under the jet stream, but we don't know the altitude accurately and you would be nearer the German flak! And you'd be trailing contrails! Err... you might try flying above the jet stream, but we don't know the top altitude accurately and you could be flying above the Allison's optimum fuel consumption altitude. Between a rock and a hard place...'* My absolute easternmost turning point must be Nysa to allow me a down sun run at the Wenceslas Mine; I'll still be 100 miles short of Katowice. It will be a one-pass-only opportunity over the mine. Get that turn wrong and you won't be coming back...'

Major Patrick 'Supershot' Guthrie had been tasked to test-fly the fuel load that Makepiece would be carrying. It was obvious that the airframe was reluctant to lift off the ground with its extra fuel tanks. Guthrie had flown the training route, without the electronics payload, and remained at altitude for the longest possible endurance. He had stayed airborne three minutes longer than 10 hours, but had to land having consumed some of his safety margin of his fuel reserve. Makepiece respected Supershot's ability with the P-38M-SP and had based his Able mission fuel calculations, and his life, on 10 hours 19 minutes flying from engines start to touchdown with dry tanks.

Makepiece had the ground crew polish his airframe until it gleamed in its special camouflage coat. Every fairing, panel and patch was made flush to use the least possible fuel. Even the spinners on the propellers had the full treatment. He had the meteorological team check, double check, and recheck their forecasts; he'd seen the high altitude weather chart himself. He knew he was going to push his aircraft beyond its limits; Messrs Lockheed and Allison had not let him down yet.

'Reflect on it, Makepiece,' he thought. 'You're breaking a written Presidential order with the most hazardous mission ever. It's only your second time over Europe... and the other time you broke a written Presidential order too. But I can't ask another Joe to fly it, not something I wouldn't try for myself. I'd never live with myself... of course, that might not be a problem if the Krauts catch me! Should I let on with Rod... why I am flying this one? No. Perhaps when I get back... He'll probably guess, but he doesn't know about Stimson's letter!'

There was no concealing it; the entire group knew he was flying tonight. But no-one knew he was under a specific order not to do it. If he brought back the goods... when he brought back the goods... perhaps Washington would forgive and forget? Some hopes...

Makepiece had cleared his desk of official business the previous afternoon. The on-call US Army chaplain had visited the Commander 1574th SPSG as requested at 15:00.

Makepiece had said, "I don't like to bother God when he's so busy, but do you think you could say a little prayer for me. I'm flying the mission tonight and I would like to get back so that I can save the world..."

The chaplain had replied that he would need an extra thick prayer mat to pull that one off, but he would try. It might help if the Colonel could spare a couple of minutes, himself, to speak with God. Miracles sometimes happen...

* * *

In a blast proof headquarters building in Görlitz, about 100 miles south west of Berlin, it was well past midnight, on March 13th 1944, that engineer and project manager SS General Hans Kammler sat with a *Deutscher Wetterdiennst* high altitude meteorological chart spread across his otherwise clear desk.

It showed the assessed atmospheric pressure pattern over Europe at an altitude of approximately 13,000 metres. By good fortune, the standard chart just happened to be centred on the Wenceslas Mine launch pad which interested him for this morning's test. The chart recorded the latest readings, among others, from a number of weather stations in northern Poland and south Finland along the planned test vehicle track.

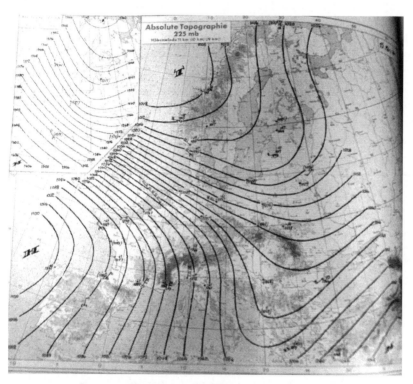

German DWR for 225 mbar on 13 March 1944
Captured German weather map courtesy of the UK Meteorological Office

The high altitude jet stream would assist the flight vehicle to transit due north into the northern Baltic Sea, where it could be tracked by ship's radar, and thence probably disappear into the snowy wastes of Finland or the Artic Ocean. The objective of today's test was to gauge the vehicle's initial rate of climb, its acceleration and therefore suitability for manned missions, its maximum altitude and its transit groundspeed. A by-product would be another proving run of the CHRONOS bell energy machine to produce the powerful electrical impulse required to launch the flight vehicle.

Confident that all the preparations were complete, the weather was auspicious and that security was intact, Kammler gave approval for the test to proceed and went to bed. He would be called two hours before the test firing — ample time to read the morning's messages before monitoring the success of his latest, and most significant, project.

'If it goes well, I should expect a summons to the Führer himself...'

Chapter 40
1944 ~ Makepiece Flies a Mission

At 02:43 GMT, Makepiece was strapped in his cockpit. The P-38M-SP had been towed to the end of the runway to conserve fuel. The engines had been warmed by the groundcrew, all systems checked, and the tanks refuelled to their limit. Makepiece's aircraft was configured with two 'borrowed' British 150 gallon drop tanks, in addition to the regular two US 125 gallon drop tanks on the inner wing mountings; none would be coming home. Internally, a single downward and two long focus oblique cameras, two wingtip mounted forward looking cameras, a full ELINT suite and full COMINT suite made up the signals intelligence role equipment. The sniffer equipment was mounted ahead of the vertical camera in the nose. A magnetic anomaly detector was fitted in the tailplane.

The Lockheed representative had warned Makepiece, "You will be 1300 lbs over and above maximum takeoff weight; your ship might not leave the deck before the runway ends. Even a cold air takeoff, with water methanol boost, might not be sufficient. You're pushing the flight envelope, Colonel."

A green Aldis lamp signalled twice from the air traffic control just visible through the mist. He was being signalled: 'clear to go'. Radio silence was strictly observed. He would not be speaking with another human being for 10 hours, when he would be checking for clearance to land. Makepiece had calculated that, on this mission, he could have as little as 7 minutes margin then the Allison engines would be running on air.

At 02:44, an anxious Makepiece showed his white gloved thumbs up to the ground crew and his twin Allison engines burst into life. This was it... he was committed. One minute later Makepiece was speeding down the runway 240. Although he could not see them in the dark, Makepiece knew that the duty watch were out of the hangar, watching him go. They would see his shape, maybe the exhaust gases and hear his noise indistinctly, but they'd know if he didn't get away with it. There was little significant surface wind, perhaps 12 miles per hour, to help him get airspeed.

'My God, this is heavy.' Makepiece knew that no one had attempted to fly a P-38 at this takeoff weight.

'Passed runway commit marker, water methanol, now!' His engines sensed something exceptional was expected. The engine boost pressure gauges in the cockpit moved into the red danger zone.

'Still weight on ground. 1000 feet left to airfield boundary. Touch of the mach flaps. She flies or I'm dead!' The P-38 lifted. With less rolling resistance the P-38 accelerated through its critical takeoff speed.

'Let's fly, baby!' The P-38 crossed the airfield boundary hedge while the tricycle undercarriage was still retracting. 'Get the flaps up… save every drop of fuel.' In the cockpit, with the gentlest of pressure on the flying control column, the rate of climb indicator showed a positive reading. Equally important, the aircraft was continuing to accelerate. The airspeed indicator was moving the correct way. Makepiece was safely airborne.

'Don't push it, Makepiece. Switch off the water methanol.'

Makepiece was making a positive effort to think clearly. His life would depend on those two engines and his clear thinking for the next 10 hours. Relaxation was not an option. 'We've got safe airspeed. She'll tell you when she's ready to cruise climb. Well done, chaplain, your chat with the Master did the trick. Gentle turn to port on to 090 away from the balloon tethers — the first heading as the fuel gets used. As she collects airspeed, it will get less hairy. Whew!'

Makepiece allowed himself to thank his guardian angel and the guys on the ground who, he knew, would now relax until he came home. He nosed into cloud at 3000 feet just as the meteorological office at Dunstable had predicted. Airframe icing was not forecast, thank goodness…

Makepiece spoke to himself, "I'd say that was pushing your luck, sunshine. Much more of that and you'll not be seeing Rosetta's Rocks again. Now, you've a job to do. Settle down. There'll be hell to pay when Washington finds out I'm flying this mission… At least the low altitude met men got their bit right. Let's get altitude and some of 'Way Blue Yonder' Ryman's jet stream wind up our arse; his radio-sonde was predicting +180 mph tailwind over the Channel. First waypoint is the Dutch coast if you can see it through this cloud."

He realised he was sweating and rubbed the backs of his gloves across his eyes. The tinted glass goggles were perched above his forehead; he would need their protection when the sun came up. In five minutes, he'd be over occupied Europe. He would be disobeying a Presidential Written Order! That was something for the future...

*   *   *

Two hours later and the sky was showing the greyness of dawn ahead. Allowing his autopilot to do most of the flying, he had flown over an allied, presumably British, bomber force on the receiving end of a German flak barrage. A blue ground based searchlight was searching the sky for a target to direct other beams on to the advancing bomber stream. As he advanced over the ground, fires raised by an earlier raid were burning fiercely in the night.

Makepiece allowed himself the luxury of thinking, 'At least I can see some of the ground below. People down there are fighting for their lives, their homes and their families. It's the same back in Blighty. We have got to stop this bastard Hitler and his cronies once and for all, before he does something we'll all regret. It's why I'm up here.'

An anti-aircraft flak shell exploded a mile below his aircraft.

"Not a hope, Kraut! I suppose it won't be long before they work out how to get those shells up here," said Makepiece.

Then he thought, 'I suppose there is a limit to how far up these P-38s can go. I reckon we could push one of the ships above 45,000 feet — today's not the day to play silly buggers like that. Perhaps Mr Lockheed is working on the next generation. I'd sure like to fly one of those.'

Makepiece checked his map. He was always grateful when daylight came so that he could read the chart more easily. Today he would be heading directly into the rising sun for over an hour, a very tiring prospect. But for now, lacking the luxury of a dedicated navigator in order that he might carry the maximum electronics, he had to strain his sight, risking night vision using his cockpit light. He noted the snow capped Harz Mountains were behind him, with now limited cloud he was able to assess his groundspeed.

'Better than I hoped. 'Way Blue Yonder' Ryman had conferred with 'Hope Not' and agreed their prediction was Force 17 on the Beaufort scale — it doesn't go any higher than that. I guess they were right! I must be careful not to overrun the first photo target. Surely that is Berlin and its lakes coming into view. Check the camera. Babs at Medmenham would like a snap of Templehof airport by dawn's early light. Looks like Berlin got a pasting recently, there's a lot of smoke. It's strange how Babs' scent comes through the pure oxygen. Imagination! It's pushing the limits of film exposure, but they can do wonders when they print it. These long lens oblique cameras really are quite effective. Don't waste film now; you may need it.'

It was time to lower the tinted glass goggles from his forehead. Straight ahead the gold orb was just breaching the horizon. Another day was dawning.

"It's March 13th — a Monday — at least it's not the *Ides of March*, unlucky for some! — that's the 15th... on Wednesday... or the full moon which was on the 10th! Concentrate, Makepiece... you've a war to win."

*   *   *

'It's time to start navigating properly,' thought Makepiece. 'I'm in the sun up here and, within 10 minutes, so will be the ground below. Those mountains have gotten plenty of snow. I've got enough visual cues to be able to do my photo run. I'll leave the electronics on automatic. That ELINT signal is just a long range radar east of Berlin, a regular scan at 4 revolutions per minute; he can probably see me but won't know who or what I am. Their communications are quiet for this hour of the day; I would expect to hear militia chattering away. Perhaps they've evacuated Silesia because they don't like the weather.'

Makepiece's eyes scanned the instrument panel beyond his gloved hands. 'Outside air temperature indicated at -52°C.' He shivered instinctively but he was, in reality, quite comfortable.

'Time to check the fuel, temperatures, oxygen, engine power and electrics; all are operating within limits. That railway between Legnica and Breslau will be very useful. A couple of snaps of Frankfurt, its river junction will give intel their fix and timing. Just follow the River Oder south east to the next major town, another couple of pictures and I'll change heading to 180 degrees to allow for the wind.' Below him was the distinctive line of clouds where southern warm air met northern cold air mass in a warm front. 'They'll be getting snow down there.' It was not his problem.

With the change of heading the sun's glare was no longer a problem to Makepiece. He slipped his goggles above his forehead. It was a clear day with no glare off the snow covered ground with the sun in its present relative early morning aspect.

The twin engines seemed to sing their contentment in doing their job well.

'Overhead Opole now, right hand down and the sun is behind at last. Another 20 miles of railway to Nysa and the Czech border and the mountains. Highest peak is 1492 metres, say safe altitude 2000 metres, let's say 8000 feet indicated on the altimeter just for the sake of it; it's only a professional formality, but you never know. Track 300 degrees from Nysa. Rod had said that I should aim to be on the line between Nysa and Gorlitz at 09:00 local time; it was his best guess at when Gerry Kammler would test his weapon leaving plenty of daylight to hang the scientists if it didn't go pop. This is the origin of where 'Edge' Cryshaw caught that COMINT reference to an explosion. Pity Cryshaw didn't see anything although he was much further west of here.'

The visibility, through the broken cloud, was excellent.

'There we are, Rod, on the button. Check the fuel...'

In this phase of his mission, where the electronics were doing the work and he was simply the driver, Makepiece allowed himself to scan the view. The industry of Brünn, about 80 miles to the south, was staining the sky with its smoke pall. Rather closer, the snow-capped Sudeten Mountains were glorious in this light. Flying at its most enjoyable, 'A bloody long way from home! I wish I could share this with Marybeth and the kids...'

The COMINT monitor in Makepiece's headset burst into life. He was reminded that he was flying, unarmed, in hostile airspace. Reality! The system indicators in the cockpit showed the sensor's recorders were running. They could give a total of 65 minutes theoretically; he would run out of fuel reserve long before he used all that. He planned to follow Rod's optimum track to keep his receivers in the radio beams. Whatever the language being used on the ground, he could not understand what was being said but someone down there was clearly very excited. The aircraft was now flying over upland mine workings five miles beneath his aircraft, some with undisturbed snow and others with obvious recent activity. Makepiece reflected that this evidence was particularly obvious in the snow covered woodlands of this mountainous region.

Makepiece caught sight of a blue flash in the ground, not a reflection of sunlight, more like an explosion. An underground explosion? There was no evidence of an explosion on the snow surface. With enough flash to show through earth and snow? To say nothing of being visible in the forest! Now there was a plume of dust and smoke rising, surrounded by a white snow storm. Radiating from the presumed centre of the explosion, the trees had shed their covering of snow standing green in a white cloud. It looked as though something underground had shaken the ground over a diameter of several hundred yards. It was too good an opportunity to miss.

'Throttle back,' he silently commanded himself. 'Cabin pressurisation to automatic, open the sniffer, do not descend below 8000 feet indicated safe altitude and let's sniff the air'.

The plume did not reach his safe altitude.

'Visibility is good, no indication of hostile activity, I'll go on down and round again to and sniff that plume. We've dropped below the COMINT intercept. Pity! Check the fuel... The sniff has priority. We'll get COMINT back when we climb. Keep the forward cameras running, should be good for stereoscopy, COMINT has caught something else. Check your flight instruments. That chatter is never ending — perhaps they've seen me. Let the magnetic anomaly kit run, it's been so much dead weight up to now.' Flying through the plume, he visually judged never below 500 feet above ground level, the sniffer filter would have collected its precious samples.

'There must have been a considerable heat there. The updraught as we went through the plume was quite marked. I'd say we gained 350 feet. But the snow cloud wasn't melting to rain. Very strange! I wonder what the camera's made of it.'

Makepiece scribbled an aide-memoir on his kneepad to ensure it was not missed when he debriefed back at base. He also wrote the word 'blue' and double underlined it.

'Time for the recovery to safe altitude and then on up to where they can't catch me.'

Makepiece eased the P-38's nose above the horizon. He realised he was sweating for the second time on this mission.

'Open the throttles and let's get out of here. Gently now... I'll let the ship cruise climb to 39,000 feet, or until we touch the turbulent wind-shear beneath the jet stream, heading due west and I shall waypoint at Dresden. A couple of frames at Görlitz on the way, just for the record. 15 degrees east meridian, one hour ahead of London. They'll have finished their breakfast by now...'

He nodded his head towards the obvious bridge across the River Neisse now visible under a rain cloud on the warm front. 'That viaduct is a good marker. Pity, the COMINT chatter has quietened down, but I am still in their radio carrier beam. They've opened up a couple of radars to watch me. Now's the time to review the options and work out what losing altitude cost me in fuel. Those radars will think I'm Russian. The external tanks are empty, dump them.'

The COMINT chatter began again. Again the language was unintelligible to Makepiece. But radio reception appeared strong and the recorders were running.

'I'll take another couple of pictures to fix time and position. It should be Dresden down there. I hope the communication chatter is related to the flash. It's obvious it's plain language, not encrypted. That flash was something pretty significant. Looks as though the magnetic gear got something — my magnetic compass seems to be misaligned with the gyro on the cockpit panel. I hope it's not damaged. It's time to concentrate on flying, Makepiece, if you want to get home in one piece. Check your instruments...'

* * *

'Fuel computation: 'Once we're cruising we're using 115 gallons per hour, call it 120 for safety — 2 gallons per minute. Allow 20 gallons extra for the climb from the mine and the extra 8 minutes flying, I reckon I've shaved 18 minutes off the fuel safety margin. I started with 7 minutes, I've gotten minus 11 to play with and no margin for 'Way Blue Yonder's' wind guess work. I did make that climb gentle, and the 8 minutes down low was not a total loss because I had to head in this direction anyway, so let's cut the 18 to 8 minutes lost. Right, Colonel, revised shaved off safety now down to minus 1. I must be on the deck after 10 hours and 11 minutes flying, which is by 12:56 GMT.'

Makepiece frowned: of course there was no-one to witness the gesture.

'Crude! Good enough for government work! Check the instruments, the horizon all round, the instruments again. No other aircraft in sight. Settle down for the long haul home! Against the wind! It's going to be a long slog home. Check autopilot... OK.'

*   *   *

"Right, Makepiece, its decision time!" Makepiece was reassuring himself.

The P-38 was cruising at 295 knots indicated airspeed and across the wind. He was flying on internal fuel now. The drop tanks had made their pock marks in the German landscape some hours ago. He was over the town of Gera and the cockpit clock showed 09:34; he was 8 minutes behind his schedule. He must be edging into the opposing jet stream. 'Not good...'

With his navigation chart showing radial distance and fuel requirement to West Malling temporarily perched on his knee, Makepiece concluded that he could route as planned, due west, then turn over the earthworks at Ohrdruf, that test range south-west of Berlin, then due north towards Magdeburg where Edge Cryshaw's systems had picked up the surface to air missile test on his Christmas flight.

"Remember, Makepiece, this ship isn't carrying any countermeasures for SAM missiles." He wished the personal equipment designers could dream up a method of giving him a drink to counter the dryness of breathing pure oxygen for so many hours.

'I wonder if this is where and why Edge Cryshaw bought it. Some sort of missile test range?' thought Makepiece. 'What did 'Sprite' Battel call it? Bad show! Typical bloody British understatement! — kinda like 'gone west' instead of saying the poor bastard's dead!'

Makepiece held his planned course while keeping a good lookout for enemy fighters or missiles.

'But at least, in this drink free environment, I do not have to use the nappy we aircrews have to wear.' That thought made him think of

Marybeth and the children back in Maryland. 'They'll be asleep now. It's the middle of the night for them. I hope they're alright. Yes, of course they're alright, why shouldn't they be? There will plenty of time to think about home when I'm on the deck. Two more hours to go, give or take. It's time to keep your eyes skinned for unwelcome company, Makepiece. At least you're flying down sun. You've gotten a coupla thousand feet altitude in reserve if you really need it, but remember you're tight of AVGAS. Check fuel… There are no refuellers up here!'

* * *

'It looks like there's something significant happening down there in the Ohrdruf barracks lines. I can't tell what it is but the ground and snow is well chewed up. Construction work? Perhaps there's something in the story about Hitler's alternative funk bunker. There's plenty of film in the vertical camera. I'll let the intel guys worry about that. The COMINT system is running again, I don't know if it's related to what's going on below. We're off to see what's on show west of Magdeburg — wait a minute — why are all those trucks going into those caves?'

Careful to keep his altitude, Makepiece turned the P-38 on its right wingtip through 180 degrees for a better look.

'I'd say those caves have got doors. Another example of Gerry using an underground factory. What for? They've gotten plenty of labour with those poor devils from Nordhausen concentration camp. Buchenwald is not so far away either. It's obviously something pretty big with all that activity. I'd better go and have a closer look. I'll keep the airspeed up. I don't want to get caught by flak over a test range. It's where the bastards got The Edge. Nose down for a single pass. It's what we've got mach flaps for. Here we go!'

All the electronic communications sensors were working as Makepiece flew past the heavy steel doors on the cave. Makepiece had opened the sniffer louvres just in case. He did not have time to see what was in the cave, his flying at extremely low altitude and high speed was too hairy. It was interesting that the men on the ground did not try to take cover as he flew by; perhaps they did not hear him coming, perhaps the guards were ruthlessly holding them at the posts. The cameras may have caught the explanation.

'Straight up, sunshine. Get some altitude under your belly. Gently does it! And get those flaps in… No more messing about until you're back at 37,000 plus. Then check your fuel and timing. Let's hope there's less jet stream at 37,000.'

*   *   *

Fuel computation: 'Oh, Makepiece, you've really blown it. Good British expression that — blown it! Fuel, aviation gasoline, AVGAS — doesn't matter what you call it, it's still fuel and you need it! Check fuel/air lever is in the fully lean position; I haven't touched it since take-off! We caught up time at Orhdruf, turned 3 minutes early, less headwind than forecast. Must nag 'Way Blue Yonder'! That down and up cost me say 10 gallons now the P-38 is lighter — say 10 minutes flying. I can shave 2 minutes passing Braunschweig to the west, just a couple of oblique images of Göring's secret test institute at Vokenrode — Babs at Medmenham will like those — then home.'

Makepiece wiped a gloved hand across his tired eyes. 'God, I'm thirsty! Check fuel…'

He heaved a sigh. It was touch and go if he would make it!

'We'll leave the autopilot to do the flying until we let down through cloud at the Dutch coast. This is going to be tight! The COMINT is running, we're going home, I shan't interfere. Thank God for the high altitude cloud; I feel a bit safer, somehow.'

*   *   *

If the *Luftwaffe* put up a pursuit fighter, Makepiece did not notice. He had no technical sensor to alert him that German radar had paid him a lot of attention, but he was moving too fast and too high to make a chase worthwhile to the stretched *Luftwaffe* resources. He crossed the Dutch coast homebound and became concerned that he had, according to his gauges, 12 minutes fuel left for 15 minutes more flying. Planned fuel margin did not matter now. This was real. Makepiece switched on his identification radio beacon to tell the RAF he was friend not foe.

"I don't want to have to dice with some trigger-happy Spitfire jockey with no fuel in my tanks," he said aloud to himself. He was still in combat airspace, gradually descending in today's return safe recovery airlane, where his special project group maintained radio silence except in the direst emergency. He crossed the English coast. Familiar territory now, in broken cloud West Malling would be visible in three minutes. Makepiece had already put the aircraft nose below the horizon to begin to lose altitude, throttled back as far as he dared to conserve fuel. His attention was now more outside the cockpit, anxious not to meet some less observant pilot going the other way.

He passed through the cloud base at 2500 feet. The fuel gauges were indicating empty when the starboard engine began to splutter. With the altimeter showing 1500 feet above the ground, now he was flying on one engine. It would be alright if the port engine could find the fuel for just 35 seconds, until he crossed West Malling hedge.

"West Malling tower, this is Able for a final landing. I'm low on fuel. I have the runway in sight. Clear for down wind landing."

Makepiece had clung to his altitude but, even so, he did not have sufficient airspeed to glide the extra four air-miles to attempt to land into wind.

"Good afternoon, Able. You are clear to land. I have no other traffic. Runway 040 wind gusting 16 knots. Altimeter 1007." Sergeant Hannah Black's calm voice welcomed home all 'her' pilots. Masking her anxiety, one of 'her' aircraft was facing the hazard of landing 32 miles per hour faster than usual.

"Able, check your landing gear, do you have three greens?"

From the runway control cabin, two miles away across the flat airfield, a pair of red Very flares arched into the sky.

The port engine spluttered to a stop. He was sweating for the third time.

Makepiece had no engine power to lower his undercarriage. He was gliding in an aircraft not designed for this type of flying. No matter how often you practice a dead-engine approach, the real thing was infinitely worse. You don't practice downwind landings. He was going to crash. He glanced at the red wind-sock on its mast.

He was going to land downwind. Only one chance...

"Able. Both engines failed. I am going to do a wheels-up, right hand side of runway."

"Understood, Able. Our rescue crews are on their way. Wind is 045 at 16 knots. Good luck."

The crash alarm had sounded and the RAF fire and ambulance crews were already climbing onto their vehicles as the American P-38 skimmed over the boundary hedge and landed on the grass beside the runway. Americans were streaming out of their lamella compound.

Makepiece held the nose high as long as he was able, trying to kill off unnecessary airspeed, but the flying attitude meant the twin fuselage touched the ground heavily, first buckling then breaking off the twin tail booms. The wings, cockpit and engines remained intact as the aircraft slithered over the grass, sheering off the propellers, screeching with friction until it came to a halt.

Silence. No fire. Silence until the crash vehicles appeared.

Makepiece slid back his cockpit canopy, moved the internal battery power switch to safe, released his harness straps, and stood to show he was alright. In his right hand he held the clip which would have pulled the igniters for the self-destruction explosives in the role equipment; with his left hand he was pulling at his oxygen mask. Under the deceleration, his goggles had slipped from over his eyes down to the mask. The RAF fireman was first on the scene, wearing his asbestos suit with his face-piece closed, approaching with a portable foam appliance. Makepiece waved him away, then collapsed against the edge of the cockpit. The crash impact had bruised three ribs against Makepiece's seat harness and both legs were badly bruised below the knees. He was fortunate that his injuries were so slight.

There was no fire — just broken metal and one crumpled pilot

The Lockheed maintainers were the first Americans on the scene. Four arrived on bicycles across the grass. One glance told them that this airframe, which had slithered over the grass on its flat photographic fairing, would not fly again. The RAF medics lifted the unconscious Makepiece onto a stretcher and into their own ambulance. By now a uniformed American officer had appeared and he took charge of the medical evacuation of the limp Makepiece back to the lamella hanger where their own flight surgeon could decide what best to do.

It was obvious the crash pilot was still alive and not visibly bleeding. In the absence of fire, the RAF agreed that the 1574th should recover the waste metal back to their compound. A second American officer had said the P-38 was not armed and he was accessing various areas about the fuselage with device safety pins with high-visibility red tape streamers. An American crew arrived in a jeep and removed camera film cassettes from the fuselage and other items whose purpose was not known to the RAF emergency team.

"There would be a minimum of paperwork if the Yanks do their own thing." A wise decision by the RAF Duty Engineering Officer clarified who would do what next. It needed a loaned crane and a flatbed trailer to get the crash remains to their hanger. The RAF helpers were not allowed to see inside the lamella hangar while the flatbed was being offloaded.

"Thanks all round."

"The incident is an American matter. You can buy us a pint sometime."

"We can take it from here."

*   *   *

In the ATC local tower, Sergeant Hannah Black's log recorded: 'One P-38 crashed at 13:13 GMT. The pilot had reported low fuel and landed cross wind without undercarriage. RAF crash crew attended. No fatalities. Americans recovered wreckage. Airfield reported clear of hazards at 15:00 GMT.'

It was routine and according to training.

Wartime calm returned to RAF West Malling airfield.

Chapter 41
1944 ~ Change of Command

Colonel Makepiece Ploughman woke. He focused on Chmielewski's and the doctor's faces. They were smiling.

"Welcome back, Colonel."

"Oh!" Makepiece hurt all over.

"Nothing actually broken, three possible cracked ribs," said the flight surgeon, David McFallis. "Your shins hit something and broke the skin; they'll be sore, but no lasting damage. Not even a nose bleed, although those black eyes suggest the other guy might not have come off worse! And you won't be flying for a couple of weeks."

"And bruised pilot pride," offered Chmielewski.

"Oh!" moaned Makepiece. "Someone get this elephant off my chest!"

"Are you fit for visitors?" questioned Doc McFallis. He was fussing over his patient in the medical tradition; he knew full well every detail of the colonel's injuries and was confident that no lasting damage had been sustained by the 43 year old body. He knew the RAF squadron leader station commander was anxious to speak with the American commander of the 1574th SPSG — '...no one else will do, I'm sorry. And alone.'

"I guess. Can't Rod handle it?" Makepiece closed his eyes to try to drive the agony away. It didn't work.

McFallis' head shook negatively. "And no alcohol for at least 24 hours... doctor's orders."

"Ooh! You bone crunchers have degree majors in torture..."

"I'm afraid Squadron Leader Wilburne insists it has to be the Colonel. You know what they're like; once the Brits've bitten, you've got to concede. Look at the rat bite that Montgomery gave Rommel at El Alamein. British bulldogs... ya know...!"

"Give me five to collect my thoughts, then... OK. I really want to talk to Rod — and the intel crew — so keep him short."

"Will do," responded the flight surgeon. "I'll limit him to five minutes on account of your condition..."

"No need to lay it on, Doc." The patient didn't need to labour his pain; it was quite clear across his face. "Now get outta here and let this here colonel ruminate. I could do with some mouthwash. Jack Daniels^{tm}? And take Rod with you!"

"I mean it, Colonel. Water, aqua pura. Doctor's orders. The nurse will put neat water on the rocks so you can pretend it's a cocktail. By the way, it's 21:45 on Thursday; you were out for 54 hours."

"Your resurrection was not quite as notable as His," blasphemed Chmielewski. "You only had two days to His three..." Makepiece's deputy was already through the door, followed by the white-coated flight surgeon, before Makepiece could reply. Already the nurse was clearing away the probes, and monitors, and drip stand and other paraphernalia. The compensation for having his hands and face washed was a delightful scent... pure American.

Makepiece's 'oohs and aarhs' generated no sympathy in the nurse.

*   *   *

Squadron Leader Wilburne had visited, delivered his urgent news, and departed. Now Makepiece's bedside was occupied by just his deputy and a reliable intelligence officer.

"Sarah. You know I would not normally do this, but this time it's for a good reason. Please understand... be patient with the old man's request. Go get me a bottle of Jack Daniels[tm], two — no — three glasses and some ice. Give Rod and me 10 minutes." Rod was already reaching for a five pound note. Makepiece continued, "I'm sorry, Sarah. I need a moment with Rod alone, then we want to hear what intelligence you've gotten — extracted — out of the stuff I brought home."

Makepiece's request of a junior officer was unusual, definitely beyond normal officer etiquette.

"Please, Sarah." No woman could resist the pleading in those blackened eyes. "All will become clear in a little while, I promise.."

"No problem, Colonel. One bottle, three glasses and ice." Her smile gave some reassurance to her injured colonel.

Sarah, who had not had an invitation to sit in the presence of her commanding officer, reached for the door. She had not yet opened it before Makepiece spoke again.

"If you can find Wing Commander Battel, ask him to join us here in 45 minutes. Request, not an order, Sarah! Better make that four glasses. Oh, and stay clear of the doctor with those goodies..."

This time Lieutenant Sarah Johansson spoke with a touch of team spirit in her voice, "You sure do arrange parties in a strange manner, Colonel."

The colonel and his deputy grinned at each other as the door closed. Their eyes had followed the form to the door.

"Good lass, that. Tcch! Women in a man's war... A commendation would be in order especially when you hear what she's got to say about your radio take. Cute arse too."

"More pressing matters first, Rod. For your ears only until I tell you different. The RAF has been told that Snodland is being given to General Patton as part of the accommodation for a new army division. We have to be out of here, totally, by 31st March. That includes everything in the Tech Block and the safe in the lamella."

Chmielewski was genuinely surprised. "Where to? You can't park some of that gear in an open field!"

"Don't know, Rod. If the RAF knows it's not saying. Protocol. American deployments are commanded by American Generals. Their balloon outfit is going too. Patton's men will be here to clean up any high-value or security sensitive stuff left behind before his grunts move in on 1st April."

"I guess it's Patton going to sort out Hitler and Rommel?"

"I reckon. I'll get on to my contact at COSSAC tomorrow and see what General Spaatz has to say from Dawes Hill. This has come right out of the blue."

"That accounts for why a General Packer is the coming over from Bushy Park tomorrow. He said to me that I was to clear your diary from 10 o'clock tomorrow and hold myself available for after he had spoken to you. No other clues."

"Well, the RAF has been told to make their arrangements under great secrecy. 'Burn before reading — pink ink on pink paper' stuff. Chummy Adrian Wilburne at Snodland does not know, or could not say, if the base commander at RAF West Malling knows we are moving out, or if they are for that matter."

"Do you think," Chmielewski was scratching the short hair on his head, "this is a play by Donovan to get 1574th into mainstream intel, flying regular missions?"

Makepiece shook his head and winced at the induced pain. "I wonder if the Sprite has got any inkling. He's not dropped any clues my way."

"Mmm!"

"Guess we'll find out more tomorrow. I'll bear in mind what you said about Sarah... talk of the devil." The quiet footsteps on the linoleum covered corridor stopped Makepiece's train of thought. A knock on the door was followed by an awkward entrance with all hands full.

Chmielewski directed, "Set it down on that table, Sarah, and pour three slugs. The Colonel ain't flying tonight! Drag up a chair... Did you find the wing commander?"

*   *   *

Colonel Ploughman was sufficiently recovered to receive General Packer in his secure office in the Technical Building. Aide Sergeant Julia Greenburg poured the coffee, left the creamer and sweetener on the otherwise clear desk and left. She closed the door behind her. She noticed the General had kept his field cap on. Trouble!

Having waved the obviously injured colonel to a chair other than his own behind the only desk, the still standing General started, verbally hitting straight from the shoulder. "And what the hell were you doing flying an operational mission? General Spaatz had Secretary Stimson on the horn screaming for your arse. Contravening written orders — his orders —your colonel's eagles aren't enough. He wants your nuts and entrails too."

The general was pacing the room, his arms held rigidly by his side. Julia Greenburg could hear that her colonel was on the end of something 'militarily gut-crunching'.

"General," began Makepiece, "I don't know how much you know about what 1574th does, or how well?"

"That's not the issue here, Colonel. You broke the rules and I'm here to collect."

Makepiece held his composure. At times like this military discipline helps.

"General. Just before I fall on my sword, just tell me. How does Stimson know I flew a mission?"

"You don't get an explanation officially." The General was removing his headdress as an indication that what followed was non-attributable. He paused his pacing while retaining the look of distaste in his mouth.

"But for old time's sake, and because you intel guys speak with special handshakes, I'll tell you that your man Bernard Weiss sent something through what's called ALSOS channels — whatever — direct to Washington and it got linked by General Donovan with a written-off P-38 on an RAF airfield."

The general shuddered, "A bleeding civilian, intelligence… spook… bypassing the chain of command…" The words conveyed his disgust with the whole business.

"One bent USAAC colonel in regular casualty records and Makepiece Ploughman is mincemeat. No ifs or buts. Chmielewski is to take command, you go to Dawes Hill for staff duties away from any and all flying — until elephants grow wings — or later."

"Shit!" Hardly a military officer's response, but…

"Quite. Something was going to happen to the 1574th anyway. We are getting ready to hit France and Ike has decided Patton is going to wave Old Glory here in Kent and East Anglia to let the Krauts know we're loading our weapons for bear. Real-estate round here is hard to come by. Snodland has been selected and out you go. I was set to come down here to tell you until your bent P-38 upset the generals. The Brits have already told their folks."

The general replaced his headdress and resumed his angry pacing.

"I heard a …"

"Whatever you heard before today, I neither know… or care. This is official. Lieutenant Colonel Chmielewski will move the outfit out to Base Aircraft Depot Warton while COSSAC decides what to do with the aircraft, staff and materiel."

"General, they are certain items that…"

"Ploughman. They're not your problem. Chmielewski gets command when he walks through that door and you leave for Dawes Hill by noon. Is that clear?"

"Crystal, General, crystal clear." A combination of risk of pain and military stoicism kept Makepiece from showing any reaction.

"Colonel. Now let's have that coffee. D'you want to smoke?" The general had moved to sit in the commanding officer's chair.

"Not in here, General. You'll blow the place and us with it, straight down the river, if you light up here. Chemicals and neat oxygen; one spark and it's curtains. It's no smoking in here, and no concession, even for Churchill."

General Packer said, "Since you mention Churchill, I can tell you that ALSOS is not going to tell the Brits what your mission brought back. No way." The cap had come off his head and was being placed on the desk. "Jesus, they won't tell me, either. The RAF will just know that the Yanks have rationalised their reccon assets, normal procedure. Now, when you are ready, have your aide bring Rod Chmielewski in."

The general paused, recognising the physical anguish of the officer seated opposite trying to begin to rise. He beckoned Makepiece to remain seated.

"I'll have your aide cut Chmielewski's orders before I leave. You stay put while I do it."

The General was already reaching for his hat as he moved around the desk. The next five minutes would be military formal.

*   *   *

"Jeez. I had no idea that was coming. I'm so sorry that you were shopped by that creep Weiss. I was never sure which side his bread was buttered. He's disappeared, into London I guess. Wrapped in the atomic bomb shroud! Someone will have to chase him down to sign off the ABLATIVE list. I don't think he ever got close enough to know the real 1574th mission. He never had access to those papers."

"No recriminations, Rod. You've gotten a tough job winding this outfit down. But I have to say that a two aircraft outfit would not be viable. I have one request. I'd like to take Sergeant Julia Greenburg as my aide, to Dawes Hill, for as long as you can spare her. I'll phone Julius Knapp and get him to clear her onto his staff, and me too I guess, and from there we can use our channels to protect the ABLATIVE level 3 material. I know we were close; that Kraut Kammler was shooting for the Moon, maybe literally. I have got to get something into FDR's hands before the invasion muddies presidential thinking."

Tenderly, Makepiece rose to shake Chmielewski's hand.

"Congratulations on your command. You sure earned your bird colonel's eagles as well. I've not heard about those. I'll get out of your short and curlies now. Give me a second to clear my desk, Julia will bring a box. Good luck. Sorry I only left you two P-38M-SPs to play with — and one toy for practice. Anything I can do to help, don't hesitate to ask…"

"Thanks, Colonel, er Makepiece. Would you please ask Sergeant Greenburg to step inside and close the door behind her? You stay put while I tell her. She's gonna have to cut her own orders to escape from here with legit paperwork to match. I'll clear it with Clarke McKing; telling the adjutant that General 'Toohey' Spaatz has reassigned his top WAAC administrator is going to blow his mind. Good luck, sir. It was a pleasure working with you and I hope we'll work together again in happier circumstances."

*   *   *

"What are we doing here, Sergeant?"

"Colonel Chmielewski says I have to take you back to the Technical Block to check your sidearm."

"That's bull shit, Sergeant!" Makepiece was still an army officer and knew a tall story when he heard one.

"Just doing as I was told, Colonel." Sitting in the driver's seat, Sergeant Greenberg was able to avoid Makepiece's eyes. He knew she was not telling the truth.

"Go along with it, Colonel, this once. Please!"

"OK. But you owe me for this."

They walked along the corridor, up to Makepiece's familiar office door. His name plate had already been removed. He knocked on the door.

"Come in."

Inside, Lieutenant Sarah Johansson stood at the desk closing a folder. There was a map spread across the surface, being leant on by Rod Chmielewski. Makepiece noted that Rod's collar lapels each carried the silver star of Lieutenant Colonel rank; COSSAC had not promoted him! Also in the room was a civilian from the electronics support area and Technical Sergeant Openshaw, a technician from the flight line. 'Wishful' Palmer and 'Way Blue Yonder' Ryman, the meteorological officers were approaching the door as if to leave. Rod Chmielewski broke the silence.

"Thank you, gentlemen. Sarah, you stand fast. Sergeant Greenberg, would you be so kind as to show the new kid on the block where you stashed the coffee and makings and then wait while I debrief your passenger? He had better bring it in, the new kid that is. Coffee. I'll be using that new skill a lot in the hours to come... coffee tasting." The visitors to the office had been effectively dismissed, except Lieutenant Sarah Johannson.

To Makepiece, Chmielewski said, "I've been summoned to COSSAC. I have to be at Bushy Park at 21:00 tonight — too late for a meal!"

While the room was settling down, Sarah spoke. "Hello, Colonel Ploughman." She made sure there was a chair, close enough to his former desk, for Makepiece to be able to view the map. There was sadness in her voice and in her eyes made darker by insufficient sleep. She knew that a change of command had happened. The whole 1574th knew. She did not know the detail. She had done her duty and produced the first level report for her commander's desk for release by telegraph.

"I guess I should have said 'goodbye'." She hesitated then thrust her hand to shake the outgoing colonel's.

Chmielewski thanked Sarah for the report and then dismissed her, acknowledging her salute, leaving only Makepiece and himself in the room.

"I thought you should see this report before you get to Dawes Hill. You might want additional detail, question a conclusion and clarify a translation, whatever. It would be easier if you could discuss the original with the analyst. Once the raw stuff gets Stateside, we won't be able to help!"

"Very good of you, Rod. Do I have 30 minutes? You're going out on a limb doing this for me."

"Take as long as it takes, Makepiece. I'm in charge even if it's only 'til the end of the month. In here it's pretty private and my new aide hasn't been out of diapers long enough to know I'm breaking any rules. The crew that compiled this report are all in the refectory until you release them. Anything you want to have explained and they'll come running faster than a Campbell on the Utah Salt Flats."

'If that officer has a fault,' thought Makepiece, 'it is misuse of metaphors.'

*　　　*　　　*

The 1574th Special Project Security Group's new commander lifted the closed folder off his desk and passed it to Colonel Ploughman. The contents were a summary message ready for the communications staff to telegraph to headquarters and Washington, a tabulated report referencing important highlights, together with formatted transcripts and translations in the style of the Intelligence Corps procedures which would be forwarded by courier. The folder also contained dozens of labelled black and white photographs. A typed text on one side at double space was titled 'Radio-nuclide Analysis'. A second typed text was titled 'Possible Einstein Engine'.

Rod Chmielewski, with a smile of his face, said, "Makepiece, you're gonna like that last sheet. It's gonna make your day! I know it's been pretty shitty so far."

Makepiece knew he could rely on Rod to have drawn out the important elements, so he gave his full attention to the formatted report.

Chapter 42
1944 ~ Ablative Mission Report

(Author's note: The full page diagram of the image Chrtonos werke is given at the concluding 'Fictional Notes' section of this book.)

MOST SECRET ABLATIVE 3 -- ULTIMATE

Partial transcription of 1574th SPSG Mission 440313/01 dated March 14, 1944.
Pilot: Colonel Makepiece Frisby Ploughman USAAC
Transcribed: Lieutenant Lorne Amhurst US Army Intelligence Corps
                 Lieutenant Sarah Johannson US Army Intelligence Corps
Media references: Sound Film: 440313/01 Channel: 5 & 6 LSB and HSB
Cross references: ELINT: 440313/01 E12 thru E43 - unusable
                 Photographic: 440313/01 strips 53 thru 126
                 Other: Telemetry: 440313/01 (6) USB
                 Particle: 440313/01 filters 4 thru 26
Time Zone: All time datums are GMT. Times in text, if any, are verbatim

Caution: This is a first level analysis and is subject to reassessment.

		Mission Phase 1: Eastbound Transit to Target Area *The intercept aircraft was over Frankfurt, SE of Berlin*
05:14	Man A	Are you ready to print radio picture?
05:16	Man B	*{faint}* go *{unreadable about 125 seconds}* have you transmitted *{it?}*
05:17		*{no traffic}*
05:17	Man B	*{unreadable }* have you transmitted *{it?}*
05:18	Man A	It went through. Shall I send it again? Stay on this channel. There will be less switching.
05:19	Man B	Yes. Herr General Kammler is waiting for the design *{blueprint?}*
05:20	Man A	I will instruct Frau *{unintelligible name}*to pass the design through the *{technical term: possibly head or reader or scan device}*Are you ready to print radio picture?

05:21	Man B	My machine is ready. The lights are green. Go.
		Analyst comment: *{there was a stream of on/off segments typical of a radio facsimile. We have played this intercept through our printer and obtained the following image}*:
		{Analyst Comment:: An improved image is available at frame 440313/01 853} (see page 366 of this novel)
05:25	Man B	That was good, Wollenberger. Standby *{for more orders?}*
05:26	Man A	*{Chronos ?}* is ready to fire, Herr General
05:27	Man B	Silence. Wait for orders. *{Silence on link}*

Rod Chmielewski had refreshed the coffee to find his former commanding officer smiling. "It gets better, Makepiece. See the next page! You'll be interested to see how it gels with what you told Sarah."

		Mission Phase 2a: Transit to target *The intercept aircraft was high altitude over Wenceslas Mine*
		Mission Phase 2b: Opportunity target flyby at low altitude *The intercept aircraft low altitude over Wenceslas Mine*
07:00	unidentified	Significant interference on all channels

		{unintelligible for 75 seconds} Aircraft was flying through 'smoke plume' ... **Transcription ends.**
		Photo analysis comment: *07:00:01 A massive explosion, probably subsurface, produced a blue flash centred on a steel structure above ground. Mensuration and shape of structure suggests radio resonance at 235 Mc/s using similar principle to a radar magnetron. Shaped object ejected from structure to higher than 450 feet in 3 seconds.* *07:00:12 frame 440313/01 890 shows structure still resonating with background earth and snow in violent shake.* *07:07:33 structure again in camera view from low altitude. Blue resonance continues. All snow to beyond 250 yards melted, all foliage stripped from conifers, many knocked down. Some vegetation smouldering.* *07:07:58 entrance to tunnel severely scorched and smoking.* *07:07:25 and 07:08:08 Wingtip cameras show considerable earth shake and a possible ventilation chimney or shaft upwards plume which aircraft flies through at 07:07:52.*
		Particle analysis comment: *Sensor apparatus clock failed. Significant radioactive particles collected: 200 to 350 times more intense radiation than background.*
		Aircraft Maintainer Report. *Significant scorching to wing leading edges. Unidentified radioactive contamination of leading edges. Cabling in port boom and all engine ignition looms show signs of induced high amperage current. Many electrical earth connection studs fused by excess current.*
		Pilot's Report. *High altitude photography from about 38000 feet, low altitude from about 400 feet*

		above ground level, tracking down-sun. Plume extended to about 1000 feet above ground level. Blue aura following initial flash sustained while I was photographing.... Engines misfired for 3 to 5 seconds at time of flash then returned to normal. Magnetic anomaly detector failed; magnetic compass gave unreliable readings after flash.

		Mission Phase 3: Transit to Ohrdruf
09:00	Kammler	*{Link in clear, Man C identified as SS General Kammler from opening pleasantries}* A good result at the mine?
09:01	Sporrenberg	*{Man D identified as SS General Sporrenberg from opening pleasantries}* Good *{pleasantries about common acquaintances}* The vehicle ejected cleanly. The launch structure survived the energy, the ground about laid to waste with all animal life extinguished to radius of 200 metres. There was no fire.
09:02	Kammler	My predictions to the centimetre.
09:02	Sporrenberg	Where you able to track the vehicle?
09:03	Kammler	My instruments gauged the vehicle to 17500 metres altitude when it was moving at 2785 kilometre per hour. It then { ... } beyond range, going north to the wilderness.
09:04	Sporrenberg	I continue to assess these mountains for protected assembly plant for your new weapons.
09:05	Kammler	The Americans' daylight precision bombing will endanger the factories in the Harz Mountains but assembly work must continue. It will save Himmler a lot of problems with the final solution.
09:05	Sporrenberg	*{laughter}* It will be safe to enter the Wenceslas cavern in three hours. The CHRONOS apparatus may have received heavy thermal shock. I shall have the Jews extract salvage for analysis in Vienna, as usual. I shall inspect the interior

		tunnels and report ... replacement bells and special materials are waiting my orders in a railway siding.
09:06	Kammler	The radio picture was sufficient for my immediate needs. Send me accurate blueprints. Maybe I can persuade Speer to do some useful work ...*{inaudible through interference}*
09:07	Sporrenberg	*{unreadable through interference}*
09:07	Kammler	The new material is proving easy to work and saves weight. We could have a manned launch ...

Makepiece commented, "So I just happened along at the moment of testing CHRONOS." He was tidying the paper sheaf as he spoke. "Good King Wenceslas sure gave me a farewell present!"

Makepiece sipped his coffee. "You don't think I could have flown through an anti-gravity beam which gave me a kick up the tailplane?"

Chmielewski was frowning. "I shouldn't suggest that if I were you. People will think you are a crank."

"I'll stick to the thermal uplift which gave me a boot."

Chmielewski replied, "It looks like it on that evidence alone. The good eggs are not the only goodies in the report pack. Maybe there was control telemetry with time coding tucked away in the multi-channel stuff we can't read. The egg-heads in Washington were ecstatic about the material that 'The Edge' brought back about the missile test. They'll love it if you've collected CHRONOS, the Einstein Engine and Hitler's time weapon in one mission! Imagine: what if you could put time back 24 hours to the day before you lost the battle...? But there is more. Don't stop reading."

		Mission Phase 4: Turning Point over Ohrdruf test range *The intercept aircraft high altitude over Ohrdruf*
09:49		***Photo analysis comment:*** *Images as aircraft climbing through 15000 feet over Mühlhausen. Second mountain entrance visible with 25 flatbed rail cars loaded with crates each 10.5*

		metres long moving away from entrance.
09:54		***Photo analysis comment:*** *Aircraft climbing through 35000 feet abeam Nordhausen concentration camp. Ongoing extension of site, new huts, more disturbed snow and groundwork. Enlarged camp compound.*
09:59		***COMINT Analysis comment:*** *Unusual military conversation about rail traffic bringing cattle freight south from Magdeburg competing for available rail clearance for armament freight moving north from Erfurt. A VIP train is claiming priority transit over same lines.* *No related photo, particle or pilot's reports.*

Makepiece's face creased with a smile. There was a final page of formatted report.

		Mission Phase 5: Opportunity target over Völkenrode Test Institute and grass airfield. *The intercept aircraft was at medium altitude climbing through 27000 feet over Braunschweig heading 280 degrees, five oblique images of Göring's (Aeronautical) Test Institute at Völkenrode.*
		COMINT Analyst comment: *Little is known about the covert Hermann Göring's (Aeronautical) Test Institute at Völkenrode. It is in a remote site, extending to an estimated 135 acres, shrouded in conifer forest with buildings resembling education blocks associated with farming. Previous imagery suggests major works (possibly underground), earth removal and electricity supply development but no explanation has been found. A small grass airstrip may be associated with light air transport.*
10:31		*{2 minutes of communications operator technical and procedural chatter.}*
10:33	Man A	Professor Blenk. I understand congratulations are in order.

10:33	Blenk	It is very good of you to say so, Herr Riechmarshall.
10:33	Man A	I read that Doktor Thome and Professor Grammel have pushed the test tunnel to Mach 4. Völkenrode is the only *{...place/site/facility?...}* in the Reich where such test speeds have been achieved under controlled conditions.
10:34	Blenk	The flow was maintained for 90 seconds, Herr Riechmarshall. The model sustained damage but the test area remained intact. We shall be able to rerun our tests with a strengthened model in 4 days.
10:34	Man A	Good. Good. And does the swept wing function as predicted?
10:35	Blenk	Grammel's forecasts were close. Our observations suggest major advantage to high speed manoeuvrability and altitude performance at Mach numbers above the speed of sound.
10:35	*Göring*	I continue to report your success to the Führer when we meet. Of course our A-4 warheads achieve greater velocity in its dive but there are problems in viewing the results *{laughter}*. You understand that your research is of great value to our new aircraft and missiles. Messerschmitt is doing good things with the Komet. You must not let anything divert you. Is the security of the institute still intact? No more unwelcome visitors, I hope.
10:36	Blenk	There were a couple of lovers who had to be frightened away with our wolfhounds, Herr Riechmarshall, *{laughter}* *{unreadable for 10 seconds}* ... cold arse, but we are confident our fence has not been breached. The tunnels are not melting the surface snow this year thanks to our control measures. We are particularly pleased with our ballistics tunnel. We can now test panzer ordinance over 400 metres flight.
10:38	Man A	All well and good, Blenk ...*{fading}* ...*priority is high Mach speed wind tunnels. Your experiments have shown ... (unreadable)*...through this so-called

		barrier and I have the pilots ready to prove it. Continue your work on *{?...delta wing ?}* for the *{? Junkers Ju 287 ?}* already has a suitable *{unreadable}*
10:39		**Transcription ends**:

*   *   *

Chmielewski noticed that Makepiece had paused in his reading. The coffee was now unpalatably cool.

"It looks as if you snapped the production line for Hitler's V-weapons and maybe confirmed a secret test range. Didn't you have a successful mission?"

"It could have ended on a sweeter note."

"Granted. This war has already shafted lots of good men and I guess you ain't gonna be the last. I'll get you a fresh jug of java while you read the final two pages. I suggest you take Weiss's paper first. Save the best for last. Take your time. I'll send Julia to the cookhouse for some travel sandwiches. I'm gonna ask you to courier this pack to Dawes Hill."

As Rod began to move, Makepiece shifted his position for greater comfort before turning to the next folio and began to read.

Most Secret - ALSOS Channels Only - American Eyes Only

Report by: Dr Bernard Weiss DPhil(Nuc), MSc(Hons)
Professor of Radio-nuclides and Researcher at University of Denver.

Analysis of Mission: - *440313/01 flown March 13th, 1944*
Pilot: *Colonel Makepiece F. Ploughman USAAC*
Location: *Western Poland, Sudeten Mountains*

Radio-nuclide Analysis

A particle collection sensor apparatus using a step-feed, 2 micron, pH neutral, filter paper cartridge was flown on a P-38 reconnaissance aircraft over west Poland on March 13th, 1944.

274

The device clock failed, perhaps due to electromagnetic pulse emanating from the relevant fission event. The collector was deliberately flown through the plume of an underground explosion emanating from a breather chimney or shaft. Significant radioactive particles were collected, which were collectively 200 to 350 times more intense radiation than normal background. Initial analysis suggests presence of uranium 235 and 238 isotopes, caesium, strontium, lead isotopes, mercury including mercury halides and permanganates, silicon and oxygen isotopes and possibly potassium isotopes, beryllium and deuterium. These substances are consistent with a fission event of uranium origin but are not, in themselves, conclusive evidence of a controlled or bomb-like explosion. Some copper and zinc, principally in halide or oxide compound, was present on the filters. Earth debris thrown up by the underground event had been exposed to intense heat and pressure, sand and clays had fused suggesting temperatures above 1000 degrees centigrade. The P-38 magnetic anomaly detection apparatus failed during the mission, consistent with an electro-magnetic pulse event-induced overload.

Conclusion. *It is concluded that the P-38 flew through a plume of exhaust detritus consistent with a fission event induced by a uranium sub-critical mass. Collateral intelligence suggests that radio-nuclide waste matter was largely contained in the underground chamber used for the test. The fission event generated considerable, not quantifiable, energy which may have been channelled into another device for unknown purposes.*

In the opinion of the author, this was not an atomic bomb test since the containment chamber evidently remained intact despite considerable seismic earth shake proximate to the plume emission.

*   *   *

"I presume that Weiss' text was dispatched without being cleared through you and was the basis of his winning a criminal record for me?"

Makepiece stood and rubbed his backside. It was obvious he was still uncomfortable from his injuries.

He chewed the inside of his cheek, the characteristic action when he was thinking distasteful thoughts. "You're gonna leave that ALSOS channels stuff in the pack? Pash and his MANHATTAN Project group will shit bricks. But the ABLATIVE team in ONI, Washington, are gonna love it."

Rod Chmielewski smiled as he poured coffee into fresh cups.

"Sure," he said. "That arsehole Weiss shopped my Colonel. If he leaves his typing carbon lying around in an intelligence outfit, he deserves everything that comes his way. It doesn't say that Hitler's got an A-bomb. On the evidence we have, Adolf may not even be trying for one. But we do know he's got a honcho called Kammler who makes things go bang and gets lots of energy as a by-product. Read the last page. I hope you like it. Maybe the author will sign a personal copy for you to keep for your memoirs."

Most Secret - ABLATIVE Level 3 - ULTIMATE
American Eyes Only

Report by: Lieutenant Colonel Roderick P. Chmielewski the Third, United States Army Air Corps, Intelligence Branch Commander of the 1574th Special Project Security Group, RAF Snodland, Kent, operating from RAF West Malling, Kent, England

Analysis of Mission: - 440313/01 flown on March 13th, 1944
Location: *Western Poland and central Germany*
Pilot: *Colonel Makepiece F. Ploughman USAAC*
Aircraft: *P-38M-SP*

Possible Einstein Engine

At 07:00 (GMT) on March 13th, 1944 in an underground chamber in Wenceslas Mine, Silesia, Poland, an explosion released a large quantity of energy. Component materials included uranium in a sub-critical mass event which was

276

witnessed by the pilot flying a USAAC reconnaissance P-38M-SP at low altitude. Signals and photographic intelligence, with particle samples returned to base, has established that Waffen SS General Hans Kammler, renowned for engineering some of the most advanced German weapons available, personally encourages the search for an energy source to power the next generation of weapon systems for the advancement of the Third Reich. The aim is to circumvent the difficulties and costs associated with nuclear fission weapons - the atomic bomb with its high dependence on uranium - for a device called CHRONOS (literally time) which might exploit a hypotheses expounded by Einstein concerning an anti-gravity concept.

There is COMINT evidence that the test in the Wenceslas Mine was channelled into a propulsion system - the so-called Einstein Engine - which caused an unpiloted metallic body measuring approximately 120 feet diameter to launch vertically, climb to altitude exceeding 50000 feet and to accelerate to greater than 2000 miles per hour.

The mechanism for generating this energy is not yet understood although a mathematical theory postulated by Einstein in 1929 appears to have been brought to fruition by Kammler and his scientists. Some fatalities among the team working underground on the tests have been reported. There is conjecture that miniature versions of the engine are already flying in devices witnessed by American pilots and other aircrew flying over Germany. These so-called 'foo-fighters', reported as being disc-shaped, with high acceleration and manoeuvrability characteristics, have eluded attempts to photograph them.

The nature and purpose of a hazardous material 'serum-525' (not identified on the intercept radio-picture of the device) associated with the CHRONOS project is not known.

It is beyond doubt that the Wenceslas Mine event of March 13th was one of a series. Preparations and resources are being gathered for the next test at a date unknown. We have limited evidence of the success or failure of earlier test firings. SIGINT and other sources tell us that, under close personal sponsorship by Hitler, Kammler intends to carry on his development of this weapon system within the tightest of security compartment.

If a practical device could realise the hypothetical potential of the Einstein Engine as a universal power source, dependence on hydrocarbon fuel would be negated at a stroke. The postulation is that by tapping gravitational energy, perhaps at sub-atomic level and under conditions of high pressure generated by extremely rapid rotation, an unlimited source of power would be available which could be sufficient to bend time. The country that wins the race to produce such a device would, without doubt, have the supreme weapon supplanting even the most extreme predictions for the atomic bomb.

Recommendation: At the very least we should continue to closely monitor this activity.

Makepiece rose, gingerly put the closed folder on his former desk, and said, "Thanks, Rod. Did you say the team are waiting? I'd like to say goodbye…"

Chapter 43
1944 ~ Chiltern Interlude

It was Sunday, his first Sunday, in the unfamiliar grounds of the commandeered Abbey School in the Oxfordshire town of High Wycombe, which formed most of the American component of Headquarters Bomber Command. The underground high security area of the American headquarters, 10 minutes drive from the British Bomber Command headquarters, was no place for a newcomer to wander around especially when he was uncertain what he might be expected to do. Jules Knapp had welcomed him yesterday, had apologised that, being Saturday, it was not a good day to pay compliments to the general and had sent him back to the Bachelor Officers' Quarters where he was billeted.

"Come in at 08:45 on Monday, Makepiece. There'll be a pass waiting for you at the piquet. We'll take it from there. Your aide will be coming in at the same time. I don't know how long you'll be able to keep her. The generals are always on the lookout for a looker with a security clearance. Enjoy a weekend's furlough. Write a letter home, give Marybeth my love!"

At the commandeered school, there was not much to hold Makepiece's interest. Yesterday's unseasonal baseball game had distracted him for an hour, but it was too cold for spectating in comfort.

So Makepiece Ploughman, colonel of the USAAC, temporarily unassigned, was at a loose end in the nearest town to Dawes Hill. Every shop and bar along the wide high street appeared closed on a Sunday morning. There was almost no traffic on the normally busy London to Oxford road at this hour. High Wycombe, a centre for furniture making and the nominal home of the RAF's Headquarters Bomber Command sited 5 miles north of the town centre, was not exactly a hive of activity. Makepiece strolled along the shop fronts, their glass windows protected against blast, their displays devoid of interesting goods. A narrow fronted newspaper shop was selling Sunday editions, but he was not tempted. The south side of the road, relatively more shaded from the sun, was dominated by the pillared Guildhall. He strolled along the north pavement towards a red brick, almost octagonal, pillared building almost opposite the Guildhall across the unusually wide road.

'Everywhere you go in this country, you trip over history,' thought Makepiece. 'This has got to be 250 years old, at least. I suppose it's one of the reasons the Brits are fighting this war, to keep this alive. It really wasn't so different in Kent, give or take a few bomb craters and an airfield here and there. Who in Washington would put up with a stick of bombs in the main thoroughfare back home? Typical Brits, it's been like this since — who knows — so why change it?'

The thought of Washington reminded him of Marybeth. She'd still be asleep. He'd written a short note stating that he'd had a minor accident, come off flying duties and would be working close to her brother at HQ 8th Bomber Command. She was not to worry, only his dignity was bruised.

He looked at his watch. A cyclist silently passed. Unseen, behind the line of shops, a steam train noisily pulled out of the railway station — that same station he'd used when he first visited Dawes Hill. It was too late to try for a train through London down to Maidstone and Aynette. He hadn't spoken to her since that recall from the hotel. He would have to be back tonight before the last train left him stranded. What would he say to Aynette if he did telephone? They had agreed that there could be no commitment in their being together. It was war!

All Saints is the Parish Church in High Wycombe town centre. A trickle of people, some in uniform, the occasional tin hat marked ARP rubbing against a navy blue colour uniform or a gas mask box slung over the shoulder, was being drawn off the north pavement towards the arched porch. There was a polished child holding his unaccompanied mother's hand; the mother was wearing a wide rimmed hat of black unadorned felt.

Today, Makepiece thought it would be a good time to reflect on his situation — to join a congregation where he might be anonymous for a short while. Beyond the entrance porch, inside the centuries old door, he picked up the duplicated history sheet which explained that an original building on a Roman site was rebuilt in 1275, with its present tower being completed in 1522. All Saints Church was the largest church in the county of Buckinghamshire. Today, such detail did not appeal.

Makepiece settled into a pew, across the nave at the back, furthest away from the door. He responded when the congregation rose to the rousing processional hymn:

God be in my heart and in my understanding...

Its theme struck a chord with him. He sat when the congregation sat and thereafter contributed no further to the congregation's activities.

'Here are folk doing normal Sunday things, in a quiet town, in a world gone mad.'

Makepiece's eyes wandered over the leaded glass windows, the ancient columns reaching to the timbered eves, the choir beyond the lectern. He did not read the polished brass memorials on the walls. His observation of the hanging ensigns would not be remembered. He was seeing, but not registering. His mind was closed to his surroundings, until from the pulpit:

"Today, as my text, II Corinthians, Chapter 4, verses 16 to 18:

For which cause we faint not; but though our outward man perish, yet the inward man is renewed day by day.

For our light affliction, which is but for a moment, worketh for us a far more exceeding and eternal weight of glory;

While we look not at the things which are seen, but at the things which are not seen: for the things which are seen are temporal; but the things which are not seen are eternal."

His thoughts were in part with his family in Maryland and in part in Kent with the momentous events of the last week and Cleeve Lyon cottage. Might he resolve his disloyalty to the woman he loved? Once, during collective prayers, Makepiece's unbowed head caught the notice of the preacher; their eyes engaged for a few precious seconds. For an instant Makepiece was at the controls of his beloved P-38, in the peace at the edge of space, touching the face of God. The preacher did not falter; Makepiece's train of thought continued, 'Have I really witnessed a test of a machine that could disturb eternity?'

When it was time to exit, the men shook hands outside the porch. Makepiece noticed the row of medal ribbons worn on the religious cassock. The understanding of soldiers' experience was exchanged in that mute contact. If the vicar noticed the residual darkening around Makepiece's eyes, he did not comment. The moment passed. The sun won its battle with the overcast and shadows appeared. Makepiece walked the few yards through the graveyard down to the High Street.

"Buy a girl a drink, soldier?"

Makepiece was jolted back to the real world. 'I know that voice.' He turned to find Julia Greenburg, dressed in civilian clothes, with a trace of lipstick, standing within 5 feet. He hadn't noticed his aide; rather, he had not recognised her out of uniform. He swallowed and suppressed a cough.

"Sergeant... Julia... I don't know what to say."

"Try 'Hello Julia...' Colonel. I find it helps break the ice."

"Well, I... err..." Julia eyes indicated she was waiting. "Err... Hello, err... Julia. Err... do you come here often?"

"Only in the mating season." There was a flirtatious highlight on her cheeks. "Talking of ice... If we turn up here, there's a quiet pub which has a private stock of malts and may have fresh ice if you want to ruin it. You said I owed you one. Well, Colonel Ploughman, this is it... a chance in a lifetime to enjoy my company... I'm paying for the first round... then the rest of the day is on you."

Makepiece frowned his query, with more than just a hint of being prepared to stay with this particular ride until the end of the line.

In a fake Atlanta accent, "Why, Colonel, I do declare that you took little Julia Greenburg from her Snodland peaceability of dashing pilots and fighting airships and such... and conveyed her to an unfenestrated accommodation that the rabbits and hares of Georgia would mindfully avoid. With vigour!"

"I plead guilty to assigning you to a windowless office underground with a hoary grounded pilot for company. Sergeant, where's this remarkable tavern? Move out! You take the point. And by the way... I prefer the Massachusetts accent. Vivien Leigh did 'The South' better..."

Later, Julia Greenburg had collected 'Colonel Ploughman's vehicle' from the transport pound, where its Friday arrival was too late to process the 'return to pool' paperwork until Monday morning and she was driving through the forests of the Chiltern Hills. Makepiece sat beside her in the unaccustomed front passenger seat. For a few hours they were Julia and Makepiece, touring the beauty of the English countryside hinting at the green splendours yet to come, stopping for a view, going into a musty 12th century church, walking along a footpath to catch sight of the Vale of Aylesbury extending 20 miles to the north and west. Julia parked in a layby off a quiet lane so they could see the late March sun set over the City of Oxford too distant to make out with the unaided eye. Daylight seemed reluctant to give up its grip on the landscape, then it was dark. Residual starlight and a sliver of moon in the cloudless sky turned the landscape silvery grey. Julia made no motion to move the car.

She had settled into the corner between the seat and door, her head resting back against the window. In this reduced light, it was difficult for Makepiece to make out her features against the silhouetted outline of her loose hair. He wanted to reach and touch. It was not easy to resist.

In a lilting voice, with more than a shade of Judy Garland, she spoke. "I was thinking that I am a lucky traveller down this particular road to meet the wizard. Why, Toto, here I have a gentle man with the brain to write reports to win a war. I have a man of iron who flies machines when there's no gas in his tanks to complete his mission." Makepiece was beginning to react, to say something, but Julia was leaning forward, her index finger on his mouth to keep him silent. "And I have a man with a heart, a man who led his men and women to the frontiers of the possible, and beyond, a man who loved his group and who was loved back."

Makepiece was dumbstruck. Sergeant Greenburg was out of order speaking to him like this. But the barrier between them had been struck down by the contact. He turned towards her, leant forward and gently at first then more firmly kissed his aide on the lips.

When they parted, for air, in her voice Julia said, "You got protection, Colonel? Are you carrying a rubber?"

"Ever the boy scout."

"Then it's all yours, Makepiece. There's a fire here that needs you to put it out."

*   *   *

Makepiece was driving the staff car back to base. They had taken dinner in a country pub, sitting in a discrete alcove where they would be unnoticed, sitting close, just a Yank officer and his girl with eyes only for themselves. There was no hurry to return the vehicle to the transport compound this Sunday evening.

Chapter 44
1945 ~ Makepiece's Underground War

1945 was seven weeks old when RAF Group Captain Cliff 'The Sprite' Battel telephoned US Army Air Corps Colonel Makepiece Ploughman at Dawes Hill. Makepiece was pleased that the former liaison officer attached to the 1574th SPSG had been promoted, that he was now 'flying a desk' in the Air Ministry — presumably in central London — and wished to re-establish contact. Makepiece became more intrigued when The Sprite indicated he wanted a private chat, away from any walls which might have ears, either British or American.

"We'll meet in front of the mausoleum at West Wycombe at 11 o'clock, tomorrow. There's a nice view up there and we can easily see that we are alone. I'll explain tomorrow. Byeee!"

*   *   *

Sprite Battel was talking. He had been delivered by taxi from High Wycombe railway station; Makepiece had arrived in a self-dive jeep. His greeting of Makepiece was just as though there was not nearly a year since they went their separate ways.

"Whotcher, Colonel, you don't mind if I call you Makepiece now that we're the same rank, what?"

"Carry on, old lad," replied Makepiece in his best fake English accent. "So long as you don't mind me calling you 'Sprite'. What?"

"OK! Or as we pilots say, 'Roger'. I'm glad to see there are no visible scars from West Malling."

"You haven't changed much either," responded Makepiece. "Well? What's the big news from the Air Ministry? You must have been doing something in London — as if I can't guess. You could have picked a better place for a meeting. It's decidedly cold up here."

"Sorry I've not been in touch since your wizard prang, Makepiece. It couldn't have happened to a nicer Yank. We have been a bit busy up in the Air Box, since you ask. The problem with the Germans is that they don't know when to give up." His gloves and his greatcoat kept him cosy. The burns to Sprite's face were now less prominent, but he still shook hands with his left.

"I think there may be the same problem with the Japs. But, you didn't drag yourself, or me, up the highest hill in High Wycombe to shoot the breeze on enemy psychology. What gives?" The colonel had slipped back to his more usual, and for him, more comfortable American delivery.

"We believe the ALSOS study is leaking like a sieve. A source inside German SS police headquarters says they know a great deal about our plans to lift their atomic scientists when this show is over. The same source says that Martin Bormann may be preparing to sue for peace, trading their know-how for his neck. We don't know if the leak is in England, USA or somewhere in Italy, but the Grove's plan is not as secret as they're making out. As for the bomb design itself, I just don't know if they've got someone on the MANHATTEN inside. ALSOS wouldn't tell the Brits anyway. Word is that the Japs seem to be pretty gung-ho about going nuclear, probably riding on Germans' know-how. The Nips want a bomb of their own."

Makepiece wondered if he detected Sprite concealing a shiver.

"As far as I have been able to check, there is no indication that your ABLATIVE project has a wider audience — here or in Germany. Bletchley Park is a good cover, any unusual intelligence can always be attributed to them and no questions asked."

"Bletchley has pretty deep cover itself, Sprite." Makepiece frowned at the concept of leaking Bletchley Park to protect the ABLATIVE concept, but he was more worried about any disclosure concerning ABLATIVE's success.

"No-one has picked up on last year's 1574th COMINT collection over West Poland and now probably won't with our heavy bomber boys stooging around Berlin having a go with manually controlled receivers and wire recorders. By the way, we are pretty sure that Bletchley Park don't know how good we were. There is no suggestion that the Germans know what your P-38s were up to."

"You were supposed to keep mute about ABLATIVE when the 1574[th] closed down."

"So I did. But my director came out with the direct question, 'What did I know about a bunch of two-screw kites swanning about Krautland, with a funny breed of Kodak[tm]s, looking for wingless lovelies? He didn't believe the foo-fighter story. Well, I could hardly plead not guilty, could

285

I? So I says to my director, I says, 'Director I says, those Yanks will go pear-shaped if I spill the beans.' And he says, 'We've got lots of spare cans for pears and beans, so spill.' You can never tell with directors how much they really know and how much they are pumping you for... but he seemed well informed that the Yanks were looking for an Einstein engine somewhere beyond Berlin. He said that perhaps they should have been looking a bit nearer to home, like in the Harz Mountains — also known as Thuringa."

"Oh!" said Makepiece. The effect of the February cold was now showing on Battel's scared face. "Really? He could be mistaken..."

"It could be," offered The Sprite without reacting to Makepeice's putdown, "that someone blew the gaff on the rather special P-38s that flew out of West Malling. I mean, it's quite difficult to confuse a night fighting Mosquito with a camouflaged P-38. The differences are a bit obvious, like a dog's genitalia. Err... especially if your mother's name is Weiss! One clever question in the right ear and the story is headline news."

"But the actual target and the precise location have not leaked? The Einstein engine is pretty specific!" Makepiece's concern harped back to his original Presidential tasking.

The Sprite's nod did not stop him replying, "No, not within the Air Ministry! I'm pretty sure I'd know about that. Let's get back to my story. Apparently the Special Operations Executive, to you and me that's our boys and girls with guns and sticks of dynamite masquerading as MI9, has got something going they call OPERATION CROSSBOW, aimed at stopping V-1 and V-2s before they takeoff. Sabotage! Their chaps have ways of looking inside mountains, particularly mountains with doors which have been photographed by star-spangled P-38s flown by eagle-toting pilots. It seems these CROSSBOW johnnies just stroll in, or something like it, lift a couple of stones to see what crawls from beneath, then walk out!"

"You are referring to my mission's images from near Ravensdorf concentration camp?"

"On the button, Colonel."

Sprite Battel reminded his former commander that all the photographs from 1574th missions were copied to the exploitation unit at Medmenham. Makepiece's last mission would have been no exception. From

Medmenham, the images would have been passed into London's military intelligence planners, via AI4, keen to find things to blow up. MI9 and the SOE would be natural customers. MI9, sharing an office in London's Baker Street, would ensure that Donovan's OSS would not get in the Brit's way for sorting out the matter.

"Oh!" said Makepiece, "I guess!"

"It seems that the SS have a general, former works and buildings engineer no less, name of Kammler I believe, who likes digging holes in mountains and filling them up with rocket works, and spare bunkers for Hitler, and heavy water plant atomic bomb making for the use of, and also likes bits or paraphernalia that we don't know very much about. The sort of research for things that might go bump in the night, you know. Perhaps flying-machine stuff, the sort that Babs at Medmenham would not recognise."

"You didn't take advantage... ?"

"No! Oh no, of course not..." The Sprite was shaking his head with unnecessary vigour.

"Oh!" Makepiece was conscious that he was repeating himself.

The Sprite said, "It crossed my mind that you had an interest in a top gerry name of Kammler — in your flying days — and you seemed awfully keen to keep your finger on said Kraut's pulse, in a manner of speaking."

"You're touching the ABLATIVE rhinestone, Sprite. You know there are limits about how much I can tell you about it."

Sprite Battel was not about to be diverted from his real purpose in meeting with the American. "So I thought that our director might like to know what the Yanks really know about all this, and I wasn't wrong. The director said to me, 'Go and talk to your American Army pilot chappie' and so here I am. Talking. Now I want to listen. To you!"

"Oh!" repeated Makepiece. "Ohrdruf, you said?"

"I didn't say Ohrdruf. You did. I agreed that Nordhausen was a good approximation for openers. As they say in the Air Ministry, they're close enough for government work, Ohrdruf and Nordhausen. I'm all ears, well one and a half ears actually. I hear that Nordhausen provides the labour pool without having to worry about inconveniences like trade unions or strikes! And Ohrdruf has a place where things explode — significantly"

So Makepiece began to recount how much further American knowledge of the extraordinary research, controlled by SS General Kammler, had advanced in the last year. It was clear that the Germans did not intend to stop their 'Einstein Engine' project because Zhukov's million strong Russian Army was pushing through Poland towards Berlin. Kammler had moved his project westwards, or possibly south into Czechoslovakia, or both. But the indications were that they were continuing with their projects.

"Kammler's research into Einstein and/or anti-gravity weapons was, and remains, certainly independent of the German drive for the atomic bomb; there have been indications that already they have tested such weapons and are assembling more."

"Are you saying that Hitler has tested an atomic bomb?" The Sprite was incredulous.

"I didn't say that. We'd have told you if we thought he had... I think!" There was some anxiety in Makepiece's voice as he developed his theme; he did not have authority to be telling a British officer any of this. The consequences of over-stepping the mark were really serious for him. Nevertheless, "But, during the German siege at Sevastopol, they may have tested an alternative, called a fuel-air bomb, equally as destructive, but without the radioactive side effects, and not dependent on expensive uranium — which they seem to have in limited quantities. It is possible that deployable systems, atomic or otherwise, will be available by the middle of this year. It is certainly what Berlin has in mind."

"Oh!" said Group Captain Battel. "That's not how ALSOS see it."

"And the Russians think the Germans were trying out such a device while they were at the gates of Moscow, in 1941!"

"That's news to me."

"Remember who pays the ALSOS pipers; they'll sing his tune. Groves's interest is seeing that his MANHATTAN project wins the race to have the first atomic bomb! Groves and nuclear are two sides of the same coin. I'll explain. I believe, but can't yet prove, that the Germans have two levels of what we might call Top Secret. There's Top Secret which is nice to keep to yourself, but which might leak. The damage is not end-of-the-world sort of stuff, just close to it! We're talking civilian stuff without the military ring of steel. They can pretend to be pissed off if the Allies find out, but — well, err... let me put it this way — if they know the Allies have the gen then that's confirmation there's a leak and they can plug it and take out the leaker, etc."

Makepiece shivered. "Look, do you mind if we move about a bit? I'm freezing."

Makepiece continued, "Reported Germanic slow progress on fission weapons falls into that category; so does missile control radar, their gas turbine engines and many others. An *'Uber Gehiem'* label provides good bait for tempting spies, too.

Sprite Battel moved slowly so as not to miss a word.

"And to cap it all, if you want to mislead the enemy on your latest success, you let a leak out that all is not well with your pet project, poor morale, can't get the materials, etc. Moths to the flame and all that."

Sprite Battel nodded his understanding of this convoluted logic.

"So while this overt activity is going on, the real show is underground — literally — don't dare utter a word about it or it is curtains — literally — for self, family, kids, friends, relatives, your village — literally. In krautspeak: *wörtlich tot!* ABLATIVE and parallel programmes were — that's wrong — are still about new science. The Germans are touching on new dimensions: time, gravity, quantum, death rays, celestial, the occult — literally — you name it and rule nothing out. This is not just Top Secret stuff; this is their 'war winning weapons' concepts wrapped up in what they label *kriegsentscheiden,* which broadly translates to *'decisive to the war effort'.* And Kammler is top-dog in this research because, first and foremost, he's a ruthless and effective organiser. *'Can't do'* does not figure in his vocabulary."

The RAF officer continued to nod his encouragement for Makepiece to continue.

"Remember the tale about Hitler's additional funk bunkers. Pure hoax! Hitler wouldn't build a funk bunker outside Germany. But constructing underground weapons' test facilities is an entirely different beast."

The emphasis and detail being disclosed was way more than any indication Makepiece had ever laid bare during their time together at Snodland.

"I'll give you another example. Gratis. Zero cost to the Winston Churchill's exchequer! An invisibility cloak!"

Sprite responded, "You're talking camouflage? Your P-38M-SP had a good line in camouflage paint that would have put Henry — *any colour you fancy so long as it's black* — Ford out of business. Our Spitfires have tried the same tactic!"

Sprite pointed, without speaking, to a steam engine pulling a train out of High Wycombe towards the Midlands. From this bird's eye view, its smoke climbed into the sky as a reminder of the solid foundations of technology far removed from the topics being discussed on the overlooking hill. Normal life was continuing while this esoteric exchange was going on.

Makepiece with a barest of facial acknowledgement of his colleague's pointing, came back with, "Not visible light. Radar! They appear to have had some success with radar absorbent coatings that stop radars seeing their echoes. Actually, that's wrong because there are no echoes because it's radar absorbent."

Sprite said, "That'll upset the boffins when the news gets out…"

"Especially if you can coat a submarine's periscope in the stuff," volunteered Makepeice.

The train had turned away from the watching two men. Its steam whistle showed a white plume five seconds before the sound reached the talking men.

Makepiece was not prepared to be diverted from his present theme. "So while this overt activity is going on, on uranium etc, the real show is underground. It's physics and chemistry beyond anything that Einstein may have had nightmares about. This is their war winning weapons' concept. New science!"

The Sprite stopped his gentle stroll and looked Makepiece in the eyes. "Are you saying that the Yanks have got something beyond ABLATIVE?"

"I didn't say that. But I'm a simple Army colonel out at the front line. ABLATIVE and the 1574th SPSG was specifically set up to get the measure of how far the Germans were going down this path. Maybe other groups are doing similar things against a different activity. Think submarines, for instance. Get your sailor chums to check on Japanese underwater aircraft carriers. I can say no more — I don't think I'm supposed to know. Who knows what goes on behind closed doors in Washington? Let's forget that line. What brought you out here where there are no walls to have ears to listen to our conversation? No coffee percolators, either!"

"OK. Makepiece! I'll cut to the chase, as they say in all the good movies. This is what we want you to do. That's me and my director want… Given 'Old Blood and Guts' Patton's intervention in the Battle of Bulge, a couple of months ago, we want you to arrange for Ike to tell Patton where to make his next home run. In payment, you'll get the information on German high technology and its associated developments that you want for your 'American Eyes Only' files and it will keep your industrial giants quiet doing reverse engineering for decades if not until the turn of the century."

Battell's head was wagging sideways in protestation to the put down he knew was coming from the American.

"Don't deny it, old son; you've had 'No Foreign Eyes' folios since Thomas Paine was a pain in our backside. Our reward? We'll get to know what's in your NOFORN files and, more important, what the Gerries were up to in their tunnels while we couldn't see through Mother Earth. How? Because you'll tell a liaison officer assigned to the Dawes Hill ABLATIVE office — me. What could be more appropriate than to assign Group Captain Battel RAF, gentleman of the realm and a thoroughly good egg, back to his Anglo-American buddies for the closing chapters of the war? It will also help us know what Joe Stalin knows because Joe's spooks will lift what Patton leaves behind: quite a lot of German scientists, maybe their blueprints, to say nothing of having the odd embedded spy in OSS, SOE, MI6 maybe, and — God forbid — Bletchley Park and in your folks' offices scattered about Washington DC."

"Just like that!" Makepiece snapped his fingers.

"Just like that!" repeated the Sprite. "But, you and me, we'll have the cream."

"You let me rattle on about two tiers of top secret, and all the time you were planning an operation to crack it yourselves!"

Sprite Battel's eyebrows rose, his shoulders shrugged and his fire-scorched face could not suppress a grin.

"Classic British approach, old lad. You had to talk yourself into this harebrained idea. Ain't war grand?"

"Go on," invited Makepiece. His lips were pursed as though he was upset by the idea being presented; in truth he remained pro-British and what he was hearing appealed to him. The two men were moving again.

"Ike will appear to give Patton his head; with the success in the Ardennes under their collective belts, the American Third Army will drive due east straight for the southern side of Berlin. Small map, thick pen is open to a thousand interpretations; that's just how Patton likes it. And no Monty, this time! Paton'll say a prayer, beg, borrow or steal extra gasoline and walk across the Rhine if necessary if he can't find a bridge or a ferry! So Patton can smirk at Monty coming second in the race across the fatherland. Then Ike says, 'Whoa, not too fast, George old lad. FDR promised Berlin to Uncle Joe at Yalta; the first of May is a red letter day to those red starred guys!' Of course Patton will be a bit upset, but this is war and Eisenhower has got more stars on his lapel. Ike will say to Patton, 'I want you to take your Third Army and look over this Ohrdruf place south of Berlin town centre, capture a few of the high priced help and generally look around. Mail me a report on what you find.'"

The train was now moving swiftly north, away from the watching officers. Its smoke remained visible, but no sound was reaching them now. Makepiece stopped, then Sprite. They continued just standing as Sprite continued his gameplan.

"When Patton's intel chaps report back, Ike will go on to say, 'The British think that all those bad things you have found in the Ohrdruf tunnels are like minnows in a pond compared with the SS great white sharks and barracuda that prowl around Prague and the Skoda factory at Pilsen, Czechoslovakia. Didn't Napoleon go straight past Prague, George? I wouldn't expect a Yank to make a mistake like that. Anyway, who better than my most able general to go and collect all those nasty Nazis and bring them back for a fair trial before we string them up? No shooting them outright, mind, George. They've got to be seen to pay for all the horrible scenes you're gonna have witnessed and filmed in the concentration camps.' What do you think, Makepiece?"

"And Patton will say… ?" The characteristic chew at his inner cheek had started.

"Oh, he'll argue. Leave Hamburg for Monty? Never! Give Bradley Cologne? No chance! Leave Bavaria and the Black Forest for Devers?

He's a good officer, but... Worse, leave Berlin for those stinking commies sons of bitches... ?"

"And Ike will say..." Up rose Makepiece's eyebrows, but the chewing continued.

"George, this is the way I see it. The US Third is the finest and quickest ground covering army the world has seen since Hannibal stopped suckling in Carthage. And there's no general since Alexander who holds a candle to its General George Smith Patton, Jr. Who else could I trust this important mission to?"

"And...?" Makepiece prompted.

"Patton will say, 'Of course you're right, sir. What a fine judge of men and commander of forces you are to recognise the limitations of those two outfielders compared to my boys. And I can protect Bradley's 12th Army Group's right flank while I'm at it.' And Patton'll hold his pearl handled Colt pistols and he'll go and collect a few German scalps, he'll agitate the Russians some and do the job he was briefed."

Sprite's upright posture relaxed just a little.

"Naturally, Ike will recall him for overstepping the mark with our gallant soviet allies and we can fill our files and write our memoirs. Piece of cake, old boy! Did you say 'death rays'?"

"Underground test chamber in Heidelberg," responded Makepiece. "It works on rats, but they hadn't tried it on *Homo sapiens* the last time I heard about it."

"Did you say bombs by the middle of the year? This year, 1945?"

"Heinkel 290 heavy bombers in generous numbers, an airfield within range of the New England coast down as far as New York, weapons production is going ahead apace. These things are coming together."

"Where?" queried an incredulous group captain.

"Oslo, Norway. Worth a look at the photos when you get back to Whitehall!"

"Jesus."

"No photos of the Son of Mary, yet, Sprite, but the Germans may be working on that too. *Der Klocken* — the time machine! Remember CHRONOS? And folks tend to forget there are 40,000 *Wermacht* in Norway, and they are not there for the skiing."

"How many other surprises do you have up your sleeve?"

"Perhaps I can persuade Washington that I should tell you."

"Oh!" mimicked Battel.

"Just before we wrap this up, I take it you know about OPERATION PAPERCLIP. Their mission is to bring out the German non-nuclear scientific know-how and apparatus."

"Routine stuff, Colonel! And so is Donovan's Operation RED STOCKING to land field agents behind the lines using B-24s and RAF Mosquitos. MI9 needs its sources, Colonel. But we both know that the real high stakes surround this Hans Kammler fellow and what he's been up to for the last three years. Ike needs to motivate Patton — a suggestion that he'll get the Pacific and take Tokyo if he takes Kammler alive. Something like that!"

"OK! You've got it all sorted... I'll give it a try. Now, lunch is on you." Makepiece was moving towards his parked Jeep^{tm} and a willing RAF group captain followed.

"Well, I know an ivy covered Officer's Mess up that way. They run Bomber Command from the bar in there. They do remarkable things to a bowl of brown windsor soup..."

*   *   *

While Patton was still advancing towards the Harz Mountains, on 3 March 1945, about 60 miles south of Berlin, there was a significant explosion on the Ohrdruf Test Range in the Thuringia district of central Germany. It was a site closely associated with Buchenwald concentration camp and its multiple lesser satellite concentration camps. Intelligence assessment concluded the blast destroyed an area of about 550 square yards, killing possibly 700 prisoners of war and concentration camp inmates. A Russian spy reported both events to Stalin just days after a second weapons test, on 12 March 1945, during which a plume was seen to rise out of ground, trailing a forked exhaust plume, which generated many lightning strikes. Intelligence speculated that this second incident was a test launch of the A-9 rocket which was the intercontinental successor to the V-2 ballistic missile then raining down on London and Amsterdam.

Reliable sources confirmed that the A-9 was intended as an attack weapon against the continental USA.

Chapter 45
1945 ~ 6th May, 1945

It was the sixth of May that Makepiece decided to telephone Aynette. Victory in Europe had been declared and would formally be signed in Rhiems tomorrow. There would be rejoicing when the news that fighting had ceased had been announced by Prime Minister Winston Churchill. A broadcast over American Forces Network radio by President Truman was expected shortly. Fighting in the Far East was as horrific as it had been at any time during the war, but victory was in sight. General Eisenhower had posted his written order of the day congratulating everyone for a job well done. Montgomery was on his way to, if not actually in, Berlin.

Patton had shaken hands with a Russian; on 5 May 1945. Pilsen was liberated by the 2nd and 97th infantry divisions and the 16th armoured division commanded by General Patton. About 90% of Czechoslovakia was denazified by the Red Army. Sadly, on the direct orders of General Eisenhower, George Patton was not allowed to advance just 60 miles to the north east of Pilsen to take undefended Prague which had been promised to the Russians. Across a meaningless border, the American general would watch the sun rise over a conquered Czechoslovakia from his headquarters in Ravensburg, Germany.

*   *   *

It was only as difficult as picking up the handset and asking the village operator on her manual switchboard to connect him to Cleeve Lyon cottage. The number was ingrained in his memory. Sitting alone in his office, Makepiece could visualise where Aynette would be standing when she picked up her handset, how she might flop onto that long settee at the sound of his voice.

He only had to pick up the handset. How would he feel at the sound of her voice? He could hardly flop on his desk…

"Hello. I'd like to make a person to person call to a Mrs Aynette Bates."

He gave the telephone number and replied to the question from the distant female operator.

"Yes, of course, that's A Y N E T T E. Bates, Mrs Bates. Yes, it is an unusual name. Yes, I'll hold on."

'I suppose she has to ask…' he thought. 'I did request a person to person call…'

"My name, oh yes. It is Makepiece Ploughman. It is unusual too. 'Make' as in make, 'piece' as in part of, all one word — Makepiece. Ploughman, as in farmer and horses and fields, one word, Ploughman. Shall I spell it for you?" He heaved a sigh as the first hurdle had been crossed.

"Yes, I'm American. Can you connect me, please? Yes, I'll continue holding. Thank you…"

He was nervous during the silence on the line until being told that a connection was not possible.

"Would you try again please? I know it's a special day, that's why I want to talk to Mrs Bates…"

Having to wait to hear Aynette speaking was not what he expected when he made the call. He wondered, 'Will she be pleased to speak to me after all this time?'

"What does that mean…'not available'? Please try again, operator… Oh, I see. The line appears to be down… The distant operator couldn't be wrong… err mistaken… could she?"

This wait was frustrating and annoying. He desperately wanted to — needed to — talk to Aynette.

"I understand. Could she give you the number of the local policeman, or warden, or vicar that I could speak to? I would like to speak to Mrs Bates wherever she is… Thank you. Yes, I'll speak to the local policeman. Thank you for your help, operator… "

A short delay, then another voice, male this time, perhaps he could help?

"Good afternoon, Constable, my name is Colonel Ploughman, I'm an American friend of Mrs Bates who lives in Cleeve Lyon Cottage and I'd…"

"Well, yes, I understand you can't speak about Mrs Bates to any Tom, Dick or Harry. You see, I'm none of those. I had command of an American outfit which flew out of RAF West Malling and… Well, we tried not to bother the police… We were a bit self-contained… I do understand your difficulty. I have been in the same situation myself."

'The officious official is trying my patience. Take a deep breath...'

"No, I'm not a relative. But if you could tell me where she, Mrs Bates is, or how to contact her, I'm certain she would say thank you to you when she next meets you..."

'Really unnecessary. Keep your temper, Makepeice... He's only doing his job...'

"The war is over, Constable. It is hardly a matter of national security. She was a successful author, you know. All I want..."

Every muscle tensed as the constable spoke. It wasn't possible...

"When?"

Makepiece's eyes closed with despair. It couldn't be true.

"You are sure she was in the cottage when the bomb exploded? Nothing left? A direct hit?

Yes... it would have been quick... mid April, you said?"

Speaking was so difficult. This shouldn't be happening...

"You mean... a V-2 rocket bomb?

Where is she... err... buried? I'd like to send some flowers.

Nothing? Ohh..."

Makepiece caught his breath as the awful details came down the telephone line.

"Yet you are sure she was in the cottage?

Oh, a fire...

I see. If there was nothing to bury it must be difficult. Thank you for your time, Constable. I'm very grateful for your help."

Even for a military man, this was like being kicked in the solar plexus.

With his eyes still closed, Makepiece returned the handset to its cradle, put his head in his hands and let the thousand questions and the million memories race around his brain.

'That lovely woman... never hurt anyone... always happy... gone in a flash.'

They had agreed 'no commitment', but neither would have wanted it to end like this.

*   *   *

Makepiece sat at the table in his billet. He couldn't do this in his office. He held an ink fountain pen, one that he reserved for special writing. A part used bottle of Jack Daniels^{tm}, and a half filled glass, were on the table. He had decided he must write a farewell letter to Aynette, to say goodbye.

May 6th, 1945
My Dearest Aynette,
For just four short months together, we escaped the horrors of this war. Our time in our shared paradise, so removed from the harsh realities beyond the cottage door, will endure in our memories. Every shared conversation, touch, embrace, kiss and loving and lingering silence brings back to me a quotation with which you will be familiar:

My life often seems to me like a story that has no beginning and no end. I have the feeling that I am a historical fragment, an excerpt for which the preceding and succeeding text are missing. I could well imagine that I might have lived in former centuries and there encountered questions I was not yet able to answer; that I had been born again because I had not fulfilled the task given to me.

Carl Jung

We were denied the chance to say our goodbyes — farewells which we knew were inevitable as we moved back to our peace time lives. I know we shall meet again, somewhere in time and space, to share...

Thinking, 'This surely is special writing,' Makepiece placed his fountain pen on his table next to the half filled liquor glass. Writing the words he wanted to say to Aynette seemed to block his throat, make it difficult to focus on the paper, to be neat as he searched for the right words. He decided he must finish his farewell letter, say goodbye to Aynette, later.

Chapter 46
1945 ~ The Next Phase of Life Begins

Two days had passed since the sixth of May's decision to telephone Aynette. The world would remember the day when the news, that fighting in Europe had ceased' had been announced by the Prime Minister in London. Every cinema would show a movie clip in the news. England was rejoicing. Gaily decorated streets were one big party despite the wartime austerity. VE Day was when 'Victory in Europe' merited a celebration. Churchill had said we should celebrate.

Makepiece would remember it as the day he completed his letter to say goodbye to Aynette — the letter she could never read. On VE Day, the 8 May 1945, he tore up his letter to Aynette; it was the day the next phase of his life began.

Makepiece Ploughman was in the Bachelor Officers' Quarters, taking respite from the intelligence cell in the bunker. Their post hostilities work would take a new direction, a rush to get at the German technology and intelligence before the Russians. ALSOS was still busy wrapping up Germany's nuclear endeavours and claimed it wanted another six months to do the job properly. Operations PAPERCLIP — concentrating on non-nuclear weapons especially rockets, and SURGEON concentrating on high-speed aeronautical research, were already launched. He could only guess how much Dawes Hill would be little more than a relaying post office for that material. Beyond doubt, there was an 'American Eyes Only' component to these missions. He felt that the scope of both operations owed something to his unacknowledged personal efforts in March '44, especially that last fateful flight, and the wider success of the 1574th SPSG before it was disbanded soon after his crash.

He missed his friend and brother-in-law. After a year working side by side, on 1st May, Colonel Julius (Jules) Knapp had been assigned to McArthur's staff in the Pacific, '...to wrap up the Japs'. He was on the move on the 3rd. Makepiece would have been grateful for Jules's experience and political knowledge to progress the case for a covert operation against the Wenceslas site now firmly in Soviet controlled territory. But Jules was not there to help.

Sprite Battel had engineered his own recall to London. The Americans were not being as forthcoming with their intelligence as he had hoped. There was, quite simply, too much pressure from Washington to save the best for their own industrial advantage. He forecast a quick post-war shrinkage of the RAF and he did not want to be a part of it.

Makepiece found it was much more difficult than he expected to get the Pentagon's interest in the German CHRONOS project in the Wenceslas Mine. Its main site was located 100 miles inside Soviet occupied Poland; the very act of showing interest would inevitably draw Russian attention to the project and possibly to its potential as the ultimate war winner. Naturally, in the Russian's mind, there would be the questions of how the American — but not the British with their lead in European Theatre of Operations intelligence — knew about the place. And how much more did the Yanks know? Such recent aerial photography of Poland that existed was keyed to industrial complexes suitable for allied air bombardment — oil and weapons plant, and the like. What could be so important about a disused ore mine? With the imminent Potsdam Conference about partitioning Germany and the whole subject of war reparations on the table, no general would propose a mission which might provoke the Russians with their deployed troops who outnumbered the allies by two to one or more. President Roosevelt would not countenance any such move. Anyway, the MANHATTEN project was about to make its first test. Not much rivalled that weapon in the priority to defeat Japan.

*   *   *

On the ninth of May, 1945 Makepiece was able to telephone Maryland for the first time since he had left 23 months before. The conversation was stilted, neither knew quite what to say after such a long separation. Both reassured the other that all was well, it was good news that the war in Europe was over and they would be re-united soon.

"…I can't say yet when I'll get home; they are making up the rules as they go along. I'll let you know as soon as I can. Give my love to the children and the rest of the family…"

They were both keen to emphasise how much they treasured each others' letters.

"Do keep writing, Makepiece my love. They bring you so much closer…"

It would be the first week of December that Marybeth caught the infection. The family sent for Makepiece who was flown home as quickly as the superlative military compassionate system could move him. He arrived 90 minutes too late.

Marybeth was buried in the family plot behind the Homestead.

*   *   *

Colonel Makepiece Ploughman's assignment to the Department of Land Warfare Intelligence in the Pentagon was to be effective from March 1st, 1946. He thought he must have been on the same aircraft from the USA as carried his assignment notice in the official mail. He would have been back in England, from burying his wife, for just six weeks when he would have to cross the ocean again. It was agreed by telegraph that all the ABLATIVE material would be bagged for couriering to his office in the Pentagon. Once back in the Pentagon, his final military duty would be to write a report on the ABLATIVE findings, draw conclusions and make recommendations. An executive summary was to be prepared in order that the Chief of Staff could make an appropriate presentation to President Harry Truman.

The assignment orders concluded:

Colonel Makepiece Frisby Ploughman will retire from the US Army Air Corps active service list on June 30th 1946.

'Just like that,' thought Makepiece. He was holding a glass of neat Jack Daniels^{tm} on the rocks, looking in the mirror on the wall of his bachelor quarters. 'Services no longer required. You give them 20 years of your life — more — and they give you 20 weeks notice — less.'

Makepiece thought, 'I would like to go back to Snodland, just one time. I'd like to tell Grandmother Susannah Catterall that everything worked just fine. I reckon she'll know even if I can't see her. Her family heritage record will live on through my own daughter, Antonia Ploughman, matriarch designate although she doesn't know it yet. I would like to do something for that old church, All Saints, Snodland, Kent. I could pay for the repair to the damaged porch, perhaps, or at least make a contribution. I am sure that Grandmother Susannah would see that as fitting. I could make it a private memorial to Aynette. No one else would know about that private meaning. Just me. If I am paying, I could have her initials ACL in small hidden letters where they would be private to me.'

Aynette would approve of Antonia landing the job. Makepiece was fighting back unmanly tears at his double loss. Marybeth would approve too, and would probably gone to the grave, in the homestead's grounds, and told Rosetta and Bernard about the plan.

'A small memorial stone as close to Grandmother Susannah, as I can get it in the repairs, is what I'll do.. No talk, just one more secret out of the 1574th SPSG technical compound where the family Hall once stood.'

In the month he had been in Maryland, Makepiece had not thought about Aynette. Now memories flooded back. 'Cleeve Lyon was not far from Snodland. I could drive up the lane, past the entrance to the lamella hangar. I would not try to go in. There would not be much to see now that Washington has paid for it to be demolished. It could so easily have been part of the history of victory. But it was not to be. Washington has its reasons, I guess. Perhaps they'll tell me when I get back to DC. Then, again, perhaps they won't.'

Makepiece planned the route he would take to Cleeve Lyon. 'Around the outside of the airfield and I'll drive past RAF West Malling gate. So much history inside that gate. Night fighter history. The RAF was justifiably proud of its night fighters. I wonder how 'Sprite' Battel will cope with peace. The RAF squadrons in there were not so much clouded by secrecy as was the 1574th. It was a good outfit, the 1574th. I couldn't have told Marybeth, or Frisby, much about it. He'll be 20 now. He'll have done nearly two years in the navy. I can't imagine life in a submarine, no fresh air, no horizons except on instruments. I don't suppose he'll want to talk about it very much; even out on the stretches of Rosetta's Rocks. I'd like that house to be his one day — when he's gotten himself a wife. It's a pity there are no images on how it looked back in Ada's time. Come to think of it, there are no images of what the Hall at Snodland looked like while she was living there. There's all her history of Ploughman folks written in the Heritage Volume and yet we don't know anything about how she really lived. I must look at that letter she wrote when she knew her time was coming. Perhaps I'll do the same, write a burial letter that is. Mm."

Makepiece raised the tumbler to his lips, but he hesitated. The liquor did not pass his lips.

"After all, it's what Rosetta did! Double mm! I quite like that idea." He began to chew the inside of his cheek.

'What will Rosetta's Rocks be like without a woman's touch? A daughter is not quite the same as a wife...' he was wondering.

There was a knock on the door.

"Yes."

The door opened and the orderly told him that his presence was required in the bunker. It was the nature of Colonel Ploughman, USAAC that all previous thoughts vanished.

"Thank you. I'll be right along." The tumbler was returned to the table top and the cheek chewing stopped. As he reached for his hat and coat, Makepiece was thinking, 'What can possibly be going wrong now? It would be just like the Soviets to cross the Rhine when I was having a quiet drink!'

Chapter 47
1945 ~ Special Category Prisoner of War

On his desk lay a solitary buff folder with its diagonal security band showing bold red letters 'MOST SECRET'. Makepiece's aide, Sergeant Toby Paul, had marked the folder's folios with visible coloured tags.

"Colonel, I've pulled the folios from their original dockets."

"OK, Sergeant, this had better be good. I'm not a fan of being extracted from my bunk when the glass is charged with a shot of Jack Daniels^{tm} finest. I'm supposed be at peace now!"

"Have faith, Colonel, Sporrenberg has risen like the phoenix." Sergeant Paul was unmilitarily relaxed in the privacy of his colonel's office.

Aide Julia Greenburg would never have addressed her colonel this way, but Sergeant Paul was not an administrator.

"Remind me, Sergeant. Not with that Greek bullshit about birds with bent wings. A Kraut general, I guess?"

"You got it, Colonel. I remembered the name from a 1574th intercept report. Up there with your General Kammler, sometime! The day 1574th caught the CHRONOS test, Sporrenberg was a SS top honcho in Poland — police wise — from the Lublin district. That's way out east, I don't know the formal boundaries of his area of responsibility. Why he did come 500 clicks west? Again, I don't know. But he was near the Wenceslas Mine when the big bang disturbed the universe."

"Slight exaggeration, Sergeant! Maybe 50 tons of metal was thrown to fifty thousand feet and perhaps it did take a trip to Lapland at Mach 4. What's so unusual about that?" Makepiece's despair at having to drag out the story showed in his face. "Buck Rogers does it every week!"

"OK, Colonel, disturbed YOUR universe, some! But it isn't every day that a communications intercept operator gets to meet the guy who's been chatting with a guy who's building — at least testing — weapons to end all wars."

Did Makepiece detect a hint of self-congratulatory smile in his aide's face.

"I just thought the colonel'd like to know the Brits have gotten Sporrenberg behind wire, in Wales."

"Give it to me from the top, Sergeant."

"OK, Colonel." Of course the aide was standing while his officer sat. "Seems that Jakob Sporrenberg made such a success of Poland that Hitler gave him a gong and then he was assigned to Norway. A source in Sweden says Sporrenberg was lucky to get out before the Russians came knocking on Lublin fortress's front door in '44. Anyway, come the German ceasefire/surrender in the fatherland, the unflustered 40,000 German troops in Norway had to give up too. It seems they were a mite reluctant, Colonel, because we know that, on 7 May 1945, General Böhme, German Commander-in-Chief in Norway, comes out with..."

The aide began reading from a translated transcript:

'We are standing here in Norway, undefeated, strong as before. No enemy has dared attack us. And yet we, too, shall have to bow to the dictate of our enemy for the benefit of the whole German cause. We trust we shall from now on deal with men who respect a soldier's honour.'

Sergeant Paul, sometime radio operator and transcriber at a US communications monitoring station in Bedfordshire and now an intelligence analyst at Dawes Hill, placed the transcript on the desk.

The aide continued, "Böhme told Sporrenberg to throw in the towel, but it took another three days to clear his desk before top cop Jakob, too, raised his hands. Anyway, into the bag goes Jakob and, in the way of these things, he gets moved between holding camps until he pitches up in Bridgend, Wales, England. Easy to get there from Dawes Hill, direct train from Reading, which is only 40 minutes drive from here."

"Wales isn't England, Sergeant. If you value your life more than you value your stripes, you won't make a mistake like that again."

"OK, Colonel, I was..."

Makepiece was quite excited that there might be an opportunity to interrogate a man who had been on the ground when he flew over the Wenceslas Mine test. He was sucking the inside of his cheek.

"Any word about Kammler? He's the fish I want to fry."

"Nothing. Anyway, Colonel," the aide was indicating the folder on Makepiece's otherwise clear desk, "the green markers are the original first level reports; the red markers are the analysed 'end product' intelligence reports back from Washington."

"Does the PAPERCLIP list include Sporrenberg?"

"No. He is not documented as an engineer or a scientist so the PAPERCLIP project would not automatically pick him up. He was more of your sheriff in a black hat — real time baddie cop that they should've sent Errol Flynn to sort out."

"Has anyone else picked this up — the Sporrenberg connection with Kammler and advanced technology?"

"No, Colonel. Not as far as I know." With his eyebrows raised, the aide emphasised his point, "General Donovan? He seems to be staying with PAPERCLIP and, anyway, he's stateside chatting up Harry Truman!"

"Let's keep it that way, Sporrenberg under ABLATIVE wraps, until I've met him."

Makepiece put his hand to his face; his right thumb rested against his jawbone while his index finger rubbed the opposite cheek. Sergeant Paul waited patiently for his colonel to speak again — it was what good aides do! The colonel did not need to think long.

"Right!" Makepiece was back in his element, facing a challenge head on. "Contact this holding camp — it says here that it is known as Camp XI for special category prisoners of war." Makepiece was holding a red marked prisoner allocation list. "He's in pretty good company — says here that Von Runstead has taken up lodgings nearby, along with a few dozen other generals. Find the name of the commandant of this camp — or whatever — and find out about visiting hours. You'll need a cover story to explain why I want to see Sporrenberg, and anyone else who was in Silesia, Poland in 1944. We're trying to trace relatives of a scientist whose wife was known to be there in March '44 — make her an American citizen — hint at advanced medicine."

"OK, Colonel." The aide made to leave; he had most of that information already.

"Wait! I'm gonna need a German linguist fluent in technical and engineering talk. Contact the Signals Security Group; they're still headquartered out near Bletchley Park…"

"The Army's 6813th Signals Security Detachment…"

"…yeh, and advise the commander at 6813th that Dawes Hill needs their best for a week. Check if Captain Bundy is still there; I'll talk with him. I'll get Washington to send authority if there's a problem."

"I've already checked that out, Colonel. There's a T/Sgt Delaney J Openshaw works there, or at least is on their books. His service number correlates with a maintainer at 1574th, so he's got an ABLATIVE clearance background. He did some time with the 25th Bombardment Group (Recon) operating B-26 signals intelligence collectors out of RAF Watton, Norfolk before the outfit folded and the RAF took the place back. His ABLATIVE clearance won't be current, but should be easily upgradeable on your say so. Language — no problem; he did a year at Heidelberg University and time with Telefuncken in Frankfurt. Neat, eh?"

"Good — err — neat! I suppose you haven't drafted Openshaw's temporary duty orders yet?" Makepiece was not sure he liked being second guessed in this way, but it was what a good aide does. Did Sergeant Paul somehow know that Openshaw had given his colonel useful advice on the Wenceslas site while they were both at Snodland?

"Give me 10 minutes, Colonel, and I'll have them on your desk. Would the Colonel like his coffee now? Just a morsel of deep background, Colonel; seems this Delaney Openshaw lassoed a GI bride name of Plowman — spelled with an 'O W'. Nice coincidence, eh?"

There was a sparkle in Makepiece's eye, and just a suggestion of a grin, "Will I be taking it white or neat? The coffee, Sergeant..."

*   *   *

Openshaw had departed two hours ago. Makepiece had decided that the T/Sgt had done so well as to merit a ride back to base in a staff car rather than face the gruelling rail journey through the austere London January – this despite grey skies heralding snow. The technical stuff had not been particularly deep, but the procedural language in Sporrenberg's field — police work — Openshaw had found testing.

While they had been travelling, there had been an exchange about Openshaw intending to take an ex-WAAF by the name of Plowman back to the States, but the US Army authorities imposing 'red tape' were making life difficult for GI brides. Apparently they had met while Openshaw had been serving in the 1574th SPSG. They had married eight weeks ago. Such emigration matters were not in Colonel Ploughman's remit. He had some recollection of a WAAF being involved in the Heinkel incident, but only because her surname sounded the same as his.

Now it was time to write up his interview with Sporrenberg. Makepiece felt the German policeman had done little but follow orders in his activities in the Sudeten Mountains. Ruthlessly maybe, effective probably in what the SS did, his detailed knowledge of the CHRONOS — *die Glocke* or *LATERNENTRAGER* — as the German had sometimes called the project did not advance Makepiece's understanding. Makepiece's lasting impression was of a creature out of the Nazi mould, a Jew hater, who had served his master, Himmler, and should now pay the price with his neck — as indeed should every SS member involved in the 'final solution'.

Sporrenberg claimed to have no recollection of special delivery trains or vehicles in the Sudeten Mountains. There were so many trains, so many individuals, that he had a staff who dealt with the detail. In that respect, clearly Sporrenberg was lying as evidenced in the intercept transcript of Makepiece's overflight. But Makepiece could not disclose how much he knew and certainly not the source of his information.

General Kammler had insisted on absolute security for his areas while Sporrenberg was SS Police Leader drafted in from Lublin in eastern Poland and there had been no breaches. He would remember that. 'Mopping up runaway labourers was routine in the isolated country,' he recalled. He did not volunteer any details.

He said he was aware that Kammler had the ear of Himmler, and maybe even the Führer himself. 'He was a man in whose good book any sensible man would want to stay.' But Kammler was an engineer, with his own agenda, and there was no room for error while dealing with him. Sporrenberg had only temporarily served on Kammler's staff and was glad when the call came for him to return to Lublin, East Poland in late March '44. He did not remember the exact date.

"The Russians were making a push for the second city in Poland and I needed to be there."

Sporrenberg remembered a scientist named Manteufle at Wenceslas, the name stuck in his memory, but not his role in *die Glocke* project. He was one of sixty or more scientists who worked or lived close to a reopened, worked out, silver mine. The mine had been enlarged by

Jewish and Russian labour brought in for the purpose. They lived in the tunnels.

"Were you present when *die Glocke* was tested?"

"*Nien.*"

"So do you know what was the purpose of *die Glocke?*"

"*Nien.* It was *Oberstes Geheimnis*, top secret."

"Why?"

"I have no knowledge of this matter."

"Would Manteufle have knowledge of the *die Glocke's purpose?*"

"Perhaps Manteufle had something to do with the design of the facility, under Kammler's supervision of course. I have no knowledge of this matter."

"Was all the research carried out underground?"

"Of course! Kammler put everything underground to protect it from allied bombing raids. He even put flying machine assembly underground. No, I do not know details."

"Was the special mine, that you were sent to guard, ever bombed?"

"I have no knowledge of this matter."

"Do you know what the research was about? Medicines or something?"

"*Nein!* Kammler did not tell me and the scientists were sworn to secrecy against the penalty of their lives. It was important work... I did not discuss the work with the Jews!"

"Was this unusual, this high degree of protection? To call for the top police general in Poland suggests it was very special."

"*Nein.* The Reich was at war. General Kammler dealt with projects which were classified '*kriegsentscheidend*' — which means — important to winning the war. You Americans had the same cloak surrounding your atomic bomb with its label 'MANHATTAN'."

"We didn't kill anybody because of a label!" Makepiece's angry comment drew the first reaction from Sporrenberg. He was seated throughout the interview, dressed in prisoner overalls, straight-back upright with his hands placed on the table between the two men. His shaved head jerked a little and then settled, his policeman's eyes interrogating Makepiece's emotions for the remainder of the time they were together.

"I have no knowledge of this matter."

"You suggest there were other projects in Poland?"

"I have no knowledge of this matter."

"Did it get very hot? In the mine? Where was the ventilation plant?"

"I have no knowledge of these matters."

"Were there dangerous gases?

No reply.

"Was it liable to roof falls in the tunnels? How many were killed in the mine?"

No reply.

"What were the medicines or chemical weapons being made in *die Glock?*"

"I have no knowledge of this matter."

"Did you ever see this *die Glock?* Did you ever go into the mine?"

"*Nien!* It was *Oberstes Geheimnis*, top secret. I had no need to know. My duties were to police the exterior." Makepiece again detected the prisoner was lying. He needed to keep up the pressure.

"Medicine research and engineering need large amounts of water. Surely that would be a problem in the Sudeten Mountains?"

"A construction of concrete support pillars resembling a street lantern, strong enough to withstand the high altitude winter temperatures, was specified near *die Glocke* project. This was suitable for additional water storage if the project needed it. It was a common design in Poland."

"Was this construction sometimes called the *laternentrager* — at Wenceslas Mine?"

Sporrenberg's head moved, but not in a decisive way — neither a nod nor a negative. Makepiece detected that the prisoner was prepared to say something, but was reluctant to volunteer anything.

"Was the lantern structure ever used for water storage or any other purpose?"

"I have no knowledge of this matter." He was lying.

"Did any of the workers talk about the *laternentrager?*"

No reply to the question. Sporrenberg shook his head. He looked as if he was about to repeat, 'I have no knowledge...' when he changed his mind. "There was a man, a Sudeten local, called Reichel, who said the *laternentrager* 'sang'. I have no knowledge what he meant, concrete does not sing. Maybe the wind, I have no knowledge of this matter."

"You are sure the man was called Reichel?"

"I remember. I am a policeman. My duty is to remember."

"Did any scientists place any objects on the *laternentrager?*"

No reply. Sporrenberg's eyes did not suggest he was concealing information. His head had not moved.

"What happened to the scientists?"

"I heard that one or two were injured during a research accident. Of the others I have no knowledge. Burying the corpses of dead Jews was not my concern."

"Did Manteufle survive?"

"I have no knowledge of that matter."

"Did Reichel survive?"

"I have no knowledge of that matter."

"What would you expect to have happened to the scientists and *die Glocke* apparatus when the Russians advanced towards the Oder River?"

"They would not be allowed to take their knowledge to the enemy. *Die Glocke* could be dismantled and moved. I understood that dismantled and moved was how it was filled for experiment."

"Were the Russians interested in your special project in the mine?"

"I have no knowledge of this matter."

"As a policeman you would have known if the Russians had a spy in the workforce."

"I would know; there was no spy." Makepiece saw no evidence that the man across the table was lying.

"Would you be surprised if there had been a Russian spy?"

"He would have been shot, but there was no spy... Russian, or English or *Amerikanischer spion*. I would have known; it was my job."

"Would anything be left behind?"

"I was not at the mine if it was dismantled. I was called back to Lublin. I was needed to prepare to protect the *Reich Vaterland*. I expect they would leave the concrete lantern and the power station buildings. *Die laternentrager* was a very robust construction. Everything else could be moved with enough Jews. General Kammler was very efficient. They would not leave any item of value to *die Glocke* to the enemy."

"Including singing concrete?"

"I have no knowledge of that matter. It would be difficult to break it down to move it."

"Was material or personnel for any other project left in the Sudeten Mountains?"

"I have no knowledge of that matter."

"So you were summoned only for Kammler's Wenceslas project, *die Glocke,* in March 1944.

No reply.

In response to a question, Sporrenberg told Makepiece, "The last I heard of Kammler was during April 1945, when he was gathering a *SS Komando* group to protect German assets from falling into the hands of the communists. Lots of people and material went to Bavaria. The Russians were across the Oder River by that date, west of your Sudeten Mountains that you are showing interest in, and occupying most of Poland except Breslaw where our gallant troops were holding out. I don't know if General Kammler surrendered as we were all told to do. I have no knowledge of any material he might have taken from Poland. I can only tell you that he was rumoured to have no interest in gold, he claimed to have something even more valuable."

"Do you know what that was? Uranium perhaps?"

"I have no knowledge of this matter."

"Was there a second *die Glocke* project somewhere else in Germany?"

"I have no knowledge of this matter."

"Near Ohrdruf, or Nordhausen?"

"I have no knowledge of this matter."

"Heidelberg?"

"I have no knowledge of this matter."

Makepiece asked Sporrenberg if he thought he had done a good job for his country while he was serving in Poland?

"I was awarded the Iron Cross 1st Class on 30 November 1944 and was appointed SS and Police Leader for South Norway. I suppose someone in Berlin thought that I did it right."

As a parting shot, Makepiece had asked, "Did you ever witness an atomic bomb test?"

"I have no knowledge of this matter."

Makepiece's last sight of the prisoner was that he was still seated, hands on the table, seated upright, presumably unaware what Makepiece's interest was.

Chapter 48
1946 ~ Loose Ends

Makepiece was looking at his draft report and was reflecting on how his high hopes to improve his knowledge of CHRONOS had been dashed by Sporrenberg's lack of technological knowledge. He now realised it had been wishful thinking to expect useful material out of Sporrenberg who, anyway, was to be moved within 5 weeks, on 25 February 1946, for interrogation in London. In that respect, at least, he had acted in time to avoid upsetting London and drawing attention to his specialised interest.

His heart was not in the chore of writing the report. More important was to write a letter home, to Antonia, about his planned movements to return to Washington. But...

Something in his memory of the visit to Camp XI was nagging. Then it registered. Sporrenberg had said, '...*a Sudeten local, called Reichel, who said the laternentrager sang...*' Openshaw had difficulty translating what Sporrenberg was saying at that point... could he have meant resonate? Circulating magnetic pulsed energy, within the lantern, was surely within the rotation torsion field concept that had been mentioned in the so-called 'gravity engine' principle.

'There had been a casual reference to 235 megacycles potential resonance by a photo-analyst reporting on his mission. The egg-heads in Washington can sort that one out!' thought Makepiece.

His train of thought was interrupted when Sergeant Paul knocked on the door with coffee. Without invitation, he sat down. Makepiece said nothing about this untoward act of indiscipline. Toby Paul obviously had something on his mind. The colonel's silence invited the aide to speak.

"I was putting some of the Sporrenberg papers away, Colonel, and I came across a Bletchley Park Police Department end product report about SS General Jakob Sporrenberg. It was marked MOST SECRET ULTRA... not military... police... in Poland... 1943. Bletchley Park tended to shy away from police because the high priced help wanted matters military, or political, or the weather. It appears there was a breakout at a concentration camp for Jews... Sobibor... the SS told Himmler, through Eichmann, that 320 Jews were on the loose and 20 German or Ukrainian guards had been killed in the breakout, their bodies being destroyed by fire. Himmler threw his toys out of the cot and ordered a reprisal."

Sergeant Paul was obviously disturbed, presumably by the document he held in his hand. Makepiece decided that he should encourage his aide to continue, "Get it off your chest, Sergeant."

"Sporrenberg, who had been appointed Special Assignment Officer to Gaulieter Eric Koch back in August 1941, got the job. He supervised 43,000 Jews being machine gunned into prepared pits in the 6 days between 3 and 9 November 1943. Then he reported to Himmler for his well done and told Bletchley Park in the process. It's probably what he got his Iron Cross, of the 1st class variety, for."

"It's what the war was all about, stopping the black shirts doing that sort of thing," offered Makepiece, feeling his comment was inadequate. Attempting to change the subject, "What are you going to do when they let you out of uniform?"

"Hunt Nazis. There's stories about a Jewish organisation setting up to bring all the nasties to justice. War crimes and all that stuff. I'd like to help."

"Yeh! That's a good mission." Makepiece relaxed in his chair; his war was nearly over.

"I reckon. Switzerland is where I'll go. I always fancied myself as a yodeller. It's where dog-collars bring you brandy not sermons! How about you, Colonel? You've seen enough of this business to hang up your hat and leave the next one to the youngsters."

"Right. I'd like to teach. Something I know, not too far removed from air power and intelligence. Maybe the fishheads will let me into Annapolis to educate the navy officers on what really happens. Take out the gung-ho and inject more thinking could be a really good idea. Reconnaissance and being prepared will win the next war, not being caught with our pants down as per Pearl Harbour. In the next shooting match, God forbid, it won't be Stukas at dawn; it'll be buckets of sunshine from the edge of space. And no second chance..."

"Heavy stuff, Colonel. And Kammler is still loose! That son of a bitch is a survivor in a game of high rollers."

"Right, Sergeant. Still loose! Did someone offer Engineer Hans Kammler a job? God forbid it was the Russians! I hope the world finds out in time..."

"You don't think there could be any truth in the story that Patton and Kammler made a deal?"

Makepiece shook his head. "Unless Kammler had the wherewithal to make Patton President, then I think Patton would have reneged on any bid no matter how much Kammler offered him. Just because George Patton got himself killed in a freak car accident, a '39 Cadillac in occupied Europe for Christ's sake, does not make for a good conspiracy except in fairy stories. No, my money is on Kammler having gotten a first class ticket in a big aeroplane and crossed the ocean blue. It needs the likes of your Swiss hunters, with time and patience, to track him down. And I don't think he'd come quietly, either."

"Right, Colonel." The aide cleared his throat, but made no motion to leave.

"Now, Sergeant, how about that coffee? I've got some writing to do... What's the problem, Sergeant?"

"I just wonder who they buried in Luxembourg, Colonel. 'Old Blood and Guts' Patton was a hero for the Luxumbourgher folks and they wanted to see him off, proper like, as the Brits might say."

"Your point, Sergeant... ?"

"Well, Colonel, it's only scuttlebutt, but... "

"I'm waiting..." Makepiece was tapping his fingers on his desk in feigned impatience. When this aide had something to say it was generally worth listening to.

"There's a story gone round that General George Smith Patton did not die in Heidelberg or any other hospital. In fact he's very much alive but contained where he can do no more damage... politics-wise. Scuttlebutt has it that he's been sectioned and is in a private clinic, Stateside..."

"Get outta here. Rumours like that are best not repeated."

"I'm just wondering who they've buried."

"It'll be you if I don't get that coffee. Let's hear no more about it... And..."

"And, Colonel?" Toby Paul had already risen from his chair, firmly clutching the top secret document.

"See if you can track down who on the staff is selecting the GI Brides to travel to the States. I think I should put in a good word for a certain Mrs Delaney Plowman — spelled with an O W — Openshaw."

"No need, Colonel. She's as near as crossed over."

"You mean she's dead?"

"No, Colonel. She's going Stateside; she's New York bound. While Openshaw was here waiting for the ride to Wales, England, he let on that he'd gotten himself a bride who collected Heinkels at little old Snodland for pleasure. It seemed likely that the Colonel would want to say thank you to a T/Sgt for helping him with his enquiries, so the Colonel's office asked the immigration office at the Embassy for a favour. She will be gone on the January 25th ship. That's today, Colonel... She's missed him."

"Sergeant, get outta here. I'll take that coffee black and strong... Err... does he know she's gone?"

Sergeant Toby Paul reached the door, grabbed the handle and turned to speak.

Makepiece quizzed his aide through his eyebrows. He could not conceal the reflex sucking of his cheek as he waited for aide to reply.

"Couldn't rightly say, Colonel. I thought the Colonel might like to know about the drafting assignment of T/Sgt Delaney J. Openshaw." Makepiece was looking for something solid to throw at his aide. "It seems that the T/Sgt's talents are required with great urgency and he has been assigned to Fort Meade, Maryland to report as quickly as Military Air Transport can move him..."

Makepiece's finger was making it plain that the aide should leave.

"...and the best they can do is to land him at Andrews Air Force Base, outside DC, about February 2nd. Fort Meade needs a security cleared escort non-com for some recon hardware... "

"Anymore?"

"His arrival stateside is dependent on the weather, Colonel, but I guess you'd know that. Forecast is for patchy snow... That'll do for now, Colonel. Strong and black, you said..."

Through the partition door, left slightly ajar, a discordant solo male voice could be heard destroying the Welsh anthem, over the sound of rattling cups and spoons.

> *"There'll be a welcome at the air base,*
> *Jenny O. helped make the peace,*
> *They missed some pretty heavy petting, when*
> *Delaney got back from Wales... Oh, yeh..."*

Chapter 49
1946 ~ No-One Asked You to Come

Mrs Jenny Plowman Openshaw, GI bride, leant out of the carriage window. She was too high to kiss, but she could just touch her mother's face as words just did not come. Their farewell kiss, hastened by the 'All Aboard' and the guard's whistle, was precious. Now their eyes were engaged and locked together. The guard's whistle twice pierced the hubbub of departure. As the noise from the steam engine increased, a hundred families and loved ones pushed the Plowman parents towards the platform edge. Jenny was determined not to cry — she wanted her mother to remember her happy face. Father Plowman stood behind his wife watching his grown up daughter departing to her new life; his initial reluctance to lose his treasured girl to a Yank had evaporated at the obvious warmth of their devotion.

The letter had arrived, its unusual envelope size and texture indicating something important from American authority. The immediate worry, that something awful had happened to her new husband, quickly faded as she realised that she had 5 days to prepare to sail to, to emigrate to, America. The cursory summary read:

Train: January 20th, 1946. Waterloo, London, England. Platform 7, depart 10:20 hours. Report to Travel Officer by 09:00 hours. Arrives about 13:00 for coach to Tidworth Transit Facility. Note: Army personnel will not be released from their duties to attend Waterloo.

Luggage allowance. Up to 200 pounds per person. Heavy luggage intended for the ship's hold will be subject to a mandatory search for weapons, valuables and contraband which will be confiscated.

Boat: January 25th, 1946. USS Argentina from Southampton, England. Transport from Tidworth to be notified.

Arrival: February 3rd, 1946 Arrive New York, NY for immigration process through Ellis Island, NY. Disperse to US destination under own arrangements.

Currency: British regulations permit only £15 (fifteen pounds) to be exported. Exchange facilities will be available at Tidworth. Amounts exceeding fifteen pounds will be confiscated.

They had been married eight weeks and spent Delaney's three weekend furloughs, and the short Christmas leave, trying to avoid her attentive parents in their desire for privacy. They had agreed that Jenny should apply for GI Bride status, fully expecting the process to take months. Now, unbelievably quickly, they were to go their separate ways, cruelly parted almost before their life together had begun. He was to stay in England, she was to go America to await his re-assignment.

A crackling trans-Atlantic phone call, followed by a confirmatory telegram, advised the newly weds that the Openshaw parents would meet their new daughter in New York. A letter with their recent photograph was in the mail.

"We'll have a proper honeymoon when I get back to the States," Delaney had promised.

Jenny mouthed the words, "I love you, Mother." Jenny was fighting to smile.

She replied, "I love you, Jenny…" The engine whistle shrilled to drown, "…Take care of yourself, my darling. And don't forget to write every day you can." The shrill echoed along Waterloo's Platform 7 and faded.

"I'll write to you every…" There were tears in Jenny's eyes.

The special train jerked into movement in a crescendo of coal smoke, steam and slipping wheels. Its precious cargo of wives and children was being transported to Tidworth Transit Camp, for onward passage by ship to the new world.

The Plowman parents' final glimpse of Jenny was her auburn hair blowing in the slipstream, her hand waving goodbye until the steam enveloped her into her journey.

Every seat on the '*Brides' Special*' train was taken, perhaps 250 wives and a quarter of that number of children en route to heaven knows what. The only respite from physical contact with a seated neighbour or a wriggling child was when a wife moved into the corridor to smoke. One sleeping baby in Jenny's compartment had been put onto the netting luggage rack as a makeshift basinette.

'Just endure it, Jenny. It will come to an end — sometime.'

After two and half hours, the special train slowed for its final tortuous five miles before jerking to a halt. They had arrived at a snow bound, isolated Salisbury Plain station called Tidworth. The children quietened.

Each compartment's carriage doors were opened to chill fresh air and unfamiliar American voices calling, 'Everyone out. Everyone out'. The unprotected platform was covered in trodden snow. Knee-length top coats would scarceley keep out the cold. Jenny was grateful she'd chosen to wear gloves.

"Ladies! Ladies…" The officer reflected that Army training had not equipped him for this situation. 'Herding cats would be easier than this,' he reflected, 'and there's another train due in five hours. And they're from Manchester. Oh my Gawd!'

At the distant end of the train from London, the luggage van was being unloaded, by prisoners of war, onto Army lorries for the transit facility.

"Sergeant, go and supervise that freight," ordered the officer.

The engine had already been uncoupled and was on the rail turntable as Jenny climbed off the snow covered cobblestones and into a coach. 'Thank heavens I chose to wear sensible shoes this morning.'

*   *   *

The formalities in the Reception Area, housed in the barracks theatre, were drawn out and tedious. At least there were chairs for most of the brides to sit on; some had to make do with their hand luggage. Many would look back on the protracted episode as a nightmare of struggling with luggage, with screaming children and unhelpful GIs barely concealing their resentment at this unwelcome duty, which they saw as delaying their return home. The whole process got off to a bad start when an officer mounted the stage only to begin his welcoming speech with, "You may not like conditions here, but remember no-one asked you to come."

Jenny was no exception to the arrival procedure. For all intents and purposes, the GI brides were now in 'little America' passing through the early phases of the immigration process. Before sailing to America, a GI bride needed to show:

Her passport.
Her visa.
2 copies of her birth certificate.
2 copies of her police record.
2 copies of her marriage certificate.

Her husband's sworn statement that he could support her, with salary details.
Confirmation from her husband's commander supporting salary details.
£15 in cash and no more — to be exchanged for US dollars.
Written confirmation from the husband's family if he was not yet in the USA that they were willing and able to house her.
Discharge papers if she had served in the military.
Evidence that she would get a train ticket to final destination on disembarking.

She needed to surrender:

Her British ration card.
Her British identity card.

Jenny, in common with everyone else, was allocated a bedspace in the barracks.

'They're all the same,' thought Jenny, 'the army organising and lists. I thought I'd escaped from all that. I should have known better...'

It became clear that Jenny's London group were soon to be joined by more GI brides from other places. This first group had to clear the reception hall so that it could accept its second batch that would be arriving after dark.

'If this is what being hurried along is like,' she thought, 'what would it be like if they were to take their time?' She checked her luggage was where she had parked it while she drank what passed for a cup of tea in an American canteen.

'At least,' Jenny thought, 'they'll be arriving when it's too late to see what a bleak and awful place this is. It beats the Kent marshes in winter and they were pretty terrible.'

Chapter 50
1946 ~ A GI Bride Sails Home

The four days long nightmare which was Tidworth had come to an end. On the 25th January, the first shipload for GI brides was coached through bomb rubble of Southampton to the dockside. Delayed for 24 hours by a severe storm, at 4:30 pm on 26 January 1946, the 20,000 ton transport *USS Argentina* sailed with 626 women, including 30 who were pregnant, and 173 children. The youngest bride was 16 years old, Mrs Benjamin Franklin Butler, who was carrying her son aged 14 months. There was said to be one 'male GI bride' who kept himself to himself throughout the voyage and whose identity would remain a mystery in the folklore which grew up about the voyage.

For one specific GI Bride it was an especially poignant moment. She had missed a final telephone call to her husband, T/Sgt Delaney J. Openshaw, on detached duty to HQ 8th Air Command and not contactable. Of course his unit would know her movements, but it wasn't the same. The letter she had sent him was little consolation. She had no way of knowing that even while she was feeling forlorn, her husband was receiving his drafting orders to be in the United States on the same day she was due to disembark. But that was for the future.

The *USS Argentina* was still fitted out as a troop transport and not yet refitted for civilian passengers. As she pulled away from the Southampton dockside, Jenny was at the ship's rails that were lined with GI brides. Everyone began to sing, 'There'll always be an England'. Many tears were shed as the young wives felt that they were seeing their home country for the last time. There were few friends or family on the quay to see the deferred departure. For the women of Tidworth Camp, it was a relief to be away from the harsh conditions, even if the forecast for the crossing was far from pleasant.

The vessel weathered an enormous storm; camp sickness, picked up at Tidworth, travelled with the passengers onto the ship. Most wives, when they had overcome those dreadful first seasick hours, were pleased to see the variety of food on offer which was a welcome relief from years of rationing for those with the digestion to eat it! Many children enjoyed their first banana on the crossing.

On 4 February 1946, a day later than scheduled because of the atrocious ocean sea conditions, the ship arrived coated in ice only to be greeted by a tug boat strike. While the temperature was recorded as 13°F, under a clear star-studded sky, some of the brides assembled at 3:30 am on the deck to catch first sight of the Statue of Liberty. *USS Argentina* was still 12 hours from going alongside. She docked at Pier 54 on the Hudson River to be surrounded by an army of newsmen and photographers.

It was time for Jenny to make ready for her first step on a new continent. The Americanisation of Jenny Plowman Openshaw was about to take a step forward.

*   *   *

'Yes,' Jenny was certain now. There they were. Jenny could see them. It had to be them. Did they recognise their son's wife from the wedding picture? There was a tentative wave and the couple came forward. This was them and they knew she was Delaney's Jenny.

"Jenny Openshaw, I guess?" queried the man. His wife was hanging back a little.

"That's me. GI bride of Delaney J Openshaw. I guess you must be my new Ma and Pa in law."

The elderly couple, together with a throng of thousands, had been waiting on the freezing dockside for several hours as the *USS Argentina* made her final manoeuvres.

"Elmer, give the girl a hug," encouraged Mother Openshaw. "She's gorgeous. I didn't know Del had it in him to net an English beauty like this. You been in the movies, Missie?"

Quite overcome by this welcome, Jenny replied with a chuckle in her voice and a mild flush in her cheeks, "Ooh no. This is what the cold Atlantic wind does to the complexion. Please call me Jenny, Delaney does."

Mother Openshaw began to pull husband Elmer off his new daughter. "I want to give this daughter a hug myself. You pick up her luggage there and let's be about reclaiming her hold trunks."

Two hours later, the Openshaw trio sat in Elmer's car, heading out of New York towards the south. Jenny was overawed, not only was the night-time New York skyline so impressive, but everything seemed so big and spacious. As they progressed out of the built up area, so the roads became quieter and the winter snow covering more complete.

"Jenny," said Elmer. "We're gonna stop at a diner for a freshen up, then we'll book a motel aways ahead. We're not gonna get through tonight and there may be some snow drifting when we get into Pennsylvania."

"Whatever you say. I am here for the ride." Jenny noted the way they spoke so easily about America — just as they did in the movies. 'Not surprising, I guess, they are American…'

When the two women were alone, while Elmer visiting the rest room, Mother Openshaw asked Jenny the burning question, "Are you expecting, child?"

"Ooh, no, Mother Openshaw." Jenny had been waiting for the question and now it was out in the open the residual tension between the two vanished.

"I had to ask. Listen, why don't you call me Ethel? Then I'll be easier when I call you Jenny. Everyone else does — call me Ethel. Elmer and Ethel, two Es in a pod. Right?" There was an impish grin on Ethel's wrinkled face.

"Right, Ethel it is. When Elmer gets back, I'll tell all I know about Delaney — Del — and how he beat the Germans single handed — well with a little help from Eisenhower and a couple of generals. You won't mind if I call him Delaney, will you? It's sort of like a habit."

"It's a deal, Jenny. It's great to have you here. If there's anything Elmer or I can do for you, please ask. If you don't ask, we won't know."

"It's a deal, Ethel. Look, here comes Elmer. Can they make a decent cup of tea? There was no proper boiling water on the boat."

As Elmer settled onto the seating bench, positioned so that he could keep a good view of his son's new wife, Ethel said, "Did you hear that woman talking as those babies were being carried down the gangway. She said something like, 'See those beautiful babies, we'll have to send our American ones over to get some colour in their faces'."

Jenny smiled. She would leave it to Delaney to tell his parents about the reality of war torn England, the wretched poverty, scarcity and rationing. Those were memories now. 'This is the land of opportunity and new love,' she thought. She noticed the Openshaws poured lots of sugar into their coffee, an unheard of luxury at home.

The Americanisation of Jenny Plowman Openshaw had taken a giant leap forward.

*   *   *

"Here we are. Home," said Elmer.

"It looks very nice," said Jenny.

"We like it," said Elmer. "Been here all our married lives... carried Ethel over the threshold here... she's never tried to run away."

"You wait until spring, my dear. Elmer's green fingers came over from England with the founding fathers a way back."

"Oh," responded Jenny. She thought, 'Perhaps they still look on England as the home country.'

"Come in, Jenny. We'll get your luggage when the car's in the garage. Ethel, don't forget Jenny's key. I had it cut special."

Ethel opened the door. "Let me show you your room, and the facilities. Then we'll get the coffee on. I'll send Elmer to the store for some tea directly. We use milk, not creamer. Is that OK?"

Jenny had learned the difference at Tidworth and on the boat. "No problem," she said. She also noticed the absence of a kettle for boiling water. She would ask how they coped later. A coffee percolator was perched on a high shelf... presumably that was not the answer.

After unpacking, during which Ethel had busied herself in the kitchen, they had been settled for about 10 minutes when a car drove up the drive. A door presumably opened because the slam of it being shut carried into the house as the sound of departing tyres drifted away. Twenty seconds later, the flyscreen squealed, the front door opened, and in strolled T/Sgt Delaney J Openshaw in uniform.

"I thought I'd find you home!"

"Delaney," screamed Jenny, almost kicking over a table as she tried to stand.

"Del," screamed Ethel — a mixture of glee, surprise and amazement carrying in the single syllable — catching the table against its fall.

"Hallo, son. Good to see you," said Elmer without rising as if a son returning from three years at war was an everyday event.

Jenny got there first, even before her man had hung up his uniform cap or undone his top coat buttons. She did not know if she was laughing or crying or kissing.

"Whoa, Jenny. I'll suffocate…"

"How? When? What…?"

"All in good time. I see you've met Ma and Pa. Good to see you, Ma and Pa." There was another kiss for Jenny, and then he had to push her gently away to embrace his mother and shake hands with his father.

"I got in to Andrews the day before yesterday. There was no answer on your telephone so I reckoned you were on your way to New York. I had a day at Fort Meade, yesterday. They are going to hold me for duties in the Pentagon. Seems my old boss, Colonel Ploughman, pulled some strings. Even got priority quarters so Jenny and me gets a roof to move into — err — this week. And I've gotten 10 days return home leave before I have to check in."

Jenny watched every word come out of Delaney's mouth. "I have so much to tell you, my love. Oh, I am so happy to see you again." Her husband wiped away her tears of joy and smiled until he needed to kiss her again.

Practical mother Ethel said, "There's a pot roast on the oven, son. Just the way you like it. You go on up with Jenny — you're in the guest room — and get reacquainted, like. You've got 15 minutes, you hear, or Elmer will be up with a watering can to stop your canoodling."

Elmer started to say, "There's a coupla of beers, Del, in the…"

"Hush up, Elmer! You got to let them young folks be. Theys got private hallos to say. They got a lot of important catching up to do and beer ain't got no place in it."

"Tchh," was all that Elmer could get out before his smiling son, carrying his kit bag, was leading his GI bride upstairs.

Inside the closed bedroom door, the couple embraced again.

"Oh, I've missed you, darling Delaney."

"I'm here now, Jenny, honey." His kiss was persistent.

"Delaney Openshaw, your wife is here. She wants you to complete a special mission — begun months ago in bombed out England."

"What's that, my love?"

"I want you to complete the Americanisation of Mrs Jenny Plowman Openshaw. Now!"

Chapter 51
1960 ~ Retirement to Rosetta's Rocks

On the November 5th, 1960, Makepiece Ploughman, being as old as the century, had reached retirement age. It was time to settle down with his second wife Denise. He called her Dee and she adored him with every aching cell in her body. She was accepted by Marybeth's children who, anyway, were now making their own independent family lives. But Rosetta's Rocks was the family anchor; any excuse would bring the family together to up date news, or celebrate a special day and what better than a birthday?

After his return to civilian life in 1946, and while instructing at the Naval Academy in Annapolis, widower Makepiece felt no urgent need to find a wife. His relaxed manner was noticed by an attractive, blonde, well-built widow at a nurses' social gathering and their relationship blossomed. She was five years Makepiece's junior, liked people, fun and partying. When Makepiece's daughters announced that they were prepared to accept Dee as their mother, Makepiece quickly popped the question. Dee's enthusiastic reply both surprised and delighted Makepiece and the couple were married in 1948.

Early in the 1950s, Makepiece and his youngest were fishing. "Daddy, why doesn't Dee smile more?" Makepiece's youngest son Bernard had asked the penetrating question.

"Son, there's women and there's women. Your new mother may tend to look unhappy, but this is not an accurate portrayal. She saves up her happy look for when there's something really joyous and then there's no holding her back."

"Will I ever get the hang of women, Dad?"

"I reckon. With two sisters you've been through the probation. Soon you'll wonder what the difficulty was. There's a song, *Girls were made to love and kiss...* and so long as you're kind to them and cherish them and be there whether they're laughing or crying, they'll just love you off your feet."

"It's sad Dee didn't have her own kids."

"It was the war, son. But you came along before those bad times got in the way for your Mom and me. Now I am as proud as can be... and I've got a wife to share it with."

"Dad? Do you miss Mom?"

"Of course I do son. Marybeth was as good a mother and wife as any man could possibly hope. She loved you all, but you know that. Anyway, she'd be happy as a songbird to see the way her children have grown up to be fine young adults and..."

"Does Dee miss her other husband? She never talks about him. There's never any mention of her first husband."

"I think that's because she loves the family she has married into. And I have never seen anyone so keen to find out more Ploughman family history."

"Dad. We kids don't want you to worry. We love Dee as being the lady in your life. We all hope you'll be very happy... as happy as a yacht on the Bay's water."

"Bernard, that's very grown up. Marybeth would have been so proud to hear..." The frog in Makepiece's throat stopped him finishing his sentence. Meanwhile young Bernard had turned away to be about young adult's business — catching that elusive catfish.

*   *   *

Dee was sitting in front of a mirror, brushing her hair. The birthday party had gone well, the guests all departed. Rosetta's Rocks was its tranquil self once more. Dee could see her husband's reflection and without turning said, "Do you realise what date it will be next year?"

"1961, it lasts all year...."

"And when did the original Ploughmans sail from England?"

"Bernard and Charity and Maria... err... autumn 1661."

"I make that 300 years, this year."

"Arithmetic was never your weak point. Where's this leading...?"

"Sounds to me like an excuse for a party. It isn't every folks that has 300 years to celebrate."

"They arrived in '62."

"I know. But they left in '61. So why don't we go over to see where they left from? And we could have the Homestead refurbished and modernised, and all, while we are away."

"I've been to Snodland. There's not much there. And London got pretty well destroyed in the blitz — at least the parts where the Ploughman roots were."

"Makepiece Frisby Ploughman. This here woman of yours wants to see for herself. And you need a good holiday. And the old Homestead needs a lick of paint. So I'll brook no nonsense, you'll take me there next year."

" 'Brook no nonsense' indeed." Approaching his reflection and, incidentally, his wife's bare shoulders, with a John Wayne swagger and an imitation of his speech mannerism, said, *"Them's mighty fine words, Missie."*

"Darling, Makepiece. I want you to make me a promise. Tomorrow, I want you to book us two tickets to England and we're gonna research your roots. The old timer, Bernard the physician, lying in the plot behind the Homestead with his own Missie Charity, requires you to do something special for the 300th anniversary of them coming here. You are retired; your time and the world is your oyster…"

"You know, Dee, I had a number two in the Air Corps who used to mix metaphors almost — but not quite as badly — as you."

"Tomorrow, my man. Now, Dee wants her refresher in… ooh… wait… ooh… for the crew to pull the chocks away… ooh."

Chapter 52
1961 ~ A Journey to Kent, England

With the pack retrieved from the safety of the county archive vault, Makepiece opened the brown paper binding, neatly bound with durable ribbon, and found the fondly remembered heritage volume.

"Here it is, Dee, just as it was when I last saw it during the war. I will try to borrow a couple of pairs of cotton gloves to stop us spoiling the papers." Dee was patient as her husband slipped on the gloves and lifted the cover. There were the folios, just as she had seen them in their photographic copies, but here, of course, real tangible history. Now she slipped on her gloves. There was something special, a frisson, when touching something that had been written three centuries ago.

"It will be all right to touch these pages, won't it?" she asked Makepiece. "Aren't you excited to be handling stuff that is 300 years old?"

"It's not new to me, my dear," responded Makepiece. "When Mrs Bates got the volume from the safety of Wales for me, she and I poured over these folios for hours. You know how difficult some of the writing was in the photocopies at home; it's no easier now, is it? That is why I had my aide at Snodland type the stuff while it was fresh in my mind. I think Julia did a good job. Look, Dee, here is Grandmother Susannah's letter which set the whole caboodle running. You read it... it's kinda addressed to you:"

Madam
Forgive this formal salutation for I know not of your family name, nor your given name, but I hold dear the knowledge that you are born from, or wedded into, good family stock. This casket records our heritage. The deerskin scroll in my own hand shows that we hold our line from John of Gaunt in 1200 or thereabouts. The signet ring was my beloved husband William's, bearing the seal that his great Uncle William earned from the Privy Council in 1463, displayed in the firebreast at the Hall and as set in brass in the memorial at All Saint's Church Snodland. You are on trust to provide documentary details of the family for the generations of your time, sealed with those who went before, the record for passing to

our descendents. Once sealed, never reopen the casket, but bequeath it on to the most likely matriarch of the Ploughman heritage. Remember the family revolves about the home you provide. Be true to your husband, be receptive for your children, be a friend to your family.
Susannah Ploughman (born Catterall)
Sealed Fifth Day of November, year of our Lord One Thousand Six Hundred and Fifteen, King James reigning.

Dee was delighted to be holding the copy of Susannah's original made by her granddaughter Abigale in the 1630s.

"The Hall has long since gone, Dee. It was pretty much where my office stood back in '43 and '44 until the Army gave it to Patton. So the firebreast with the crest has long since gone to the great chimney in the sky. Except that the firebreast would have been carved in stone... but you get the idea."

"Isn't is marvellous? I wonder what happened to that signet ring? And the casket? Look Makepiece, inside the back cover there is a single sheet of typescript within an unsealed closed envelope. Go on, you read it; I just can't bear the excitement. After all, this is your bloodline. I'm only in it for the duration."

"You are in it because I love you, Dee. Now, madam, I'll charge you not to forget that." He gave Dee a tender kiss on her cheek and took the typed letter. His heart skipped a beat as he looked first at the signature and then read the text:

11th March 1945
Cleeve Lyon Cottage, Near Maidstone, Kent, England

To the Reader. Greetings.
Grandmother Susannah Ploughman's family heritage volume has been safeguarded through the centuries within the County Archives. Its longevity is as assured as it can be. It should be a matter of record that two photo film copies of the texts were made during 1943. Colonel Makepiece Frisby Ploughman (American national born 5 November 1900, stationed in Kent on American Air Corps war business) visited the County Archives seeking information about

his family. We found this material which had been handed to the Archive, when it was founded in 1933, by a legal firm of Maidstone. Colonel Ploughman had the facilities to make copies when I accidentally mislaid the pack while I was researching my second novel: 'Warranted Traveller'.

While it is locked away in a stuffy vault, Susannah's message to her family progeny is denied transmission to the next generations. The mystique of the casket has been lost, but its theme lives on through the set of duplicates. I kept one copy of the original, now in your hands. The second went with the American colonel whose personal fate, and the fate of that copy, I do not know.

I hold, as did Susannah, that a woman's support to her man in no way diminishes her ability gladly to give her love, share her intelligence and donate her comfort. Treasure your family, be there in your children's time of need, and bear witness to our common heritage for the future wellbeing of your family and Grandmother Susannah's trust.

Aynette (born Cleeve Lyon)(widowed) Bates
Archivist Assistant, Kent County Archives, Maidstone.

"Makepiece, she writes as though she is a part of the family..."

A second sheet was folded into the envelope. Makepiece carefully unfolded the single sheet and read what obviously had been hand written at about the time that she had typed the previous text. It was what Aynette, in the style of Rosetta Makepiece Ploughman 150 years before, had written as what she called her confession. Makepiece read the text silently, savouring every word as if Aynette was there, speaking the words in his ear.

Revelation of a Ploughman's Lover

I loved a fighting man, a married man, whom I could never have as my own exclusive man. He was a pilot, a senior commander of a very secret USAAC group with unimaginable burdens he kept unto himself. I could not share the burden of his mission. Mine was the role to provide but a short-lived bolthole from the pains of war, release from the pressure of command, succour from the absence of dear ones and the loss of friends. I took Makepiece Frisby Ploughman to my heart and body as I had taken no one before or since. I was keeping him for his family across the ocean. They do not need to feel jealousy or contempt for me or my Ploughman man. It was war, total war, when none knew if this day was to be the last. We both knew that our closeness must end. There was never a suggestion of commitment, either way, beyond the immediate needs of the moment. This I affirm with all my being, confident that heaven knows we both lived only for our time together, not as sinners, but as seekers of peace of mind and body.

Out of our love came a boy whom I christened Bernard Makepiece Bates. Makepiece Frisby Ploughman did not know his boy was conceived when his war took him away from me. Perhaps, one day, the ocean will divide to bring my son to meet his father. For the record, Bernard Makepiece Bates was born at Maidstone, Kent, England on 5ᵗʰ November 1944.

Aynette Bates

There was silence. Dee's eyes interrogated Makepiece's face. Was there a hint of tears there? What could possibly have brought about such a reaction in her strong husband reading of a simple hand-written page — a page she could not herself read at this distance? She tried to communicate sympathy, touching his arm, but somehow that did not seem to be possible in this extraordinary moment. Makepiece would not let her make eye contact; this was his exclusive moment with history. She reached out with an open hand and took Aynette's once private letter so that she could read it.

Dee did not hesitate. She went over to the central counter and asked if she might have copies of the two documents in her hand.

"We have to make a charge for copying, madam. It's the rules."

"That'll be OK. Whatever. Make it two of each. I'll be over there with my husband when they're done."

"Is he alright, madam? He looks poorly."

"Oh I think so. He's a strong fella. I think his war has just caught up with him. He just wants to be quiet for a moment. Do you have a restroom?"

"There is a staff canteen which you are welcome to use. It serves hot snacks between twelve and two. There are facilities for... ladies... you know... just through that door on the right. The 'Mens' is next door to the 'Ladies'."

"Thank you. We'll be fine." Dee returned, her heels echoing in the otherwise absolute silence, to sit next to Makepiece.

He had not moved and did not react when she took his hand. He was staring at the window, its lowest pane made of obscured glass, its upper panes covered in combined weather and traffic grime. Unseeing. Unfocussed. It was obvious his mind was somewhere long ago, with innermost private thoughts which Dee hoped he would share with her when he was ready. Now she was there for him, just as Aynette had written, just as Grandmother Susannah had written. Dee squeezed Makepiece's hand.

He slowly turned his head to look at her. He tried to smile at her support, but there was an internal anguish he could not control. Both cheeks were sucked in. He was fighting back tears, tears he could not explain, tears a grown man needed to shed.

"I'm sorry, Dee. It came as a bit of a shock to see Aynette's writing. Let's go and finds a coffee someplace. There is something I want... I need to tell you. Ask the staff to put the papers aside for a while, Dee. Tell them we'll be back when I've had a breath of fresh air."

Chapter 53
1962 ~ The Family Celebrates 300 years on Warranted Land

It was the week of the reunion. Ploughmans, Plowmans and acceptable variations thereto from worldwide, were en-route to assemble at the Homestead plantation. Dee Ploughman was delighted by the response to her invitation; tickets had been issued and now it was all over bar the shouting. Makepiece was surprised at the energy Dee put into her project and was not at all pleased with the telephone bill she accumulated. But it was all in a good cause.

Unknown to her husband, she had planned a secret surprise for her husband, but the way had to be cleared with his and Marybeth's children.

"While your Father is socialising with his Association of Old Crows chums, from the electronic warfare and intelligence community though heaven knows what those wrinklies find new to talk about now the war's long since gone, I wanted to speak with you about a secret visitor I have invited. Your father is not aware of this and I hope that you will give me the support to pull this off."

"Dee," said Frisby the eldest at age 38 years. "I've hightailed over from Rosetta's Rocks to hear what you have to say. Dad's happy talking electronic warfare to his cronies because it's getting to be big business in South East Asia."

"OK, Frisby. Look, you are all adults and have read stories of things that crawl out of the woodwork. But you and Antonia, Abigail and Bernard — if he were here, but is now over in Annapolis as we talk — all being children of Makepiece and Marybeth may find what I am about to tell you... well... unexpected."

"Come on, Dee. You're making me nervous. What's the big deal?" Antonia, the eldest daughter taught in high school across the Bay; she believed that no-one could make any pronouncement more difficult to comprehend than the things she heard in her classes.

"I guess there's no easy way to tell you this, kids. Makepiece found it and, believe me, it was a surprise when he found out in England when we visited."

"Grandmother Susannah's risen from her grave and is coming to the party here in Maryland?" offered the younger daughter Abigail.

"That would be easy. Try this for size. How about if I told you that your baby brother is coming to our pig roast?" Dee waited for a reaction.

Abigail came in with, "It ain't no big secret that Bernard will be here. There's been a Bernard here, for every pig roast, since Charity dropped her kid in 1670. Why if it weren't for the Bernard Ploughmans, the whole shooting match would…"

Dee shook her head. "I take that point. But I am referring to another brother, one that you don't know nothing about until I tells you now. It's one that your Father didn't know about until our trip. You've gotten a baby brother, sired in England, when Makepiece was fighting the war."

There was silence. Frisby made to stand from his chair, but Antonia laid a hand gently on his arm.

"Are you telling us that Father was playing hooky while Mom was still alive?" Abigail's voice combined shock with disbelief.

Antonia's head was shaking in disbelief.

Frisby's reaction was the most direct. "That's gotta be the biggest load of rubbish since…"

Dee gently shook her head in rebuttal of Frisby's outburst. "It's true — all true. Your Father found a paper stashed in the archives in Maidstone, Kent County, England. It was written by a lady for who your father had great attraction while he was fighting and flying in England. They say that lots of folks do things they might regret when they goes to war and your Father was one of them. It seems that Makepiece did not know about his son until he found the paper when the boy was already 16 years old. So he could not have owned up to Marybeth because he did not know, and any naughtiness on his part was only between him and Marybeth and she had died before he got to tell her."

"But…" Frisby was unwilling to accept this story. Antonia was fighting back tears while Abigail was momentarily struck dumb.

"No 'buts' Frisby… and you girls. Your Father told me some of his story while we were England-side, and made me swear to keep it a secret. But secrets have a habit of slipping out and I reckoned it was time for you to know. You're all of an age to understand these things and maybe, privately, you have ventured off the straight and narrow yourselves. I'm not askin' and I don't want to know."

The was a pregnant silence, until…

"OK, Dee. What's this bastard's name? I guess he has a name?" Antonia's hand was still resting on her brother's arm although he was no longer trying to rise from his chair. The gesture was as much a search for family reassurance as a restraint. "And where is he now? Are you gonna bring the brat out of a hat tomorrow?"

"Your brother... your half-brother... has a name. He's called Bernard Makepiece Bates and was born at Maidstone, Kent, England in 1944 on November 5th."

Antonia was visibly shocked at the announced use of the name 'Makepiece'.

"I know, it's your Father's birthday which don't make it easier, none. And I know, it's the Ploughman fifth of November curse again, but it's all coincidence really. His mother's name was Aynette Bates, a widow and an author; she was killed by a flying bomb two months before the war ended. I found the boy through his uncle — his mother's brother."

"So?" questioned Abigail. She, of all the siblings, had remained calm, so far.

"He's with your brother Bernard in a motel downtown in Annapolis. I paid his air passage and it happens to coincide with an interview with MIT he had on the cards."

"So?" repeated Abigail. "I think I've gotten enough brothers. Another out of the blue could break the camel's back."

"OK, Abigail. I understand your point." Dee sought to make eye contact with each of the gathering. But this is your father's business and sooner or later he's gotta face up to the problem. That means we all have. Now, these days, there's no stigma to being born the wrong side of the blanket. All I ask is that you all give the boy — Bernard Bates — a Ploughman fair wind. We might all like the boy. Let's take the lead from your Father. If they can't touch base, we'll all know a little more of the truth, fewer lies and we'll rest easier at nights."

"How many more skeletons are you going to drag out of our cupboard, Dee?" Frisby was not too sure if Bernard Bates's appearance on the scene, tomorrow or whenever, was going to make much difference to his life. Surely the lad was no threat to his inheritance? The kid had no birthright, no claim in law. Surely?

Dee said, "I needed to get this problem out of the way tonight ahead of tomorrow's party. All I ask is that you don't talk about it with your

Father until after he's met the lad. Bernard has given me his promise. Now please, Frisby?"

After a moment's hesitation, "I'll play it your way, Dee, but I'm not happy."

"Antonia?"

"I'm with big brother." She lifted her hand away from Frisby's arm.

"Abigail?"

"OK. But only because you ask. It's not gonna be easy. I don't know if I could look Father in the eye knowing what I know, and knowing that he don't know what I know. You know?"

"We all understand, Abigail. It's only a short time and then we can talk about our feelings and give our support to Makepiece. He will need every ounce of family support he can get. But, as I said, it's better and easier now than later." She paused. "It will be easier for him if you are all about, giving him your support and love. It's what families do."

Frisby made to rise. Dee said, "Frisby, would you please just check that the drinks are right for tomorrow? We've got 205 acceptances so far and there'll be more when the mail gets collected tomorrow, and that's a lot of booze. Abigail, would you please make sure the cook knows where everything is? He's got to light the fire at 9 o'clock and start cooking at ten tonight if we're gonna eat at one tomorrow. That's two mighty generous sized pigs we're going to eat in one sitting, over 200 pounds without their heads. Why, he didn't choose to go for one carcass I just don't know. Thank you both. There's something I need to talk to Antonia about, nothing about the lad from England, I promise. It's a woman's family matter." Her eyebrows went in emphasis. "Honest, cross my heart."

When the two women were alone, Dee having moved to the seat next to Antonia, before she could begin, Antonia attacked.

"If you pull another stunt like that again, step-mother or no step-mother, I'll throttle you with my bare hands."

"No stunts, Antonia, I promise. This is Ploughman family business. Heritage stuff which goes back as far as 1615, and the old country. It doesn't matter that I'm a second wife. You know some of the story about Grandmother Susannah Catterall, she was a fourth wife. You'll see how to find out lots more in a minute. She set up a collection of heritage documents stowed in a casket where the matriarch of the family put pen to paper to record the births, marriages and death. Her granddaughter, Abigale, spelled old English manner differently from our Abigail, started a duplicate.

Antonia was wondering what this had to do with her. She was not sure she liked the way Dee had dropped the half-brother on the family.

"The casket was lost in the English burning of our Washington DC and the White House in 1815, but the duplicate papers survived and found their way to England courtesy of great, great and some, grandaunt Ada Ploughman Wilmer. Your Father, with the help of Bernard Bates's mother, found these duplicates during the war and had them photocopied in his office. I have those original films and prints and have been adding my knowledge of the Ploughmans on paper family trees and index cards since we came home from England a while back."

"What's this got to do with me?"

"Your father wants you to be the family heritage matriarch, to take over from me. You've gotten Ploughman blood coursing through your veins. Some day you'll live in the Homestead, this very house, since Frisby wants to stay out at Rosetta's Rocks. So you'll become the matriarch in two ways. One day, you'll pass the documents on to the daughter of the blood who you judge will best keep up the records; that was the trust Grandmother Susannah Catterall placed on her granddaughter Abigale Ploughman 300 years ago and some. Some responsibility, eh?"

"You don't do things by half, do you, Dee Ploughman?" She took a deep breath. Antonia's face showed she was deep in thought about what she was being told.

"'tain't in my nature, beloved daughter Antonia; half is not in my vocabulary. But I love this family. I love your Father more than I can describe. And I love all his children too. Makepiece would be the proudest man on warranted land to know that his eldest daughter was going to pick up where Maria and Rosetta, who are lying buried in the family plot out back there, and Susannah with Ada lying alongside in Snodland, England all left off."

Dee reached to clasp Antonia's hands.

"You'll see their own writing in their own hand and the confession that lies buried with Rosetta and the confession prepared by Aynette

Bates too. It's family, Antonia, and I would be so proud to hand it over to you to maintain."

Anxiously, "Do I have to talk to father about this?"

"Let's say it's a done deal, woman to woman. Makepiece'll know I have spoken with you, you being the eldest daughter and all, and maybe one day he'll mention it to you, just in passing. He'll dismiss it as another concession to the Women's Rights Movement: the Equal Pay Act is going to be passed by Congress, promising equitable wages for the same work, regardless of the race, colour, religion, national origin or sex of the worker. Of course that has nothing to do with our family heritage' but that's the way he'll say he sees it. But I think the old English women had a saying about such matters: '...it's women's work...' so enough is said."

"When?" There was still anxiety in Antonia's voice.

"We'll get the pig roast out of the way, and the brother from England too, and then I'll pull the papers out of my desk. Soon, Antonia, I promise. Soon. Don't worry, it'll be fine."

"It's easy for you to talk," challenged Antonia. "The twins are boys... and I ain't proposin' to have anymore, thank you very much."

"Grandmother Susannah's rules are that you pass the heritage onto your choice of a daughter of the blood. It'll be your choice when the time comes and doesn't have to your natural born child. You'll get the notion when you study the folios. I promise it will work out just fine and fitting for the lady who's gonna live in the Homestead house when we've gone. I've been doing it for 10 years."

"Oh Dee. I just don't know. When do I get to see all these papers?" Her step-mother's clasp of her hands did not fully reassure her that she was up to the job.

"When all the guests have gone, I'll tell you a tale about a 375 year old scarlet silk petticoat."

"Enough," begged Antonia. "you'll be telling me next that Rosetta tamed the old west single handed."

"There might be some truth in that..." replied Dee as she ducked the cushion hurled at her head.

*   *   *

The next day, by 11 o'clock, there were more than 250 people in the grounds of the Homestead plantation. Dee and Makepiece made fine hosts to many familiar faces and to the many more strangers. The children seemed to get on well and the air was full of reminiscences. Cameras and notebooks were in abundance. Dee, especially, took copious notes of who did what to whom, where and when, excusing herself with the explanation '...hatches, matches and dispatches, you know...'

Makepiece was particularly pleased to meet again with Delaney J. Openshaw and his wife Jenny with their boisterous twin teenagers. The Openshaws lived in a suburb of Washington where he ran an electronic assembly business specialising in work for the National Security Agency at Fort Meade. Another face from the past was Rod Chmielewski who was suggested to Dee by 'Jules' Knapp as a surprise guest — a sort of honorary member of the Ploughman family. Rod had further surprises for his host up his sleeve.

From within the groups that formed, and disbanded, came joyous exclamations of recognition and enlightenment: the area in front of the old colonial style building resounded to 'no', 'really', 'she didn't', 'how many?', and similar family banter. Twice there were shrieks of enlightenment as a family secret was breached to open the floodgates of more 'no', 'really', 'I don't believe it...'

*   *   *

Three days of intensive effort had prepared the riverside lawn. By the dusk of day preceding the gathering, three marquees were up, their weather protection demonstrating, on the eve of the party, welcome effectiveness in a sudden downpour.

"I hope we don't get weather like this on the big day, my Darling." Dee was fussing with all the details to make sure the unprecedented event would go off without a hitch. The last thing they wanted was a washout. The tables and chairs, the glass and the cutlery, the dance floor and a stage all came together with the military precision.

The banners along plantation access drive were up and secure: 'Welcome to 300 Years' and 'The Ploughman family — 1662 thru 1962' and Dee's favourite: 'Grandmother Susannah says Hi'. There were some pre-arranged mobile homes to be parked on the plantation; the hotels for miles around began to fill.

The mobile latrine, the garbage skips and copious litter bins had been deployed. The mobile power generator was silently doing its job.

Step-daughter Abigail assured Dee that all the necessary emergency precautions were in place. The air-conditioned tent had been erected in case anyone should be unwell from too much sun or the heat of the day.

The refrigerated container had been ordered by the ever practical Bernard and was now providing plenty of ice and keeping the food fresh.

The cook lit his fire at 10:00 pm on the evening before and his choice of two spitted pigs in lieu of the more difficult singleton were beginning their slow roast, under his careful attention, at midnight.

Dee had invited the assembly of 293 members of the global Ploughman family — including the Plowmans of course and one family who styled themselves Ploman. From across the United States they came, in mobile homes or by car. Two yachts were moored offshore in the river. A couple had flown in from Hawaii; there were two family couples each from Australia and New Zealand, and three more from England. One family of five flew in from Barbados.

The deputy sheriff had placed road signs at the plantation entrance and positioned two deputies to turn away gatecrashers. "The Eastern Shore ain't seen nothing like this before...", she claimed.

Family and a few selected friends, young and old, guests or helpers, black and white — and a few indeterminate — and four native American Indians, joined in with the rest of the family, would gather to celebrate 300 years of family heritage at the Homestead plantation. From as early as half-past nine on a mercifully dry day, they assembled chatting, drinking, socialising, greeting, exchanging addresses, showing family pictures or simply exploring the plantation grounds and buildings with its burial plot.

One child fell off the jetty into the river.

Smoke from the roasting fire rose vertically in the still air into the near cloudless sky. The ancient trees provided welcome shade from what could have been unpleasant direct summer sunlight. Somehow the special aroma of cooking meat permeated the gathering. The musicians provided background music of the Glenn Miller era.

Most listened to Makepiece's three-minute welcome speech, delivered with confidence from the stage, with Dee standing by his side holding his hand.

"I just want to say how much I appreciate you all coming to the Homestead where my predecessors — Bernard and Charity Ploughman —laid down American roots 300 years ago. There have been a few changes beyond the fence since those days... 13 generations have been rooted here... some are buried out back where they will never leave the Homestead..." Bernard concluded with thanks to Dee for making the gathering happen which drew resounding applause and whistles from the audience and a blush to Dee's cheeks.

At midday, with an imitation dress sword, Makepiece cut the first slice of pork and the feasting began. There was a burger and hot dog grill for the less adventurous or those that just could not wait. A whole table was dedicated to the widest selection of salads: potato, coleslaw, curried rice and mixed tossed green leaf with a variety of dressings. At another, there was a selection of breads, potatoes, carrot strips with dips, sauces and relishes. Since pork was the central meat, a 10 pound basin of apple puree was placed on the sauces' table. A reserve was discretely hidden under the table.

A local mobile ice-cream vendor had been brought in, for the day, to serve to those who craved the delicacy. And there were multiple tables supplying iced beer, wines, soft drinks and even Homestead well-water for the thirsty.

"Makepiece, don't you over tire yourself. It's a long day." Dee knew the strain Makepiece had been under just assembling the contributing facilities. "Look, Darling, they're still coming in..."

"Dee, my love, this is all down to you. Ike could not have invaded Normandy with better planning. Not bad for a second stringer."

"I know all that. Don't forget the kids. They were great..."

"Their mother would have been so proud..."

"You think Marybeth would have liked to celebrate this way?"

"You bet. Marybeth enjoyed a good party. It's a pity that she ain't..." The lump in his throat cut short the thought. "I reckon she's watching and cooing from a cloud, up there," tossing his head skywards, "holding Grandmother Susannah's hand for comfort, I reckon."

"You old softie, Makepiece Ploughman."

He reached across to kiss her cheek, but she turned to meet him full on the lips.

"Another time, or in a more convenient place, Mr Ploughman, and I do declare there might be some serious taking of familial advantage..."

"You'd get laid, you mean..."

"Later, my love. Look — there's Rod Chmielewski. He's made it. My, it's nearly 12:30 already. Let's go make sure his glass is wet on the inside..." Dee knew this was the time for Makepiece's first surprise treat — one which Rod had played a major part in putting together.

Chapter 54
1962 ~ Wiffenpoof's Salute

The sound was unmistakable. Twin Allison engines purred in unison to announce their arrival, mounted on a blue P-38, skimming the flat surface of the river. Their pitch rose as the aircraft's nose went up and the twin boom machine seemed to hang in free space.

"Max chat," waved Rod ending in a USAF salute to the passing aircraft, appreciating the historic sound of the engines at maximum throttle.

The manoeuvre was the signature of Whiffenpoof Cuthill, an expert pilot flying his machine — his way. After what seemed to be an impossible loiter, the nose dropped and the aircraft advanced trailing white smoke into a flat orbit to pass over the jetty into an upward climbing roll. The crowd clapped with excitement as the aircraft gathered itself, rolled onto its back and shook its wings before diving towards river in a half loop. The river surface shimmered a bit at the disturbance. Cameras were clicking, children would be cheering. The musicians stopped playing to watch. The surprise had worked. The pilot put on an impressive three-minute low-altitude aerobatic display for the gathering, but experienced pilot Makepiece had seen it before. He only had thoughts for his former number two from Snodland days.

"Rod, you son of the gun, it's great to see you." The firm grip of the hands while their eyes engaged brought back happy memories. "I guess I've gotten you... and Whiffenpoof?... to thank for that? I counted 15 breaches of air safety law and he's still going!"

Rod shrugged. "Maybe... You put on a good party for a retired spook. Have you met my wife... she'd like to say hello?"

"The party's down to Dee. You're a surprise — just like that war-bird up there." His head was nodding in the general direction of the sky. His whole body language betrayed the pleasure of the moment. "You... married?"

"I guess... It's a good gathering. Sure looks as if the Ploughmans know where it goes, procreation-wise!"

"Hush up, you — I don't know what! Ladies present! Where's this wife then?"

Rod ignored the question. "Hi Dee! I see the old fellow is still in good shape. Must be something to do with his diet — or his love life."

"Oh! He's OK!" Dee was beaming. Rod had turned up trumps organising an air display — as much a surprise to her as to her husband. As Whiffenpoof completed his final upward charlie climb away, Dee was gripping Makepiece with both hands, holding him close to her in combined affection and excitement. "There's plenty of steam in his boiler yet. Talking of which, where's Mrs C ?"

There was a twinkle in her eyes as she continued, "I've heard it said that a man is only as old as the woman he feels. My critter, Makepiece here, is pretty good at feeling... and I'm only 21..." Dee's mouth creased in a smile.

"Enough of such talk, Mrs P ! How could a man be happier?" Rod was enjoying this banter... he knew what was coming shortly. "A loving wife, friends and family gathered, a P-38 strutting its stuff over his piece of the river..."

"Rod, you've obviously met Dee?" queried the host.

"Sure have! We're old chums..."

"Heh! Not so much of the old." Dee's smile just stayed there on her face. It had come together, her reunion plan for her beloved, as she had hoped it would. Her man was happy and therefore she was too. "This is one helluva party to add to the family archive. I hope the kids are using their cameras! I'll leave you warriors to exchange scars and war stories. I've gotten 300 guests to get chowed down."

She began to move away, even her walk gave away that she was as content as a mother bear that has found the honey. She was 15 strides away when she turned and returned to stand by her man.

"Now don't you dominate my man with your flying" she commanded Rod Chmielewski. "He's got lots of family hands to shake before this day is out. Where are you hiding your other half?"

Nonplussed, Rod was pointing at the climbing P-38. "Oh she'll be by, by and by... Don't miss this, Makepiece." The smoke went off as the aircraft continued upwards and away.

"A pilot's salute by the finest of the elite — none better."

The aircraft had reached 2500 feet — half a mile above the applauding gathering. The dark underside plan-form was a distant hash-shape against the clear azure sky and now too far away to be heard. It seemed to settle into horizontal flight so as to show its lower surface to the ground until it began to roll. It disappeared.

"Ooh!" exclaimed the crowd. "Where's it gone?"

Rod was still pointing. Makepiece was smiling. The special paint, his selection for camouflage, had rendered Wiffenpoof's inverted machine invisible from the ground.

"Keep looking," prompted Rod.

Across the sky interrupted trails of white smoke appeared.

Long, long, space, short, long, long, short. Then nothing.

"Morse code — M P — Makepiece Ploughman. Wiffenpoof's salute to the Commander, 1574th SPSG. Not bad, eh?"

There was a knowing smile on the face of the retired colonel, a recognition of excellence by one professional of another. Makepiece was choking back emotion, sensed by Dee through his arm held firmly against her body. The emotion defocused Makepeice's vision for a moment then he realised there was another lady in the group.

"Buy a girl a drink, Soldier?"

"I know that voice... Julia Greenburg. Oh my God... Julia... how?... Rod? You didn't?... Are you two spliced? Well I'll be doggoned... I didn't recognise you..."

A left hand sporting a wedding band was raised in answer to the questions.

Makepiece took the initiative. He reached for both her hands and kissed his former aide on the cheek.

"Hi, Colonel. It's great to see you again. I couldn't let Rod loose on the ladies of the USAF, so I had to hangar him myself. Quite a challenge, it was, but I'm used to it."

However, there was a more immediate matter. With Makepiece protecting his eyes from the sun's glare, with the other he pointed at the receding aeroplane.

"Where did he get that ship? That was no ordinary P-38! Not in that paint job — with those engines — and those wing stubs!" The aircraft was now in normal flight, dark side down and receding towards the west across the open water of the Chesapeake.

Rod answered, "When Bushy Park said the outfit had to fold, we had three machines. The regular P-38L went into the pursuit pool somewhere in Suffolk county, England. We had two P-38M-SP after your pancake at West Malling. Orders were to get them to BAD Warton to be used for spares after the electronics had been stripped out. One made it — I flew it there myself. The other was trusted to Captain Wiffenpoof Cuthill US Army Air Corps and didn't — make it. He said he'd had engine failure off-shore from Liverpool and had ditched in the oggin. Said he'd had his flying suit washed by a local lassie so he'd look presentable when he checked in. He's actually landed on a sheep farm in North Wales and parked his machine in a sheep shed until he'd sorted out Hitler and Hirohito. He went back in '49, kicked the tyres, lit the fires and flew back Stateside for unspecified duties with the confederate air force. Some say he married the farmer's daughter, but that's only a rumour."

Makepiece listened to the tale with complete disbelief. Dee could not contain her amusement at the enthusiasm with which Rod told his tale. Makepiece looked at Julia for confirmation. She shrugged. It was what all the men in her life did — something oddball!

"What about fuel? Flight planning? Air traffic?"

"Don't ask," rejoined Rod.

"Airframe number? Registration documents? The USAF?"

"Same answer! The answer to all those airmanship questions is, 'It's what Wiffenpoof does best... push the envelope beyond the limits...' Your beloved ship would have ended up as scrap; that's no fitting end for Lockheed's finest. I know they're making some new beast, but it won't have the edge over one of your specials."

"Enough said!" Makepiece was shaking his ahead and not too sure if he believed it. "Come and have a cold beer, Rod, and regale me with another tale of misdeed and daring-do. Whatever happened to that intel officer, Sarah Johansson? You didn't marry her... ? I thought you might've... Or worse...? No, of course not..."

The two former air corps chums strolled towards the beer table; Dee was still holding Makepiece's hand and was almost dragged along by the men folk. Julia excused herself and made for the ice cream. They passed Delaney Openshaw, standing with Jenny, clutching their twins.

"Some flying, Colonel — err — Colonels?"

"You've got it, son," replied Rod with a nod, "...in spades!" Then he turned to Jenny, "Flown any balloons recently, Mrs Openshaw?"

Jenny's cheeks flushed with memories, conceding just a hint of a smile and then she turned to the child on her arm who was demanding popcorn.

Chapter 55
1962 ~ The Late Arrival

Makepiece looked around the family gathering. He could see Frisby, Alison and Abigail with their families and friends. He asked Dee, "Where's Bernard? It would be a shame if he was to…"

Dee slipped an arm under her husband's making reassuring noises about probably being delayed at the toll gate on the Chesapeake Bay Bridge, while she steered Makepiece towards the veranda and his favourite swing seat.

"Sit down for a moment and enjoy the view. Here, in your favourite chair overlooking the gathering, and all. G. G. Grandfather Bernard would have approved this gathering 300 years ago and so, I'll warrant, would Grandmother Susannah Catterall from across the ocean. Now I'll get you a couple of fingers of Jack Daniels^{tm} while you get your second wind. We've got a long afternoon ahead."

"You know, Dee, this view has hardly changed in 300 years. I guess some of the river bank reeds have been cleared away. But it pretty much as Bernard and Charity would have seen it. I reckon I'm the luckiest man in Maryland…"

Behind the house there was a crunch of tyres on gravel followed by the sounds of two car doors being closed. Two men came around the house; both casually dressed, wearing sunglasses against the road glare. One had shortish blonde hair, the other a full fashionable head of auburn, worn to shoulder length, casting a shadow over his face. Makepiece recognised the silhouette of his youngest son Bernard, his companion was more broadly built about his shoulders and some 4 inches taller.

There was something about the way the second lad moved as the pair approached. Something familiar, something stirred deep-seated memories in Makepiece's mind. What…? The first lines of an old wartime tune came to the forefront of his thinking:

In all the old familiar places…
…I'll be looking at the moon
But I'll be seeing you.

"Dad," said Bernard, removing his sunglasses in an action mimicked by his companion. Makepiece was rising to stand to greet the visitor without having the chance to speak. "May I introduce you to Bernard Makepiece Bates with whose name you may be acquainted? Bernard, meet our Father."

The lad's handshake was firm and confident against the bewildered figure standing before him. Makepiece was grateful for the reassuring support from his chair against the backs of his legs.

Makepiece looked into the newcomer's eyes. They were unmistakably Aynette's...

To be continued...

Now you have enjoyed the story of *Makepiece's Mission*, you will wish to learn what happened next to the Ploughman and Plowman *Warranted Land* families in Maryland and the Medway valley of Kent.

The following sample chapter of the *Warranted Land* saga is taken from the saga's sixth novel *Piers' Cadetship* due to be published late in 2012. The novel primarily concerns the British son of the family, with roots along the Medway estuary, who chooses to join the Royal Air Force with a strong ambition fly as a pilot. The east/west cold war is a major factor in Piers' life and his chosen career which will eventually take him across the globe. Among the challenges ahead is the advanced technology demanded in air power while sustaining a sensible balance of family life. Inevitably, family history research will carry Piers towards Grandmother Susannah's archive. But, first, Piers has to join the Royal Air Force...

See http://www.warrantedland.co.uk for further information on publication details.

Sample Chapter of *Piers' Cadetship*

Chapter 8
1956 ~ 'You have been selected…'

Daedalus House at RAF Cranwell, Lincolnshire, was the final selection centre for Royal Air Force Officer Cadetship, not exclusively aircrew. The letter from the Air Ministry, now re-titled Ministry of Defence (Air Force Department), instructed:

> *Mr Piers P. Ploughman … be at Grantham Railway Station by 12:30 on August 26th for transportation to RAF Cranwell. Bring a pair of casual slacks for physical activity exercises.*
> *A rail warrant from your postal address to Grantham is enclosed herewith…*

The building probably had something to do with the former Royal Naval Air Station on the site back in 1916. This was of no interest to Piers or any other candidate for RAF officer selection, not necessarily aircrew or cadetship. The selection process repeated the same techniques as the Aircrew Selection Centre Royal Air Force Hornchurch, without the medical component, and this time Piers was successful. A final pre-enlistment visit to Hornchurch during the summer of 1956, confirmed that all his medical bits were in the right place and that the nasal operation had been successful. An officer cadetship at the RAF Technical College would be offered where, subject to final confirmation of medical fitness, he would have up to 120 hours of flying plus the opportunity to go on to 'Wings'.

Piers' ambition was back on track! Pilot training, as an engineer, could lead to test pilot for the newest aircraft…

And the bonus: through the RAF Technical College, Piers would have an engineering officer's qualification so that he might follow in his father's footsteps when he was too old to fly.

*   *   *

The beach at Clacton-on-Sea was not an exciting stretch of East Anglia coastline. Piers had said to Helen that the most interesting feature of the whole place was the horizon when you could see it. From where they were sitting, on a bench 'In loving Memory of Harold the Scotch Terrier — passed away 23rd May 1938' according to the corroded plaque, the pebble beach extended for nearly a mile to the pier adorned by the vertical ring of a big wheel amusement ride. Today, even the sea seemed reluctant to roll ashore against the dismal Essex coastline. The pier had somehow survived the war and the weather, but now definitely was in need of a coat of paint. From this bench, the distant amusements on the pier, even when illuminated in coloured night lights, was beyond hearing range. That suited both Piers and Helen who, anyway, had only ears for what each other said.

On their days off from school vacation work, they rode a bus or hired a tandem bicycle inland, away from the crowds at the coast, to the quiet fields where the sun was ripening the corn and where the birds sang enchanting songs. On workdays, there was only spare time sufficient to find solitude on a windy beachside bench.

Both teenagers had completed their schools' sixth form, sat exams and had been advised they had achieved the grades necessary for Helen to proceed to University, in Exeter, and for Piers to enter officer cadetship in the Royal Air Force. The requisite documentation had been mailed and written confirmation of a place was awaited. Now they were on work experience, with Butlin's[tm] Holiday Camp, in the catering support areas. They had been at Butlin's[tm] for six weeks when they each received their letter of offer; Helen's required a telephone call to confirm her wish to go ahead. Piers' letter was rather more formal; it had been forwarded from the River Medway town of Gillingham, Kent where his grandmother lived and which he used as a mailing address while his parents were on Royal Air Force duties in Singapore.

Telephone: Holborn 3434

Air Ministry
Adastral House
Theobalds Road
London   WC1

TC.1956/21/A.R.1a.   *30th August, 1956*

Sir,

1.   *I am commanded by the Air Council to inform you that you have been selected for me to offer you a Technical Cadetship (Henlow) at the Royal Air Force Technical College following which, upon your successful completion and graduation following the three years course, will qualify you for appointment to a permanent commission in the Technical Branch (General List) of the Royal Air Force.*

2.   *Subject to satisfying appropriate medical checks and your confirmation of willingness to undergo flying training, this letter includes the offer of additional training during and following your Technical Cadetship (Henlow).*

3.   *You will be required to attend the Aircrew Selection Centre located at Royal Air Force Biggin Hill, Kent for medical assessment of your continued fitness for service in the Royal Air Force.*

4.   *If you wish to accept this offer, please return a signed and dated copy acknowledging receipt of this offer. I enclose an envelope and second copy of this letter for the purpose. Please also enclose a short letter of acceptance and state from which railway station you wish the return rail warrant to be made. Our letter with the warrant will advise you of the date for your appointment at Royal Air Force Biggin Hill which will include an overnight stay in service accommodation.*

5.   *If you wish not to accept this opportunity, please write a short letter advising me of your rejection of this offer.*

I am, Sir,
    Your obedient Servant

L C Aubruy

Mr P. P. Ploughman,
c/o 16 Debden Lane
Gillingham
Kent

Piers' reaction was to sit on the bench, close to Helen, re-read the letter and enjoy the moment. He was oblivious to the sea breeze, the sun's glinting on the breaking waves and the background noise of the holiday camp behind them.

"You've gone quiet," said Helen. She could feel his excitement bridging the proximity of their position. "What does it say? Come on... don't keep it to yourself..."

With great difficulty, Piers controlled himself. Very quietly, he said, "I've got it."

"What?" She guessed his letter was official; she had to wait for him to tell her.

"I've got it. The RAF is going to let me fly. I've got it."

"Well done," whispered Helen and planted a kiss on his cheek. To her surprise, Piers did not react to the kiss. He re-read the letter, and then again.

"They've done it. They've offered me a cadetship and they are going to let me fly. It means pilot training."

"Can I see your letter? Henlow is quite a long way from Exeter, isn't it?"

"I'm going to fly. It's what I've wanted to do ever since... I don't remember when... all those cinema films... school... Dad... the war... the sound barrier... books. And all those medicals... and fixing my nose... I am going to fly. Whee!" Helen clung more tightly to his arm, but Piers was not moving. She could feel the pent-up excitement coursing through his body. Helen had to take the letter out of his grasp to read and that provided Piers with the excuse to move his head to read it again while she held it.

"Gosh that nose job was awful... but it was worth it... as a pilot. Great!" Their heads were now so close they could feel the others' warmth radiating and the lingering kiss became inevitable, their eyes wide open searching for each others' innermost thoughts.

"Do I say congratulations? Or what?" Helen's sea blue eyes looked deeply into his, telling him of her shared joy at his good news. She did not know how the news would affect their lives; separation for a while maybe, but there was the phone... and letters... and the train... and holidays. For the moment, her man was happy and that made her happy too. The future would look after itself.

"And for you, too... you're off to wear a mortar board and learn to count numbers bigger than 10. My oh my! ...I'm in love with a swot... What was it the man said? The future starts here. Wow!"

"Sh!" Even her first attempt at a kiss could not silence him.

"And never again to have to go to that miserable Hornchurch..."

"Sh!" she mouthed with their lips just touching. "You'll wake up the gulls or even Butlin's^{tm} happy campers."

Piers received another kiss and the couple quietened, looking at the horizon, their heads joined at their temples. Each had private thoughts — thoughts to be shared at some later time.

Their teenage lives together had just become much more complicated.

Closing Notes
Historical Footnotes

Evolution of the US Signal Intelligence Service. By December 1941, the previous inter-service rivalry between the US Army Signals Corps and the US Navy OP-20-G branches had achieved a measure of cohesion to mutually address the decryption of the Japanese diplomatic message network. Intelligence from this source was given the protective handling caveat 'MAGIC' which controlled access to the collection and exploitation methods. Partnership with the British attack on German radio messages conducted at Bletchley Park, with its protective handling caveat 'ULTRA', allowed the two nations to exchange intelligence derived from enemy communications 'COMINT'. It enabled the USA to concentrate on the Far East theatre while Great Britain concentrated on the European sector. In July 1943, following a series of re-organisations under Colonel Carter W. Clark, the US Army's group name changed to Signal Security Agency. It was managed at Arlington Hall, Virginia. By 1949, additionally the USAF, the FBI and the CIA each had developed independent signals intelligence departments; Secretary of Defense James V. Forestall directed that all such activities were to operate under one authority. It was President Harry S. Truman who, on 4 November 1952, signed the memorandum establishing the National Security Agency which adopted Fort Meade, Maryland as its headquarters site.

Royal Air Force Balloon Command. RAF Cardington, Bedfordshire was responsible for training in balloon handling from 9 January 1937. Balloon Command was formed on 1 November 1938, with the purpose of protecting major population centres and industrial areas, ports and harbours. Each barrage balloon required about 20000 cubic feet of hydrogen per fill to inflate to a nominal 66 feet long and 30 feet high envelope. The three fins self-inflated by air entering scoops on the fins. A valve released hydrogen to compensate for reduced pressure with altitude; a rip chord removed a panel at the top rear of the balloon for emergency deflation. By 1944, the number deployed had risen to nearly 3000 balloons with 1000 ringing London to combat the V-1 of which 300 foundered on the balloons' cables. Balloon crews of up to sixteen strong, mainly Women's Auxiliary Air Force, had the task of launching then tethering these balloons at various heights on steel cables. The working conditions were difficult and dangerous; some balloons were positioned above mobile launchers such as barges or lorries. The initial intention was to protect ground targets from dive-bombers. Later, barrage balloons were flown at heights of up to 5000 feet to force bombing aircraft to fly high, making them less accurate, and bring them within range of the anti-aircraft guns. The Balloon Training Unit closed in 1943, when it had trained about 22000 RAF and WAAF operators and operator-drivers. From September 1944, Balloon Squadrons began to disband and Balloon Command ceased February 1945.

Archibald McIndoe. Born in Dunedin, New Zealand on 4 May 1900, McIndoe was appointed the RAF's consultant in plastic surgery in 1939. Hurricane and Spitfire pilots suffering major burns were taken to what was to become the world famous hospital in East Grinstead. Burns and reconstructive surgery was experimental; someone suggested the name "Guinea Pig Club" for the patients of plastic surgeon Archibald McIndoe. The first verse of The Guinea Pig Anthem (provenance unknown) is:

We are McIndoe's army,
We are his Guinea Pigs.
With dermatomes and pedicles,
Glass eyes, false teeth and wigs.
And when we get our discharge
We'll shout with all our might:
'Per ardua ad astra'
We'd rather drink than fight.

Over 640 patients were treated. Sir Archibald McIndoe died in 1960.

R V Jones. Reginald Victor Jones, born in Dulwich on 29 September 1911. He attained first class honours in physics in 1932 at Oxford. In October 1936, he joined the Air Ministry, was temporally assigned to the Admiralty Research Laboratory, Teddington, Middlesex leading, in September 1939, to intelligence duties to investigate the German application of science to air warfare. An early success was the identification and jamming of the radio navigational beams' systems guiding German Luftwaffe bombers to their targets. In 1941, Jones was promoted to be Assistant Director of Intelligence (Science) and the CBE in 1942. He has been credited with inventing radar jamming chaff (window) despite the Germans having a similar technology. Jones travelled widely to lecture and attend conferences, often visiting the USA where he was highly regarded in intelligence circles. He was appointed a Companion of Honour in 1994. He died on 17 December 1997.

P-38 Lightning. Clarence L 'Kelly' Johnson designed Lockheed's fighter designated P-38, nicknamed 'twin-tailed pursuit ship', called the Lightning by the British. It survived rejection by the RAF to become one of the most deadly American pursuit fighters of the war, serving with distinction in the Pacific, the North African desert, the Mediterranean, and the final assault of Germany. The engine glycol coolers were mounted in the tail booms. The American designation of the P-38 photo-reconnaissance variant was F-5B/C/E.

The P-38M was derived from the P-38J, through the high performance P-38L, then fitted with a two man cockpit and nose radar.

Of a total of 9923 P-38 airframes built, 75 were converted to the P-38M night fighter variant.

The P-38's nominal performance, dependent on model and weapon configuration, was:
Max speed: 414 mph
Cruising speed: 275 mph
Range: 1,100 miles
Engines: Two Allison V-1710s of 1475 hp each.
Ceiling: 40,000 ft.

Constance Babington Smith. Section Officer Constance "Babs" Babington Smith WAAF began her photographic interpretation training as one of five women at Wembley on 1 December 1940. Within weeks she was issuing live reports. In 1941, her unit was reformed at Dansfield House, Medmenham on the Thames north bank between Marlow and Henley. From 1942, she was interpreting American imagery taken by USAAC P-38 variants (later designated F-4 or F-5), and others, in addition to RAF specialist Spitfires. In 1943, she reported on German experimental aircraft and missile work at Peenemünde on the Baltic coast. Later she concentrated on aircraft production plant in Germany including identifying the experimental He 280 jet fighter dropped in favour of the Me 262. Her autobiographical war story, *Evidence in Camera* was first published in 1957, wherein she volunteered frequent use of Guerlain's *L'Heure Blue* perfume. Constance Babington Smith died in 2000.

Hitler's Atomic Weapon. Allied planners were aware that Germany had the scientific and material facilities to manufacture fission products essential for nuclear weapon production. In parallel, they were working on delivery vehicles should a device become available. The German approach was to develop the dual routes to weapon grade materials through developments of various competing atomic pile facilities; the result was that insufficient uranium^{235} or plutonium was made for a practical weapon. It has been suggested that Hitler may not have been confident that an atomic weapon was economically feasible (perhaps because he was incorrectly advised on the quantity of fissile material to achieve criticality) and that he preferred known armament technologies and/or the promising 'war decisive' anti-gravity weapon under investigation. Nevertheless, throughout the war, the Germans continued to exploit reserves of uranium ore in Silesia and elsewhere. There is conjecture that, in 1944/45, German nuclear devices were tested in which any fissile material present did not attain criticality for nuclear chain reaction. Under the MANHATTAN Project umbrella, America's top secret nuclear weapons programme, in December 1943, General George Marshall established the ALSOS Mission in London comprising military, scientific and interpreter personnel to assemble intelligence on German nuclear progress, and to capture resources for their own weapons programme ahead of the Russians. Led by Lt Col Boris T Pash, the ALSOS team was denied information of the MANHATTAN programme for fear of disclosure should any be captured.

Wartime Rationing.   During WWII, the British government adopted food rationing to ensure everyone received their fair share of the limited food available. Food rationing started in 1940, and finally ended in 1954. Beginning with just a few items, more foods were included as the years passed. The rations of food varied throughout the war with additional allowances given to certain groups. Special arrangements were made for young children, expectant and nursing mothers to receive cod-liver oil, orange juice and milk from welfare clinics. Each person was given a ration book, although some foods such as fish, offal, fruit and bread were off the ration, but were frequently in short supply. A 'points' scheme was introduced for unrationed foods which, on 8 February 1943, was extended to include tinned fruit. Each person was allocated a number of points and a selected range of foods was given a points value. The consumer could choose how to spend their points. Many people were better fed during wartime food rationing than before the war years. White bread became a rarity as the 'National Loaf' was introduced; made with whole grain, it produced a brown loaf. Many people grew their own vegetables and kept hens to supplement their rations. Infant mortality rates declined, and life expectancy from natural causes increased. A similar rationing scheme based on individual points was introduced for clothing. An individual was issued with 60 points annually: 2 points were required for a pair of ladies stockings, 7 for a typical dress and 26 for a man's suit.

Daylight Saving.   During WWII, the British government adopted a regimen for daylight saving, a routine it had practised since 1916. Its purpose was to save energy for heating and lighting and to give more summer daylight hours to the farming industry, especially the production of milk. During WWII, between 25 February 1940 and 07 October 1945, the clocks were held one hour ahead of Greenwich Mean Time (GMT) throughout the winter months; at this time the regimen was sometimes known as 'daylight saving' rather than the less accurate 'British Summer Time'. However, on 4 April 1941, an Order in Council amended the

Defence (Summer Time) Regulations, 1939 to provide for double summer time, during which period the time was two hours in advance of GMT, starting at 1am GMT (rather than the previously used 2am).

yy mmm dd:	Daylight Saving Regimen
39 Apr 16	British Summer Time GMT + 1 begins until 19 Nov 39
39 Nov 19	British Summer Time ends until 25 Feb 40
40 Feb 25	British Summer Time GMT + 1 begins until 07 Oct 45
41 May 04	Double Summer Time GMT + 2 (BST + 1) until 10 Aug 41
41 Aug 10	Double Summer Time ends until 05 Apr 42
42 Apr 05	Double Summer Time GMT + 2 (BST + 1) until 09 Aug 42
42 Aug 09	Double Summer Time ends until 04 Apr 43
43 Apr 04	Double Summer Time GMT + 2 (BST + 1) until 15 Aug 43
43 Aug 15	Double Summer Time ends until 02 Apr 44
44 Apr 02	Double Summer Time GMT + 2 (BST + 1) until 17 Sep 44
44 Sep 17	Double Summer Time ends until 02 Apr 45
45 Apr 02	Double Summer Time GMT + 2 (BST + 1) until 15 Jul 45
45 Jul 15	Double Summer Time ends until 13 Apr 47
45 Oct 07	British Summer Time ends until 14 Apr 46
46 Apr 14	British Summer Time GMT + 1 begins until 06 Oct 46
46 Oct 06	British Summer Time ends until 16 Mar 47
47 Mar 16	British Summer Time GMT + 1 begins until 02 Nov 47
47 Apr 13	Double Summer Time GMT + 2 (BST + 1) until 10 Aug 47
47 Aug 10	Double Summer Time ends.
47 Nov 02	British Summer Time ends until 14 Mar 48
60 Apr 10	British Summer Time GMT + 1 begins until 02 Oct 60
60 Oct 02	British Summer Time ends until 26 Mar 61

American Broadcasting Service in Europe. ABSIE began broadcasting from London at 17:45 on 4 July1943. Using BBC emergency facilities, the first radio broadcasts included less than five hours of recorded shows, a BBC newscast and a sportscast. Later styled the American Forces Network in London, part of the Armed Forces Radio Service, it used land lines and five regional Medium Wave transmitters to reach US troops in the United Kingdom. During the next 11 months, AFN broadcast day expanded to 19 hours, 50 additional transmitters were installed and six more soldiers joined the original staff of seven broadcasters and technicians. Because Nazi V-1 bombs repeatedly interrupted broadcasting, AFN London relocated from its original BBC studios, at 11 Carlos Place, to 80 Portland Place in May 1944.

Whiffenpoof Song. The *Whiffenpoof Song* was written for the Yale University Whiffenpoofs (a male singing group without accompaniment) when they formed in 1909. The theme provided a background in the 1948 motion picture *Twelve O'Clock High* and has featured in other movies and recorded songs of the post war era.

GI Brides

USS Argentina **20500 tons**

In the first 4 months of 1946, she made four return brides' trips to Europe.

On 26 January 1946, the American former troopship *Argentina* left Southampton for New York carrying 452 brides, 30 of them pregnant, 173 children and one war groom. This was the first official GI war bride contingent. It was nicknamed the 'Diaper Run,' and 'The War Bride Special.' Winter Atlantic gales thrashed the ship causing the women and their children to suffer violent seasickness.

The first official war bride ship arrived in New York, in freezing conditions, on 4 February 1946.

During the next 6 months a total of 55000 GI brides, many transported in the luxury of the liner Queen Mary, emigrated from Europe and a further 10000 from Australasia.

Civilian use of Tidworth rail station in Hampshire ceased in 1955, but continued in military use until 1962. The trains' engines were turned around on a turntable and then shunted back to Ludgershall to wait for further use. Tidworth railway station closed in 1963, and was then removed with the tracks being lifted in 1964. The site is now (2005) a supermarket.

Office of Strategic Services. The OSS was America's first 'central' intelligence and covert action agency. Instigated by President Roosevelt in June 1942, it was pioneered by a cavalier Wall Street lawyer named William 'Wild Bill' Donovan. The OSS seemed to take on his maverick personality. Donovan was interested in results, had no patience for bureaucracy, and was willing to try any new idea. As a result, the work of the OSS ranged from the enlightened to the bizarre. Success was paramount, its hard-hitting methods legendary. Civilians were organized into partisan militias, and psychological terror was considered a weapon just like any other in the military's arsenal. The US OSS, from England, clandestinely supplied tools and material to anti-Nazi groups in Europe under OPERATION CARPETBAGGER using modified bomber aircraft for their mainly unescorted missions. Between April 1944 and May 1945, 492nd Bomb Group (Heavy) flew 3,000 sorties between RAF Harrington, Northants and occupied Europe continuing their effort right up to VE Day. President Harry S. Truman established the Central Intelligence Group in January 1946, directing it to coordinate existing departmental intelligence, supplementing but not supplanting their services. This was all to be done under the direction of a National Intelligence Authority. Under the provisions of the National Security Act of 1947, the National Security Council and the Central Intelligence Agency were established.

SS General Hans Kammler. Kammler, born 26 August 1901, is widely credited with being a driving force behind the V-1 and V-2 rockets transition from experimental models to practical weapons. Trained as an engineer, he has been associated with many German high technology projects including the German nuclear programme and the search for the 'gravity engine'. He oversaw the demolition of Warsaw following the Ghetto Uprising in 1943, and has been associated with the concentration camps' gas chambers and incinerators. He disappeared from Germany in April 1945; his body was never recovered although there is unsubstantiated rumour that he personally negotiated his own escape from Germany in a meeting with US General Patton. He was closely associated with many underground weapons' development and assembly plants, notably the German rocket and flying disc projects. The German flying saucer project's principal members Schriver and Bellonzo are known to have died, and Habermohl was captured by the Russians. Of the research group at the Wenceslas Mine, Kammler is said to have ordered the killing of 62 German scientists, technicians and labourers to prevent their knowledge leaking into Allied military hands. Eisenhower admits in *Crusade In Europe* that the Nazis were within 6 months of developing advanced weapons that would have changed the outcome of the war. Yet Kammler's name is absent in the Nuremberg war crimes trials' record. Kammler has yet another distinction; as the officer most responsible for the manufacture of the enormous long-range, in-flight refuelling capable, air transport Ju 390; one such aircraft 'went missing' at the end of the war, was reported to have unloaded its passengers and cargo at a private airfield 195 km north of Buenos Aires and may have ended its flying career at a short airstrip in Paysandu Province, Uraguay. Miethe, who worked on *'Projekt Saucer'*, went to work in Canada and America. The prototype of the Canadian AVRO flying saucer was handed over to the US. Considered an uncontrollable failure in the days before flight control computers, it is located in the US Air Force Museum at Fort Eustis, Virginia.

SS General Jakob Sporrenberg. Sporrenberg, born 16 September 1902, joined the SS in 1930: he was appointed, between August 1941 and March 1943, as Special Assignment Officer to Gauleiter Erich Koch in Poland. During this time some 40000 Jews were murdered in his area of control. After receiving his ultimate promotion to the rank of SS Gruppenführer und Generalleutnant der Polizei, between 16 August 1943 and 25 November 1944, he commanded the 'Lublin' Division in Poland for which he was decorated with the Iron Cross, 1st Class. His oversight of the Wenceslas Mine site security, during March 1944, is evidence of the high security value of the facility. However, Kammler had responsibility for another top secret, munitions assembly, underground complex nearby, the largest in the Reich, thought to have been capable of accommodating 40,000 slave workers and resourced through the Gross-Rosen concentration camp. Sporrenberg may have been called in to check that facility's security too. On 21 November 1944, he was moved to become SS Gruppenführer and Generalleutnant of Police, South Norway, until his arrest on 11 May 1945. After being held for a time at Special Prisoner of War Camp XI in Wales, he was tried in a Polish court in Warsaw in 1950, and was hanged on 6 December 1952.

Electromagnetic Pulse. The Electromagnetic Pulse (EMP) effect was first publicly acknowledged during the early testing of high altitude airburst nuclear weapons above the Pacific Ocean. The effect is characterised by the production of a very short but intense electromagnetic pulse of energy producing a powerful electromagnetic field, particularly within the vicinity of the weapon burst. Techniques have been developed to produce EMP by non-nuclear detonations. The field can be sufficiently strong, over geographic radii of 20-40 miles, to produce short-lived transient voltages of thousands of volts on exposed electrical conductors, such as wires, railways, or conductive tracks on electronic circuit boards and radio or radar receivers where exposed. The damage inflicted is similar to that experienced through exposure to close proximity lightning strikes requiring complete or partial replacement of the equipment. Even a weak EMP not inducing thermal damage will readily be sufficient to complete the destructive process. Any cables or metal pipes behave much like antennae, in effect guiding the high voltage transients into the equipment. Telecommunications equipment and electrical distribution grids and unprotected aircraft are particularly vulnerable.

The Bell (*die Glocke)* and the *Laternentrager.* There are no known surviving blueprints of the device tested in the Wenceslas Mine between 1942 and '44. It is believed to have comprised a metallic bell-like vessel containing one or more mercury-coated cylinders rotating at high speed about a central axial pillar holding a radioactive source. By inducing a circulating plasma, excited by a sequence of very high voltage direct current discharges, there was created a possibly self-sustaining energy flux which might be focussed for weaponolgy or propulsion. Sporrenberg testified that mathematician Elizabeth Adler, rocketry expert and Luftwaffe officer Herman Oberth, plus SS officer and high voltage specialist Dr Kurt Debus were said to have been aboard a Ju 390 flight when it departed an airfield near Opele, with the Nazi Bell, for Bodo in northern Norway. One unsubstantiated claim has it that General Kammler escaped, with the dismantled device via Norway, to America where development continued under the auspices of the US 'Black Projects' programme. The 'lantern' structure external to the mine remained in situ, photographed now rather overgrown, in 2010.

Fictional Footnotes

MOST SECRET ABLATIVE 3 -- ULTIMATE

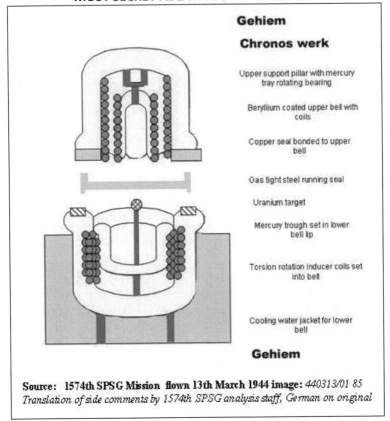

Gehiem

Chronos werk

Upper support pillar with mercury tray rotating bearing

Beryllium coated upper bell with coils

Copper seal bonded to upper bell

Gas tight steel running seal

Uranium target

Mercury trough set in lower bell lip

Torsion rotation inducer coils set into bell

Cooling water jacket for lower bell

Gehiem

Source: 1574th SPSG Mission flown 13th March 1944 image: *440313/01 85*
Translation of side comments by 1574th SPSG analysis staff, German on original

This is a representation of the possible Einstein Engine believed to have been used to generate a very large energy pulse at the Wenceslas Mine. This image was created from a radio facsimile intercept frame (440313/01 853) which was the subject of an analyst comment at the report datum 05:21

*   *   *

Aynette Bates' Novella. Aynette's novella, set geographically in her Kent cottage during 1605/06, was the first of two, intended for publication, fictional works with strong historical overtones. Makepiece Ploughman was able to read the text of the first: *A Kentish Cottage in 1606,* during his visits in the winter of 1943/44. Aynette wrote her second novel: *Warranted Traveller* sometime after Makepiece had been posted away from Kent during 1944. She wrote the stories as a fictionalised biography of the Ploughman family based on the material in the family heritage documents founded by Grandmother Susannah Catteral Ploughman. The manuscript for *A Kentish Cottage in 1606* was tied to the stored Ploughman Heritage Volume in the Kent archive, where it survived. Inexplicably, Makepiece missed it when he visited Maidstone in the 1970s and it remained 'undiscovered' until Piers Ploughman found it during a genealogical research, but was denied a full copy by a diligent archivist applying copyright laws. (Piers' daughter, Philippa, Ploughman was less concerned about copyright; she surreptitiously 'borrowed' the original and arranged for its publication in about 2013, under the title: *Novembers' Fifth.).* Aynette's second, full length, novel manuscript was destroyed when she died in the flying bomb incident and was never published.

About the Author - J N Cleeve

This page introduces J N Cleeve, the creator of the fictional Ploughman family, whose story is told in the *Warranted Land* saga's novels.
J N Cleeve served a full career in the Royal Air Force as a ground engineering officer specialising in electronic communications. This was followed in related defence consultancy until, taking a holiday in Virginia and Maryland in 2002, he asked the question: "Why did those colonists come here?" There proved to be no single or simple answer.

The five novels thus far of the *Warranted Land* saga have given some insight into the history of post-Elizabethan colonialism and the strong ties which still bind Great Britain with the United States of America. We have seen how sensible folk left England for what was little better than a swamp on a distant, sometimes hostile shore. Their fictionalised opportunities, tribulations and happier episodes across thirteen generations have been portrayed in 660,000 words. The archives of England and around the Chesapeake Bay did disclose hidden concepts — related ideas which spanned centuries and oceans. Some of these have been adapted and incorporated in saga so far.

With Makepiece retiring to the Chesapeake, this author could have let the sun set on a saga's happy ending. But, as Jenny Plowman demonstrated, there was part of the extended family still resident, in Kent, England, at the beginning of WWII. It would have been churlish not to have told their story and so the theme for the sixth novel in the series, *Piers' Cadetship,* was conceived. We should expect Piers Ploughman to be ambitious and lead a colourful life; he's sure to marry, perhaps have a family. Could they, in turn, be the subject of Book 7 of the saga? Piers is almost honour-bound to seek out Grandmother Susannah's heritage. No doubt there will be an American dimension as those tales evolve.

"In the ten years constructing this saga, I have found it enthralling to write about how close history came, so often, to being nudged along completely different tracks. I have not reinvented history, even if I have taken a few liberties with geography to keep the plot moving. The fictional players in my tale interface with actual characters who did their bit for what they thought was right."

I hope you are enjoying reading the *Warranted Land* saga.

PS   Why the pseudonym?   When I started this saga I lived in a village called Cleeve, in a cottage called Juniper.   J N Cleeve stuck and I see no reason to change it."

J N Cleeve
31st August 2012

The Warranted Land saga tells of the proud heritage sustaining the family and its continuity, through 3 previous and 10 subsequent generations, in England, America, the East Indies, on the high seas and in the air. The full saga has been edited to be presented in six novels, each designed to be free-standing. Any novel in the saga could be read individually, or the whole sequence could be taken in any order, although there is a chronological structure to the six titles:

Warranted Land	broadly 1605 to 1662
Bernard's Law	broadly 1662 to 1730
Rosetta's Rocks	broadly 1752 to 1799
Ada's Troth	broadly 1770 to 1840
Makepiece's Mission	broadly 1943 to 1965
Piers' Cadetship	broadly 1938 to 2001.

Has the saga concluded with the sixth novel? Allow me to misquote T E Lawrence (of Arabia), onetime airman, of renowned indiscipline but considerable authoring skills, as evidenced in an autobiography *The Mint* (understood to be out of British copyright 1 January 2006*):

I can't write 'Finis' to this work while I am
still writing. I hope, sometimes, that I will never write it.
* http://telawrenece.net/ telawrenecenet/te_copyright.htm updated 2 July 2006

A seventh novel, with the working title:

Philippa's Licence   broadly 1974 to 2018,

is gestating for possible publication in 2013. My editor has suggested I consider a prequel to saga, but any author knows it is arduous to construct a novel when you already know how it ends. She has even suggested a working title:

Susannah's Petticoat   broadly 1574 to 1615

The significance of the title will not escape readers of the Warranted Land novels. Further release information will be given on the author's website www.warrantedland.co.uk when appropriate.

The text of the fictional Aynette Bates' novella, re-titled:

Novembers' Fifth   broadly 1594 to 1620,

is in course of preparation for publication during 2013.